The Wrong Woman

By
Brenda J. Brown

TWCS
PUBLISHING HOUSE

First published by The Writer's Coffee Shop, 2014

Copyright © Brenda J. Brown, 2014

The right of Brenda J. Brown to be identified as the author of this work has been asserted by her under the Copyright Amendment (Moral Rights) Act 2000

This work is copyrighted. All rights are reserved. Apart from any use as permitted under the Copyright Act 1968, no part may be reproduced, copied, scanned, stored in a retrieval system, recorded or transmitted, in any form or by any means, without the prior written permission of the publisher.

All characters and events in this book—even those sharing the same name as (or based upon) real people—are entirely fictional. No person, brand or corporation mentioned in this book should be taken to have endorsed this book nor should the events surrounding them be considered in any way factual.
This book is a work of fiction and should be read as such.

The Writer's Coffee Shop
(Australia) PO Box 447 Cherrybrook NSW 2126
(USA) PO Box 2116 Waxahachie TX 75168

Paperback ISBN- 978-1-61213-204-4
E-book ISBN- 978-1-61213-205-1

A CIP catalogue record for this book is available from the US Congress Library.

Cover image by: © Depositphotos / Damiano Poli, © Depositphotos / Sergey Pristyazhnyuk
Cover design by: Niina Cord

www.thewriterscoffeeshop.com/bbrown

Dedication

For Gaye.

Chapter 1

It was a life-altering moment, or more accurately a *potentially* life-altering moment, and everything hinged on what she did next.

Norah Rothe was the thirty-four-year-old single mother of Ella—the nearest-to-perfect two-year-old daughter ever—and she knew a life-altering moment when she came across one. Ever since she had discovered that her morning sickness was more significant than mere gluten intolerance, she'd developed a healthy respect for life-altering moments and, more importantly, when to grab on to one.

She had been routinely passing through the small, homey café that she ran with her younger brother, topping coffee cups and sending polite greetings to the regulars, when she'd noticed them. Two men—strangers, so far as she'd been able to tell—sitting across from each other at a window table, engrossed in a clearly stressful conversation. Their heads had been lowered, shoulders hunched, voices weary, and they'd hardly given a second glance to the lunch specials in front of them. She could see the melted Brie congealing on top of the grilled asparagus from ten paces.

"The crew is standing by, the clock is ticking, and we do not have time for her to consult so much as a Magic 8 Ball, let alone her agent, her manager, her freakin' psychic—"

"What difference does it make? We don't have a prayer of finding another actress worth her salt, much less have her on the set in the next hour."

That had been the moment Norah's brakes had grabbed hold.

Ever since she could remember, she had loved the theatre. She'd studied, auditioned, and pounded the boards in every school, university, community, and professional stage that would have her. She'd received good to excellent reviews and even won awards in regional festivals from time to time. If all those years of checking audition notices and callboards had taught her anything, it was that this was *not* the time to keep walking.

Sure, it had been years since she'd acted in anything seriously, and she had no idea what these men were looking for, but it couldn't hurt to ask.

Could it?

She was probably setting herself up, getting her hopes up for no reason. This sort of thing didn't happen in places like this, to people like her. These guys could be perverts or deviants looking to drag some unsuspecting neophyte into a life of exploitation and ruin.

Look, either keep walking and wonder what if *for the rest of your life, or turn around and find out what the deal is.*

"Excuse me, gentlemen. I couldn't help but overhear . . ."

****

As the limousine door shut softly behind her, the ramifications of being trapped hit her full in the chest. She'd asked if she could sit facing forward to avoid getting carsick. Seeing as she was on the edge of hurling as it was, she saw no need to tempt fate. Now she found herself strapped in, staring at two strange men who looked even more freaked out than she felt.

One of the men, Steve Frost, was the movie's production manager—or *bean counter*, as he'd put it. He was a stoutly built fellow with fine, thinning hair the colour of mild cheddar, and wore his golf shirt—to no advantage—tucked over his massive belly and into the straining waistband of his trousers. His shoes seemed to be of two slightly different tones, as though he'd made it halfway through polishing them, and then changed his mind.

The other fellow was the local representative for the Hollywood-based casting agency. Ted Lui was a diminutive man, in his midthirties, of Asian descent, and flawlessly pulling off the West Coast Casual style seen on all the trendiest shows.

She'd had an idea what they were up to long before she had agreed to accompany them on this stress-inducing thrill ride. A film crew setting up for an actual Hollywood movie had been common knowledge among the locals before the ink had dried on the contracts, thanks to the ever reliable, small-town verbal telegraph system. There was never a baby born, a nose bloodied, or a marriage failed that wasn't announced there first.

According to the local gossip, they'd chosen Whitecourt to take advantage of its Anytown, USA, workability. And its dream rates, of course. Despite some studio backing, this was an independent movie and costs had to be contained to prevent trouble.

And at the moment, the film was in trouble.

The actress due on set that morning had been injured and was out of commission, and the isolation that had originally drawn them here wasn't helping matters.

Steve rummaged through his briefcase for a copy of the pages they were set to shoot today, so that Norah could have a look. He handed them to her with a pained expression. "I know it's a bit much to ask you to memorize it, but if you could, that would be amazing for us."

She glanced down at the official sides—one quarter-sized copies of the script for the day's shoot, stapled together. On the front page was listed the cast that was necessary for the day, the crew that was to be called, as well as all the particulars like location and call times. She had played a number of roles in student films, so she recognized the format.

"Who am I playing?" she asked, trying to quell the tremor maliciously tickling her voice.

"Oh, right!" Ted half smiled and gestured to the character sheet. It was clear he was nervous about the risk they were taking. "You are reading for Clare. She's around your age, maybe a bit younger. Kind of a sad case, you know the type—dowdy, low self-esteem, a bit homely—n-n-not that *you're* homely," he said quickly, as a flush of dark pink blazed across his cheeks.

"Thanks. Who was originally supposed . . ." She turned back to the first page of the cast list. "Cl—Helen Crandall! *Really?* Wow. What happened?"

"She was on her way here last night and tripped on the escalator at the airport. Fell eighteen feet and broke her collarbone. Now she's stuck in one of those casts that makes her look like she's saluting everyone for the next six weeks."

"Bummer." An understatement, but she couldn't think of anything else to say as she opened the script and started reading, all the while digging around in her purse for a pen. She made notes in the small margins—first impressions, character analysis, basic information.

She, or rather Clare, was initially introduced to the story via a scene in an interrogation room. Two police officers—correction, *detectives*—were questioning her about someone. Someone she was reluctant to talk about. Someone she was involved with that they believed committed a crime.

"Did he do it?"

"Sorry?" Ted glanced up, looking lost. He and Steve had been talking in hushed tones. "Did who do what?"

"This guy that they're questioning her about. Did he do something illegal?"

He smiled indulgently. "Have a look at the title."

Embarrassed, she flipped back to the front page. There it was, as they say, in black and white.

KOSMA.

One of the most notorious serial rapist–murderers of the twentieth century.

"Oh. So that would be a yes," she muttered, feeling more than a little stupid.

"No worries. You're coming in naked . . . pardon the expression. A bit of background—he is who he is, doing what he does. As it turns out, a few months before the real Kosma got arrested, he met this woman, Clare—not her real name, obviously. Anyway, they're guessing that because she didn't look or act anything like the pretty, blond college girls that were typically his victims, he didn't, you know, strangle her."

"Go on." She tried to ignore the prickle of sympathetic fear that ran up the back of her neck.

"Well, the story goes that Kosma developed a thing for her. Naturally, she didn't have a clue who he was, and they ended up getting pretty close. But the way the *real* Clare tells it, when they went to have sex for the first time, he flipped out. The poor bastard just couldn't do it unless he was thinking about how he was going to off her afterward, and since he really liked her too much to kill her . . ." He substituted the conclusion of his story with an indifferent shrug. "Anyway, it's one of the most messed up love stories in history."

"So at this point in the story . . ."

"At this point, the police know she's connected to him. It's been a couple of weeks since he ran screaming out of her bedroom, or whatever, and they want to know if she's going to give him up, what does she know, that sort of stuff. For her part, she doesn't believe what they're saying about him because she still kinda loves him and all that baloney."

"Okay, that helps. Thanks." She went back to the pages, jotting down more notes and growing excited as she fleshed out more of the character.

It was a well-written script—excellent dialogue, sharp repartee between Clare and the two policemen, with the plot points revealed in tiny increments to keep up the tension.

She'd always had the enviable gift of learning lines quickly, so by the third pass, she had them almost down cold. Before going through it a fourth time, she checked the cast list again to see if she could put a face to the men she would be playing against.

DETECTIVE MALCOLM . . . DENNIS JAMES AUSTIN.
DETECTIVE SALVATORE—SAL . . . NICK COSTELLO.

She felt her backbone turn to liquid.

No. Way.

"Miss Rothe?"

Her tongue felt as if it had swollen to twice its normal size. She managed a small whimper as she pointed at the front page of the sides. These were true actors—artists she would sit through a crap film for—and in a matter of minutes, she was expected to audition opposite them?

The two men smiled at each other before Ted spoke.

"Sorry, I guess we should have mentioned who the director was from the beginning. He's going to be playing Kosma, too, but only because the money men insisted. He really only wanted to direct. He'd had his heart set on this project for about a decade now, so you can imagine how big a disaster this business with Helen and her arm is. Not that I'm trying to pressure you, right?"

Not wanting to draw attention to the misunderstanding, she muttered, "No, of course not. No, I'm cool."

Cool, yeah, sure. Uh-huh. I'm c—nope. No, I'm very much not cool!

Unable to imagine whom Ted and Steve thought could be more impressive or intimidating than Dennis James Austin and Nick Costello, she retreated back to her script, the words blurring as she battled the overwhelming temptation to peek. In the end, curiosity got the better of her, and she gave in, turning casually back to the front page. There it was: first name in the crew list, typed in a paradoxically simple manner, in a nondescript column along with a bunch of people she'd never heard of.

DIRECTOR . . . DAVID RAURKE.

She blinked once, twice, three times, and willed the logical side of her brain to interpret what she was reading to the swooning, starstruck, non-comprehending side of her brain. It was necessary to accept and to embrace this information with grace and maturity.

Instead, she laughed. Even worse, she punctuated said laugh with a decidedly unfeminine snort.

Hysteria. No question.

She attempted to cover with a clumsy cough, as two pairs of eyes looked her way—one worried, the other maybe a little frightened. "Sorry. Just a— never mind." She dropped her gaze back to the pages and tried to keep them from fluttering in her visibly shaking hands.

The magnitude of the situation dragged her from the safety of the harmless fantasy she'd intended this little caper to be to a reality of soul-sickening proportions. Her brain was so rattled that she was barely cognizant of the rest of the trip to the location. She was remotely aware of Ted and Steve muttering away and glancing at her in turns, no doubt wondering if they were backing the right horse.

Before Norah could decide whether to breathe and get through it, or surrender to panic and fling herself from a moving vehicle, she looked out to see a bored-looking PA in a reflective vest, waving them through the gate.

Inside the barbed-wired perimeter and taking it all in, Norah saw exactly why it was known in the industry as *the circus*. They parked a short distance from an enormous corrugated metal structure, with several smaller buildings and numerous trailers arranged neatly to one side. To the immediate left of the main building, the on-set caterers had set up their mobile kitchen complete with a large tarpaulin tent sheltering the tables and chairs, and the aroma of coffee and cooking easily reached her as soon as the car door was opened.

The gentlemen gestured for her to precede them out of the car, and it was her deepest hope that her legs wouldn't drop her on her keister the minute she stepped onto the lot.

Ted arrived at her side and took her elbow to guide her, or keep her from escaping—she couldn't be sure—toward the main structure.

Steve, meanwhile, made a beeline for the craft services table, where he started up a conversation with a young man laden with pens, radios, cell phones, and clipboards. Steve pointed in Norah and Ted's direction, and within seconds, the young man was hurrying toward the trailers, rapidly speaking into one of the radios.

"Steve's having one of the assistant directors gather up the actors playing opposite you," Ted said in a calm and even tone, as though she was on the edge of bolting.

Very astute man, that Ted.

"What we're hoping for is a chance for the three of you to run through the scene a few times before showing it to David. That way, you won't be so, you know . . . nervous."

"Excellent idea." Norah suspected that their actual agenda was to make sure she didn't stink up the place. If so, they could sneak her out the back door before David Raurke was any the wiser.

David Raurke. Jesus tap-dancing Christ.

Just the thought of how that gorgeous, talented, intelligent, sexy, did she mention gorgeous, brilliant, funny, dream of a man was somewhere within spitting distance, had her seriously rethinking her moxie. Fat lot of good her heroic initiative was going to do her if she vomited all over his shoes.

Are those the toilets?

Norah excused herself and dashed into the ladies' room, at the very least, happy to remove *wetting ones pants* from the list of potential opportunities to embarrass herself. She leaned against the sink for a moment, and then slowly met her own eyes in the mirror.

Remember why you're doing this. No regrets! This could very well be your moment, whatever the hell that means, so suck it up, pull yourself together, and go kick some ass.

Three deep breaths and she was off.

Ted escorted her inside the ad hoc soundstage, and she took a moment to allow her eyes to adjust to the darkness.

A cavernous building, it had been used at one time to house oil rig machinery and still had the stink of crude hanging in the air, despite having sat empty for years. About halfway along the right wall, the near blackness was broken by a solitary pole light directed at one of the interior sets they had built for the production—a series of what looked like offices.

Ted hurried forward while Norah trailed behind, picking her way carefully through the tangle of cables, ropes, and cords lining the floor. She arrived at what she guessed was the interrogation room of the scene she'd been studying.

The walls were painted a dreary battleship gray, broken by a battered door and the classic two-way mirror. Both the walls and the speckled linoleum floor looked as though they'd had many years of wear, tear, and neglect, which contrasted sharply with the smell of wet paint and pots of flooring epoxy sitting just off set.

Ah, the magic of movies!

She took a quick look around as Ted set up a few more work lights, trying his best to focus them on the main area.

The interrogation room door led into the squad room, which was packed with a half dozen desks littered with computers, in/out trays, multiline telephones, personal mementos, and other office specific items. File cabinets lined one wall, painted the same tedious gray as the interrogation room, and another wall was nothing but a row of large grimy windows.

A flash of sunlight from behind grabbed her attention, as the main door opened and three people walked in, two of whom Norah identified with a certainty that made her stomach clench—Dennis James Austin and Nick Costello. Once the door closed, the area outside the immediate set was plunged into darkness again. Though momentarily blinded, she was able to pick out enough of Steve's mutterings to determine that the actors were being introduced to the limb they were all about to climb out on.

They made their way onto the interrogation set as Steve broke away and headed straight for her. "How's it going? You get a good look around? Can I get you anything? Water? Coffee?"

"No, I'm fine. Thanks very much."

"So, Nick and Dennis are waiting on set for you. Shall we go?"

"Absolutely," she replied, only slightly more confidently than she felt.

The men were waiting and both approached her smiling, hands outstretched, as she followed Steve onto set. The introductions were warm and jovial, and put her at ease.

Nick Costello was wiry and small, far smaller than he looked in his films, she realized with a shock. He had a pointed, angular, rodent-like face that only a mother could love. With his dark hair and complexion, he easily fit any number of different ethnicities with nothing more than a change of accent.

He was the perfect counterpoint to Dennis James Austin, who was nearly a natural platinum blond, with a pallor that could barely aspire above pasty. He had a more rounded physique, only about twenty pounds shy of doughy, and while Nick was very much a type—a kind of fidgety, smart-ass with rat-terrier tenacity—Dennis was the quintessential blank canvas. He had a versatility in his look and talent to take him into any conceivable role then walk the streets afterward in near anonymity. The downside to that particular gift was that people frequently forgot who it was that they so loved in his films.

"Well, let's have a kick at this cat." Nick smiled and gestured everyone toward the set.

****

"Damn it!" He punched a button on his cell and longed for the days when you could slam down the receiver of a phone and end a pointless conversation properly.

"So, is no luck?" Jozef Koziak sounded more bored than concerned as he smiled at something on his own phone, and punched more buttons. The director of photography, a giant bear of a man from the Czech Republic, had a gift for grasping the obvious in record time.

"No," David replied in a tone just short of a whine, and roughly rubbed eyes that were more red than brown at this point. He caught himself wondering for the hundredth time since starting this project why he had ever quit smoking. "Her psychic said it was a bad time to start a new project."

"Question, Dafid. This actress talking to voodoo man. Why you want . . . how you say . . . *crackpot* like this on film?" Jozef asked, while his thumbs never missed a beat on his phone's keyboard.

"That's nothing. I worked with a woman once who wouldn't take a role unless her hairdresser okayed it first. No, Raya's good. It's a trip to some kind of psychedelic amusement park getting her signed, but she delivers. Have we heard anything from Ted and Steve?"

"Yeah, they back on lot 'bout half hour ago."

"They must have come up bust, then."

"Not sure. They call the boys to set. Dunno." Jozef shrugged, mumbled a curse at his phone, and slid it into his pocket as he met David's stare.

"To the set? Which boys? *My* boys? What for?" Not waiting for an answer, David jumped up, hooked his radio to his belt, grabbed his clipboard, and ran out the trailer door.

The second AD, Jason, appeared at his side, half jogging to keep up as David hurried to the makeshift studio. "So, David, I sent the crew to lunch forty-three minutes ago, and now they're on standby."

"Standby for what?"

"Um, well, Steve seems to think we may be shooting something this afternoon."

Not wanting to sound like a total ass, or as though he didn't have clue-one as to what was happening on his own set, David kept his mouth shut and stepped up his pace.

Jason ran ahead and opened the door for David, and then closed it quietly behind them.

The lights focused on the interrogation room drew David's attention, and even from a distance, he could make out a number of people in the area. Before he'd taken more than a half dozen steps inside, Ted glanced up and broke away from the group.

"David, David. Glad you're here. We were just about to send for you. It's incredible . . . this woman . . . out of thin air, swear to God, and what a talent." Ted was on the verge of hyperventilating.

"What woman?"

****

Norah was seated at the table where she would stay throughout the scene. The fact that she didn't have to worry about treading on someone's foot or tripping over a piece of furniture made her giddy with gratitude.

They'd stumbled through the scene the first time adjusting to each other's rhythms, coming up with blocking ideas for the guys, pacing suggestions, places in the dialogue where overlapping would be the most effective, as well as where to place the pauses. Seeing as it was nothing more than a rehearsal, they didn't want to peak too early. As Nick so indelicately put it, "We don't want to blow our wad before the boss sees."

The mere mention of David Raurke caused her tummy to do a little flop. She stared down at her fingers, trying to focus on something besides the little white dots popping off behind her retinas like flashbulbs, while at the same time willing her legs to stop shaking.

"Me and Dennis've got your back, sweetheart." Nick leaned in companionably to Norah, and Dennis gave her arm a little squeeze.

****

David stepped within earshot and worked out that Dennis and Nick were running dialogue with someone. They were all so engrossed in what they were doing that he was able to remain in the shadows, observing without being observed himself. Unfortunately, because of the way Nick was sitting on the tabletop, David still couldn't see the third person.

Steve quietly joined him, smiling broadly. "David, my friend, you must be doing something right."

All at once, a burst of laughter erupted from the set, and Steve and David turned to see the performers huddled together as if they were old friends, cutting up and cracking jokes. Steve took the opportunity to interrupt them and, while he was speaking low to the mystery guest, Ted took Steve's lead and coaxed David toward the group.

There was a woman seated at the table—small, a bit younger than his thirty-eight years, with warm brown hair cut to gently frame the jawline of, from what little he could see, a pleasant face. She seemed to be fascinated by her fingers, which were drumming frenetically on the table in front of her, but as he came within arms' length, she took a deep breath, raised her head, and smiled.

He froze midstride and was completely taken aback.

He blamed her eyes—an unprecedented shade of green, sparkling and full of intelligence, lighting up her face and half the room around her. He realized, to his mortification, that for the first time in his life, he knew what the poets meant when they wrote about drowning in a woman's gaze. He desperately needed air.

Ted stepped forward. "David, please allow me to introduce our Clare, Norah Rothe."

"Where did our guys find you?" David asked, trying to keep his voice level as he attempted to understand the tightening in his gut.

She cleared her throat and opened her mouth, but nothing came out. She blinked a few times, opened her mouth again, but Ted and Steve jumped to her rescue by talking over each other and sounding like two enthusiastic toddlers as they relayed the details of their discovery and what a great story it was going to make.

"Well, David, what do you think?" Ted asked, smiling.

What do I think?

All eyes, including hers, turned to face him, but he didn't know what to say.

All right, pal, take stock. Could you be in a bigger mess?

No.

What are your options here?

Bupkes.

So what exactly is your problem?

. . . I got nuthin'.

He was expected to make a decision . . . he was the boss, after all, and people—*lots* of people—were waiting for him. He put his focus on the script, on Clare, on who he visualized her to be, and he was finally able to find his voice.

"I don't know. I think you're just too attractive."

She rolled her eyes. "God, if I had a nickel for every time I heard *that* one."

****

The entire exchange sounded as if it took place through a wall of mud. Norah was so transfixed by David Raurke that she'd completely missed his greeting. When he'd offered her his hand, she vaguely recalled standing and wiping her soggy palms on the legs of her khakis before taking his hand in what she could only hope had been a firm, yet feminine grasp. She prayed that she'd said something about being pleased to meet him and not any of the hundred-and-one sophomoric suggestions that flooded her frenzied brain.

She was terribly aware of David's scrutiny, sadly not in the way she wanted. In fact, she had the distinct feeling that at any minute he was going to reach over and pull down her lower lip to inspect her teeth.

She was desperate to reclaim the elation she'd felt while rehearsing the scene, so she needed to give it her best shot and pull out all the stops. If he cut her loose, it would be a story with a sad ending but she'd always know she had tried.

"With all due respect, Mr. Raurke, I'm a character actor, and I think, a pretty good one. I expect you have excellent hair, makeup, and costume departments, and with the support of these fine fellows here," Norah nodded toward Dennis and Nick, "and, naturally, *your* expert guidance, I can be whoever you need me to be." She leaned in and stage-whispered, "That bit about your expert guidance was me sucking up, by the way."

Dennis shifted in his seat. "David, we've been rehearsing for the last half hour. She's terrific, isn't she, Nick?"

Nick jumped up and moved toward David. "Listen, Raurke, what've you got to lose? The crew is standing by with their thumbs up their butts, and the production is hemorrhaging money at the moment."

Steve nodded mournfully.

"So why not shoot a few and see what we've got?"

"Film costs money, too, bud." David knew he was being petty, but he didn't like being ganged up on either.

Nick, sounding like a car salesman, took a deep breath and began the negotiations. "Okay, tell you what, you shoot the scene. If you see that she's the cat's ass, like we do, we're all winners. If it turns out she's a big honkin' floater, then I'll cover the cost of the wasted fil—"

"I can't let you do that, Nick." Norah shook her head. "Thank you, but if I don't deliver then I'll pay for the film."

Steve leaned close and said, "Honey, film runs about a hundred dollars a foot, developed."

The colour drained form Norah's face like a cartoon. "Seriously? Er, hmm . . . umm, heh. Well, as Mr. Costello so generously offered . . ." she stage-whispered to Nick, "I promise not to, you know . . . *float*."

David chuckled in spite of himself, then announced to a room charged with anticipation, "All right, let's shoot something. But I'm not making any promises."

He watched as Dennis gave Norah a brotherly hug and Ted and Steve shook each other's hands in anticipatory congratulations for a job well done.

"Jason!" David bellowed. "Take Miss Rothe to wardrobe, please, and get the crew in here for setup."

Jason scrambled from the wings and led Norah off the set.

Nick followed David to his chair. "This is a good thing you're doing, boss. You won't be sorry."

David looked across the soundstage as Norah was led out, and felt something stir inside him, something he didn't recognize that had a smile twitching his lips upward once more. "Hey, if nothing else, she's had me laughing for the first time in a month."

Chapter 2

An hour and twenty minutes later, they were ready to shoot. The crew had swarmed over the set, laid camera track, hung lights, and then crept back into the shadows. The on-set teams had put the finishing touches on the extras, props, and dressing. Finally, Jozef, who had happily lumbered around the main area bellowing orders cheerfully at the gaffers and testing light levels, nodded at the set with a satisfied grunt.

David sat in his chair, gulping coffee and watching the organized madness. With so much chaos, it continued to amaze him that movies ever got made at all. With everything that went into making a film, and the infinite number of things that could go wrong at any given moment—the odds of creating a *great* film were astronomical.

Grace, his first assistant director, sidled up to him. "We're about ten minutes away, boss. Jason's on his way in with the talent."

"Thanks. Can you ask Jozef to come over when he has a sec?"

"Copy that." And she was off.

David smiled.

Grace was the most ill-named person he'd ever met. At about five foot nothing and packed into a pair of size sixteen khakis, she was, as his grandmother would say, easier to step over than walk around. She had the face of an irritated bulldog, and hands like a pair of baseball mitts, but man, she knew her job. She had been AD on a film he'd acted in about sixteen months ago, and he'd sworn he would steal her for his next project. No one kept a shoot running as smoothly as Grace.

Jozef arrived at David's side, pulled a bottle of water from the pocket hanging off his own chair, and then heaved himself into it. "Is good," he stated, before taking a huge swig.

"Good. Here's the thing, though. Our new Clare is, well, *prettier* than I'd like. Maybe she needs a bit of bottom lighting or something, you know, dowdy her down a bit?" When his suggestion was met with silence, David turned to see Jozef staring at him as if he'd suggested that he grow a third arm and dance the funky chicken. "Or maybe . . ." David called on his dialect talent to pull off his best thick Czech accent. ". . . Dafid should mind own business and let DOP do his job."

"This is what I am thinking, too."

"Fine."

Jozef slapped David on the knee, hard. "You are good boss. Smart man." He tromped off, pointing and yelling half-English, half-Czech commands to his crew as they prepped for finals.

David fought the urge to rub his stinging leg while looking around for a place to toss his coffee cup.

Jason appeared at his side, took the cup from him, and fired it into a bin before returning to David's side.

"How is she?" David asked.

"Ready," Jason said.

"I hope this isn't a colossal error. I mean, this woman, she's too . . . I dunno." David's uncertainty was getting the better of him, and it was a feeling he detested.

Taking risks was a big part of who he was. It was impossible to gather the reviews, the acclaim, or the little golden statues he had, without jumping in feet first once in a while. Since he'd taken on this new role, however, where he was responsible for a hundred people and a hundred decisions every single day, his courage had been taking a shit-kicking.

He glanced toward a group of grips standing off to one side—all garbed in tatty jeans, various styles of steel-toed shoes or boots, dark T-shirts with vintage art prints and rock band insignias, and although generally clean, their hands and faces were grubby. The guys were unshaven, the women un-made up, and hardly any of them had seen the business end of a comb today.

"That's what I need," David said, pointing to one of the female grips. "Plain, lacking the feminine . . . thing. No sexual confidence. You know what I mean?"

"Yes, sir," Jason said with a nod.

Just then, the woman David had picked out turned toward them. When she noticed him looking her way, she sent a bright, somewhat shy, smile in his direction.

"Jason?"

"Yes, sir?"

"That's her, isn't it?"

"Yes, sir."

"Thank you, Jason."

"Anytime, sir." He walked off, listening closely to his earpiece before calling out, "Okay, lock it up. Picture's up! Everyone, first marks, please."

David watched Norah walk quickly to the interrogation room and take her place at the table. He marveled at the transformation since she last sat there. The hair department had arranged her hair so that it kept drooping into her face and had added something to it, making it look stringy and unclean.

Makeup had thickened her nose a touch, taken the luster out of her skin, and made her lips appear raw and chapped. And wardrobe had made her look precisely like he needed her to. She appeared shabby, sexless, and without conceit—the sort of unremarkable woman that fades into the background no matter where she is. The visual was more than he had hoped for.

Now, if only she can act.

Nick Costello took his place in the chair opposite Norah, and they began a friendly chatter.

The scene was set to start with Dennis' character, Detective Malcolm, in the squad room, grabbing a file off his desk. With the camera following him, he was storyboarded to make his way along the wall of windows, past the filing cabinets, and through the interrogation room door where the dialogue between Sal and Clare was already underway.

It had been David's plan to do the entire scene from start to finish in one continuous shot—no stops, no editing—but he'd resigned himself to the fact that it may no longer be a viable option. There had been a number of shots that he'd looked forward to on this project. He'd wanted to play with light and camera angles, bust through some of the boundaries of cinematography, and push the limits of filmmaking in order to prove he was more than just an actor playing a director. But from the start, there had been one setback after another. This latest one—Helen Crandall's last minute accident—had been the capper. He'd been on enough sets to know that disruptions were the norm, but would it turn the universe on its ear to cut him a bit of slack?

He hopped to his feet and moved into the squad room, slapping one of the bit players on the back, wishing a cluster of background performers well, and then made his way to the centre of the room. "All right, everyone, this is the shot."

The cast and crew went silent and listened attentively while David blocked the camera's path and how it would trail Detective Malcolm into the interrogation room. He made suggestions to the background players— get coffee, answer phones, do reports on the computer, discuss a case with another officer; in short, look busy but not frantic, and be interesting but don't pull focus.

Dennis, who preferred to be called by his character's name once he was on set, stood on his starting point, quietly mumbling to himself.

Nick paced back and forth in the interrogation room, gesturing wildly with his hands, muttering, and appearing quite mad.

Norah, on the other hand, sat stock-still, hands flat on the table in front of her, barely blinking.

As an actor, David had never participated in any artistic process beyond learning his lines and blocking. All this self-imposed internal strife had always struck him as slightly ridiculous, but as a director, he tried to respect it and kept his distance. He figured he'd let them all blunder through the

first take and then put his spin on it.
He returned to his chair and gave a nod to Grace.
"Stand by." She never had to shout. "Quiet everyone."
Everyone fell to first positions like sprinters at the beginning of a race.
"Bell."
A shrill clanging went off to insure that no one came in or out of the soundstage once they were filming.
"Roll sound."
"Rolling," replied the boom mic operator.
"Roll camera."
"Rolling," replied another voice from behind the steady cam.
"Mark it."
The clapboard snapped down in front of the camera—one of David's favorite sounds.
He felt his blood pound through his veins and couldn't stop his knees from jumping.
"Background," Grace said.
The extras sprang to life, performing their various tasks and business.
Finally, David took over the commands. "And . . . action."

Detective Malcolm flips through a number of papers on his desk and finds the file among them. He pulls it out from the pile, clutching it to his chest, hurries across the squad room and toward Interrogation, closing the door quickly behind him.

Too quickly, it turned out.
"Cut."
Dennis, caught up in the moment, had shut the door on the camera, cut off the shot and nearly hit the lens.
"Fuck. Sorry, David."
Everyone laughed and the screwup eased the tension.
"Never mind, bud. Let's do it again, everyone."
And so it went, seven more false starts—the classic boom mic in shot, a cable tangled in the steady cam, a background police officer slammed a file cabinet drawer so hard it rocked backward and hit the wall with a loud bang. At one point, Nick hissed a line with such force that spit flew into Norah's hair and cracked the cast and crew up for several minutes.
David was cautiously optimistic. The girl could act, and the three of them played off each other much better than he could have imagined. During breaks, he rushed over and, while offering Norah bits of direction, would put a hand on her back or he'd squeeze her shoulders or touch her in some way. For some reason, he couldn't keep his hands off her and it unnerved the hell out of him.
At last, the scene was ready to go.
The interview between the detectives and Clare started off polite, almost

friendly. Norah played her role cooperative though confused, and it gave her somewhere to go once the details began to reveal themselves. Some actors fell into the trap of playing the ending right from the start. David was glad she wasn't one of them.

He watched the scene from the monitors set up at the video village, and as each line unfolded, he became more and more impressed with Norah's ability. She was always aware but never played to the camera, subtly relaying her internal dialogue. No question, this woman knew her stuff.

Detective Malcolm places the gruesome crime scene photos in front of Clare as Detective Salvatore's voice shatters everything she thought she knew.

The result on the monitor was stunning as David quietly directed the painful, almost undetectable slowness of the camera zooming in on Norah's face.

Clare's eyes dart from photo to photo, her breath rapid and shallow. She pushes her fingers into her hair and drops her head in her hands as she stares into the faces of the victims.

David never focused the camera on the photographs. The horror of what she saw and what it meant was more brutally portrayed by this actress than anything a photograph could reveal.

Her eyes well up and huge tears begin a steady stream down her face. She roughly wipes them away with her sleeve and attempts to recover. She looks up at the detectives and, with a voice as flat as her eyes, she tells the detectives what they need to hear.

"And, cut."

There was a silence as everyone held their breath.

"Print that," David said. He leaned over to Jozef and whispered, "What do you think?"

Jozef shrugged his huge shoulders. "We watch playback, but I think we can no improve on that. Is good, this girl."

"Good. Grace?"

Grace knew her next command. "Standby, everyone, video playback, please."

While David, Jozef, and a number of other crew members watched the scene as it played back on the monitors, the cast stretched and mumbled quietly to one another.

Craft services moved through the groups, offering trays of sandwiches, drinks, and sweets, and everyone helped themselves.

David waved the tray away, but Jozef reached over him to snag a handful

The Wrong Woman

of sandwiches, jammed an entire half in his mouth, pointed to the sequence running, and said something—obscured by pastrami and seven-grain—about moving a hair slower.

David disagreed.

They got caught up again in the drama and skill of the scene. At its close, they were more than satisfied with the results.

"I think that would be pretty hard to top. Where are we at with the time, Judy?" David asked his script supervisor, the hyperefficient, amazingly organized, spookily observant Judy Evanston.

She checked her stopwatch, her wristwatch, and then her notes. "Well, we were scheduled to start shooting at eight this morning but didn't actually roll until just after one. It is now only ten after six, so I would be inclined to say that puts us in pretty good shape."

"What time?" asked David, astonished.

"Six ten."

"So even though—"

"We're still almost two hours ahead of schedule." She was clearly impressed, and not much impressed this lady.

David smiled and then his smile turned to a chuckle. "Check the gate."

If the gate wasn't clean, if even a speck of dust or a hair was on the camera's lens, the scene had to be re-shot.

"Gate's good."

An expectant hush fell over the soundstage. Despite the equipment and the crush of more than forty people packed into a few hundred square feet, all that could be heard was an odd shuffle here or there. All attention was focused on David.

He took a deep breath and kept his focus on her. "Norah?" He ignored the fact that he held the power to change her life. That wasn't what this was about, though one look at her hands clenched and white knuckled on the table, or her eyes—soft and locked on his—told him that she knew it, too.

"Yes, David?"

The tiniest grin touched his lips. "You're hired."

Any chance of mentioning starting fresh tomorrow was drowned out by the enthusiastic round of cheers, whistles, and applause.

David smiled broadly as Norah clapped her hands over her mouth, barely containing her gleeful squeals.

The boys on either side of her spiritedly jostled her until she emerged, her glorious eyes bright and shining. Her laughter reached him across the stage.

"Okay, everyone." Grace clapped her hands to quiet the din. "Good work today. That's a wrap."

There was a blur of activity as lights went out, grips briskly hustled to the trucks with stands, cords, gels, and lamps, and everyone made their way out into the evening.

David watched as Norah, sandwiched between Dennis and Nick, was all but carried off the set. He stayed back in his chair, quiet and reflective, and went over the events of the day, unable to believe that it had turned out so well. Better than he'd dreamed, in fact.

Norah was phenomenal, and that was not a word he used often. He couldn't remember a time when a single performance had blown him away like that. He was excited about the project again, couldn't wait to see what happened next, and it had everything to do with her. It was as though her energy and talent had ignited a new fire in him. Strange how five hours ago he hadn't even known her name, and now he couldn't imagine the film without her.

He checked the sides for tomorrow, had a quick meeting with Judy to determine any pickups that were needed, and then he consulted his binder for the current schedule. His stomach took a dive when he read which scene was to be shot the day after tomorrow.

He struggled to keep his voice neutral. "Jason?"

"Yes, sir."

David had long since given up asking him to stop calling him *sir*. Even though Jason was only twenty-four, he was old-school, and the sir thing was hardwired into him.

"Where is Nor—Miss Rothe?"

"Stand by." He turned slightly and spoke into his radio, "Jason for Gail."

"Go ahead," replied the disembodied voice.

"Gail, do you have a twenty on Norah Rothe?"

"I just saw her in your office. She was picking up her script and a schedule, and I heard Ted say he needed her to sign off on some stuff before we wrapped her for the day."

"Copy that."

It occurred to David and Steve, who had apparently overheard, that Norah had worked the entire day without the benefit of anything in writing.

"Oh, shit," said Steve, his face morphing from smug satisfaction to grimace.

David knew precisely what Steve was thinking. They had both been held by the short and curlies often enough to know when someone had a good grip. What that woman could ask for to finish the film could flatten them.

He shook his head and smiled. "I wouldn't worry about it." He turned back to his AD. "Jason, ask Gail to let Norah know I need to speak with her before she leaves. I'll be over in ten."

Jason relayed the message as he headed toward the door.

Steve had already taken off, and David knew he would be insinuating himself into the meeting between Ted and Norah. David was on his own, but for a couple of PAs doing a bit of last minute cleanup, and he took the time to consider his next move.

Wednesday—the love scene, so-called in any film, whether love has anything to do with it or not. It was going to be a tricky shoot, with a lot of demands being made on him in all areas. As a director, he was thrilled at the opportunity to guide Norah through such a complex, volatile, and even violent scene. As an actor, however, playing with her in front of the camera intimidated him in a way he couldn't explain, and he realized that he was more than a little nervous.

He employed a bit of self-deprecation to shake himself out of his funk.

I'm an award-winning actor, damn it, not some inexperienced, mime-school dropout!

There was no denying it, though. The girl had raised the bar.

Maybe they could talk it through, rehearse a little. They needed to be comfortable together, or rather their characters did. For her sake, he needed to spend some time with her.

Yeah, that's right. For her *sake.*

He rose from his chair, tugged on the legs of his jeans, and walked with as much confidence as he could muster toward the AD's office. En route, he spotted Norah, laughing and looking over her shoulder as she exited the trailer.

Ted followed her out, obviously pleased with the day as he jumped down to shake her hand, then pulled her into a clumsy hug. He released her as he saw David arrive, but kept an arm draped companionably across her shoulders. "So what do you think of our girl here, David? Was she fabulous, or was she fabulous?"

"She was fabulous," David said, smiling and hoping he didn't sound insincere.

Norah, for all her fabulousness, looked embarrassed.

David asked, "Are you two finished with your business?"

"Yes, quite finished to the satisfaction of all, I believe. I'll leave you to it and, Norah, good luck, not that you'll need it."

Ted ducked back into the trailer, and they were alone—or as alone as you could be on a lot full of people still milling about. They stood, awkwardly facing each other for a moment, and David cleared his throat.

"Um, how did you get here?"

"Ted and Steve . . . oh! Right. I guess I'll have to call someo—"

He laughed. "No, no. I'll walk you to transport. We'll get you a ride."

"Perfect. Thank you."

They walked slowly in silence for a few moments. She had obviously taken a shower and her damp hair had been pushed back off her face, fully revealing her amazing eyes. She didn't have any makeup on, but she was naturally radiant and, in own her way, quite beautiful.

"Actually, I'm the one who needs to thank you. You were . . . well, you really were fabulous today. I'm . . . we're all happy to have you, you know, on the show." He was furious with himself, stammering like a teenager.

"Oh, please, Davi—may I call you David?" Before she could even finish asking the question, he was nodding emphatically, and she grinned. "This was one of the most amazing days of my life. I can't even tell you what it's meant to me to be a part of this, what it means to be coming back on Wednesday. I'm out of my mind, really."

"Good. Actually, that's what I wanted to talk to you about, the, uh, the Wednesday part. I know you haven't had a chance to read the script yet," he said, gesturing to the thick envelope in her hand. "But on Wednesday, I know this will be a bit rough, but that's the day we're shooting the, uh . . ." He cleared his throat. ". . . the love scene." He wasn't sure if he'd imagined it or not, but he thought she might have stumbled a bit.

"Oh." She audibly gulped and her face, which moments before had been flushed and pink, shifted through several shades of green.

"Of course, it's not your typical love scene."

"No, I know. Steve briefed me a bit in the car coming here."

"Good, so you know their relationship was not run-of-the-mill."

"Right. Well, no, it hardly could be, could it?" She attempted to chuckle but it sounded more like a small, nervous snort.

He sensed her encroaching panic and rushed on. "Exactly. So here's what I was thinking. Maybe we should get together, for a sit down, work out some of the dialogue, character stuff, you know, like what you did with the guys today. I mean that was helpful, the shoot went so well, and I know it was because you had the chance to work on it beforehand." He noticed her smiling. "What's so funny?" he asked.

"Sorry, as primarily a stage actor, it's always amused me how impressed film actors are with the magic of rehearsal. Again, sorry, I'm not making fun. Honest."

"No, please. As primarily a film actor, I feel confident and entitled enough to say we are fundamentally the laziest group of people on the planet. And when you work into that how much money we make, it's practically criminal." He sighed, feeling easier now. "So what do you think, about what I said, you know, the getting together thing?"

"That would be fine. When do you suggest?" she asked.

"I guess it'll have to be tomorrow. It'll be an easy day here, mostly second unit. I'll shift some stuff around and free up my afternoon. I have an idea." He knew his attempt at sounding as though the idea had just occurred to him was his crappiest performance to date, but he pushed through.

In for a penny . . .

"Why don't I pick you up around five? We'll drive into the city for dinner. That'll give us a chance to talk in the car. It's, what, an hour there, an hour back?"

"Closer to an hour and a half, but that sounds fine. I mean . . . very nice, in fact. Thank you."

They arrived at the same car that had brought her in that morning, and the driver made a move toward the car door.

David waved him back and opened the door for her. Leaning against the window frame, he smiled and said, "Great. Until tomorrow."

"I look forward to it. Do you need my address?"

"No, that's okay. Jim here will be driving us so—"

"Oh, right! He'll know."

"Yeah."

"Good, then. Well, good night."

"Good night."

They stared, grinning at each other like a pair of fools.

At last, he asked himself how he'd treat any other actor after a great day of filming. Relaxing, he reached out and pulled Norah into a warm embrace.

Nothing more than thanks for a job well done.

"Thank you again, so much," he whispered against her ear.

"You are so very welcome." She sighed, pulled away, then climbed into the car and was gone.

Chapter 3

As the car pulled out of the lot and onto the road, Norah risked a quick peek behind her. David stood where she'd left him, hands shoved deep in the pockets of his jeans, watching her drive away. He tucked his head and kicked at a couple of rocks, looking so much like a little boy, before he turned back toward the circus.

She faced front and tried to breathe through the cacophony of emotions that reeled inside her.

Has there ever been such a day?

Not even twelve hours ago, she had been biking to the café expecting another ordinary morning. If Ella learned nothing else from her, she hoped she learned to take advantage of every opportunity that presented itself, no matter what the risk.

With Ella's little face clear in the forefront of Norah's mind, she grabbed her cell phone and dialed home. "Hi, Peg. How's she been?" She smiled as her aunt shared the minutia of a busy two-year-old—the newest word, amusing act, any and all of the things of interest to those who adored her. Reassured that all was well, Norah promised to be home soon and ended the call.

Thank heaven for Aunt Peg!

She wasn't technically her aunt, but the widow of her father's best friend. Norah and her brother, Brett, had known Peg their whole lives, and loved her to bits. From the time they were very little, Peg had been a constant source of support and a buffer between them and their quiet, distant, somewhat grim father and their overbearing, self-involved mother. Whatever the crisis, you went to Peg first, and she got you through. Whether it had been a bad grade, an inappropriate CD turning up mysteriously in Brett's backpack, or a ding in the door of the family car— all right, slightly more than a ding, but it had been a *huge* spider dangling from the rearview mirror, and that had been a stupid place to put a mailbox anyway. No matter, Peg had your back.

The most poignant episode had been when Brett had gone to their parents

The Wrong Woman

to declare he was gay. Norah had known since before Brett had been ready to admit it to himself. She was two-and-a-half years older but, without hesitation or judgment, she'd made it a point to step in when he'd been teased by school mates. She had squelched rumors and even knocked a couple of bullies on their asses. And the day Brett had faced Vic and Mona, she and Peg had been right by his side.

Vic had sat at the kitchen table, jaw clenched in white-hot denial, and Mona had screamed down the house about shame and embarrassment.

Norah had tried to rationalize, to keep the conversation geared toward truths rather than speculation, to point out that this was the reality of who Brett was and not a choice he'd made simply to piss them off. She'd hated that they'd made it all about them, as usual.

Brett had been fifteen at the time, full of hurt feelings, and he felt betrayed. The combination had naturally made him belligerent. A few cracks from his chronically smart mouth and Vic had been on his feet with his hand raised.

Peg, all five feet of her, had launched herself in his path. "That'll do, Victor. You'll not touch one of these children in anger so long as there's breath in my body."

Peg had a real flair, and under different circumstances, Norah would have applauded.

Many years later, when Norah had learned she was going to be a parent—and a single one at that—Peg had been the first one she'd shared the unhappy news with.

After crying herself out against Peg's cable knit cardigan that always smelled of rose oil and bread, she'd declared, "I won't abort. That doesn't feel right for me. But I can't keep it either. It'll be better off, you know, with a family. With people who can offer it everything. What have I got?"

"My darling girl, I would never dream of telling you what to do."

That was how Peg began every speech that ended with her doing just that, and Norah had begrudgingly smiled, secretly rolled her eyes, and then braced herself.

"But you say you've nothing to offer, and I must say, *nonsense!* You are a bright, funny, talented, loving woman, and any child would be lucky to have you for a mother. Did you know that Buddhists believe all the little unborn babies wait up in heaven, checking everyone out, until they find the one special person or people that they think they'll learn the most from during their lifetime? If that's so, this little baby looked down and saw you and said, 'That's the one! That's the mama for me.' Who are you then to give it away when it went to so much trouble to find you?"

Who am I, indeed?

Norah settled back in the plush seats of the limo, her eyes misting at the memory, and realized how exhausted she was. When she reflected on all that had happened since she'd first gotten into this car, it made her head spin, but at the same time she was terrified of forgetting a single detail.

Though she'd never been one for keeping journals, she determined that this was one for the books and promised not to sleep a wink until she'd recorded every moment. Not that she'd be able to sleep anyway. As if today wasn't enough, the fact that tomorrow night she'd be going out to dinner with David Raurke . . .

How is that possible? Mind you, it's not like a date or anything. Men like David don't ask women like me out on dates.

Not that she wasn't a catch. She knew she was. It just wasn't always immediately evident. An ex-boyfriend had told her that he would have walked on by, but she had looked up at him and smiled, and he had kissed his heart goodbye.

So maybe . . .

No. She had more than enough on her plate without letting herself get all gooey over a man. She had a job to do, and she was smart enough to know that this was a once-in-a-lifetime opportunity. She wasn't about to screw it up.

She was giddy all over again with the memory of the shoot. Working with Dennis Austin and Nick Costello. The scene had been pure, real, unforced—everything she could have wished for. The energy between the three of them had positively crackled.

Better than sex.

Her musings returned to David as she nestled deeper into the cushiony backseat. She knew it was her lusty imagination, but she could have sworn there had been something in that hug.

Hmm.

The scent of him lingered in her nostrils, sending a little thrill down to her toes, and if she closed her eyes, she imagined she could still feel his arms around her, pulling her, holding her against him, his voice close, his mouth against her ear, moving lower and lower still . . .

"Mama. Mama bed?"

Norah forced her eyes open and looked around. She was in her room, in her bed, and the lamp was still burning. She had fallen asleep face down on the notebook that she had been writing in. Unfortunately, she now had a painful imprint of the metal coil binding running down her cheek. She winced at the ink stain on her sheet where the pen had come to rest as she dozed off.

"Damn, damn, damn."

"Mama loud."

That's what woke me up.

Ella stood at the side of her bed, adorable in her footsie pajamas, her tousled hair a study in chaotic cute.

"Hey, pooper, did you hear Mama swear?"

"Yeah," she stated, matter-of-factly. "Mama bed?"

"You want to come into Mama's bed?"

"Oday."

Norah reached over, dragged the little bundle into the bed, and covered them both with the duvet. She set the book and pen onto the bedside table, turned out the lamp, then snuggled up next to her darling daughter. For a moment, though, Norah permitted herself to revisit her dream before drifting off once more.

****

David forced his eyes open and looked around, certain he wasn't alone.

How can that be?

He was sure he'd felt the weight of her upon him, her lips hot on his neck, her hips demanding against him.

"Crap!"

He fell back against his pillow. He couldn't remember having a dream that intense since high school, and he relived the same level of frustrated disappointment in waking up.

He looked at the clock on the bedside and moaned. His wake-up call wasn't due for two more hours. He pounded on his pillow, flopped onto his side and tried to relax, but found that was futile. He lowered his hand to the source of his frustration, and while finding the familiar rhythm of his body, he let his mind wander back to the dream that had started it all. Though he never saw the woman's face in the shadows, he knew it had to be Norah.

The pressure from her small body when he'd held her yesterday had imprinted against his like a brand, and for the rest of the evening he had been sure he could smell the clean scent of her all around him. Now, he imagined her again pressed tightly to him, imagined that it was her sweet hand working the tension from his aching body. Blessed relief washed over him, and he happily drifted off.

****

"Morning, boss, how'd you sleep?" asked Jason cheerily, checking something off his clipboard.

"What?" David asked in a tone far testier than normal.

"What what?" Jason looked startled. "I just asked if you, you know, had a good sleep what with the shoot yesterday going so great and . . . never mind, none of my business. Jozef, Steve, and Geoff are waiting for you in your trailer. Grace has second unit filming the pickups from the crime scenes with Katarina and your stand-in. They needed Kosma's footsteps walking away and the weapon landing in the dirt. They have a half a dozen other setups scheduled for the rest of the day, seeing as the weather's so good and they're calling for rain by Friday."

"Anything that needs me specifically?" David glanced at the list of second unit shots.

"No, sir. Kat has it covered. Light day for you." Jason started to walk away.

"Jason?"

"Yes, sir?"

"I slept like a baby, thanks."

Jason smiled and his whole body seemed to sigh. "Yes, sir. You're welcome."

David made a quick stop at craft services for a coffee, before he crossed the compound and hopped up the two metal stairs leading into his standard issue trailer.

He'd never been comfortable with the elite caravans that the producers had tried to ply him with. What a guy needed with a hot tub and a recording studio while shooting a film was beyond him. All he required was an area to change in, a shower big enough that his ass didn't poke through the curtain when he bent down to wash his feet, a bed in case he had a couple of minutes to grab a quick nap, and a decent-sized seating area for production meetings.

These were usually held on Monday mornings, but with the crisis over Helen's accident yesterday, everyone who might have been useful had spread out to see what could be done.

"Gentlemen." He grinned and nodded at each of the men waiting.

Everyone was in high spirits after their good luck yesterday, and far be it from him to be a buzzkill. In fact, he realized he had every reason to be in a terrific mood himself.

Great shoot yesterday, easy day today, interesting evening tonight, and tomorrow?

The possibilities were endless, and he was a man who loved possibilities.

"What are we starting with today?"

"We were just discussing Norah," Steve said.

David coughed a little as his sip of coffee found its way up his throat rather than down. "Really?" He grabbed another breath in between coughs and, without sounding too strained, managed to ask, "What about her?"

"Well, I was telling Geoff what a stroke of luck it was to find her, and all that."

Geoff was the scriptwriter who had based this work on a short story he had started developing during his last year of college.

At the time, David had been dating Geoff's sister, when her little brother had taken the opportunity to mention the script to the then rising star on the off-chance that it might come to something one day. Ironically, David's relationship with Geoff had outlasted the one he'd had with Geoff's sister, by more than a decade so far. One of those odd little twists of fate, he loved the story and had encouraged and even supported the young writer—once he had been able to—in the hopes that he might one day accumulate enough clout to direct the work.

The first time he'd had a studio interested enough to back *Kosma*, he and Geoff had been ecstatic. The ecstasy died quickly when they'd learned that production costs would only be covered if David played the title role. He had fought against it, desperate to keep himself exclusively *behind* the camera. He had already signed Nick, Dennis, Helen Crandall, a handful of other notable names, and he had another very able actor on board for the lead. The money men had found that all well and good, but none of those names put bums in the seats like David Raurke.

David had been furious and unable to understand what the point was of gaining his level of positive notoriety if you still couldn't do a project the way you wanted it done. He'd wanted to pull the plug, go strictly independent, raise the money himself without the studio, but everywhere he'd gone had been the same story—*Sure we'd be happy to sign on, but you have to play Kosma or it's no deal, and I want my sister to play the part of* . . .

He would have called the whole thing off if it hadn't been for Geoff. For him, this wasn't just another film, and there might not be another opportunity like this right around the corner. This was his life's work, and at thirty-one years old, if he was going to break out it had better be soon.

So, hat in hand, David had gone back to the studio who, even if they didn't give a crap about the story, would back it without interference. Providing he stayed under budget and met the deadlines, they had promised to handle the distribution and hadn't given a damn if David cast their sisters or not.

Movies, like life, were a series of compromises.

Geoff pushed his glasses back up on his nose. "Jozef showed me yesterday's dailies, and I have to tell you, that scene really rocked. I'd written it as a means to an end, a way to get Clare on the stand, but now I'm really excited about this Norah woman. I'm thinking of expanding her role. If you've got a minute, I can run my ideas by you. Nothing major, but there have been a couple of holes that I've never been happy with, and I think I've got the patches figured out."

"Sure, let me get through the rest of this first." He turned to Steve. "How would that affect her contract? What did you guys finally cobble together yesterday?" He was curious as to whether or not she had tried to exploit the situation, as Steve had expected.

"Basically, she's settled for scale. All she's asked for is a car and driver, which we would have given her anyway, so that she can spend more time on the script. Having come on board so late, she feels at a bit of a disadvantage, and I couldn't fault her there. I'm throwing in a trailer for good measure. It'll be here and ready when she comes back tomorrow. Certainly, a larger part for her won't hurt us in any way, and if it helps the film . . ."

"So she didn't go for your throat?" David asked, smiling and a little pleased that his instinct about Norah had been dead on. He'd known she would settle for the minimum pay because that's the kind of person he thought she'd be.

Steve, looking slightly remorseful, said, "No. She's a good girl, a real pro."

Jozef concurred. "She is beautiful artist, should have bigger part, make her big star."

David nodded in agreement. "I'll see what I can do, my friend."

They went on for the next three hours discussing scheduling, equipment issues, creative worries, for which Jozef had no end of excellent solutions. Grace joined them to give an update on the second unit during her lunch break, and Jason was called in for status updates concerning the upcoming location and how things were moving on the new set—Clare's apartment—which was needed for tomorrow.

"They're dressing it now if you want to take a look."

"Yeah, in a minute. What time is the call tomorrow morning?"

"Seven, for an eight o'clock start."

"And we're still looking at a day-and-a-half, right?"

"Well, that's the plan. It's a tricky scene."

"Don't I know it?" he grumbled.

Everyone else grinned.

No one knew an actor who enjoyed shooting a love scene, and David was no exception. "I don't have to mention I want a closed set, do I?"

Grace was quick to reassure him. "The notices are already out, boss. It'll only be Jozef, Judy, Bruno on the boom mic, Keith on camera, the focus puller, and me getting a gander at your fine, fine ass."

Everyone guffawed, and David laughed in spite of himself.

Jesus! Did I actually agree to show my ass?

He sighed and made a mental note to read the fine print on *his* contract. "Right, let's get some lunch. C'mon, Geoff, you can tell me about your ideas and then I'll take a look at the set. After that, I'm going to bugger off. I have some prep to do for tomorrow."

"Butt clenches?"

"Grace!"

"Going, boss."

"Yes, let's get food." Jozef hauled himself out of his chair, and the group made their way to the catering tent as Jason dictatorially herded everyone else back to the second unit set.

The men enjoyed their meal while Geoff described the scenes where he was planning to flesh out Clare's character, and strengthen the relationship between her and Kosma. It would also add an unexpected element to Kosma's character, a more human element, increasing his complexity.

David realized the changes meant tomorrow's scene would be even more pivotal than the original plan. He figured out the pieces that they would have to go back and pick up—a couple of brief moments, but nothing second unit couldn't handle. David would mention the changes to the producers, but since he doubted they'd make much of a stink about it, he gave Geoff the go-ahead to write them.

After lunch, Geoff dashed back to the trailer to write, while David and Jozef walked to the soundstage to have a look at the new set.

Construction had been completed last Friday, and Margaret Ulman, the lead decorator, supervised the two dressers on the finishing touches, stepping in from time to time to hang a picture or plump a pillow. She stopped long enough to show David and Jozef around the small, modest, studio apartment.

Keeping in mind that the real Clare had been a dockworker in shipping and receiving, Margaret had been very particular about the pieces and their placement. Clare had a good job with a decent wage, but her tastes were simple and plain, much like herself. A single bed was set against one wall, with cushions piled in a way that allowed it to serve double duty as a sofa. An antique wardrobe stood next to a narrow window which was dressed with a venetian blind. The tiny kitchen was made up of a bar fridge, a hot plate, a small sink, and a microwave oven, banked by only the barest minimum of cupboards. Through an open door, there was a partial bathroom. The small, overstuffed easy chair sat opposite the bed, with an oval rag rug covering hardwood flooring.

Jozef was in a corner near the bed and David joined him to discuss where the action would take place and how it should be lit, based on the mood that David wanted to establish.

After half an hour of lighting talk, David checked his watch for the umpteenth time. "Gotta run, Jozef. I'll see you tomorrow."

He managed to get to the car with only half a dozen crew members catching up to him to ask this or that, and he answered them all without slowing his pace, even if that answer was nothing but a hearty, "Go ask Grace."

By half past three, he was in the car and headed back to town, in his hotel room by just after four, in the shower by seven after, and out again a mere seven minutes later. A quick toweling off, a thorough swipe of deodorant, and he was in his boxers and socks by four eighteen. Next the shave; taking a bit of time there.

No good showing up looking like I've had a run-in with a weed whacker.

Aftershave lotion.

Not too much. Brush the teeth then sort out the hair. Okay, back to the closet.

Black slacks, black mock turtleneck, black sport coat?

No, too severe. It's not a funeral.

Tan slacks, white T-shirt, navy sport coat?

Too preppy.

Black slacks, white button-down, no tie, camel sport coat.

Good, nice.

His sister had picked the jacket out for him a few months ago because she thought the colour brought out the golden tones in his brown eyes.

Whatever.

The white shirt was dressy without being formal, and he had only brought black shoes. He checked his watch again while he fumbled with the buckle.
Shit.
He'd check with Jim, and if it looked like they were going to be late, he'd call her from the car.
Wallet?
Check.
Watch?
Just did it, stupid.
Keys?
Check.
Condom?
Huh, now there's an interesting question.
He dropped the thought immediately and headed quickly for the door.
It was four fifty-eight precisely as they pulled up in front of her house. A handsome, sturdy, two story plus attic, likely built in the early forties. It was pleasantly situated on an acre of land, lined with mature trees, and framed with a tall, wooden, gated fence.
He turned down Jim's offer to collect her; his mother didn't raise him to let another man do his job. Once through the gate, he stopped dead in his tracks. There, in front of the veranda, was a tiny tricycle laid on its side. To his left, a tree swing with a belted safety seat, and to the far right, in an area of the lawn that would receive constant shade, a small inflatable kiddie pool littered with all manner of multicoloured accessories.
It had never even occurred to him.
Why not?
He was pretty sure he hadn't misread the signals . . .
There were signals, right?
He was certain there had been . . . something. Though it wouldn't have been the first time that he'd been on the receiving end of a suggestion that should have been reserved for a significant other.
Still . . .
He was sure he looked as if he'd somehow managed to get lost between the gate and the house, and after a couple of false starts, David stomped up the steps with much heavier feet than the ones he'd slipped into his shoes not a half hour before.
Never mind, David. You still have a film to make, and you can't very well turn around now, can you?
He'd been so sure. And worse, he couldn't deny the fact that he was disappointed. Really disappointed.
He looked for a doorbell and found one of those old-fashioned chimes with a key—the kind that made a merry little sound, which thoroughly mocked his now foul mood.
The door opened and David's stomach completed its drop to the floor.
A man stood before him, early to midthirties, dark hair, darker than

Norah's, not quite as tall as him, David noticed with some satisfaction, but certainly good-looking enough.

He fixed David with a steady stare mixed with a little surprise, maybe a shade of suspicion, and a touch of . . .

What?

"Hello, I'm Brett," the man said, holding his hand out and giving David a very delicate handshake.

Holy crap! I wonder if Norah knows her husband's . . .

"Uh . . . I . . . yeah. How do you do?"

"Won't you come in?" Brett stepped to the side and allowed David to enter through the porch, which was framed in beautiful stained glass, and into the front hall.

He gestured to an entryway on the right, and David found himself in a lovely room with high ceilings, a small fireplace, and finely finished dark oak floors. A large window to the front overlooked the yard, and to the rear, french doors led into what looked like the dining room. Two sofas flanked the fireplace and Brett invited him to sit in one.

"Forgive me," he said, feeling completely flustered. "I'm David Raurke."

"Yes, you are, aren't you?" Brett said pleasantly as he sat down across from him. "May I get you anything? A drink, a cigarette . . . a change of plans?"

"Pardon?"

"Never mind. Small joke."

Just then, David heard footsteps on the stairs.

Chapter 4

She heard the doorbell ring as she slipped on her shoes. She didn't trust herself to rise, not yet. She prayed Brett wouldn't make a total ass of himself, but she sure wished she could see his face when he opened the door and saw David Raurke standing there.

She'd spent the past three hours trying to describe every detail of yesterday to him, since she'd torn out of the café with barely more than a phone call home to Aunt Peg and a shout to him that she'd explain later.

He'd bombarded her with questions and tried to trip her up or catch her in a fib, as she had clearly gone out of her mind, according to him.

They'd continued their argument through the bathroom door while she had showered, and through the closet door as she'd dressed. He'd even refused to zip her up, saying he wouldn't enable her sad little fantasy, but watched from the end of her bed instead as she twisted and writhed and bent her arms in all manner of unnatural angles to get the job done herself.

Talking out of the other side of your ass now, aren'tcha?

Then she realized that he might indeed be talking and figured she'd better step on it before the silly twit sent David screaming down the street.

Facing the armoire mirror, she had to admit she looked very nice. She'd styled her hair with care and taken some trouble with her makeup. She stared at her eyes, as the reflection looked back with a smoky allure. Her dress had been custom-made for her for a play she had been in several years ago, and it was a point of pride that, even after having Ella, the black crepe dress with its subtle dotted print, still fit her perfectly.

A shallow scoop neck in the front, it fitted her through the bodice, and flared away gently from the waist to just below her knee. A modest, classic design. At least until she turned around. The back made the impact. It was cut very low—more than halfway to her waist—and required a special bra, but she had a nice back and the cut only complimented it. She might not be a knock-out, but she had a decent figure—small but strong.

She had grown up in a neighbourhood of boys, so it was boys she'd hung out with and boys' games she'd played. By the time she'd gotten to junior high, she had been too involved in sports to get caught up in the body anxiety that many of her female peers had suffered through. Besides, she hadn't been interested in girlie things or girlie clothes, so it hadn't mattered. Unfortunately, when the day came that she had started to look at the boys differently, they had still looked at her the same. Norah had been the one the guys came to when they'd wanted one of the other girls to know they had a crush on them.

In retrospect, it had been for the best.

She'd grown up fit and healthy, never bothered to diet, and could not relate to the fingers down the throat crap from her teen years. True, she'd never acquired the art of girl talk, but she could count on one hand the number of women she'd known who she'd had any interest in talking to about anything that mattered, apart from Peg.

No, she still preferred the company of men.

She enjoyed most of the things they did. She understood their language and loved the hard, hairiness of them. The fact that she wasn't a size two and could crush them in a leg lock didn't slow her down a bit. She'd maintained friendships with all of her ex-boyfriends through the years, because they respected her, and that was good enough for her.

She took one last nervous look before grabbing her purse and wrap, then making her way to the stairs.

She held the handrail all the way down in an effort to lighten her step, certain she sounded like a shod horse, and peered into the parlor where she'd firmly instructed Brett to invite David when he arrived.

Brett had looked at her as if she had lost her mind and said, "Yes, Blanche, honey. When your gentleman caller comes, I shall have him wait in the parlor and offer him a mint julep."

God, give me strength.

David rose to his feet as she entered the room, and the look on his face was worth the extra effort she'd put into her appearance. He also appeared a bit shaky, but she put it down to what was likely a typical exchange with Brett.

"I see you've met my brother," she said with an acidic sidelong glance at the cretin.

"Your brother?"

Something she couldn't quite name flashed across his face.

Surely, he didn't think . . .

"Yes, well. Brett, *David Raurke*," she said pointedly.

"Yes, fine, you win. Please excuse me, David. It was lovely meeting you, but I must hurry if I want to cancel the ambulance. Have fun." With a grin, a wave, and something resembling a bow-curtsy hybrid, Brett was gone.

David turned to her. "The ambulance?"

"I'll tell you in the car. Shall we?" She stepped toward the door and thought she heard something catch in his throat. She looked back and caught a small smile play about his mouth.

"You look very nice."

"Thank you. So do you."

Soon they were settled into the car and coasting along the highway.

"So . . ." he said.

"So," she replied nervously.

This is going to be a dull drive if someone doesn't smarten up.

"Brett is pretty . . . *interesting*."

She laughed. "That's one way to put it, I suppose."

He reached into a compartment in front of them and expertly opened the chilled bottle of champagne, pouring them each a glass.

This is pretty interesting, too.

He took a deep breath and paused a moment, obviously putting a bit of thought into what he wanted to say. "I've come a long way in life believing that hard work and a positive attitude would get you everything you needed. So I'm guessing I got the message across because, just when I needed something the most, you walked in." With a smile, he gently clinked his glass to hers and took a sip.

She stared at him then closed her gaping mouth with an audible click. "Wow." She took a bigger drink than she'd intended as she'd suddenly gone completely cottonmouthed. She tried to suppress a sputter as the unexpected hit of bubbles tickled her throat and nose. "That was just about the finest thing anyone has ever said to me, and I thank you. Um, well, I believe that as well, and although I didn't ask for this *specific* opportunity, I am so grateful that Ted and Steve waltzed into my gin joint yesterday. Thank you, again, for taking a chance on me. That was very brave. I think it's going to be a fabulous film, and I feel blessed to be even a small part of it. So . . ." She clinked her glass to his. ". . . cheers, tally ho, whatever."

"Whatever." He chuckled, and they sipped some more champagne.

"Tell me something. Did you think Brett was my . . . partner?"

"Um, yeah, I guess I did."

"You didn't get the gay vibe off him?"

"No, no. I did. I thought . . . I don't know what I thought. Now, what was that about an ambulance?" he said quickly, changing the subject.

"Oh, right. Well, in his defense—and you have no idea how many conversations I have about him that have to begin that way—I did have a pretty unusual day yesterday. It sounded even more so when I tried to tell him about it. The icing on the cake was when I told him, 'oh, and David Raurke is picking me up at five o'clock to take me to dinner'. He was basically ready to tie me into one of those jackets with the sleeves in the back."

David laughed outright. "So he thought you were right off your nut, then?"

"Can you blame him? It sounded like pure lunacy coming out of my mouth and I *lived* it. It's a good thing that you didn't stand me up. He would have made my life a nightmare. Can you imagine?"

The Wrong Woman

They both laughed.

After a moment, he looked as if he had something else on his mind but seemed to shake it away. Instead, he smiled. "So you think we have a good movie here?"

"Uh-huh," she answered, grateful for safe territory. "It's such a good read. The plot line is compelling, and I love how human Kosma's been written. It goes a long way to explaining how all those girls were lured to their deaths. I mean, who wouldn't get into a car with that guy? Top it with the fact he's going to look like, well . . . *you*, and it's all over but the yucky stuff. I haven't read a lot of movie scripts but I expect they're quite a bit different than stage plays."

"Why do you say that?"

"Well, in a film, there seems to be so much more said visually. I mean, there were a couple of areas that seemed a bit unclear in print, or maybe I'm being a bit sensitive. I have some questions about Clare that aren't answered in the screenplay, so far as I can see. I'm not criticizing," she said, as she reached out and lightly touched his knee. "I have to dig a bit deeper. God, wouldn't it be great to talk to her?" She realized David was looking at her with an expression she couldn't quit discern. "What?"

"I'll tell you later, I promise. So, any thoughts on our scene tomorrow?"

She took another deep drink of her champagne.

She had read the scene many times over the course of the day. She had even called Ella's paternal grandparents last night to see if they could take her for a while this morning, so she didn't feel as though she was neglecting her child for the sake of some scene work. She'd told Brett she wouldn't be in the café at all, turned off the phone, made herself a bucket of tea, and curled up on the sofa.

It was a painfully raw scene with two horribly damaged people trying desperately to find comfort, contact, maybe even love, and neither believing they deserved it or were worthy of the other.

"It's going to be a tough one." She reached into her clutch purse and pulled out several pages of folded notes and flattened them out on her lap. "My first thoughts were that the interaction had to proceed very . . . tentatively, you know? Like, for my part—Clare's part, rather—there's this total disbelief. I mean, I simply can't comprehend how someone like you could be interested in someone like me." She looked up to find a bemused smile on his face, and she felt the heat rise up to her cheeks. "Obviously what I mean is—"

He placed his hand over hers on the seat between them. "Don't worry about it. I prefer it when actors speak about their characters in the first person. It's easier that way. More personal, less confusing. So why do you think he's with her? I mean, why am I with you?"

"I don't know. I've considered the possibility that maybe you feel sorry for me. I expect that's happened to me before. I'm even a bit worried that you're having some fun at my expense, like maybe you'll get together with your friends afterward and laugh about going slumming. That sort of thing. What I want more than anything is to believe that you have seen what I only suspect—that I'm actually a lovely person, but I don't think I trust that possibility."

He nodded. "Interesting."

"So why are you with me?" she asked.

This is getting tricky.

It was impossible to miss the parallels, and she was very aware that he hadn't yet removed his hand from hers.

A flash of confusion in his eyes told her he was having trouble, too. Then there was that shy-boy smile that made her all wobbly.

He cleared his throat before answering. "I think you're one of the most honest, kind, and endearing people I've ever met. You've none of the superficiality that I've come to expect from women. You don't flaunt your sexuality like the others, and most important of all, when I'm with you I feel like I can be . . . a normal man, that I can be the person that I want to be, and that I don't have to hurt anyone anymore."

She had watched his face as he spoke. Listening to the smooth, deep timbre of his voice, she felt hypnotized by him. She put down the champagne glass.

"More?" he asked indicating her glass.

"Oh, thank you, no." She flipped through her notes and pulled her hand out from under his in an effort to refocus on what he had said and get her imagination back on the script where it belonged. "Yes, yes, that's good. That'll put me at ease. If I sense that you're sincere, I'll let my guard down, a little bit anyway."

David pulled a copy of the script out of the binder on the seat across from them and drew a crude rendering of a floor plan.

They discussed blocking the moments of the scene—when they're coming in the door, does she take his coat? Is there a coat rack or a hook, or maybe he hangs it over a chair? They imagined Kosma was hyperaware of leaving evidence behind and therefore cognizant of exactly where he stood, what he'd touched, and where his belongings were. It was a trait that would radically change the way Kosma would move about the room, how he would handle things, or where he'd allow his hands to rest. They spent a lot of time finding their way to their first touch.

David was adamant about the moment being organic and unforced. He refused to have one of those hackneyed movements where they bumped into each other while making coffee and fell into a bodice-ripping grope-fest.

They bantered possibilities back and forth, but nothing felt right.

"Maybe it should be a conscious decision," She said.

"What do you mean?"

"I think one of them chooses to reach out . . . something completely unrelated to the moment in the scene—"

"So it comes as a surprise. To both of them."

"And, if we're lucky, to the audience."

He scribbled notes on the pages, his excitement evident. "That's great. Damn, I wish Geoff were here."

"Geoff?"

"The screenwriter."

"Oops, sorry."

"Don't apologize. I'm impressed that you've managed to read the whole script. Skipping the writer's name is forgivable, to me anyway, and I promise not to tell him."

"Thanks. So why do you wish he were here? Do you think there should be dialogue?"

He thought for a long moment and then, with a very sexy glint in his eye, he said, "You know what? No. We don't need dialogue. I know exactly how it's going to happen." He started rifling through the script but she interrupted him.

"Don't tell me."

"What?"

"Don't tell me. When we run it tomorrow, let's just play it. It'll help with that element of surprise thing."

"Good idea. We might even get a chance to do some improv?"

"Improv?" She smiled at him.

"Yeah, improv. You know, when . . ." He looked up from his notes, caught her amused expression, rolled his eyes, and grinned. "Oh right, I forgot, we got us a know-it-all stage actor. Aren't you a *big* deal? Aren't you the artist?"

"Shut up." She gave him a playful shove and was pleased when he shoved her back.

The rest of the trip was spent in a similar, casual manner. They laughed and regaled each other with horror stories from both theatre and movie productions—lines lost, props falling apart, walking into walls, fellow actors and their bizarre mannerisms or behaviors. Before they knew it, they were seeing the outskirts of the city on the horizon.

Norah felt great. And hungry. "Where are we going, by the way?"

"There's a very nice place a friend told me about, Sampson's or something."

"I've heard of it. Pretty schmancy."

"Ah, well, nothing but the best for . . . what did you say your name was?"

"Hardy-har. Do you think we're going to be bothered? I mean, one of us is kinda famous and all."

"Yeah, but they have a private room here. I called last night to reserve it."

"Oh."

"You don't mind, do you? It's not for me, really. I couldn't care less, and around here it's not so bad, but there's a chance you might get a pretty bad time."

"You're probably right."

"You sure?"

"Sure. No problem."

Or was there?

Never one to pay attention to that nasty little voice that drives some people to seek therapy, religion, or gym memberships, Norah was bewildered to discover that she *was,* in fact . . . what? Offended? Hurt? Indignant? But why? Did she think he was hiding her? That he was ashamed to be seen with her?

We're colleagues, for pity's sake. What possible difference does it make where we eat?

She felt preposterous, and yet the bone-deep insecurities nurtured by a lifetime of less than supportive parenting made it clear, in no uncertain terms, that a man like David Raurke was a million miles out of her league.

Not that it matters.

She felt rather than saw him watching her battle her demons. She turned and forced a smile.

Their eyes locked in a flash of total intimacy, and then he reached up and gently touched her cheek.

The car came to a halt and broke the moment.

Jim jumped out and opened the door on David's side.

David got out and reached back in for her hand. He instructed Jim that he'd call and reminded him to get something to eat as well, before taking her elbow and escorting her through the front door.

It was a beautiful room—dark oak paneling, heavy brocade draperies, high-back chairs or lush settees placed on either side of tables laden with crisp linens, gleaming crystal, and fine china. Only a few elegantly dressed people were seated here and there, since it was still fairly early on a Tuesday evening.

A maître d' approached them. "Mr. Raurke, such a pleasure to have you with us this evening. And the lovely lady. We have your private dining room ready, if you would—"

"Actually, we'd rather have a table in the front here. If you have something available."

The maître d' didn't miss a beat. "Certainly, sir. Right this way, if you please." He led them to a gorgeous semicircular sofa, a high-backed and deep-seated booth arrangement against one wall.

The server had to pull out the small round table and, once settled, David ordered a bottle of wine then placed his left arm on the back of the bench so that he was half facing her.

She sat very still, certain that her pitiful demeanor had brought about this change of plans.

"I'm sorry," he said.

"Why are you sorry?" she asked softly, and looked into his eyes.

He took a deep breath. "Because. Listen, I am thrilled to have you in my

The Wrong Woman

cast, and I would be proud to have you as my . . . as my friend. I never want to do or say anything that would make you feel like I wanted to hide you away. That wasn't . . . I took my twin sister out to lunch a couple of years ago, for our birthday. Some people took photos. They got in the rags, and absolutely trashed her. I thought I was . . . I don't know . . . protecting you, I guess."

She placed her hand gently on his, moved by his admission and perception. "David, I can't begin to imagine or understand what it is to be in your world. To suffer through that kind of scrutiny day after day, I really can't. And I know it's ridiculous for me to think that I can handle whatever might come my way as a result of working with you on this film but, for the duration of this shoot, I *am* in this world, your world, and I might as well face what I need to face and hope for the best." She gave his knee a warm squeeze. "I do appreciate your wanting to save me from it, and the story about your sister helped, but more than that, I appreciate you taking my feelings to heart and getting a seat here. That was . . . that was good. Could you do one more thing for me?"

"Sure."

"Order."

"What?"

"Order. Dinner. I'm famished."

****

Their appetizers arrived in short order, and they discussed safe subjects over a lovely cheese arrangement, salad, and the first glass of wine—hometowns, first jobs, favorite songs.

Then he decided to revisit the elephant in the room . . . in his room, at any rate. He wasn't sure what was going to happen with her. He knew that he was enchanted by her, and he needed to be certain whether or not there was a possibility, because he was a man who loved possibilities.

"Tell me about your child."

For the briefest second, she seemed to freeze, then she put down her salad fork and gave him her full attention.

"Her name is Ella. She turned this many . . ." She held up two fingers the way small children do. ". . . three months ago. She has copper-coloured hair and blue eyes, and she is the love of my life."

He enjoyed the way her face lit up when she spoke of her daughter. He wanted to ask her more, but for now there was an important question that he needed answered. "And where is her father?" He tried to sound casual, but he doubted he pulled it off.

She smiled at him, and he had that feeling again that she knew more about him than he was comfortable with. She took a small sip of wine then rested her chin on her hand. "He was in Kazakhstan."

"Oh?"

Her silence filled in the blank.

"Oh! Oh, God." He felt like a perfect ass. "I'm sorry. I—"

"No, don't feel bad. Well, not for me, anyway. I mean I'd known him since . . . forever. We started dating in high school, but after eight years or so our families started to pressure us to marry. We both knew that would be a disaster, so we split up. We stayed friends, of course, very good friends. In fact, I was his best *person* at his wedding."

"Really, how was that?"

"Oh, the wedding was a riot. The marriage? Not so much. It lasted about four years or so, which I could have told him. Anyway, he'd signed up with the Reserves right after graduation, and when Canada started sending her troops into Afghanistan, off he went. The day before he was shipped out, we got together to hoist a brew, that sort of thing. I can't honestly tell you how it happened, but in retrospect, I think we both knew he wouldn't be coming home."

"He was killed."

Obviously, idiot.

"Four months later, just ten days after my first prenatal ultrasound."

"Did he know?"

She shook her head. "No, I worried that it would make things worse for him over there, and, to be honest, there was a long while when I was considering giving her up, so there mightn't have been any point. Before I could make up my mind about any of it . . ."

"I'm . . . I don't know what to say."

"Ach! Don't worry about it. It's all been said. He was a nice man, and Ella will know that. I feel bad for his folks. He was an only child, so naturally, they're in pieces."

"At least Ella's around." He made an effort to sound sensitive though he still felt like he'd stepped in it. "You know, she's a piece of him. That's gotta be a good thing."

Norah's face broke into a wide, warm smile and she touched his arm.

He took her hand and placed it in his. "Norah?"

"David."

"Are you . . . involved with anyone?"

"No. You?"

"No."

"Interesting."

"Very."

"David?"

"Norah."

"May I, please?"

"What?"

"May I please have a bite of your cheese?"

He laughed the laugh of a happy man. "Oh, honey. You may take a bite of whatever your heart desires." He cut off a piece of the crispy morsel and

fed it to her.
"Mister, I might just take you up on that."

Chapter 5

Hours later, they reluctantly got up from the table. It wasn't late, but they had a long return trip and a very early call in the morning.

She was fairly sure the meal had been splendid. She'd gone all gaga halfway through, and her taste buds had stopped communicating with her brain.

He guided her to the door with his hand resting on the small of her back. Then, as they waited outside for the car, she felt his fingers trail little lines on the bare flesh between her shoulder blades, causing a shiver to run through her. She glanced back with a smile and caught him looking at her in a way that made her breath catch.

He leaned in, and with his mouth nearly touching her ear, he whispered, "I very much like this dress on you, but I prefer the parts of you it isn't on."

It was all she could do to keep her knees locked under her.

****

She slid into the car and waited while he took a moment to remove his jacket before settling in beside her. She noticed that the partition between the passenger seats and the driver, which had been only halfway up on the trip in, was now completely closed. She raised her eyebrows and wondered if it was common practice.

"Did you have a nice time?" he asked as they pulled away, interrupting her reverie.

"You know I did. Did you?"

"In every way. Do you feel okay about tomorrow?"

She thought for a few minutes and then she realized there was something that was nagging at her. "Is there going to be nu-nudit-ity?" she asked, and he chuckled. She took a deep breath and tried again. "I mean, there aren't any actions or stage directions. Just the destination, not the journey, as it were. *'They attempt to have sex . . . the end.'* I mean, I know that's one of the things we'll work out tomorrow. I just thought I'd like to have some idea, you know, going in."

"Well, I'm doing butt clenches as we speak," he said, then he laughed as fear and trepidation met head-on across her face. He took her hands between his own. "I don't know for sure. I guess it depends on what we do with it tomorrow, like you said. I take it you're not comfortable with the idea?"

"It's not that I'm uncomfortable with nudity as a rule." She was going to wisecrack about being quite comfortable unclothed around him, but thought better of it. "And I know I signed the damned contract saying that if it were integral to the story . . . blah, blah, blah, and I kind of like the idea of a woman who is not a supermodel getting it on in a film. However, you've got to admit, it is a pretty interesting way of-of-of getting to know someone."

Smiling, he kissed the back of each of her hands. "Do you know why I asked you out tonight?"

"Not to discuss the script?"

"Nah. I could have easily had you come to my trailer." He wiggled his eyebrows, winked, and clicked his tongue.

"Nice. Fully loaded with your very own casting couch, no doubt?"

"No way, baby, that's old school. Nowadays we just have a cushion."

She looked confused.

"For kneeling."

She laughed. "Funny. One hitch though . . . I already have the part."

"Curses. No, I wanted to go out with you like this because . . ." He seemed to lose his train of thought, or was it his nerve? "Obviously, I thought it would help the scene if we got to know each other better."

"But we could have done that in your trailer, too." Imitating him, she wiggled her eyebrows, winked, and clicked her tongue.

He laughed, but it was clear he was struggling "Yes, yes, we could have, but . . ."

"You don't have to tell me," she said softly.

He looked into her eyes and took a deep breath. "I wanted to kiss you. I don't know when it started—maybe before we were even introduced. You looked up at me and it was like . . . cut to David making an ass of himself by hauling actress across the table and kissing the life out of her in front of the crew, fade to black."

There was a long pause while that delicious little scenario got settled all nice and cozy in her belly.

"Well, that's . . . wow! That's pretty flattering."

And hot.

"Yeah, well, when I learned that we'd be shooting that scene tomorrow, all I've been thinking about is yes, I want to kiss you, but there's more to it than that. I don't want . . . I don't want their kiss, Clare and Wayne's kiss, to be *our* first kiss."

"You wanted us to have one of our own." The words slipped from her lips so softly they were practically a whisper.

He winced. "Too corny?"

"Absolutely." She reached up and tenderly stroked his face and turned his chin so he was facing her. "And about the most romantic thing I've ever heard in my life."

"Really?"

"Really."

"Okay." He breathed a sigh, smiled into her eyes, and leaned in. "Norah Rothe, I'm going to kiss you now."

She reached up and placed a finger on his lips. "No, you're not," she said, with a small smile.

"Excuse me?" He looked more than a little alarmed.

"David, we are in the backseat of a car—"

"Technically, the backseat of a *limousine*."

"Okay, the backseat of a limousine, but there is a man sitting six feet away."

"Oh. Don't worry. He can't hear us, he can't see us, and he wouldn't care if he could."

She glowered.

"Fine." He sat back with an exaggerated pout.

"Tell you what, you may walk me to my door like a gentleman. Won't that be nice?"

"Yeah, but that's, like, over an hour away."

He laughed, and she was sure he knew how ridiculous he sounded. "Listen, I've been watching you on television and in the movies since you first started."

"So?"

"So I've wanted to kiss you for the last decade or more. I think you can handle waiting one hour for me."

He grinned. "You've wanted to kiss me for the last decade?"

"You betcha, baby."

"That's pretty cool."

With his arm still around her, she laid her head against his shoulder, breathed in the masculine scent of him, and they chatted quietly about nothing in particular.

In a gesture more natural than it probably should have been, she laid her hand on his chest and traced the patch of skin visible above the top of his shirt with a fingertip. She felt his heart beat under her palm and was aware that her touch caused it to pound faster and faster. She smiled.

"Are we there yet?" he moaned.

She giggled but agreed with the sentiment. She'd never known this trip to take so long.

He pressed his free hand over hers for a moment then lifted it to his mouth and, while she watched, he slowly kissed every knuckle of each finger before turning her hand over and kissing every inch of her palm at the same agonizing pace. Never taking his eyes from hers, he moved his mouth to that small sensitive area where her hand met her wrist, and danced the tip of his tongue along her pulse.

She drew in a ragged breath and sighed. "Are we there yet?"

He smiled and moved his mouth along her wrist to her lower arm. By the time he reached the inside of her elbow, she was sure she'd lost her mind.

"Listen," she said, trying to keep her voice from quavering. "I've had a little change of heart. People have been having first kisses in the backseats of cars since the Model T, so who am I—"

His smile broadened as he shook his head. "No, you were right. You see, I happen to have a lot of respect for the art of anticipation. Not to brag, but it's not a dance I get to enjoy very often, and I'm very much enjoying this dance with you."

"Really?"

"Really."

The rhythm within the car changed, and after peering out the window, Norah recognized the town's outer limits. She grew aware of an almighty blush washing over her and was disquieted to feel her yummy dessert turn to rocks in her stomach. She sat back to replace one of the shoes she'd kicked off, and effectively avoided his gaze. As she leaned forward for the second one, she felt his touch on her bare back once more. She couldn't suppress a sigh and peeked up shyly.

He looked at her with such tenderness before pulling her into his arms, and with her head against his chest, they covered the last few blocks to her house.

Jim opened their door and waited patiently.

"Good night, Jim," she said, before heading for her gate.

"Good night, Miss Rothe. I'll be here at six thirty sharp."

"See you then."

While fiddling with the latch, she heard David briefly mumble something to Jim before he joined her.

David caught up to her at the gate, and they slowly made their way along the walk and up the steps to the veranda. He had not quite reached the landing when Norah turned to face him, stopping him on the step beneath her by placing both her hands on his shoulders.

As light and animated as her voice sounded, she was certain that she wasn't fooling anyone. "Have you ever gone to a movie and seen the trailer for an upcoming feature that looked so terrific, you couldn't wait to see it, only to discover when you finally get there, all the best bits had been put in the trailer?"

He stared with confusion, then laughed out loud. "Sweetheart, I don't know about you, but I prefer to save my best bits for the movie. My trailer is just a tease, I promise."

She smiled sheepishly and turned to continue up to the veranda, but his hands tightened on her waist. Standing this way, a step above him, she could easily look up at him without straining.

It felt as though everything was suspended in time, quiet and still, waiting. Once this line was crossed, they could never go back.

Her hands slid from his shoulders to his neck, and she tilted her head ever so slightly, meeting him halfway.

He pulled her body to him with one arm as his other hand caressed her hair.

Their lips touched, barely brushing, but the heat was unmistakable.

He pulled back and looked over every inch of Norah's face then his mouth was upon hers again, firmer this time.

Norah was overwhelmed. It's not every day that a woman finds herself in the arms of a man who represented all that was desirable—tall, handsome, sexy, wealthy, talented, internationally renowned.

He's a movie star, *for crying out loud! David frickin' Raurke is kissing me good night on my front porch.*

More than that, though, in an admittedly short period of time she'd learned he was kind, compassionate, sometimes charmingly awkward, and really, really funny. She liked him. For him. And that first light touch of his lips on hers had started a buzzing in her head that required her to stop doing so much ridiculous thinking and pay attention.

She leaned in and took the kiss one step deeper.

He responded by teasing her, visiting the corners of her mouth with the tip of his tongue and feeding the hunger that was building inside her. Her hands, once timidly around his neck, found their way down his body. One pulled him ever closer, and the other explored his chest through his shirt. She felt tremors vibrate through him as she drew his bottom lip between her teeth.

She felt something claim her, something compelling and dangerous at the same time. She knew she had to stop, but before she could pull away he released her with a gasp and stumbled, nearly falling, as if he'd forgotten he was on the steps.

She leaned against the railing, gripping it tightly, and noted that he looked almost as shocked as she felt. "Oh my . . . goodness." She touched her lips lightly, half expecting to find them ablaze.

He shook a finger at her. "What the hell do you call that?"

Her hand flew off her mouth. "I'm sorry, *what?*"

He spun around and sat, hard, on the fourth tread.

She struggled to get her quaking insides under control.

He reached for her hand and tugged her down until she sat beside him. He put both his arms around her small body, and she felt his lips on the top of her head.

He laughed. "Well, I would have to say, that kicked the hell out of the trailer."

She laughed along with him and cuddled into his arms.

They sat quiet for a few moments then she turned toward him.

"I need to ask you something. It's really stupid, and I want you to feel totally free to lie to me, but have you ever—"

"Never," he answered, shaking his head emphatically, and she could see that he meant it. "Not even close. You?"

"Hell, no," she replied without hesitation.

"Well, we're going to have to revisit this soon . . . and *often*, I think. For now, we should both get some—"

"Sleep?"

"Yeah, sleep."

"Yeah, good luck with that." She rose from the steps and rooted through her bag for the key.

He stood and turned her face to him. He looked deep into her eyes for several long seconds before leaning in and placing the softest kiss on her mouth.

She savoured his taste only a moment before she wisely pulled away. Still, that brief tenderness set her insides quaking again.

How am I ever going to get enough of that?

She felt his eyes on her as she went through the door and shut it behind her.

Chapter 6

Norah stood at the beverage table in craft services, a breakfast burrito in one hand and a cup of strong tea in the other, when she felt a familiar hand on her back. Without looking up, she knew who it was.

"Good morning," she said, trying to sound casual while getting the riot in her stomach under control.

"Good morning. How are you?"

"Great. I have a trailer. How cool is that?" Then she went back to scooping her tea bag into the waste receptacle.

"Congratulations. When do you go into wardrobe?"

"Yuckity-yuk, you're such a funny fellow."

She had been in costume for the past forty-five minutes, her hair completed thirty minutes ago, and she had only just come out of the makeup chair. She looked dowdy, frowsy and plain . . . in other words, perfect.

"It's true. I'm a terribly funny man. So can I borrow you for a moment?"

"Sure. Where?"

He gestured over his shoulder. "My trailer."

They started walking toward the circus.

She took a tentative sip of her tea before she asked, "This doesn't have anything to do with a cushion, does it?"

He laughed and then took a breath as if to say something, but thought better of it. "Yuckity-yuk."

They arrived at his caravan and he held the door open for her. She climbed in and took a cursory look around before turning to face him. He was so serious all at once. Her stomach began to pitch in the other direction.

This is it. He's going to tell me he's ashamed of his behavior last night, can't work with me, and I've been replaced by someone with really big tits.

He stood in the galley kitchen, leaning with his hands braced on the countertops on either side. His head was tilted down, as though it took great effort to put into words what he needed to say.

At the precise moment she was convinced she would collapse from dread, he looked up and said in a small voice, "Kiss me."

Her eyes widened and she was sure the relief showed in her face. She paused only long enough to set all her stuff down on the table, then walked slowly toward him, all the while expecting him to make another joke. He said nothing, there was only the tiniest flicker in his eyes as she placed her hands on either side of his face and kissed him with all the tenderness that she felt.

He sighed and placed his hands on her hips.

She couldn't stand the thought of getting lost in the intensity of last night and withdrew as the dizziness started clouding her mind.

He pulled her into an embrace and they stood breathing each other in for a full minute before he released her.

"Not that I'm complaining or anything, but what was that about?" she asked.

"I needed to . . . to touch base, I guess."

"Okay." She tried to sound like she understood.

"It's going to be a pretty rough day for us, and I wanted to go into it—"

"Knowing where we stop and they start?"

He smiled. "Perfect. Exactly. Thank you."

"No, thank *you*." She held onto the moment one extra beat before getting back to the business at hand. "Don't you have to get into costume?"

He frowned. "I am. I only need a minute in Hair."

Naturally, he was as beautiful as ever, dressed in a paprika-coloured V-neck sweater and snug-fitting jeans, and she was the queen of frump in sweatpants and flannel.

"Aw, man," she whined. She had the feeling she was never going to be the pretty one in this setup. She gathered her things and headed toward the door.

"Oh, Norah?"

"Hmm?"

"I know I don't have to tell you, but we should keep this, keep us, you know, under wraps . . . for a while."

She tried to come off less insulted than she felt. "Oh, you mean I shouldn't have posted my declaration of love for you on today's call sheet?"

He stood, grinning sheepishly, and folded his arms across his chest. "Yuckity-yuk."

Twenty minutes later, David arrived onto the soundstage.

Norah had come straight from his trailer and spent the time wandering Clare's apartment—*her* apartment—until it got under her skin. She performed small tasks—came in the door as she would every day from work, turned on the lights, hung up her coat. She walked through fixing a cup of coffee, read a magazine in the chair, walked to the bathroom, as though she'd done these things a thousand times.

Jozef came over at one point, took her by the shoulders, and kissed her on the forehead. He looked down at her, nodded a few times, then wordlessly returned to his business.

Okeydokey.

She went back to her script.

The electrics and grips clambered about, following Jozef's instructions for lighting as he faced the challenge of getting it all set as well as possible, since everything that had been blocked with stand-ins the day before was thrown out.

Today, they were going to make it up as they went along.

This also meant the camera operator had to be on his toes. He had to grab the action and hang on. It was going to be an interesting day, full of stops and starts, dialogue and action rejected on the spot, and lots of unknown variables muddying up the works. It was a risky venture, but it was exactly the kind of by-the-seat-of-your-pants filmmaking that kept the industry interesting and alive.

David claimed that Norah had inspired him to the point that he'd decided they were going to improvise this scene.

Inspired, inschmired. He wants a good scapegoat should the whole thing land in the crapper.

David joined Norah on the set, and they worked out their entrance to Clare's apartment, keeping in mind all of the things that they'd discussed yesterday.

The filming of the first sequence went fairly smoothly.

Clare unlocks her door and removes her key from the deadbolt. As she steps inside, Wayne Kosma stands in the hall outside.

"C'mon in." Clare dips her head as Wayne steps past, and she hides behind her curtain of hair.

She switches on the overhead light, and Wayne casually takes in the room.

He places his hand over hers on the doorknob, and she pulls away as if burned. He smiles then closes the door.

She peeks at him through her hair. "Can I take your coat?" she asks, while shrugging off her own heavy parka, trying to maintain a calmness in her voice that she clearly doesn't feel.

He reaches over to help her and the strangeness of the gesture stops her short.

"I've got it," he replies, his honey-smooth voice.

She lets her coat drop off her arms and steps quickly away, leaving him to hook it on the tree before removing his black pea coat and hanging it carefully alongside.

She moves toward the kitchenette, pausing to turn on the lamp next to the easy chair, then turns to him. "Oh, I thought I'd make some coffee. Would you like a cup?"

"Coffee would be perfect. Thank you."

She smiles with timid delight then turns to the task at hand. She flexes her fingers, whether to warm them into working order or to shake out the tremors of her nerves is anyone's guess.

He wanders around her tiny, spartan apartment, giving the impression he's taking in the evidence of her life, but he seldom takes his eyes from her. His look is full of intrigue, curiosity, and maybe a hint of something softer.

"I hope instant is okay?" she asks, as she prepares their cups.

"Yeah, in fact, I prefer it. Weird, huh?"

She smiles back at him. "No. I don't think it's weird." It's clear in her soft tone that nothing this man did would ever be weird in her eyes.

He stands a few steps away, his hands folded in front of him, watching her every move. The rich colour of his sweater deepens his skin tones so that he resembles a bronze statue.

She sighs a tiny sigh, then before he can witness her adoration, goes back to the coffee.

He catches it and smiles to himself. Taking a deep breath, he gestures around the room. "This is a nice place. Have you lived here long?"

"Uh, yeah. Seven years next month. Um, thanks." Stirring the water and coffee together, she winces each times the spoon clinks against the edge of the cup. "What do you take in your coffee?"

"Black is fine, no sugar please."

She smiles and grabs the cups by their handles. She turns back to the kitchen, looks at the cups then around the room. Her head drops slightly and her chin quivers.

He sees her dismay. "Here, let me help with that." He reaches for one of the cups.

"No, thanks, I've got it." In her attempt to show she could at least get the crap coffee to the crap coffee table, she sloshes a bit onto his hand and wrist.

"Oh, damn it!" Clare cries out.

"Whoops. Cut."

"Oh, for fu—sorry, everyone," Norah called out.

"Actually, I think that's lunch, everyone." Grace checked her watch before announcing, "One half hour, please."

"Sorry, David," Norah said quietly.

The idea had been to spill as little as possible, but quite a lot had gone onto the cuff of his sweater and some had even spattered onto his shoes and the floor. It was a continuity nightmare. It meant someone had to make sure that the stain stayed the same in every shot and, since they tend to change colour as they dry, the coffee stains had to go.

Barb, the wardrobe mistress, swooped in with a T-shirt and loafers for David to wear during lunch, while they cleaned and dried the sweater sleeve and attended to his shoes.

"Don't worry about it, the last four screwups were my fault. It was your turn." He smiled and then casually pulled his sweater over his head. He stood, shirtless, in front of Norah, trying to figure out the opening in the T-shirt and rattling on about how they should try it a couple of times after lunch before he changed back.

Her eyes feasted on the lovely cut of him. As he lifted the garment over his head, her fingers itched to reach out and touch the smooth hardness of his chest. She averted her eyes as he popped through the opening.

"May I join you for lunch?" he asked.

"Oh, you don't have to meet with crew or anything?"

"Nope, today I'm just a lowly actor."

"Nice," she replied, playing his game.

A few moments later, she had gathered a few things from the buffet, but now that it sat before her, she realized she had little appetite. She put her face in her hands in an effort to rest her eyes for a moment, but was aware of movement around her.

David seated himself beside her and began casually rubbing her back.

She smiled gratefully up at him and forced herself to eat a little.

Grace sat to her left, Jozef across from David, and Jason to Jozef's right. They fell into a companionable conversation, laughing about the flubs of the day. It had taken nearly five hours to shoot what would turn out to be less than five minutes of film, but everyone seemed in good spirits, which told her things were going pretty well, and she was eager to get back at it.

Twenty-three minutes later, she was back on the set. She found a corner of Clare's apartment and eased into some stretches in order to ward off the post-meal fatigue. She sat with her legs straight out and had lowered her forehead to her knees when a sultry whisper came from beside her.

"Mmm, I love a limber woman."

She raised her head and hoped he'd interpret the redness in her face as the result of exertion. "May I help you?"

He chuckled at her. "Do you want to work on that bit of business?"

"Right. Absolutely."

He helped her to her feet and they crossed to where the props master had prepped the cups.

"Thanks, Colin," she said, carefully taking the cups from him. She took a deep breath, and stepped into position. "Okay, I'm standing here, facing the sink. I turn to the room, my nerves get the better of me, and I turn back a bit . . ."

"I come up from behind . . . 'here let me help with that.' I'll reach out to take them . . ."

" 'No thanks, I've got it.' I move to pull back—now *I'm* wet."

"Maybe if I tug on them a bit?"

"Or if you have a firmer grip when I pull back?"

"Yeah, let's try that. Less contrived."

After three more runs, they managed to splash the appropriate amount of liquid onto his hand and only his hand. They were ready for the take and, after final adjustments were made to the set and lighting, the excess crews dispersed.

Norah stood next to Judy, chatting about kids and dogs, while Barb approached David with his clean gear. Plopping his shoes on the floor and laying the clean sweater over the arm of his chair, she stepped over to rearrange Norah's tank top and flannel overshirt.

David, who had changed his shoes unobserved, started to remove his T-shirt and became very much observed.

The three women froze in the middle of their tasks—Judy peeked over her half glasses, pen suspended over her notes. Norah still had her water bottle to her lips but had ceased swallowing, and Barb's fingers were anchored to Norah's top. The women watched in rapturous delight as David, his back to them, pulled the shirt up over his head giving this small but very appreciative audience full view of his broad shoulders, smooth back, and tapered waist.

He discarded the shirt onto his chair then wriggled his arms into the sweater, causing his back muscles to ripple deliciously. He raised the sweater over his head, at the same time turning just enough to treat the ladies to a lovely view of his abdomen up to and including that lovely thin line of hair trailing the underside of his navel into the waistband of his jeans.

Hmm, I missed that the first time.

"God, I love my job," the chorus sang on either side of Norah.

She nodded in lusty agreement.

"Places, please!"

All three ladies almost jumped out of their skins as Grace's voice echoed around the room, and she grinned at them.

In an effort to not spit water down the back of Judy's neck, Norah clamped her mouth shut, forcing it up her sinuses and almost out her nose. She sputtered and grabbed a towel from the nearest chair.

They all shot Grace a filthy look as she walked away, cackling, before resuming their respective tasks.

Deliberately disheveled once more, after hair and makeup's last minute touch-ups, Norah made her way back to the kitchenette to take her first position.

David came up behind her, gorgeous as usual, and gave her a cheerful wink.

Once they were given the cue for action, they carried through the scene just as they had rehearsed, with beautiful, natural ease.

The coffee splashes over Wayne's hand, scalding him.

"Oh, damn it," Clare cries out.

Wayne hisses in pain, and Clare grabs him by his arm, pulling him to the sink where she runs cold water over his hand.

"I'm sorry. I'm so, so sorry," she exclaims.

"Please, don't worry, it's not that bad," he says, drying his hand on the dishtowel.

"No, it's just . . . nothing, I'm sorry."

With his good hand, he reaches over, brushes the hair from her face, and lifts her chin to face him. "It's no big deal, really. See? Why don't we have our coffee now?"

"All right. Let me get you some ice, though."

"Okay."

He carries their cups to the sofa bed and places them on the coffee table. He sits with his back against the cushions, allowing her plenty of room while keeping her within arms' reach.

She hurries in with an ice pack and sees how he is situated. Handing him the pack, she makes a move toward the armchair on the other side of the coffee table.

He sees her intent and, as she releases her grip on the cold pack, he clutches her wrist.

She gasps but stops and looks into his eyes.

"Please. Sit beside me."

She nods, sitting on the edge of the mattress and reaching carefully for her cup.

Wayne silently observes her and she observes her drink.

"May I put on some music?" he asks, rising.

"Sure, I've only got the radio, though." Again her head droops and a frown furrows her brow.

"The radio is fine."

Clare cannot take her eyes off him as he moves from the radio to the door.

His fingers turn the lock into place, and he flicks the light switch, plunging the apartment into darkness, save only the soft glow of the floor lamp. He stands unmoving, watching, as her whole body starts to tremble, hearing each breath catch in her throat, almost gasping for the next.

Her desperation to be loved is palpable, and she is absolutely aching for his touch. She stiffens as he moves toward her.

He seems to be willing her to look up at him as he stands before her. When she doesn't, he kneels on the floor at her feet. Gently prying the coffee cup from her clenched fingers, he sets it on the table beside him. Turning back to her, he dips his head in order to put his face in her line of sight.

"Clare?"

She is completely silent.

"Clare, are you crying?" He coaxes her head up and finds tears falling freely down her cheeks. "Clare, I don't understand."

"Neither do I."

He shakes his head and a soft moan escapes his lips as he's moved by her

The Wrong Woman

distress. Slowly, he leans in and kisses the tears from her face with an unexpected tenderness.

She whimpers softly and permits her hands to rest on his shoulders.

Encouraged, and with his hands still on either side of her sad face, he moves in and kisses her fully on her mouth.

She melts into him, and they both gasp, astonished when she kisses him back.

He eases her back on the sofa bed.

She fights the action and snaps upright as if cold water is poured on her. "No. Stop. Stop this."

"Why? Why do you want me to stop?" His voice is gentle but commanding, his hands still touching her, smoothing her hair from her face. "Look at me, Clare. Tell me why you want me to stop."

"Because . . ." She struggles to find the words.

"Because, why? You have to know I don't want to stop."

She looks at him, a picture of confusion and anxiety. "Why?"

"Why, what?"

"Why do . . . why are you here? Why are you here with me? Why do you—"

"Why do I want to make love to you?"

She nods, looking hard into his face for any trace of a lie or mockery.

He smiles openly and free of guise. It was very likely the first one of its kind in his life. "Because, sweet Clare, I think you're one of the most honest and endearing people I've ever known. You're not . . . superficial like the other women that I meet. You don't flaunt your . . . yourself like they do, and even more than that, when I'm with you I feel like I can be . . . that I can be the person that I want to be."

"You're not . . . please, tell me you're not . . ."

"I'm not going to leave you, Clare. I don't want to hurt anyone anymore."

"What do you mean?"

The darkness flickers in his eyes for a second. "I have a tendency to be a bit of a heartbreaker. But I won't hurt you, I couldn't. I just want to be with you." Sighing, he lays his head in her lap.

She looks down at him and, unable to resist the impulse to touch him, allows her fingers to move gently and tentatively through his hair.

He turns his head into her touch and lays so he can look up at her. She sits upright, but he doesn't linger. Instead, he begins moving up, kissing a trail along her stomach. Both of his hands reach up until they find her breasts, fumbling, frustrated by the ungainliness of her overshirt. Slowly, he pops open one snap after another, ripping the last two open with one quick pull. Beneath her flannel is a man's style, ribbed muscle shirt, which clings with surprising femininity to her curves.

In a move of shocking confidence, she lowers the overshirt off her shoulders, all the while watching his face for any sign of rejection or *disgust.*

He notices that she isn't wearing a bra and her nipples are barely concealed through the thin fabric. He enjoys a very long moment of simply looking at her, allowing his eyes to wander from one lovely breast to the other. His hands come up to touch but pull back, then move in again, then . . .

"Cut, please."

"Cut and print that. David, you okay?" Grace asked.

"I'm fine, sorry. Gimme a minute, please."

"Take five everyone."

The crew took advantage, dispersing in all different directions. The two cast members remained where they were.

David dropped his head and sat back on his heels with his hands on his hips.

Norah sat forward and pulled her shirt back up over her shoulders. She glanced at the camera operator as he attempted to clamber off the bed from where he had been perched capturing Wayne's reactions. "Keith, you sly dog, I didn't even notice you were there. Fancy sneaking up on a girl's bed without her knowing."

"Honey, you have no idea." He winked and placed the camera on its safety stand before heading for the soundstage door.

She waited until everyone had cleared before addressing David. "So what happened?"

He didn't move for a moment, then he lifted his head and started to laugh. "It's just so frigging juvenile."

"What is?"

"I'm *mortified*. I froze because," he leaned in and whispered, "because I saw . . . your boobs."

"You're kidding!"

"Oh, I wish I were."

"David," she chided.

"I know!" He jumped up and paced the set.

Norah pulled on the neckline of her shirt, and glanced down at her chest. She shrugged and decided to go after him and jolly him out of it.

"Okay, so you went to a lot of trouble to make our kiss special last night, which I will always think is the most romantic thing ever, just so you know. Do you think maybe we should have taken the time for you to cop a feel as well?"

He turned on her, decidedly not amused, or at least trying to appear so.

"David, they're boobs." She opened her overshirt wide and flashed him another peek. "See?"

Laughing, he seemed to get caught up in her silliness. He looked down at them, first from this angle and then the other. He bent over to view the undersides then tried to peer over the top of her shirt before she gave him a

The Wrong Woman

shove.

"All right already. Better?"

"Yeah. They're very nice, by the way."

"Thank you," she said curtly and returned to the daybed, blushing a little.

He trailed after her. "I look forward to getting to know them."

She felt the tiny bit of heat on her cheeks flush all the way into her hairline.

As the crew trickled in, David and Norah sat side by side, chatting quietly amongst themselves.

"You have to admit it's a bit creepy, though," he said.

"What is?"

"These scenes. I hate them. It's almost like getting it on with someone when they're not really there, like they're asleep or something."

"Why? It's not technically us. We're playing different people."

"Right, that's my point. Wayne is mauling Norah's body even though Norah doesn't have anything to say about it because, for the time being, Clare is in charge. You're kinda being violated."

"You're kinda nuts, you know."

He jostled her with his shoulder and she jostled him back.

"Are we ready?" Grace asked, looking at her watch.

They had three hours left for shooting and a lot of difficult ground still left to cover.

Makeup came in briefly to give the pair a touch-up here and there.

"Drat. I should have gone—"

David shouted, "Hold camera! Norah has to pee."

"Back in a sec, everyone. Sorry."

When she returned, David was already in position, kneeling in front of the sofa. She gave him a playful cuff on the back of his head as she crawled past him and took her seat.

Judy came over and reminded them that Clare's shirt was off her shoulders and, using a video playback still of the final shot, they arranged themselves accordingly.

Keith got repositioned behind Norah as they called out the rolling sequence.

Wayne touches her on each side of her breasts with the palms of his hands, learning the shape and softness of her. He rests one knee on the mattress beside her, opening her up to view. He covers her mouth with his own, moaning softly as her hands reach up and pull him toward her, not resisting at all when he lowers her back onto the bed. He throws a bunch of pillows off to the side.

There was a muffled grunt as a cushion hit the camera and knocked the viewfinder into Keith's eye.

"Shit, shit, shit. Sorry, man."

"Never mind, David. Take it from there," said Grace. "Keith, do you want to find another vantage point?"

"Nah, I'm good."

Jozef stepped up and nudged David's arm. "Maybe I need to get him helmet. Dafid, is expensive this camera. Even more expensive than Keith. Ya?"

"Ya."

David and Norah shared a laugh. She lay on her back and he was propped up on one elbow, gazing down at her, waiting for the call. He had his hand on her stomach, and she saw no point in removing it.

The last pillow is shoved to the side as he buries his face in her throat, and her head rolls back with pleasure.

She moans aloud, encouraging him.

He places his hand fully on her breast and runs his thumb in small circles over her nipple causing it to peak unmistakably beneath the muscle shirt. He reaches under the hem of her top, walks his fingers along her body until she feels his touch directly on the skin of her soft breast.

Even with a camera lens less than an arm's length from her face, Norah thrilled at the contact with him. She twisted her head to the side and forced herself to concentrate on the scene, the camera . . .

Concentrate on Clare.

She turns to face him, forcing eye contact.

Wayne breathes heavily and retracts his hand from under her shirt, surprise and confusion in his eyes. Her expression softens as he meets her gaze, and he lifts her shirt to fully expose her round, ripe breast, which he quickly covers with his mouth.

Norah gasped in shock.

Did not see that coming.

David's mouth wasn't open but simply against her skin. She assumed that he was counting on the angle of the camera so she played to the stimulation, holding his head to her breast and letting a whimper come from deep within her. Once he released her and moved his mouth back onto hers, she took her cue to move the action forward. She rolled, shifting him a bit, so they were both on their sides.

Clare uses her leg to coax Wayne's knee between her thighs. She tentatively starts a rhythmic movement against him with her hips as her free hand begins to explore him—first his chest, shoulders, back, over his sweater, under his sweater, then slowly moving around the edge of his waistband to the front of his jeans, before continuing lower and lower and . . .

Norah rolled back and covered her face. "Sorry. Argh! Cut, please."

"Cut. Print that," Grace commanded. She consulted her watch and glanced over at Judy, who nodded. "That looks like a good place to wrap for the night. Check the gate and shut 'er down, folks."

Jason ran over to unlock the soundstage door and allow the rest of the crew back in, all the while giving the wrap alert on his radio.

Keith stepped off the bed and received a pat on the back from Jozef as he passed by the two actors still reclined in their last position.

David looked up at him and asked, "So how does it look?"

"Is erotic masterpiece. Must go back to hotel now and sneak up on wife. Poosh!" With a grin, he turned and quickly walked out of the stage.

Norah, giving herself credit for being more intelligent than an ostrich, knew that, despite hiding behind her hands, she was still visible. "This is all your fault," she mumbled.

"What is?"

"You got me all creeped out with that stuff about violation and whatnot, and I couldn't . . . you know . . . *grab* you." The heat washed over her cheeks as she gestured suggestively.

"Why not?" He grinned like the proverbial Cheshire cat.

"Because . . . because maybe you—not the Wayne you, but the David you . . . you didn't want—oh, forget it." She scooted down the length of the mattress, hopped off, and stuffed her arms back through the worn flannel, wrapping it securely around her.

As she started for the door, she heard Grace call out to David.

Back in her trailer and in her street clothes, Norah sank into one of the club chairs in the lounging area and tucked her feet under her. She knew she should remove her makeup, but a small smile crept onto her face as she realized she didn't want to wash him off her.

Damn, this is complicated.

She understood why he'd been so reticent this morning. How had he put it? *It's going to be a pretty rough day for us.*

She gave in after a bit, washing her face and comforting herself with the fact that, until she took a shower, there was plenty of him left in other areas. She felt her stomach jolt at the memory of his touch on her, his tongue on her throat, his weight on top of her.

A light knock on the door shattered her train of thought.

"Come in." She put away her lotions and turned, pleased to see David standing there, even if he looked somewhat lost.

"May I come in?"

"Of course."

He stepped inside and closed the door before looking around. "Very nice."

"Yeah. Not as nice as yours, though."

"Naturally."

They smiled at each other and the last bit of tension lifted.

Issuing the plea in barely more than a whisper, David sounded like the shy boy once more. "Kiss me."

Only two steps and fewer seconds and she was in his arms, his mouth warm and welcoming on hers.

Chapter 7

David sat in the playback room—a dimly lit trailer near the soundstage. It had a large monitor, a stack of video equipment, a half dozen uncomfortable folding chairs and little else. He was accompanied by Jozef, Geoff, Steve, Grace, and Katarina, the second unit director. They had watched the dailies—the uncut, unedited video from the day before. There wasn't any kind of sound score yet, only the raw footage starting seconds before *action* is called, to just after *cut* and including all the flubs, outtakes, and technical gaffes. It took a great deal of imagination to see a movie at this stage of the process, but this particular group of people *had* a great deal of imagination and they saw not only a movie, they saw a very good movie.

Jozef hit a button as the last shot faded to black.

No one spoke; like gourmets after a magnificent meal, they sat and savoured.

Steve broke the silence first. "It's . . . it's . . . great. Just great. Chilling, gripping. David, you've never been better. And Norah! Let me say for the record, and you can all quote me on this, that is an Oscar-caliber performance. A thousand dollars . . . I'll bet anyone, come nomination day, if she's not on the list—great. I have to call the studio. I won't have any trouble pushing through the extensions for Geoff's rewrites after this. And you can take that to the bank." He was already dialing before the door had closed behind him.

"Will he get the go-ahead?" Geoff asked. He'd completed most of scenes he'd set out to write, and letting go of them now that the script flowed so beautifully would not be a happy task.

David had sat through the playback with his chin on his one hand, a pen in the other, and a clipboard on his knee. He had yet to move. He spoke through his fingers when he replied, "I already received the go-ahead late last night."

"Thank you, David." Geoff sagged with relief. Then, sounding a bit hurt, he asked, "Why didn't you tell me that first thing?"

"I hadn't seen the dailies yet. If they'd sucked . . ."

"Right. Well, I have a bit of tweaking to do. May I borrow your trailer again?"

"Help yourself."

"Thanks again, David. I'll be able to show you after lunch. Or maybe we could have dinner together?"

"Yeah. Wait. I might have plans. Let's take a look at them after lunch."

"Right," Geoff said with a quick wave as he headed out the door.

Grace, a woman of few words, heaved herself off the wall she'd been leaning against, walked over to David, and gave his shoulder a squeeze. "Good show, boss, good show. Twenty minutes to call, by the way." She nodded and made her way out the door.

Katarina, who also happened to be Jozef's wife, chuckled and David turned just in time to catch her slowly taking him in, head to toe, as if something about him amused her.

Katarina was a striking-looking woman of forty years or so. She was easily six foot tall, with alabaster skin and unnaturally red hair cascading past her waist. Layers of crochet and beads covered her upper body and dangled over her bohemian-style peasant skirt.

She clomped up behind Jozef in serious, size twelve combat boots, wrapped her arms around his bearish neck and whispered something in Slovak, then gave David a sly smile as she left them.

Without knowing exactly why, David felt exposed. "What was that all about?"

Jozef smiled. "Well, mostly she see now why I come home last night in such good mood."

David shoved his fingers in his ears and shook his head. "Too much information."

"But also she think she see something there with you and girl."

Definitely exposed.

"Oh, she think that, does she?"

"Women. They so full of the horse shit, but is good to have one. Better to have two, but one good, too." He rose to his substantial height and stretched, nearly filling the room with his mass. "Is good. Now picture has . . . how you say? Heart. Yes, will be good film now. Coming for food?"

"In a minute."

"See you at tent, then."

David sat in the dark, alone, staring at the blank monitor. The minutes ticked away and he was bombarded with emotions—a confusing swirl of pride in the work he had done, astonishment at the performance this woman had produced, frustration that he hadn't had her on board from the get-go, worry that he might have to go back and reshoot a shitload of footage because she'd raised the bar of the entire film, excitement at Jozef's stunning lighting and camera work turning what had been, for all intents and purpose, a high-rent slasher movie into an art house thriller.

And then there was the other stuff, the really complicated stuff. He glanced down at the notes he'd jotted on his clipboard while the video had been running. Beside comments like *Take 4 too fast, splice Take 9 with end of Take 2*, he had doodled Norah's name three times in the margin of the page. He took some comfort in the fact that he hadn't turned the *O*s into little hearts.

"What is this? Eighth grade?" He tossed the clipboard on the floor, buried his face in his hands, and felt an overwhelming desire to put Norah out of his mind for two minutes in a row.

Ever since their first meeting, he hadn't been able to shake her from his mind. Her acting abilities, which were formidable, were only a fraction of what he admired about her. Jozef was right—now the picture had heart. The larger truth was that David *liked* her. He liked her very much.

He liked her talent. He liked her enthusiasm and the pure joy she brought to her work. He liked that she challenged him and made him a better actor and director. He liked her intelligence and her friendly manner with the crew. He liked that she didn't look in the mirror every ten seconds and didn't call for makeup and hair after every take. He liked the look of her— no artifice, just a lovely face on a lovely little body that moved well, and she didn't get all self-conscious about it. He even liked that she didn't let him get away with anything. He liked—no, he *loved* the way she made him laugh. That, he loved more than anything. She surprised him with her wit, be it a quirky attitude, a slash of sarcasm, a spicy zinger in his direction, or the ability to tell a funny story and make it even funnier. He had laughed more since she had come along than he had in the last two years.

And he loved the way she kissed him.

How did this diminutive, small-town, single mother with a smart mouth and nice eyes send his world reeling with the slightest touch of her lips? None of it made any sense. He'd kissed starlets and legends, royalty and harlots, dancers and doctors, and never felt that blissful fog descend on his brain to chase all reason away.

He checked his watch. She would be on the lot by now, and he still needed to get to wardrobe. As he left the trailer, he shook his head and fought back the impulse to tear about the grounds looking for her.

****

In the end, he was quarter of an hour late to the soundstage after he got waylaid by a call from the studio to confirm the extensions, despite his best efforts to put them off.

He saw her on the set in that sexy tank top with the flannel thrown over her shoulders. She was walking circles around the apartment and looked deep in thought. Not wanting to interrupt, he walked to his chair, sent a greeting to Judy, and asked Grace the status.

When she confirmed everyone was ready, he realized his problem. The conversation with the studio had taken his head out of the acting game and into the producing game, and he was having a devil of a time getting it back.

Damn it.

He took a swig of water and launched himself toward the set.

Norah looked up as he approached. "What's wrong?"

"Nothing. Everything's great in fact."

Her expression told him that she didn't believe a word of it.

"No, seriously." He stood in front of her, his hands on his hips when all he really wanted was to place them on hers. "Everything's good, I've seen the dailies. They're brilliant. You're brilliant. In fact, I have something pretty exciting to tell you later. It's just . . . I had to take this studio call, and I'm all fucked up." He tried to laugh but barely managed a choked chuckle. "I feel like a big baby standing here whining about it to you."

She put her hands on his shoulders and pulled him down to her height. With her forehead against his, she spoke low and gently, "Listen, you need to take all the time you need to get here."

"We've got to start rolling."

"David, you're the director, and as director, your lead has told you he needs a few minutes to get into character. Christ, you held up shooting for five minutes because I had to pee. They can wait. We can all wait for you."

Oh yeah, and I like that about her, too.

He pulled her into a big bear hug, lifting her right off the ground, and with a laugh she wrapped her arms around his neck and hung on. "Grace!"

"Yeah, boss."

"I need ten."

"You got it, boss. Take a break, folks."

The crew dispersed and Norah and David walked toward where their scene was set to pick up. Norah nudged him toward the sofa bed and she sat on the coffee table facing him. She held his hands in hers and took him through breathing exercises. She asked him how Wayne Kosma felt about himself, about Clare, how he saw her, what had happened between them, and what he wanted to do to her, to focus his energy back into the role.

Within minutes, he was *centred*—a theatrical term that translated to *get your shit together and get rolling 'cause this crap is costing thousands of dollars an hour.*

"Okay," he said to her. "I think I'm good."

"Good? You're the best, baby."

He laughed in spite of himself and called Grace back into action who, in turn, got everyone else hopping.

Judy coached them back into position using a still camera shot. "There, on your sides facing each other, that's right. This leg was here, your arm there. Oh, and your top was kinda up, you know . . ."

Once everything was where it ought to be and the camera was traveling over, they had a moment of quiet to themselves.

"May I break character for a moment?" he asked.

"Sure."

"I thought I should ask first because I didn't want to disturb the process of the gre—"

"Get on with it, smart guy."

"Do you remember when we cut last night? When you didn't feel like you could grab me because . . . what was it? I think you were about to say, 'maybe David doesn't want me grabbing him'?"

"Yeah?"

"Well, for the record, David wants."

She sighed heavily.

He laughed and gave her a friendly nip on the neck.

Oh, yeah, baby! I'm back.

Whether it had been character driven or a chance to get even, he never knew, but grab him she had and with a good deal more exuberance then he had thought necessary. He'd actually had to suppress a yelp at one point.

When they called the scene to change reels, he turned to her. "Easy now. That's not a prop, you know?"

"Hey, it's not me, it's Clare."

So many comebacks popped to mind, but he fixed her with a cool stare and readjusted himself instead.

****

They decided that Clare's sexual modesty falling away would be the catalyst for Wayne's demons to reassert themselves. Through the scene, there were moments she was tested and failed—when she kissed him back, when she allowed him to touch and expose her, when she touched him, and finally, when she clumsily undid his jeans and slid her hand inside.

Wayne reacts as if scalded again. He grabs Clare's wrist and bends her arm painfully back.

She cries out.

His anger is obvious, and he rolls on top of her, pinning her arms to the mattress with his knees.

Grabbing her face hard in his hand, he rages. "You slut! I thought you were different. But you're a whore! You're a filthy, fucking whore." *Wayne leaps off her and stumbles into the middle of the room as if startled by his own outburst.*

Clare sits up quickly. "What did I do? Please, tell me what I did wrong."

Wayne's eyes dart back and forth, and he grabs either side of his head as though he's in terrible pain.

"Please, tell me what I did wrong."

He mimics her with a sharp edge to his voice, "Please, come home with me. Please, do this, please, do that. Please, forgive me for being a stupid, *pathetic cow!"*

"I don't understand," she cries.

He crosses the room and grabs her by the shoulders, shaking her hard. His voice is suddenly calm and quiet and more threatening than ever. "No, that's right, you dumb bitch, you don't understand. You don't understand that I couldn't possibly stomach being near you, let alone . . . you make me sick. You're so fucking pathetic you make me want to puke."

"No, you said . . . you said . . ." Her sobs are so uncontrollable, she can't speak.

He throws her onto the bed and stands tall, staring down at her in disgust. He tilts his head to the side as if hearing a voice, perhaps a voice telling him to finish her, that she deserves it. But as the part of him that was soft with her, smiled for her, and was touched by her, wins the blatant inner battle, he backs away. A look of horror crosses his face and he rushes to the door. He struggles to unlock the deadbolt then, taking one last look at her curled on the mattress, flees into the hall.

Clare muffles her agony by burying her face into the cushions and wailing like a wounded animal. As though she's suddenly terrified he might come back, she runs for the door to bolt it against him. She manages to stumble a few steps back before her legs give out and she folds to the floor in unyielding grief.

"And . . . cut. Print that. Check the gate, please."

David had left the scene and come around to chairs to watch the agonizing end of it. He turned to Jozef, who nodded his approval.

Judy let him know that they were good on all points.

Keith called out the clean status of the gate, and David signaled Grace to wrap the scene.

Grace ignored him. "Boss . . ."

David turned and followed her gaze to Norah.

She hadn't moved from where she had collapsed on the floor. She was attempting to rise but couldn't, as wave after wave of sobs crashed over her.

David ran to her side and gently pulled her against him. "Norah, sweetheart, what is it?"

Grace quietly set a box of tissues on the floor beside them. "I've seen it a hundred times. It's always the tough ones. You get going and you can't stop." She leaned over and began stroking Norah's head with a tenderness David had never seen. "You've been packing it all around for so long, haven't you, honey? Everybody wants a piece of you, and there never seems to be any left over for yourself. Well, you've got yourself some good luck now, Norah, and don't you dare try to tell yourself that you don't deserve it, 'cause you do."

David saw his first assistant director with new eyes. Norah's tiny body heaved against his, and he looked at Grace helplessly.

"Let her have her cry. Best thing in the world for her. She'll feel like a million dollars when she's done." Grace stood, cleared her throat, and took command. "All right, everyone. Clear out. One half hour for lunch, please."

David sat on the floor with Norah and lost track of time, rocking back and forth until her sobs turned to whimpers, her whimpers to sniffles, and her sniffles to sighs. When he was certain his questions wouldn't shatter her, he slowly pushed the hair off her face.

"I'm so embarrassed," she said, unable to meet his eyes.

"Hey, never mind that. Are you okay?"

"Yeah, I think so."

He eased her away from him, helped her stand, then pulled her back into his arms with a sigh of relief. "You scared the hell out of me."

"Me, too. Sorry."

"You sure you're all right? What do you need?"

"A face wash and some air."

He nodded. "All right. Why don't you go to your trailer, get changed, wash up, and I'll do the same? I need to have a quick word with Jozef then I'll come by and get you, and we can take a walk . . . somewhere. How does that sound?"

"That sounds perfect." She hiccupped once and patted his sweater. "Wardrobe's going to freak when they see what I've done."

He was soaked. He leaned down and kissed her on her forehead. "See you in a minute."

****

Twenty minutes later, David had Jozef working with Katarina on a few precinct moments with secondary characters. It would keep things moving and still free him and Norah up for a good hour. Before the second unit was finished, he'd have to be back to go over rewrites with Geoff and then be on set for the scenes that involved Nick and Dennis. With everyone else taken care of, he knocked on her door.

She greeted him in a pair of khakis, a white cotton V-neck, and a light jean jacket. She looked great, all fresh-faced and smiling.

"How are you feeling?"

"Fabulous. Grace was right."

"No kidding. Wasn't she a surprise?"

They talked and laughed about the new incarnation of Grace and how she had Norah down to a tee, as they walked toward the wooded area beyond the circus. Within ten minutes, they'd left the craziness behind and arrived at a small clearing along the edge of the Saskatchewan River. The water cut in front of them, with evergreens and leafy poplars standing protectively on three sides.

David sat against the remains of a huge fallen pine and guided her to sit between his knees and lean against his chest. He wrapped his arms around her and squeezed her tight, breathing in the perfume of her neck. He felt more than heard her sigh, and he smiled.

She fits. Like she's meant to be here.

In the past, he'd always been attracted to much taller women with seemingly endlessness limbs, so he marveled at how much he enjoyed the smallness of this woman—how he towered over her as they walked, or how comfortably his chin rested on the top of her head while her fingers traced delicate circles on the back of his hand and sent chills through him.

He didn't want to check his watch, afraid he would disturb the moment, but he was keenly aware that he needed to get back soon. He was loath to end their time together and wondered when they could meet again properly, away from the circus, the sets and the cameras. The weekend was coming up, and he didn't have any plans that he couldn't get out of.

He idly tried to recall how they'd spent last weekend. He chuckled out loud.

"What's so funny?" she asked, tilting her head to look up at him.

"I was just thinking about what we should do this weekend and was trying to remember what we did during the last one . . ."

"Um, well . . ." She suddenly spun around to face him. "Oh, my God!" she exclaimed.

"I know," he said, amused by her reaction.

"Oh, my God. We didn't even know each other last weekend."

"We only met Monday."

"That was . . . four days ago."

"I know."

"So what does that mean? I mean, time's supposed to fly when you're having fun. I've been having fun. Have you been having fun?"

He chuckled again. "Oh yes, I've been having fun." He snapped his fingers. "I've got it. We make time stand still."

She stared at him then reached into her pocket and mimed pulling out and opening a cell phone, hitting a button, and putting it up to her ear. "Hello . . . yes? Really? Okay, I'll tell him." She closed the cell phone and, staying in character, placed it back in her pocket before turning her attention to him. "The cheesy romance movie of the week called. They want their cornball line back."

He threw his head back and howled with laughter.

God, I like this woman.

She had him figured out and he didn't mind one bit. "Okay, smart-ass. I have to admit you've got me worried."

"What do you mean?" she asked, settling back against him.

"I've got a terrible feeling that none of my stuff is going to work on you."

It was her turn to laugh. "Well, if by 'stuff' you mean overused lines, pathetic seduction maneuvers, and basically, a lot of bullshit, then no, I'm afraid you're hooped. You might have to resort to sincerity."

He gasped in mock despair before giving her exactly that—sincerity. "The thing is, Norah, I like you. I *really* like you, and I don't want to screw this up."

She turned to face him again and read the seriousness in his face. "Jeez, I didn't mean right this minute."

He recognized the humour defense she hid behind, since he did it himself. He understood her, and it was nice.

He grinned. "Here's my problem. I've always, you know, been in some . . . *thing* with one woman or another. I mean, I've been around, you know?"

"Okay."

"But they've never lasted. Obviously. And I take full responsibility for it. My thing is to move pretty fast into the . . . physical." He gestured wildly as if trying to get his point across in a crude game of charades. "My friends, my family, they all keep telling me 'you've got to have something to build on,' and . . . I guess what I'm trying to say here, very badly by the way . . . I think . . . I think with you, I'd like to build something."

"Oh, David." She leaned in and kissed him. "I really like you, too, and I don't want you to screw it up either."

They smiled at each other.

"So what's the plan?" She asked.

"Oh! Um . . . I dunno. I've never tried this before, to be honest. I guess we . . . we don't rush things?"

"You mean sex?"

Plain and simple. No beating about the bush. Shoulda known.

"I dunno, I guess. Is that all right? I mean . . . do you think that's a good idea? I'm flying blind here."

"I think there's no secret recipe for a successful relationship. Sorry, you won't get nervous if I use the *R* word will you?"

"I'll try to quell the tremors."

"Anyway, if you believe that rushing into the sex is what wrecked things for you in the past, then certainly, I haven't any problem with putting that on the back burner for now."

"Really?"

"Well, for my part, I'm relieved. I mean, I don't have only myself to think of, right? I have Ella to work into the equation."

"I'm sorry. I'm not sure I understand."

"I'm somebody's parent, David, and I have to keep that in mind. I like you very much. I like the way we laugh together and how we work together, and I very much like the way you make me feel. But I'm not interested in a fling."

"Oh."

"Maybe 'not interested' is a bit strong," she said with a flirty grin. "Let's just say, I really appreciate your honesty and agree with you that we should move slowly. It's good."

"Oh. Okay. Good then. Good."

"You need to get back, don't you?"

"Hmm? Oh, yeah, right."

They had started back down the path when she turned to face him, a wicked smile playing about her lips.

"David? Were you expecting an argument? About the 'no sex' thing?"

"Well . . . I was expecting a bit of resistance to the idea, yes, if I'm being perfectly honest." Truth be told, he was feeling a bit of an ass at the moment.

"I'm sorry," she said, not sounding sorry in the least. In fact, she was doing a very poor job of keeping the laughter out of her voice. "Wait! I know, let's go back a bit . . ."

"Oh, never mind." He smiled in spite of himself and tried to push past her.

"No, no, I don't mind. Let's see . . . um . . ." Norah stomped her foot and threw her hand on her hip. "What do you mean you don't want us to do the nasty? But, David, how can you say that when you must know it's all I think about, night and day?" She grabbed the back of his belt and pulled at him like a lunatic.

He laughed and tried to break free.

"Please, David. I need your manliness, your guy-ness, and your super cool dude-ness. Make me a woman, *please!*"

"Oh, God. I'm having flashbacks to last year's film festival." He spun around and drew her roughly to him. He looked down into her adorable face. "Aw crap, wouldn't you know it? Now I want nothing more than to throw you to the ground and take you, right here, right now."

She blushed. "Well, that's what's going to make it interesting, isn't it?"

"Yes. Yes, it is."

With his arm around her shoulders, they continued on their way, and he breathed a sigh of something unfamiliar.

Is this contentment?

"So what would you like to do this weekend? Is there a movie house here?"

"Yeah, you could say that. We do have to take a particular two-year-old into account, though."

"I can't wait to meet her." He felt her snuggle deeper into his side. "Did I score big points there?"

"Big, *big* points."

"Excellent."

"I have an idea. Why don't I make you dinner tomorrow night at my place? You can meet Ella on her own turf, and we can have a nice relaxing evening."

"That sounds perfect."

And it really did.

Chapter 8

Norah came through the front door laden down with grocery bags and baskets. She barely managed to get the door closed behind Ella when the phone rang.

"Oh fu—*heck.*"

Sheesh! A few days on-set and my vocabulary's right in the toilet.

She dumped the bags unceremoniously on the hall rug, stumbled over them in her rush to grab the phone, and called over her shoulder as she went, "Ella, take off your coat and boots, okay?"

"Oday."

She reached the phone by the fourth ring. "Hello?"

"Hello there."

She was positive she had actually heard her stomach go *whoosh*.

"Hey, handsome. How's your day?"

"Fine. It looks like we're going to shut her down around four o'clock."

"Wow, that's early. Is the shoot going so well, or is the rain getting in your way?" She tried to shed her coat without drenching the floor or dropping the phone.

"It's going pretty smooth. Mostly everyone's anxious to get cleaned up, hit the bars, and get their weekend started. After four, they're pretty useless."

Norah knew the crew would do whatever he needed them to, but the thought of him trying to hang the impatience on them made her smile. She played along. "Yeah well, everyone's looking forward to spending your money."

"You're right. I should have bought shares in a beer company . . . and then maybe I could recoup my losses."

She laughed. "So when can we expect you?"

"I'd like to go back to the hotel and change, so . . . about five thirty? Is that too early?"

"No, that's great. Never too early to start kicking back."

Jesus, did I really just say that?

"Okay, I'll see you in a little while. Bye."

"B'bye." She hung up then pressed the heels of her hands into her eyes.

"Never too early to start kicking back?" Holy cow, that's one for the books.

She plopped down at her desk and grabbed her journal, which, as promised, she'd been keeping meticulously. She jotted down her asinine comment as Brett came through the front door.

"What the hell?"

She remembered the pile of groceries she'd abandoned in the hall. "Sorry, I'll get it. I wanted to write this down before I forgot it. You'll never believe what I just said to David."

"Well, one of the things you'll be able to say to him tonight is, 'the reason my daughter looks like that is because she spent the afternoon stuffing blueberries up her nose.'"

"Aw, no! *Ella*." Norah slammed the journal shut and ran for the hall.

****

The doorbell rang five minutes ahead of schedule, and Norah all but skipped to answer it.

Dressed in an emerald green button-down sweater that complimented her eyes and a pair of light cotton pants, she'd taken extra care with her appearance again. David had spent most of their time with her as Clare, so she thought it wise to remind him that she cleaned up pretty good.

She opened the door and couldn't subdue her smile. David looked breathtakingly handsome dressed in a caramel-coloured trench coat over a navy blue V-neck shirt and tan slacks. He smiled and held a bottle of wine and a bouquet mix of deep orange lilies, blood red roses, and dark purple freesias. As soon as he'd handed her the flowers, he reached behind her neck and pulled her toward him for their first kiss since yesterday.

They lingered until she reluctantly stepped back, allowing him into the hall, then helped him off with his coat.

"I hope this goes with dinner," he said, and gestured to the bottle of wine.

"Very nice. Brett will be impressed."

His face fell a touch. "Brett? Is Brett joining us?"

She couldn't stifle her giggle. "Don't worry, he's not staying for dinner. He's giving me a hand with the meal. He thinks I'm a culinary dolt."

David was audibly relieved as he sighed heavily.

"I heard that." Brett came out of the kitchen. He walked toward them, wiping his hands on a tea towel. He scrutinized David with a small smile. "Well, don't you look yummy."

"Brett!"

Norah was about to apologize for her brother's behavior, but David intervened. "Listen, Brett, we seem to have gotten off to a bad start. I'm not sure why, but there it is. I, for one, would like to start over." He put out his hand.

She couldn't have been more pleased as she turned to Brett and gave him a pointed look.

Relenting, he shook David's hand. "All right, I can play nice if I have to. Let me put a few more touches on dinner then we can have a nice cocktail together before I toddle off to Make-myself-scarceville."

David nodded and smiled. "That sounds great."

Norah handed Brett the wine and heard him murmur his approval before he headed back to the stove. She took David by the arm and led him to the parlor. "By the way, that was a pretty awesome thing you did."

David shrugged. "I think he'd make a better friend than an enemy."

They entered the living room and found Ella busily engaged with her zoo—a collection of beautifully hand-painted animals of all species; jungle, farm, birds, sea life, even a dinosaur or two, all cohabiting happily in her very active imagination. She looked so tiny, kneeling on the mat in front of the fireplace, her wee feet poking out from under her little bum, her head bent in concentration.

"Ella?"

Ella turned her head around in response to her mother and saw the large man beside her. She took him in with all the guilelessness of the innocent, before pointing a chubby finger in his direction.

"Preeetty," she stated emphatically.

David laughed.

"Oh, fine. She's never called *me* pretty." Smiling, she brought him over to meet her daughter. "Ella, this is David. David is a friend of Mama's."

David squatted in front of the little girl, smiled, and reached his hand out to her.

Ella observed it for a moment then shook it as she had seen the grown-ups do. Naturally, she thought that was hilarious and clapped her hands over her mouth, giggling.

David laughed along with her, thoroughly charmed.

Ella patted the floor beside her. "Day-day, sit."

David looked up at Norah, who nodded. He worked his way into a sitting position beside the tot who proceeded to introduce him to her menagerie.

"Ewwafunt," she said, holding up the pachyderm.

"That's a terrific elephant. Does it have a name?"

He's trying. Bless him.

Ella pointed to herself. "Ewwa." She held up the toy in her hand. "Funt." She placed her finger back in the center of her chest. "Ewwa." She held her toy back up and wiggled it back and forth. "Funt." She repeated the motions and names until David got the joke and laughed. She clapped her hands over her mouth again, clearly thinking herself the cleverest girl ever. She picked up a goat and declared, "Day-day."

"Oh, I'm a goat, am I?" Smiling up at Norah, David asked, "Why am I a goat? What have you said?" Then he frowned. "What has Brett said?"

Norah shrugged. "Don't feel bad, she calls the penguin Mama. Brett is the lemur."

Ella bounced David the goat around on his hooves, making baaing noises.

David the man picked up another creature and started asking questions about it, which Ella patiently answered.

Norah was more than relieved, she was elated. Ella had been the easiest child—easy pregnancy, easy infancy, and now an easy toddler. Never dull, always exploring, thrilled with anything new—she was a delight in a thousand different ways.

Now, she belly laughed as David helped an ostrich munch-munch-munch at her neck. Norah didn't know if he'd ever had much experience with small children. He'd certainly seemed somewhat ambiguous when he'd learned that she was a package deal, but to watch as he galloped a giraffe around the hearth, trying to work out what sound a giraffe actually made, he looked as though he'd been at it forever. Not only that, but he seemed to enjoy the game as much as Ella did.

Norah left them together in the parlor and rejoined Brett in the kitchen.

He had done most of the cooking, and she'd simply followed his instructions for the salad. They laughed and talked conspiratorially about what sort of silliness Ella might drive David to, when she heard him call out.

"Norah, do you have any paper? Ella and I want to draw."

"Sure." Her hands were all mucky from cutting the tomatoes. "In my office, David, across the hall. There's all kinds in there. Just grab anything. Oh, and her crayons are in that basket under the coffee table. She'll show you." She was midway through chopping garlic when she heard David call out again.

"Norah, what's this?"

"What's what?"

"Well, you told me to grab anything so I thought I'd tear a couple of pages out of this notebook, but . . . it seems to have my name in it."

The knife clattered on the countertop as Norah spun toward Brett. The blood drained from her face as she grabbed her brother by his shoulders and started shaking him frantically. "That's my journal! He has my journal! Why does he have my journal?" she whispered hysterically.

"I don't know! But you'd better get it off him before he rea—"

"Oh my God! Help me!"

"Norah?" There was no denying the humour in David's voice.

Norah and Brett tried to run, but like an old black and white Marx Bothers' comedy, they only spun out in nothing but their sock feet. When they finally reached the other end, those same hard-to-start socks became hard to stop.

Once they'd pried themselves off the foyer wall and untangled their limbs, they turned to face David.

Seated in her chair, at her desk, and with the classic cat-who-ate-the-canary smile on his face, he held Norah's journal in his hands—the detailed report of absolutely *everything* that had happened to her since the moment she'd met Ted and Steve in the café, just as she'd promised herself. He casually turned the pages one by one, but his eyes were glued to Norah and Brett standing wide-eyed in the doorway.

"David," she said, sounding like a negotiator talking a jumper off a rooftop. "When I said grab anything, I meant from the scanner or the printer."

"Ah, well, my mistake then." He showed no sign of releasing the book as he turned yet another page, getting closer to their private conversations, private meetings, private—

"David! Give me the book."

"He's not listening to you. Not so well trained, this one."

Brett's gift for stating the obvious earned him a sharp elbow to the ribs, and Norah turned her focus back on David and the very real possibility of every last one of her secrets being revealed. "David, I mean it. That is . . . private in nature, and I want you to hand it back to me. Please."

"But, honey, how can it be private from me? I seem to be . . ." He thumbed rapidly through the pages. "Gosh, *everywhere*."

She nearly sobbed with embarrassment. "David, either hand that over now, or I'll take it off you, I swear."

"Suit yourself." His smile had broadened considerably.

"Bastard." She turned to Brett. "Okay, I'll take the front, you get him from behind."

"Ooh! This reminds me of a dream I had." He looked at Norah and made a sour face. "Obviously, *you* weren't in it." He aimed a cheeky smile at David. "But *you* sure were."

David's smile faltered.

Norah laughed and launched herself at him, got a grip on the journal and, while straddling his lap, tried to jerk it away from him.

Brett rounded the chair and grabbed David in a very girlie headlock with one arm and tickled his ribs with his free hand.

David laughed and doubled over, folding Norah under him and pulling Brett over the back of the chair.

It proved to be too much for the poor garage sale acquisition, and with a resounding crack, the pedestal base of the chair snapped in half and spilled the lot of them howling onto the floor.

David braced for a hard fall and lost his hold on the journal.

Norah latched onto it and tried to make her escape by crawling out the door on her knees.

David's hand shot out, and with a shout of victory, he had her by an ankle.

She screamed—half laughter, half terror—as she twisted on the floor and attempted to drag herself, and consequently him, out of the office.

Brett still had David by the back of his shirt and tried his mightiest to pull him off his sister, giggling like a maniac the entire time.

"Mama loud." Ella stood in the door with her cup of crayons, taking in the madness with a casual eye, as if this sort of nonsense was a daily occurrence. She was, however, unimpressed with all the noise. Turning her attention to David, who was squished under her uncle and had her mother by her leg, she said with a charming smile, "Day-day, draw picture wif Ewwa."

"Be right there, honey," he answered, his voice muffled against the throw rug.

"Oday." She turned and padded back to the parlor with her crayons.

Norah sat up and slapped David's hands until he released her leg, and stuffed the book down the front of her pants.

On his elbows now and panting, David said with a chuckle, "Baby, you don't honestly think that would stop me, do you?" With a leer, he climbed her legs despite her renewed squeals of protestation.

"Ewww, breeder stuff," Brett whined. "Lemme out of here. Must check dinner." He made his way toward the kitchen, but not before sending a wink in David's direction. "That was thoroughly exhilarating."

David waited until he was out of sight and earshot before continuing his trek upward, a look of pure determination in his eyes. "In fact . . ." His face was directly above the book's hiding spot. "I've been looking for an excuse."

She gasped in mock horror and clapped her hands over her crotch, then over the book, then over her crotch again. The comedy of it was too much, and they rolled on the floor with laughter.

David rose slowly to his feet and held out a hand to help her up. He gestured to the front of her pants. "You might want to tuck that somewhere I won't be so keen to get at."

Her eyes flitted down the front of his body, and she replied with the naughtiest of grins, "I could say the same thing to you." Norah bolted out of the office and up the stairs. She heard his attempted pursuit, but the tiny voice calling out to him brought him to a halt.

"Daaay-day!"

She watched from the top of the landing as he sighed with a grin.

"On my way, sweetie." He smiled and wiggled a finger in Norah's direction before reentering the office.

Giggling, she turned, tiptoed into her room and stuffed the notorious journal under her mattress.

Chapter 9

David decided that he liked Norah's brother for a number of reasons.

First, Brett clearly adored his sister and little niece. During their cocktail hour, he regaled David with stories of growing up, and how she'd completely had his back when he learned he was different. It told David that Norah had a brave and loyal nature—something he very much admired. And it was a kick to hear how crabby Brett had been when he'd learned there was to be a *"puking, pooping, little ankle-biter in their house,"* all the while witnessing how tender he was with Ella.

Second, he kept his end of a bargain. He played very nice indeed, asking David casual questions about the industry—what direction did he see American films going, and had he ever met Byron Robbins, the current twentysomething flavor of the month?

Third, he honoured his promise to make himself scarce. He'd been out the door with a hearty *ta-ta* before dinner had been served.

And finally, he was an amazing chef. Their chicken roasted in lemons and garlic—"If you both eat it, it'll cancel itself out," he'd explained when Norah had protested—with creamy potatoes, grilled crispy on top, and a kind of spicy ratatouille, had been first rate. For dessert, Ella's favourite, *"ice keem."*

Through Brett, David had learned that he and Norah had inherited the café and—as an extra bonus—the house, from their parents when they'd decided to retire nearly a decade ago. Norah had been living in Vancouver, British Columbia, trying to break into the booming film industry there. She had landed an agent and been auditioning, taken classes with exciting instructors, and had even featured in a couple of commercials. Mostly, she had been loving her life by the ocean, after having lived the majority of her life landlocked in this "fly-infested dust bowl." Then she got the call.

Their mother had always fancied herself a kind of homespun gourmand, and pored over ethnic and avant-garde cookbooks before experimenting well into the night to put her own twist on some exotic dish. Eventually, she'd convinced their father to commit, full throttle, to her dream and purchase a shabby little greasy spoon downtown, with nothing to recommend it but its location.

With Mona working her magic in the kitchen, it had fallen to Vic to run the business end, which meant keeping the place stocked, staffed, and in good working order. He had paid the bills, plumbed the dishwasher, and helped build the deck when the 80s rolled in, and it was time to go *alfresco*. Basically, he had done everything his wife had asked of him, so she was able to do what she'd wanted to—cook the best damned whatever-it-was she'd chosen that day, and as a result, her café had found itself featured in major newspapers, foodie magazines, and international guidebooks as "a place worth going off the beaten path for."

The trade-off, however, had been that when Victor Rothe said "enough is enough," Mona had hung up her whisk and called it a day.

Their children, both of whom had worked in the café ever since either could remember, had known that the day would come. Brett had certainly prepared, having gained a degree in the culinary arts right out of high school and even studied two terms in Italy. He'd never known an occupation outside of the café and never desired one.

Norah, on the other hand, had wanted nothing to do with the place once she'd left Whitecourt for the coast. She'd come home once or twice a year for holidays and had even waited tables if they had been stuck. But when Vic had called to say that he and Mona were ready to turn it over, and Brett —for all his artistry—had no head for business, she had felt trapped. She'd tried to convince him that her life wasn't in Whitecourt anymore, but Vic would have none of it.

"This is where your roots are. This acting thing . . . well, if you're serious, you can always go back to it later on."

In the end, she had agreed to come home just long enough to train someone to take her place. That had been eight years ago.

"Something always seemed to come up," Norah said, shrugging.

David discovered a newfound respect for Norah. She was someone who, to quote Brett, "was handed the shit end of the stick yet still made a pretty good life out of it." It seemed such a waste to David. She had all this talent holed up inside of her, waiting. But for what?

As it turned out, she'd been waiting for two industry flunkies to park their asses in her diner.

What are the odds?

He didn't even like to think about it. He wasn't a gambling man, but he never wanted to learn how big the chances were that he might never have met her.

After dinner, while Norah was upstairs putting Ella to bed, David felt restless, unsure what to do next. He wandered around her living room and poked through her CDs. He found a selection of pleasant classical piano and put it on. He considered lighting the fireplace, but the warmth of the evening after the rain had let up dissuaded him. Instead, he lit the candles placed randomly about the room and switched off the rest of the lights, save one floor lamp. He sat on the sofa, shifting this way and that, trying to look comfortable, maybe even a little alluring. He gave up and sat with a moan of frustration.

What am I doing?

She had already assured him that his seduction maneuvers wouldn't work on her.

He looked around the room and was about to start blowing out the candles. He simply wanted to . . .

What? Hold her in my arms and kiss her until the last breath leaves me? Surely that deserves a few candles?

Reflecting back on his past romantic life, he knew he had been a very lucky man. Women had come easily to him, sometimes aggressively, and always enthusiastically. His conquests had seldom required more effort than a smile. Yet here he was, nervous as a virgin, waiting for a woman with whom the sexual act had been taken off the table. He was good with that decision, and he knew it would be put back when the time was right.

Besides, nothing wrong with anticipation. It's certainly worked its magic so far.

Absorbed in his own musings, he missed her soft footfalls on the back stairs, but he heard her call out from the kitchen.

"How's your beer? Would you like another?"

"No, I'm good, thanks."

Seconds later, she stopped in the doorway of the living room and took in the ambiance.

He worried she might take it the wrong way and prepared to explain himself, when her face broke into a broad smile.

"It's perfect. Thank you." She set her glass of water down then stood in front of the sofa looking at him, an enigmatic grin playing about her lips. He was about to ask her what was on her mind when she jumped up on the couch and sat across his lap facing him. With both arms around his neck and a very mischievous smile, she asked, "So. Whatcha wanna do?"

He laughed. "Gee, I dunno. What do *you* wanna do?"

"Ooh, I dunno," she said, screwing her face up thoughtfully. "We could watch a video. Discuss current events. Play a rousing game of Crib . . ." She continued listing ideas, all the while running a finger absentmindedly along the edge of his ear, down the side of his neck, and along the collar of his shirt, turning him inside out.

"Well, that all sounds like big fun." He was terribly aware of how her proximity had added huskiness to his voice—and by her smile, so was she. "I'll tell you what, while I'm deciding, why don't you just kiss me? It shouldn't take more than an hour or two to make up my mind."

She nodded and leaned in to him. Her mouth was devastating—soft, warm, perfectly moist.

They moved against each other in harmony, teasing each other with tender little nibbles.

He pulled her against him with near crushing force, half afraid of snapping her in two, half afraid he would never be able to hold her close enough.

They broke apart, breathless.

Dizzy with arousal, he asked between gasps, "What *is* that?"

He had kissed a lot of women, between his job and his personal life, but nothing had ever made him feel like the bottom was dropping out from under him as it did when he kissed her. Even the mere memory of their kisses ran through him like a jolt of electricity. Whenever she was within arms' reach, it was all he could do to resist pulling her to him. On one hand, he was afraid that one day their passion would fade, but he was almost more afraid that it wouldn't.

"I don't know." She drew a jagged breath against his cheek. "I remember seeing a documentary or something once."

Is she kidding? I'm about to suffer a socially embarrassing incident, and she's talking documentaries?

"It was about debunking the concept of soul mates. Scientists were speculating that rather than a spiritual element drawing two people together, there was, in fact, a biochemical link."

He traced the outline of her sweet lips with his thumb, causing her to garble every fourth word. He tried hard to focus on what she was saying as he suspected it might be important, and there was always a chance she might ask questions later.

God, her mouth! Even watching her speak turns me on.

"It's like there's something wired into our DNA. I can't remember if it's a *similar* genetic connection or an *opposing* one, but it communicates to the other person through our basic senses. Sight—which naturally, makes sense. Sound—even hearing the other's voice is a compelling force. Smell—likely the most primal. Taste and touch, which, well that goes without saying," she said with a chuckle, as her hands wormed their way under the sleeves of his T-shirt and stroked his arms and shoulders.

"That's pretty terrifying."

"What do you mean?"

"Well, if that's right, and I'm connected to you all the way down to my DNA, then I might as well give up now. Lovely lady," he said, and kissed her again, "I surrender."

"Mmm. You've gotta love a quitter." She kissed him back with force, and he relaxed against her as the world fell away.

****

Norah went around the living room slowly extinguishing the candles that David had thoughtfully lit so many hours before. She had kissed him goodbye at the door, stood in the window as he'd gone down her walk, and waved when he'd turned at her gate to see if she was still there.

She powered off the CD player but continued to hum as she turned out the lamp and took their glasses into the kitchen. She vowed to wash up tomorrow, as she turned that light out as well and made her way up the back stairs.

She stopped on her way to take a peek at Ella, who was sleeping deeply, face down on the mattress with her bum in the air and her hands tucked under her.

Norah stroked her cheek and led a few stray curls of shining copper away from her brow. It was moments like this that Norah felt her heart was filled to bursting with the love she had for Ella. Nothing in the world surprised her more than the almost consuming devotion she had to this wee soul who had captivated her since she'd first known of her. She knew it was a ridiculously prideful thought, that no mother had ever loved a child more, but on some level she believed it nonetheless.

She backed quietly out of Ella's room and, leaving the door ajar, went across the hall to her own. Once she'd completed her toilette, she changed into a pair of flannel drawstrings and a ratty old T-shirt. She dug the journal out from its hiding spot under the mattress and laughed at the memory of the events that led to it being there.

Settled in and comfy, she turned to the last entry—her telephone conversation with David earlier that day. With pen in hand, she completed the thought and moved on to the remaining events. She stopped often, collecting the memories, focusing her thoughts, and recording it in a way that would be pleasing to read later on. Perhaps when she was old, or maybe for Ella after Norah had passed away.

The evening had been magical first to last. It had been so different from their relationship on-set and working. That was where they challenged or infuriated each other then laughed it off. It was where they tried to keep a professional distance.

In her home, however, with no clock ticking, no one watching, no pressures, no interruptions, no defined roles, they had been free to be who they were as individuals, and able to explore who they might be as a couple. They were a very different David and Norah, and it was very nice indeed.

By the time she finished, it was nearly two o'clock in the morning. She closed her journal and pitched it into the semidarkness, shut out the light, and snuggled down under the covers. She remembered reading a quote by a famous actress who'd said something about how only good girls kept diaries because bad girls didn't have the time. Truer words had been never spoken. If she'd been half as naughty as she'd wanted to be, she wouldn't have spent the last two hours with a notebook in her bed, that's for sure.

David had left just before midnight, and she could honestly say that she missed him already. Her hand reached over to where he would have been lying right now if she had surrendered to the heat of the hours spent on the sofa. She hadn't had a make-out session like that since she'd been a teenager, and she had certainly never enjoyed one so much.

She pressed her lips together and smiled at their tingling numbness.

Quite the workout, and I'm sorely out of shape.

She sighed into her pillow and vividly remembered the feel of being in his arms, his hands caressing her skin where he had found it, and the precise texture of his fingers on her body.

He had never ventured beneath her clothing, and she'd congratulated him on his restraint.

"Honey, you have no idea," he had answered.

In fact, she did.

She'd never wanted it to end, but despite their hunger, they had both recognized that he needed to leave soon or not leave at all. She had moved off his lap and sat near him and waited for their fevers to cool. He'd held her hand as if not willing to part with her completely, and she'd smiled.

They had discussed plans for tomorrow, and how to include Ella. In the end, they had decided he would come to their house for brunch before they headed into town for the local matinee. After that, who knew? She didn't want to presume that he would want to spend another evening with them, although he did say something about a Blu-ray of a yet unreleased movie he had that he thought they would enjoy together, so maybe . . .

As she lay dozing, she let her thoughts wander back to their goodbyes.

They had been holding each other when David had pulled back and smiled at her and said, "I can't remember ever having such a hard time getting out a door."

She nodded. "I know."

"And the irony is that the only reason I'm leaving is because I care so much about you. If I liked you even a little bit less, you'd be getting your clothes shredded right about now."

"It almost makes me want to do something to piss you off."

He had laughed, and after one more sweet parting kiss, he'd opened the front door and crossed the veranda.

She had never allowed herself to imagine that they could have a full future together, but for this time, in this place, with this amazing series of events unfolding before her, she couldn't imagine a happier woman alive.

****

Late the next morning, she was upstairs putting the finishing touches on Ella when she heard the doorbell.

"I've got it," she heard Brett grumbled from downstairs, as he thumped toward the front door.

She wasn't sure what time he'd finally stumbled in that morning, but it had been nearly three before she had drifted off, and he still hadn't come up the stairs.

She heard male voices in the hall and some laughter as she moved back to the mirror to take one final glance before heading down.

They wore very pretty summer dresses. Norah's was the colour of heather, quite long, nearly to her ankle, and very lightweight. It billowed out behind her when she walked and was cut flattering to her figure. Ella's was a soft mango yellow with tiny birds on it. It had a matching sun hat, which Norah could never get on her for some reason. Instead, Ella chose a rather tatty cap with a wide brim the shade of a robin's egg. It gave her the look of a bereft fisherman, but Ella loved it and it kept the sun off her.

They followed the sound of the voices to the kitchen where she found Brett sautéing something in a skillet and David leaning against the countertop, coffee cup in hand. He grinned and listened as Brett regaled him with details of his antics from the previous night. As they entered, both men turned to greet them.

"Hello there." David smiled warmly at them.

"Day-day!" Ella toddled toward him.

David set his coffee on the counter and squatted down to accept her hug. He was clearly touched by this display of affection, and looked up at Norah with surprise and tenderness.

Norah smiled back, well pleased with the picture, and then moved to pour herself a cup of tea.

David scooped Ella up and listened attentively as she explained the intricacies of her hat, pointing at and naming all the different cartoon characters embroidered around the rim.

Norah crossed to them with her drink, and went up on her tiptoes to place a good-morning kiss on this wonderful man.

"Go in and sit." Brett gestured to the others with a wave of napkins. "I've set us up in the sunroom. Norah, grab the toast, will you?"

Norah collected the basket filled with warm slices of freshly buttered toast, balancing the jam trivet as well as her tea as she led David, who was still packing Ella, into the solarium with its large round table set with dishes in a bright tropical print. There was already a pitcher of juice and glasses, a couple of covered chafing dishes, and in the centre were the flowers David had brought to Norah the night before, beautifully arranged in a large ceramic jug.

Norah took Ella off David and fastened her into her booster seat. When she turned to take her own place, he wrapped her in his arms.

"You look lovely, by the way, and I've been looking forward to this since I left last night." He bent down and kissed her thoroughly.

"Please, you two, not on an empty stomach." Brett entered, laden down with a platter of omelettes, a dish stacked high with thin griddle cakes, and a decanter of warmed syrup.

Norah and David untangled to help him distribute the bounty around the table before they all sat and filled their plates.

Norah cut up a griddle cake for Ella and laughed as the little girl offered

David a slice from the end of her little plastic fork.

David made a loud growling sound as he gobbled the morsel, making Ella giggle.

Their conversation was light and lively and continued well into the lunch hour before Norah checked her watch. She apologized to Brett for sticking him with the dishes.

"Screw that, I have Theresa coming over."

Theresa was the woman who lived down the street and worked as a freelance domestic. Usually Brett and Norah had her in only once a week to do the vacuuming, dusting, cleaning the bathrooms, windows—all the loathsome stuff that they would much rather pay someone else to do. This week, with Norah occupied elsewhere, the place had fallen down a little in the areas they did manage to keep clean on their own. Seeing as she would make a nice bit of cash off the movie, she had told Brett to farm out anything she wasn't holding her end up on, and clearly that meant the dishes.

Fair enough.

He had prepared a fabulous brunch, and he hadn't had to in light of his late night, so she was terribly grateful.

They entered the lobby of the theatre with more than ten minutes to spare.

David stopped short as he took in the diminutive scale of the place. To the far left stood the box office—barely big enough for a whole person to fit inside—and next to it a snack bar where two staff members practically stood shoulder to shoulder behind a crowded counter displaying all the classic treats.

"Man," said David. "I feel like Gulliver."

Norah laughed and stood in line for popcorn.

"Norah, I just watched you put away eight pounds of breakfast. Are you telling me you have room for a snack?"

She huffed in mock indignation. "Certainly not. I simply don't know how to watch a movie without popcorn."

The longer they stood, the more aware she was of the surreptitious glances and whispered conversations pointed in their direction.

"Doesn't that look like . . ."

"Is that—"

"I'd heard he was, but no. It can't be . . ."

Norah cast a sideways glance at David, who looked as though he hadn't heard a thing. He held Ella's tiny hand as they discussed the poster advertising the movie they were about to see. She wondered if he had trained himself to block out the droning buzz to avoid being drawn into it.

Hopefully, I'll have the need to add that skill to my repertoire.

The film they chose was standard children's fare—live action mixed with animation. Ella was entranced, oohing and ahhing at all the best parts, and joined all the other children clapping her hands at the end.

The Wrong Woman

They waited until most of the house had cleared before making their way out.

Norah asked David to get Ella settled in the car so that she could use the facilities before they left.

Taking her keys, they headed outside.

Just as Norah was about to exit the stall, a conversation entered the washroom and she stopped dead.

"You didn't see him, Kelly. I'm positive it was him leaving just now."

"David Raurke? In the Whitecourt Theatre? Gimme a break."

"I'm serious. My uncle told me that he was making a film somewhere between here and Mayerthorpe."

"But what would he be doing here?"

"I dunno. I think he was with Norah Rothe and her little girl."

"Okay, now I know you're cracked. What the hell would he be doing with *her*?"

"Why? She's all right."

"She's all right, but David Raurke wouldn't be caught dead with *all right*. I mean she's no Corrina Biblios, that's for sure, or Sandy Gishler—"

"Or Marianna McCoy."

"Now, see, I don't think she's very pretty at all."

"No, but she has *huge* boobs."

They both howled with laughter and Norah listened to the cackles fade as the door closed behind them.

"Ouch." Norah sat down on the toilet lid with a thud, propping her chin on her fist. A short pity party later, she slid back the latch and took a few tentative steps toward the mirror. "So that's what 'just all right' looks like."

Her reflection sighed back at her.

Once they made it home again, David followed Norah through the gate and sat beside her on the step as they watched Ella run around the yard.

"What happened?" he asked.

She looked in surprise, then realized that she hadn't said a word the whole drive back. She toyed with the idea of shrugging it off but stopped herself.

If you can't be honest with him, especially about this, then where can you go?

She took a deep breath. "I overheard something in the bathroom."

He braced himself. "Okay. What did you hear?"

"That David Raurke wouldn't be caught dead with someone who looked 'just all right.'"

"Is that all?" he asked dismissively.

"David—"

"Norah, I told you, people are going to say things—filthy, horrible, inexcusable things that you can't begin to imagine. You told me that first night that as long as you were in my world, you'd handle it. Well, welcome to my world. You'd better find some way to handle it because *it* is not going to go away."

Okay, that stung.

She sulked a little on her side of the stoop, but reflected on what he had said.

He's right, of course. Those two idiots in the can were rank amateurs, and if I can't take a little sass from a couple of pissy cows I'll never survive the big guns firing at me.

"You're right, and by the way you should take note of this, because it isn't very often *that* is going to come out of my mouth."

He laughed and moved closer to her, tucking her arm in his as they watched Ella plucking the petals off a daisy.

"Lumme, lumme not, lumme, lumme not . . ."

"I guess what got me was that I . . . I worried that they might be right."

"What? That I wouldn't date someone who's 'just all right'?" He shrugged. "That's entirely possible."

"Pardon?"

"Yeah, I don't know. Maybe." He took her face in his free hand, pulling her full focus to what he was saying. "Norah, you are not just all right. Every minute I'm with you, you become more and more beautiful to me."

Her lips twitched as she fought the smile. "But what about at the beginning? When we first met? Honestly, what did you think?" She watched him dig deep for an answer, and then he smiled.

"It's hard. Every memory I have of you is influenced by the way I feel about you now."

She nestled against his arm, reveling in the sweetness of the sentiment.

"Okay, I think I remember. I came up to you guys sitting at the table, you had your head down a bit, and I thought you looked very . . . pleasant."

"Pleasant?" she asked.

"Yeah, pleasant. Pleasing. You raised your head, you fixed me with those eyes . . . and then you smiled." He shook his head and smiled. "Fa-get abou'dit." He even took on the gangster accent and posture.

She laughed and kissed him, grateful he'd quieted her anxiety.

They settled back and watched Ella, who had plunked herself into her sandbox under the tree.

"I'll be honest with you though, honey."

She stiffened slightly as she imagined her bubble of contentment meeting up with this needle of honesty he threatened her with.

"Ten years ago, hell, maybe even five years ago, I might not have looked at you twice. If we were working together, I'd have thought you were funny, smart, talented as hell, and I likely would have tried to set you up with one of my best friends. Which is a huge compliment, by the way. I almost always take better care of them than I do myself, but . . ."

Hmm, this honesty crap may be overrated.

". . . to go for you myself, not likely. You aren't—"

"Corrina Biblios?"

"Oh, fuck me!" He clapped his hand over his mouth and jerked his gaze to Ella. "Sorry. No. Let me tell you something about Corrina Biblios. I never, *ever* talk about my exes unless I have something nice to say, but in this case . . . talk about high maintenance, vain, bland—damn! We'd be at a party or something, and the whole time you're talking to her, she's looking over your shoulder to see who else might be walking in, you know? I'd suggest something fun to do, something that didn't involve the 'in' crowd, nothing crazy, a walk or whatever. She'd look at me and roll her eyes like I'd gone nuts. But that's what I'm saying, back then, that was all I wanted. I was just looking for someone who looked good on my arm at a party, was hot in the sack—which plenty of times they weren't but, whatever—and didn't force me to take too hard a look at myself."

"And now?"

"And now I'm looking for more." He leaned in to her and, with his lips practically touching hers, said, "Now *I'm* the best friend I want to set you up with."

They kissed long and tenderly, her arm still wrapped around his and holding his hand, her other hand softly stroking his face.

"Mama, Day-day, come pway."

They drew apart slowly then, still holding hands, walked over to the sandbox.

****

Dinner that night was a good deal more casual than the night before. Brett had been needed at the café, since Saturday was their busiest night, and Norah knew she could still put together a mean salad to go with the delivery pizza, which was on its way.

She wished they could go outside, but the flies and mosquitoes this time of year were relentless. A blanket on the living room floor gave the illusion of a picnic, accentuated with a CD of forest sounds, a dusty leftover from the days Brett had considered taking up meditation. David had begged for mercy halfway through her story about the mini shrine and chants Norah and Ella had been subjected to during that phase. Once the food was in place, the fun and laughs had carried over into their very own bug-free outing.

While they cleared the spread away, David informed her casually, "By the way, I hope you didn't have too much planned for the next few weeks."

She took the dirty plates from him and tucked them into the dishwasher with their used glasses and utensils. "I don't . . . why?"

"Well, Geoff—you know, the man who wrote the script?" He laughed when she turned and stuck her tongue out. "Seems he liked your work so much that he wanted to write a bunch more scenes for you. I got the green light from the studio, and I read them Thursday afternoon. They're really good. I think you'll be pleased."

She stood, frozen, clutching the empty pizza box. "I'm sorry, could you repeat that?"

He leaned against the counter with his arms folded across his chest, grinning. "Well, if memory serves, you'll have . . . let's see, two, three, five, six, yeah, six more scenes. A couple of them are substantial, and that's on top of the ones you're already signed up for. Oh, and I think this'll interest you. In about six weeks, you'll be needed for about ten days of shooting . . . away from Whitecourt."

"What away? Where away?"

"New York."

"New York, New York?"

"No, New York, Nebraska. Of course, New York, New York."

"David, what does this mean?"

"Well, it means you've gone from a fairly meaty bit part to a really good supporting role. It means quite a bit more money. It means you and Ella had better have your passports in order, and if you ask me, it means you're gonna be a star, baby."

She stared at him.

This can't be true. He had to be teasing. But . . .

He wasn't joking. He was thrilled for her, and she could see it in his eyes. She spun toward the counter, shoved the pizza box to the side, and leaned on the butcher block fighting to contain her tears.

"Norah, honey." He came up behind her, turned her around, and folded her into his arms. "Sweetheart, don't cry."

"I'm n-n-not." She hiccupped again. "David, you've no idea—"

"Yes, I do." He pushed her back and looked at her with feigned seriousness. "I wasn't always internationally famous and beloved throughout the universe, you know."

She threw her arms around his neck and, with a squeal, hung on while he spun her round the kitchen.

****

They waited until Ella was tucked into bed before they popped in the Blu-ray. David sat with his back against the sofa arm and his legs stretched out along the seat, and Norah made herself comfortable, lying with her head against his chest and their legs intertwined.

She breathed deeply the musky scent of him and turned her head up to kiss his neck, right under his fabulous jawline.

"Stop it." He never took his eyes off the screen.

"Stop what?" she asked innocently.

"That. What you're doing. I want to see this film. My friend's in it."

"Okay."

"My really good friend."

"Okay!"

She smiled to herself, happy that even though neither of them had discussed it, they were together for another evening. She tried not to think about what would happen when the evening ended this time.

Chapter 10

David woke to a feeling of happy . . . strangeness. He opened his eyes and blinked a few times to clear his vision. It was dark all around him but for a television screen, which was eerily blank outside its bright blue background. He heard an echoing *tick-tock* of a heavy pendulum swinging somewhere far away and the sound of an appliance, maybe a refrigerator, kicking on. Then he heard a soft sigh and felt her move against him, and the last piece of the puzzle fell into place.

They'd dozed off . . . watching a movie.

Right, Terry's movie.

He looked down at her. Her head felt right on his chest, with her hand buried between the buttons of his shirt so that he could feel the warmth of her fingers against his skin. He tried to adjust and relieve his left arm, which had fallen asleep wedged between her and the sofa back, without disturbing her. She looked so peaceful, and if she woke up, he would have to leave.

He thought about the night before—getting off the sofa, holding hands as they had walked to the door, saying goodbye. It had taken superhuman strength to continue down that sidewalk and through the gate, especially when he had turned at the last minute and spotted her standing at the window. She had been so lovely in the glow of the streetlight. He didn't know if he'd be able to go back to his cold, impersonal hotel room and crawl into a big empty bed alone and lonely for a second night. That experience had given new meaning to the word *desolation*.

Without thinking, he moaned out loud at the memory and then stiffened, cursing as she began to stir.

"Mmm. What happened?" she asked, not quite awake.

"We fell asleep." His voice was low and soothing, partly because he hoped she'd drift back off.

"No, in the movie. What happened?"

"I don't know. I faded about twenty minutes in."

"So that means . . ."

"Terry's in a turkey."

"How excellent for you."

He smiled at her comprehension of his particular sense of humour.

She lifted herself to a halfway seated position and pushed the hair off her face. She smiled down at him and then . . .

He read it on her face as if she'd spoken it aloud. It wasn't just that her smile had faded, there was sadness in her eyes.

He worked his way off the couch and, taking her hands in his, he pulled her to her feet and asked, "Do you trust me?"

She hesitated less than a second, long enough for his words to translate through her still foggy brain. "Of course."

"Then trust me when I say, I can't do it. I'm sorry, but you are involved with a weakling, a coward, a . . . how do they say it in England? 'A big girl's blouse.' That's it. You are involved with a big girl's blouse."

"My mother would be so proud. David, what are you talking about? Am I dreaming?"

"No, honey, you're not dreaming. I can't walk away from you tonight. I can't. So what we're going to do is this. We're going to go your room, get into your bed, and then we are going to fall asleep. Now this is where the trust thing comes in. I promise nothing more will happen, and I am willing to suffer the madness that will result from making such a promise, but I know . . . I know, I can't do another night like last night. So, unless you're going to toss me out on my—"

"Okay."

"I'm sorry, baby, but 'okay' what? 'Okay' you're going to toss me or—"

"Okay, let's go upstairs." She didn't say it in a sexy or remotely suggestive way, just plain and simple. "I trust you and I trust the decision we made, but I don't want you to go either. We'll try it once and if it's, you know, impossible, then we'll revisit the issue. So you turn off the TV, and I'll lock the door." Then she walked off.

He stood stock-still for a fraction of a second, a little disappointed that he didn't get to present his entire argument, then he realized he still wasn't moving and mentally cuffed himself in the head.

He turned off the television, the Blu-ray player, the sound system, and all but dashed into the hall where she was waiting at the foot of the stairs.

She smiled, another simple little smile that said nothing more than she was glad he was there. She took one step up.

He clasped her hand and stopped her.

She turned to face him, a question in her eyes.

"It's nothing," he answered. "I just wanted to kiss you good night . . . here. I don't want to risk, you know—"

"You *are* a big girl's blouse." She giggled, wrapped her arms around his neck, and pulled him into a warm, sweet, still sleepy kiss.

He buried his face in her neck and inhaled the delicious perfume of her before pulling away. With one hand on the small of her back, he followed her up the stairs, and realized that this was one of the happiest journeys of his life.

****

She led him toward Ella's room where he waited in the doorway, watching as she adjusted the covers over the tiny sleeping form, stroked the little head, and then touched it with a kiss. He was entranced—this lovely woman gazing down at her slumbering child with only a small nightlight illuminating them—and he wished more than anything for a camera to capture the beauty of that moment.

She looked back from the hall, left the door opened a crack, and held out her hand to guide him across the hall.

The room was a good size with a sloped ceiling on the far side. Tall, but narrow windows to the left appeared to overlook the front street. There was a dressing table at an angle beside him, a large armoire with mirrored doors just off the washroom, and dominating the space between the windows was an old-fashioned canopy bed with four, thick posts and draperies hung all around it.

She went to a drawer in the dressing table, pulled out a bundle and headed for her bathroom, when she turned to him. "Is there something I can get you to wear? Maybe something of Brett's?"

While David liked Brett just fine, there was something about his bits being where another man's had been that had him shaking his head before she finished the question. "No, thanks. I'm good. I'll just do my shirt and boxers . . . if that's okay?"

"That's fine. If you like, you can use the washroom across the hall next to Ella's room, or wait and use this one after I'm finished."

"Okay, I'll go . . ." He jerked his thumb, gesturing behind him.

She disappeared inside and closed the door.

She still hadn't come out when he returned, so he stripped down and turned to face the bed. Standing at the foot, he looked right, then left, then he rocked from to one side to the other. Giving up, he tapped lightly on the door. "Norah, which side do you prefer?"

"Oh! Thanks. The side closest the door, if you don't mind. In case Ella wakes up."

"Okay." He turned and faced the intimidating bed again and gave it a wry smile. "Okay, buddy, I want us to become good friends." He piled the eight hundred extra pillows on the chaise and tugged down the covers.

He tried not to stare as the door opened, but she was so cute in her baggy plaid pajama bottoms and a T-shirt that looked as if it had seen better days.

"Not very sexy, I'm afraid," she said, as she shut off the bathroom light behind her.

One day he would tell her that seeing her in those ratty pajamas was a thousand times sexier than Corrina Biblios in a negligée could ever hope to be.

Just as he began to worry that she might have changed her mind, she glided toward him, delivering the play-by-play in the perfect movie announcer voice.

"In a town, that no one has ever heard of, there was a house. And in the house there was a room. And in that room, there was a woman. An ordinary woman who was about to embark on a very extraordinary adventure. For here, in the room, in the house, in the town that no one had ever heard of, was a man that *everyone* had heard of. And he was in her bed."

"She glided toward him, purposefully clothed in her frumpiest, in a feeble attempt to stave off the animals lusts that she knew raged within him."

He laughed out loud at her performance and watched as she climbed on the bed and faced him, sitting on her knees.

Her voice reverted to normal. "Little did she know that he was, in fact, perfectly calm and cool, and no threat to her precious virtue whatsoever."

He sighed. "Not calm, hardly cool, but a promise is a promise."

"Are you sure?"

"Hey, I'm just glad to be here."

"So am I," she whispered. She scooted between the sheets then reached for the lamp.

Darkness flooded the room with only the streetlights casting a pale glow across them. He shifted toward her, barely able to make out her profile amidst the shadows, until she turned, and he got lost in the shine of her eyes.

"Norah?"

"Hmm?"

"May I hold you?"

She answered by slipping into his arms. A small sigh escaped as she nestled her head under his chin, her hand softly on his chest, and her leg draped over one of his.

He kissed the top of her head and placed his hand on top of hers and snuggled close.

Last night, desolation. Tonight, bliss.

****

The first time you wake up next to a woman is a daunting event, as David was well aware. So when he opened his eyes and was unable to focus on anything remotely familiar, the cold hand of dread reached out and squeezed him by the balls as if to say, "What have you done, David? You naughty, naughty boy."

He propped up and tried to blink away the fog enough to make out his reflection as it blinked back at him from the armoire mirror across the room. He slid his gaze to the woman sleeping next to him. So many times in the past, he'd found only regret there. Not today, however.

Definitely not today.

Norah was on her stomach, facing away, and sound asleep. The bedding had pooled to her knees and her shirt had ridden up toward her shoulders, treating him to a lovely view of her naked back. His morning erection cheered on his fantasy of leaning over, caressing that delicious display of flesh with his mouth and tongue, and turning her over and filling his hands with her breasts, of hooking his thumbs in the elastic of her bottoms and . . .

"Put it out of your head, buster."

His erection collapsed like a fat man on a lawn chair. "I beg your pardon," he said, falling back on the pillow, spooked by her perception. "I'm sure I don't know what you mean."

She turned and faced him with a smirk.

He grinned foolishly back at her. "How did you know?"

She pushed onto her elbows, shoving her tousled hair out of her eyes.

My God—she is gorgeous.

"I heard you breathing."

"What?"

"You breathe funny when you get . . . you know."

"No, I don't know. How do I breathe?" He felt a bit picked on.

"I'm not going to tell you."

"I don't breathe funny."

She took the bait. "Yes, you do." Her face went slack and she breathed through her mouth, sounding like an asthmatic camel, and they both dissolved into laughter.

Once they'd recovered, he reached over and smoothed down her hair a bit and sighed. "I have to meet Jozef for lunch today."

"Okay, do you want to shower here or back at the hotel?"

"I'll do it there, I guess, all my stuff . . ." It was too soon to suggest leaving a few things here. "What are your plans for the day?" he asked, as he crossed along the foot of the bed to grab his pants.

"I think I'm taking Ella to my folks' for dinner. Other than that, I'll be working on my script, maybe catching up on a bit of paperwork for the café."

Inwardly, he pouted at the idea that he couldn't spend the evening with her, but he had to get some work done, too. He shook off his disappointment and scouted around for his socks.

When she crawled to the edge of the bed and wrapped her arms around his neck, he leaned his head onto her shoulder and stroked her arm. "Thank you for letting me stay."

"Thank you for staying," she whispered against his ear. "Not too difficult?"

"No, not too bad. Well, maybe a bit this morning." He mimicked her imitation of his camel-breathing, which made her laugh uproariously, with a snort even. He dragged her out from behind him and into his lap, and he smiled, watching every movement of her face, until her laughter faded.

The Wrong Woman

"Mama . . ." came a soft plea from across the hall.

Norah raised her eyebrows and let him help her to her feet. "Will you stay for breakfast?"

"Umm, sure. Maybe some toast and coffee?"

"I'll meet you downstairs, then."

He needed to get on with the business of the day, and could have waited until lunch to eat, but he'd cut out on too many women on too many mornings during his life, and this was one lady he was not going to give the bum's rush to. Besides, he really did want to stay, say good morning to Ella, and leave properly, not like some thief skulking out with the silverware. Also, this would give them the chance to set something up for later in the week without having to sneak into some corner on set. He had the master schedule in the car and was aware of an upcoming day that was strictly second unit filming, so he tossed some ideas around his head as he continued getting dressed.

****

After breakfast, after goodbye kisses and chubby little arms offering sweet hugs, after showering, after Jozef, after paperwork, after script work, and after scheduling, he threw himself down on his hotel bed and groaned. Looking at the clock, he wondered if Norah and Ella were on their way to dinner yet. He sulked a bit, then sat up and reached for his cell.

"Don't be an ass," he said, and tossed the phone away. He pacified himself with a promise to call her before he went to bed. He'd never been so scattered before. If he wanted to call a woman, he called her. If he didn't, he didn't. None of this, "I want to, but I shouldn't, it's too early or it's too late, or I don't want to wake her or bother her or interrupt something, blah, blah, blah." He barely recognized himself.

Another thought occurred to him and he reached for his cell again.

"Hello?"

"Hey, it's me."

"David. To what do I owe—"

"It's not too late, is it?"

"Nope. We just finished dinner. What's up?"

"Why does something have to be up?"

"All right, I'll play. How's the picture?"

Definitely the right call. Now, be casual!

"The picture is going good—great, in fact."

"Okay, so? Oh, I know. What's her name?"

Maybe not.

"Now why would you think—"

"Hey, buddy, it's your dime. If you want to play cat and mouse all night . . ."

"Norah. Her name is Norah, with an *H*."

"Nice. How did you meet her?"
"On set. She's on the film."
"Norah who?"
"She's brand new. You've never heard of her."
"Who's she playing?"
"Clare."
"Clare? What happened to whasserface?"
"Broke her arm at the airport on the way over."
"Nooo!"
"Yep."
"Well, that really . . . how did you find this . . . Norah?"

He relayed the details of Norah's discovery with great emphasis on his resistance to the whole idea.

"So how is she doing in the role?"
"She's abso-frigging-amazing actually. Better than Helen would have been."
"Wow. So when did you know?"
"What?"
"That you liked her, dummy."
He chuckled. "Instantly."
"Seriously?"
"Seriously."
"Humph. So what's she like then?"

He struggled for the words. "Lovely, smart, talented, so funny, kind. She has the most fabulous little girl . . ."

"Wait! Stop, stop, stop! There's a child?"
He sighed. "Yes, there's a child."
"Okay, I have to sit down."
"Oh, please don't make a big deal—"
"David. What do you . . . what are you doing?"
"What, what am I doing?"
"I've asked you probably a hundred times about the women you've . . . whatever it is you call it, and do you know how many times you've used the words 'smart' or 'kind' to describe them?"
"Not too often I'd say."
"Or *ever*. This is a whole new side of you, I have to say."
"That's kind of why I called you."
"How's that?"

He tried to think of an original way to describe what he was feeling, but in the end fell back on clichés to do the work for him. "I'm . . . I feel like a fish out of water. I'm really out of my element here."

"A stranger in a strange land?"
"Yeah, that's a good one, too."
"Okay, so that's a bad thing?"
"No. I guess not. I'm really nuts about her."

"I can tell."

"Really?"

"Yeah, really. She sounds like a real person, not one of your usual cardboard cutouts. I don't mean this in a demeaning way, David, but you don't usually involve yourself with women who are very—how should I say this? *Challenging*, I guess. It sounds like she's got you on your toes, and I think that's good. It's what we've all been wanting for you, actually."

"And here I was hoping you'd make me feel better."

"Afraid you might lose your cool, David?"

"Oh, we're way beyond that," he said, chuckling.

"What have you done?"

"Well, we were having breakfast and working out when we could get together, you know, away from the set. I mentioned to her that Thursday was all second unit stuff so both of us could get away and maybe, you know, whatever . . ."

"Yeah?"

"Well, I told you she has this café, right, where she met Ted and Steve."

"Right."

"She tells me that she has to go get supplies and stuff from one of those big box warehouse stores . . ."

"Okay."

". . . and that it takes pretty much the whole day, with the drive into the city and all . . ."

"Sure."

". . . and that Thursday would be her only chance . . ."

"I've got it. So?"

"So I said, 'Gee, that sounds really fun,' or some idiot thing like that . . ."

"You're kidding?"

". . . and she says, 'You mean you'd like to come along?' as if, what kind of fool would want to spend a day doing that if they didn't have to? But did I take the out? No, I did not. Instead, I said, 'That'd be great.' That's what I said. 'That'd be great.'"

"So, basically, what you're telling me is that you're a girl."

"Pretty much."

"Dude, what are you doing?"

"I don't know! What the hell am I doing?"

"Well, you're going shopping, for one."

"Right, thanks."

"For big bargains."

"Thank you."

"So . . . how's the sex?"

"I beg your pardon?"

"You heard me."

"What would compel me to discuss *that* with my sister?"

"Oh, don't be an ass."

"Well, if you must pry—I don't know."
"What does that mean?"
"We decided to, you know, wait awhile."
Dead silence met him from the other end.
"Beth?"
"Are you serious? You sound serious. Are you *serious*?"
"I guess I'm serious."
"But wait . . . you said you had breakfast with her this morning."
Of course, she caught that.
"Yes, I know. We slept together, but we don't . . . *sleep* together."
"Well, David, I couldn't be more astonished. Honestly, you could knock me down with a feather."
"Oh, come on!"
"No, I'm terribly impressed with you. And her." He heard her shift the phone and then the muffled commands to "wash it first", then she was back. "When do we get to meet this unprecedented woman?"

He couldn't remember the last time he had introduced someone—a *woman* someone—to his family. Strangely, he was okay with the idea.

"Soon, I think," he answered. "Yeah, soon."

Chapter 11

Early Thursday morning and everyone else was still asleep. The house was just the way Norah loved it best—that almost unearthly quiet—only the grandfather clock within, and the first waking birds without. She sat in the solarium, feet propped up on a neighbouring chair, her thoughts and a large mug of tea keeping her company while her pen found its way across the pages of her journal. She was grateful that she'd decided to chronicle her experiences, since it was all becoming a bit of a blur and she didn't want to forget a minute.

It had been an unbelievable week. Working three straight days on set was a dream come true. Knowing that shooting days are almost always twelve hours long, frequently longer, she'd asked David—as actor to director—if it would be all right for Ella to be allowed on the lot, with Aunt Peg to care for her while shooting. That way she'd at least get to see her at meals and during all the downtime. He'd said it would be fine, that people did it all the time, and that he very much appreciated that she had come to him as an actor to her director and asked, rather than as his girlfriend.

I'm David Raurke's girlfriend! Inconceivable.

She had watched his career from a distance for over a decade. As a fan, she had never viewed him in the same league as Dennis and Nick, especially since a number of his earlier films had been ill-conceived, but there was no denying his appeal. She'd bought magazines because he was on the cover and watched talk shows when she'd heard he was a guest. He had always been dazzling to look at and a funny, charming man—the ultimate mega-movie star.

There was no way she was *that* David's girlfriend.

But *her* David—the one who cracked her up all the time, brought her flowers and wine, carried her daughter around on his shoulders, and whose kisses made her dizzy with desire. Her David who had stood behind her in chairs this past Monday and whispered, "happy anniversary," because he remembered that they'd met exactly one week ago.

She was absolutely and without a doubt that David's girlfriend. The rest was incidental.

The grandfather clock struck eight. Norah knew she'd have to get moving soon in order to wake up Ella and get them on the road, but first she wanted to revisit yesterday. She took a deep breath and, pen poised, let her memories slide onto the page.

****

She had wrapped early, and after lunch with David and the gang, she collected Ella and Peg and set off for the café. There were cheques to write, invoices to sign, payroll to get to the accountant, and—the most tedious of all—inventory to count, before she headed off into the city bright and early the next morning.

Peg volunteered to take Ella shopping, and then over to Mona and Vic's for dinner. That was far more exciting for Ella than another afternoon at the café, so Norah gave her an extra big hug and kiss and waved goodbye.

It had been a sticky, dusty walk home after she'd completed her work, and Norah let out a moan of pleasure as she stretched out along the length of the enormous claw-foot tub and let the water work its magic. She reached up to the taps, conveniently positioned on the centre edge of the rim, and added just a bit more hot water.

She wasn't sure if she would be picking David up in front of his hotel tomorrow morning or if he were coming here first, so she hoped he'd call sometime this evening for clarification. Just in case, she'd brought the phone in with her, and it was sharing the window ledge with her wine.

After a very long relaxing soak, she let herself slide under the water, wetting her hair before shampooing. Amid the burbling sound, she heard something shrill outside her watery cocoon. She rose up amid much splashing, heard the phone ringing, and quickly flicked as much water as she could off her hand before she picked it up.

"Hello?"

"Hello."

Whoosh. Humph. Every time . . . stomach whoosh.

"Hey, I was just thinking about you."

"Oh, you were, were you? What were you thinking?"

She grinned. "I was thinking about how handsome you looked sitting in the stand today and how very badly I wanted to come over and bite your buttons off."

Where did that— must be the wine.

He coughed slightly. "Oh, really? Well, that would have made for an interesting take. You sound funny, kind of echo-y. Where are you?"

"I am right now, you gorgeous hunk of man, lying naked in a bubble bath."

Definitely the wine.

"You don't say."

"I *do* say."

"What do you do with Ella when you're in the bath?"

"She's with Peg, having dinner with my parents."

"Aw, so you're all alone."

"Yes, and terribly, terribly lonely."

Note to self, must get more of this wine.

"How about you? Are you still on set?"

"No, as a matter of a fact, I've just come through your gate."

She jerked upright and water sloshed everywhere as her free hand instinctively covered her chest. "You're where?"

"Yep. Coming up the front steps. Ah, the front steps . . . good times here. I don't suppose there's any chance you left the door unlock—oh yes, you did. You really should be more careful, you know. You can never tell who might walk in on you."

She heard the front door squeak and heard boots on the hall floor. Her heart was racing so fast she felt it pounding in her ears. Her voice lost its sexy allure. In fact, she could have done a fair imitation of a cartoon rodent. "If you want to make yourself comfortable, I'll be down in a minute."

She heard him chuckle softly, followed immediately by the creak of his tread on the stairs. "I have a better idea . . . what's that noise? Is that running water?"

"I'm making more bubbles."

"Well, don't fill it too much. We don't want it to overflow."

"David, you're not thinking . . ."

She heard his voice in stereo, from the handset and the general direction of her bedroom. "No, I'm not thinking. I am, however, taking off my pants. Do you want me to leave my shirt in here or would you rather bite my buttons off?"

She turned off the phone and flung it onto the mat in one move, then clapped her hands over her face and half screamed, half laughed in a dizzying combination of terror and excitement. She heard him approaching the door and, like a late night horror film, watched as the doorknob turned in slow motion.

The door drifted open and there he was, leaning against the jam in bare feet, shorts on, and his shirt undone to the waist. His arms were folded across his chest and he looked so sexy she could have died.

"Sorry, I only saved you a couple." He motioned to the bottom of his shirt. He stepped inside, shut the door behind him, then secured the lock.

Like a deer caught in headlights, she couldn't look away as he approached.

He saved her dental work and unfastened the remaining buttons himself, then shrugged the shirt off his shoulders and let it drop. "May I?" He gestured to her wine.

She reached a shaking hand beside her and handed the glass to him.

He took a long deliberate drink, handed it back, and never took his eyes off her as she took a steadying sip before returning it to the shelf. He waited until her gaze returned to him before he hooked his thumbs in the waistband of his boxers and dropped them to the floor.

"Oh, David, I'm not sure this is such a good idea . . ."

"I'm sure it's not. Move over."

She drew her legs up to her chest and waited as he stepped gingerly into the steaming water then sank slowly into it.

"Ouch! You like it hot."

"I would have thought that was obvious by now," she replied.

He sat back with both arms resting on the sides of the tub, his chest shining wet. He stretched his legs out to either side of her then propped his head onto one of his hands. He began a slow study of her, and Norah was proud that she didn't shrink away from this thorough going over. He gazed at the point where the bubbles barely concealed her breasts, as if the intensity of his stare could melt the suds away. "What am I going to do with you?" he questioned, and cocked his brow.

"I would ask, what do you want to do with me? But I know that would be asking for a world of trouble."

He chuckled.

"So what are you doing here? I mean *here,* at my house, not *here,* in my tub." She hoped to break the sexual tension that was nearly choking her or, at the very least, bend it a little.

"We wrapped at six, and then I puttered around for a while. The crew wanted to hit the bar, but I knew you, Ella, and I had an early morning, so I thought I'd come here and ask you to make me some dinner."

"Aw, you should have gone out if you wanted to. I mean, I'm really happy you're coming with us tomorrow, but I'm afraid you're going to be bored out of your tree."

He shook his head. "I'm exactly where I want to be, Norah."

She smiled, touched by his earnestness. "But how . . . you couldn't know I was in the tub."

"Nope, just a very pleasant surprise." Then he leaned forward.

She held her breath, but he reached past her for the wineglass and took another drink. Then he slowly tipped it toward her lips, and let her take a sip before setting it aside. Rather than leaning back, he gently captured her ankles, and then pulled her feet to his chest. There, he began a gentle massage of first one foot then the other, causing her to relax even deeper into the water. She placed her hands on his shins beside her and firmly rubbed the muscles of his lower legs. Then she sat up in order to attend to the sensitive region behind his knees.

She was naughtily aware that this posture brought her breasts clear of the water, so she raised her eyes blatantly to meet his, and was met by a look of passion so raw that she trembled. He guided her feet to each side of him, then walked his hands, with painstaking slowness, up her legs to her hips, then slid her gently toward him. She relaxed into his embrace, and thrilled at the feel of their naked flesh fusing together. She moved against him, causing her nipples to gently tease his bare chest, before she leaned her head back exposing her throat. He hungrily complied, as his hands moved from her back, along her ribcage, to the front of her, then up.

A moan escaped her when she looked down and beheld the greatly anticipated view of her breasts in his hands. They watched together, fascinated, as her nipples hardened beneath the featherlight touch of his circling thumbs. He looked up into her face and would have seen eyes slightly glazed with the beginnings of pleasure. He captured her mouth with his. They locked together in a frenzy of lips and tongues for several breathtaking minutes, and she pulled her body even closer to his until there was nothing but the rock hardness of him against the softest part of her. It was as if an electric current shot through them both and they were shocked to their senses.

"How far can we take this?" she asked, her lips against his mouth. She very much wanted to go further, but she also knew that in going too far they could destroy everything.

"This is a very dangerous game, my lovely."

"You're the one who climbed into my tub," she accused with a smile.

She could see him mentally running through scenarios, discarding this one, disregarding that one. Finally, in an irritated huff, he let himself sink back, splashed water on his face, and ran a couple more handfuls through his neatly cropped hair.

"It's no good," he said, clearly exasperated. "Everything leads to . . ." Then he looked at her and a small growl resonated in the back of his throat. He rubbed his eyes with one hand as if trying to wipe out the vision of her sitting there, bare-breasted and longing for him.

She reached over and pulled his hand away, forcing him to look at her, and invoked an earlier conversation. "Do you trust me?"

"Yes, baby, of course." He grinned.

"Then you need to trust me to keep our boundaries . . . intact."

"What . . . I don't know what that means."

"It's like when I was in high school. In a small town, if a girl goes all the way, she's ruined. So there were all these girls, clinging to their virginities like they were life rafts, terrified of being labeled the 'town bike' or whatever."

"Okay. What's that got—"

"Well, we just couldn't go all the way. That was the . . . boundary. And what that meant was, we had to use our imaginations, sometimes for years."

"You mean all that time you were with Ella's father . . ."

"Oh, God no! I didn't quite make it out of high school. But that still meant roughly two years . . . maybe a little less."

"Christ. That's impressive. What . . . how?"

She smiled at him provocatively. She definitely had his attention. "Oh, lots of things. I doubt I'm going to teach you anything new . . . well, maybe a thing or two, now that I think of it." She had risen up on to her knees, and braced her hands on the sides of the tub.

She looked firmly into his eyes. "I just need to know if that's where you're comfortable. Is that the point where you feel this is threatened? Because, David, as much as I want this to keep moving forward, as much as I want us to go just to the next level, I wouldn't want to hurt what we have for the world. So if you think that anything beyond what we've already done is risking what we have, then say so, and I'll put anything else out of my head until we're ready, I promise."

He laughed sardonically. "You say that like I'm capable of making a clear, rational decision right now. My God, Norah, you're naked, you're wet, really wet, and you're right here. All I can think about is how badly I want you, all of you . . ." He broke off in frustration.

"All right, baby, it's okay. Let's just cool down a bit." She sat back at her end of the tub, took a sip of wine, and offered the glass to him, which he accepted with a gratefully smile.

"I'm sorry, David."

"Why are you sorry?"

"I don't know, I feel like I'm . . . I don't know."

"Please, honey, don't ever apologize for driving me wild. I know I'm coming across as a bit of a dick just at the moment, it's only that I'm a little . . . pent up, shall we say? I've done a lot of thinking, I really have, about the decision we made about holding out on the sex for a while, and I'm sure we made the right choice. Mind you, you're never in the room when I'm doing all this thinking." After a moment of charged silence, he said, "I'd better go."

"Why?" She was heartsick. The last thing she wanted was for him to leave her tonight.

"Honey, I don't want to go, believe me. It's just . . ." He gestured to his nether region. "I've got to take care of something."

"So take care of it," she stated, matter-of-factly.

He looked at her as if she'd gone mad. "Here? In front of you?"

"Why not?

"Well, I . . ."

"David, you're blushing."

"Yeah, I think I might be."

"Well, I am . . . stunned."

"I am, too, a little."

They laughed, and the relaxed and comfortable sense of calm that they'd both come to rely on when they were together was back. They spent the next several minutes in general chitchat blended with happy quiet.

Combined with this was the frequent passing back and forth of the wine, which gave her the courage to ask, "So have you never?"

"What? Oh, in front of . . . no, not really. I mean a bit, you know, just to keep the show going between acts, so to speak."

"But, and not to beat the metaphor to death, but not as a, um . . . performance of its own?"

"Certainly not with an audience. Plenty of private rehearsals . . . especially lately." The last bit he said half to himself, half to the wine.

"Well, I think that's interesting," she said, taking the glass off him in order to steal another sip.

"Why?"

"I dunno. I would have thought you'd done it all."

"Madam what do you take me for?"

"Oh, sweetie, no. I don't think you're a man-whore or anything . . . I just . . . how's the wine? Good, right?"

He laughed and she was grateful that she hadn't offended him. "No, no. Quite right. I've had my share . . . and, very likely, a couple of other guys', too. Is there more?"

"More?"

"More wine, nitwit."

She giggled, feeling quite giddy. "Just behind you, on the floor."

He twisted to look over his shoulder and spotted the bottle. "Hmm. If I lean over to get that, you're going to see my ass."

"Damn." They both thought that was hilarious.

He got up on his knees and reached over the side of the tub, still laughing, in order to retrieve the bottle, top up their glass, then replace it onto the floor. She was taking a long, luxurious drink, but before she had tipped the glass away, he said, "So you want to watch me pull my pud, do you?"

It was the perfect spit take; wine was everywhere—over him, in the water, down the front of her, up her nose. She was sputtering, choking, laughing, and gasping for air. He quickly grabbed the goblet off her before the thrashing caused there to be broken glass in the water, chuckling at his own joke and the effect it had on her. Then, as she was trying desperately to recover, he took note of the wine running in rivulets down her throat and between her breasts.

"Here, let me get that." He crawled over to her and started to playfully lap at her chest. She was thinking that she still might drown, and was trying to shove him off, all the while laughing in between the coughs.

"Stop it, you maniac! David!" She braced her elbows on the sides of the tub and raised herself out in an effort to escape him, providing a lovely view of her all the way down just beyond her navel. She watched as his gaze travelled the length of her, saw reflected in his eyes his desire at seeing her aglow in the candlelight, glistening wet, her face flushed with wine and laughter.

"See, now you've gone and done it." He reached up and took her around her waist, then pulled her, none too gently, back into the tub, and pinned her under him. His mouth was on hers in a blistering display of passion. Her own hunger was immediately reignited and she met his tongue, thrust for thrust, before she shamelessly guided his head to her breast, urging his lips to redirect their delightful work.

There was no camera this time, no feigned manipulation, no imitation of arousal. David reminded her of a man starved as he all but consumed one mound of trembling flesh before moving on to the other.

She became aware of an ache building low in her body, the primal pull in her deepest place. Aware of the tremors his mouth and tongue caused wherever they touched. Aware of his hands as they kneaded her back, keeping her upper body just above the water. As one hand wandered lower, it cupped her buttocks before moving still lower to lift her thigh, and he braced one of his legs between hers. Then she became aware of this hand as it stroked her inner thigh, and progressed with mind numbing slowness higher and higher.

His fingertips grazed the fine hairs of her before tentatively, and with almost incomprehensible tenderness, finding their way between her secret lips, and he moaned aloud against her throat. Her head floated back against the rim of the tub as she submitted, willingly, to his touch. She felt his fingers slip in and around her, testing, teasing, and learning this most private of lessons. His touch was tender, yet confident; he needed no guide to find her most delicate spot, where a single touch found her pulsing with desire.

"Sweet, sweet Norah . . ." he whispered into her ear. She was slick with the want of him, and his fingers moved with ease around and over her swollen bud. She was already so close to cresting she could hardly comprehend anything but her own mounting excitement, until she became conscious of his beautifully engorged member as it moved rhythmically against her hip. She reached down wanting to take him in her hand, but he stopped her.

"You first," he breathed. Smiling, she relaxed against his shoulder, and enjoyed, uninhibited, the magnificent strokes of his skilled fingers as they became more concentrated, her sighs and light gasps giving him knowledge of what touch pleased her best. The glorious ache within her built, layer upon magnificent layer, until her breath left her in a visceral cry and her back arched, lifting her torso clear of the water.

The sight and sound of her climax was too much for his strained self-control, and before she got a chance to touch him, his passion burst against her, surprising them both in the severity of its attack. He clung to her as they both rode out this most luscious assault.

As their respective breakers ceased crashing and ebbed onto silent, breathless shores, he lifted his face as if to kiss her, and she was shamed to present him, not with a dreamy satisfied smile, but with tears streaming from her closed eyes.

"Baby, what's wrong?"

She gulped back a sob, and then looked at him smiling, shaking her head, unable to speak. She wrapped her arms around his neck and knew pure happiness as he drew her tightly to him. She kissed his face and gazed into

his eyes as he tenderly smoothed her damp hair from her forehead.
"Are you all right?" he asked softly.
"I'm fine. That was just a little . . . intense, is all."
"You're not kidding."
They became aware of the water having grown uncomfortably chilly. Norah pulled the plug and, while the tub drained, she turned warm water on through the hand-held showerhead. Kneeling, they slowly soaped, sponged and rinsed one another off, growing comfortable in their nudity. There was nothing sexual in this act—their appetites for each other sated for the moment—just a tender, loving task done with affection and respect. Moments later, while they dried themselves off, she became aware of him staring at her, and struggled against self-consciousness.
"What are you looking at?" she asked finally.
"Nothing, I mean . . . you surprised me, that's all."
"I did? How?" She had finished drying, and wrapped her towel around her.
"I don't know. I can't even think what I expected. You are an extraordinarily lovely and very exciting woman, Norah Rothe." He took her hand and kissed the palm of it, his eyes full of sensuality and promise of more to come. She felt herself shiver.
"Do you still feel like some dinner?"
"Mmm, I'm starving. What time is it?" With his towel around his waist, they went across to her room; she directly to the closet, and he to the dressing table where he had removed his watch while he was undressing.
"Norah, it's nearly nine."
Her head popped out of the closet. "You're kidding? Where's my baby?"
She remembered that the phone was in the bathroom, so went back across the hall to retrieve it in order to call Mona and find out what was up. Something in the hallway caught her attention, and she altered her route. Within a minute she was back in the room, her face a picture of animated alarm.
"Norah, what's wrong? Is Ella—"
"No, no. Ella's fine," she said quickly, touched by his concern.
"Then what?"
"Ella's in her crib."
"Pardon me?"
"Yep, sound asleep."
"How . . . how did she get there?"
"Um, Peg would have brought her. She knows Ella goes to bed between eight and eight thirty, so . . . and she wouldn't have left her unless she knew I was home . . ."
". . . while we were in there . . ."
". . . my aunt was . . . in there . . . with my baby . . ." She could tell that he wanted to laugh, but didn't know if he should.
"So do you think she heard . . . anything?" he asked, having a very

difficult time.

Her face went into her hands at the picture of her gentle, widowed aunt hearing their orgasmic cries coming through the bathroom walls.

"Oh, David."

****

"Is that what I think it is?"

Norah jumped and snapped the book shut.

"Maybe."

Warm hands slid around her neck then moved lower as strong fingers massaged her shoulders, relieving the tension caused by so much writing.

"Are you ever going to let me read that?"

"Maybe." She looked up into smiling eyes then burst out laughing. David stood in the solarium in one of her bathrobes. The collar was decidedly unmasculine, the sleeves rode halfway up his arms, and it barely closed around his waist, so the prospect of an indecency at the breakfast table was pretty much a certainty.

"Perhaps you'd like to keep a few things here, just in case?" she asked, and placed her hand over her mouth to stifle her giggles.

"Thank you. I wasn't sure it was appropriate to ask."

"But this you think is appropriate?"

"What's not appropriate?" Brett came around the corner with his coffee cup. He halted when he saw David. "Oh, my. What do we have we here?"

David walked uninhibited to the nearest chair and sat down.

Brett turned and headed back the way he came.

"What are you doing?" Norah asked. "Aren't you staying for breakfast?"

"I'm sorry, you can't expect me to face eggs with David Raurke's schmenky peeking out at me from my sister's robe. There's not enough therapy in the world."

Chapter 12

David sat at the table in his trailer with the master schedule spread out in front of him. Another week of shooting had come and gone, and David was elated with the results. The energy that had been injected into everything when Norah arrived was still burning strong. The crews were giving it their all, Jozef's work was surpassing even his own considerable expectations, and even David himself found his creative juices flowing at full force.

They had three weeks left of shooting in Whitecourt, with a one week extension to accommodate Clare's new scenes before moving to the New York locations, and they were well within their deadlines. He should be elated, but it was the uncertainty hanging at the end of those three weeks that worried him. Yes, Norah was scheduled to shoot ten days in New York, but then what?

David had had on-set affairs in the past and they had almost all followed the same path—lots of fun and heat at the beginning, followed by dwindling interest, until he was waiting, anxious for the shoot to finish and the relationship to dissipate naturally. The standard promises to keep in touch, a call next week, "I'll look you up when I'm in town" sort of stuff. There was no doubt in his mind that this was not one of those

He realized with a wry smile that he couldn't get through a day without seeing her, even if it were only on the lot during filming. He enjoyed the sweet agony of not touching her when she stood next to his chair chatting with Judy. Even as he tried to concentrate on the next shot, all he wanted to do was gather her in his arms and dip his hand inside her blouse.

He marveled at his desire for her. Since the evening in her tub, their physical relationship had evolved beautifully. They hadn't progressed beyond what they had shared that night, but the nature of their promise kept them—more or less—satiated until they decided to move forward again. As a result, the poor woman couldn't stand, sit, or lie still for more than a second without his hands on her. It had become a bit of a game with them, actually.

For added fun, he hadn't allowed her to touch his cock. He enjoyed her eager petting him through his pants, but whenever her fingers tried to find their way inside, he'd *tsk, tsk* and lift her anxious digits away while listening to her growls of exasperation. He loved teasing her and sustaining the anticipation for himself. Besides, it presented him with the focus to develop his skills for bringing her from orgasm to earth-shattering orgasm without allowing his own needs to interfere.

Lost in his thoughts of whispered words, her arms over her head and her soft slipperiness pressed against a tiled shower wall, it took several moments for David to recognize the rhythmic beat wasn't his blood pounding but some yahoo knocking on his trailer door.

"Who is it?" David asked.

"Jason."

Isn't this terrific? I'm sitting here with a hard-on and the AD wants to talk.

He adjusted himself and tried to look casual. "Come in."

"Hey. There's a problem, sort of. Dennis' wife has gone into labour. He's found a red-eye flight back to San Francisco so he'll have to leave around ten, eleven at the latest. We figured if we pushed through, we could wrap the arrest scene tonight then he won't have to come back until the middle of next week. What do you think?"

I think I planned to go to Norah's in an hour, and now I won't be able to. And, what kind of a big baby am I that I'm nearly prepared to kick up a stink about this?

He forced a smile. "Good idea," he said. "Let's get rolling."

"Thanks." Jason fired off the word into his radio.

David sighed, rubbed his forehead, and picked up his cell phone from the table.

"Hello."

"Hey, honey."

"Hey, yourself. How's it going?"

"Good. There's a bit of a hitch though. Dennis' wife has gone into labour—"

"Wow, that's a bit early. Is she okay? Is he heading home?"

"Yeah. There's a red-eye tonight, but it means us pushing through until about eleven so he can have a few days at home."

"Oh. Well, that's a shame. I mean, nice for him, of course."

"Yeah. So I guess I'll see you tomorrow, then."

"All right. You'll call me in the morning?"

"As soon as I wake up."

"Okay. Good night."

"Good night."

He hung up and thought about how much he missed her and how much more he'd be missing her come eleven o'clock. He thought about how he would go back to his hotel room, how long the night would be, and do what? Maybe he could phone Geoff about the changes and rewrites.

Except Geoff's in New York and, with a two hour time difference, it'll be the middle of the night by then. Damn it

He didn't really want to talk to Geoff, anyway. What he wanted to do was pick up the phone and tell Norah he was coming over after the last scene was shot, regardless. Maybe it would be after midnight by the time he got there, but he absolutely ached at the thought of going back to his room and trying to sleep without her. He shook his head, grinned, and considered how radically his life had been altered in a few short weeks. He had never imagined himself sulking like a teenager because he couldn't see his girlfriend on a Friday night.

He grabbed his clipboard and headed for the door, determined to get this bloody shot underway. He got about five paces from his trailer when he stopped short and stood frozen for about ten seconds. He cursed under his breath, turned around, reentered the trailer, picked up his cell phone from the table, and hit redial.

She picked up after two rings and, without even a hint of greeting, said, "Please tell me you're calling to say you're coming over later."

I should have known she'd say the perfect thing.

"It'll be very late, but I'd very much like to."

"I'll see you then."

"You're sure?"

He heard the smile in her voice. "David, I'll see you then."

"I'll see you then." He was overcome with relief. He bounded out of his trailer and bellowed across the compound, "All right, people, let's get this show on the road!"

****

He pulled up to the curb just after one in the morning. Dennis had made his flight, but David had extra shots to take care of, production decisions to make, and general dicking around before he'd been able to get away from the circus.

As his hand found the latch in the near total darkness, he looked up and saw her in the window of her office. Filming had kept her busy so she was, no doubt, taking advantage of the time to catch up on some of the paperwork for the café. She had changed into her bedclothes and was draped in a long, white, old-fashioned nightgown with a low V-neck trimmed in lace, which matched the trim on the cuffs. Metres of soft cotton fell around her as she sat in the new desk chair that he'd bought, her feet tucked under her as she concentrated on her work.

He stood, unobserved, watching her and marveling at the joy he felt simply being here. He couldn't believe he'd given a second thought to going to his hotel tonight.

She stood and took a step toward the other side of the room, but she must have caught the hem of her nightie on something because her gown stretched out behind her, and with a jerk, she went down hard on her hands and knees.

He winced and hurried through the gate, concerned that she'd hurt herself. He glanced back to the window and noticed she'd pushed herself up, but instead of worrying about her wounds or being angry, she had thrown back her head and laughed out loud.

He stopped and smiled as he realized, without fear or hesitation, that this was the girl for him.

****

He fought against consciousness, wanting to stay immersed in his dream. He felt movement beside him, a warm hand on his shoulder, and the dream was gone.

"David. David, are you all right?"

His eyes opened and he smiled at her.

Maybe not such a bad thing.

"Something woke me and I thought maybe it was Ella, but it was you. Were you having a bad dream?" she asked softly.

"No. A very nice one. In fact, you were in it," he murmured as he ran his fingers along her cheek.

"Really?" She sounded flattered. "What were we doing?"

He smiled drowsily and closed his eyes again, then he took her hand and moved it under the bedclothes. "Let's see, we were walking hand in hand in a field of—" He casually laid her hand on the front of his boxers. "—freakin' daisies."

She giggled. "Let me see if I can guess what happened next." She slid her hand up his belly, her fingers lightly grazing the tiny trail of hair that he knew she loved, before her hand snuck under the elastic of his shorts.

His eyes shot open as her hand enclosed him in a firm but tender grip.

"Did we, um, find a basket of puppies?"

A moan of pure pleasure escaped him as her hand began to move. He thought about his game, how he should remove her hand, but he couldn't see the point. "Not . . . exactly."

"Why don't you tell me what really happened then?" she whispered in his ear.

He shook his head, unable to speak.

"Why not?" She poked her bottom lip out. "I'm clearly not a prude."

"And to that, please permit me to say, 'yay.' " His head rolled back as she concentrated her fingertips in a particularly sensitive region.

"Then tell me."

He groaned. "No, men's dreams are dumb."

"Well, you seemed to enjoy it. Maybe I can improve upon it."

"Oh, God. Honey, you already have."

She stopped and lifted her hand.

He looked up. "Oh, you can't be serious."

She gave him a small smile and a half shrug.

To his credit, he wasted no time considering his options. "You, augh . . . we were walking somewhere." Her touch returned and he sighed.

"Where?"

"Umm. Uh, I dunno . . . trees."

"Like that place by the river we went to?"

"Yeah, yeah, I'll bet that was it. Sure." Even through his haze, he could tell that she was fighting to keep her laughter contained. She obviously loved her power over him as well as pleasuring him.

"Then what happened?"

"Um, it's dumb, like I said. You pushed me against something."

"What? A tree? A rock? A yeti?"

"Yeah, I guess. Then you ripped open my shirt, your shirt, and . . . ugh . . . opened my pants and . . . you know, kneeled down."

"Aha! The casting cushion." She nodded like an analyst.

His hands flew to his face. "There is no casting cushion! I'm sorry I ever brought up the frigging casting cushion."

"Then what happened?"

"Nothing, that's when I woke up. That's when I *always* wake up." He growled and opened his eyes enough to give her a frown.

"What a pity. Why don't we see if I can't take the sting out of that for you?" She dipped her tongue into his ear.

He suppressed a shiver and grabbed her face, pulling her into a passionate kiss. His hand began a slow descent over her nightgown to her breast, but she stopped him.

"Nuh-uh. This time is just for you." She pushed his hand onto his pillow. "Do me a favor, though?"

"It's tough to say no to a woman who has your balls in the palm of her hand."

"Literally *and* figuratively, just so we're clear."

"Whatever . . . what's the favor?"

"Lose the shorts. They're getting in my w—"

His boxers sailed across the room.

"Did you hear that?" she asked.

"Hear what?"

"That sonic boom that followed your underwear to the floor."

They held each other and laughed until they ached.

"Aw, don't make me laugh," he whined as his mood altered somewhat.

"Don't worry, honey, I'll get him back." She pushed his T-shirt to his shoulders and, keeping her eyes locked on his, she teased his nipples with her mouth, moving from one to the other while her hand returned to its intoxicating task.

He moaned at the multiple assault.

"Hey, do you remember that movie?" she asked.

His eyes flew open again. "You are the damned chattiest woman."

"Quiet . . . that movie where those two guys are sword fighting, and it's an amazing duel, but then they laugh and reveal that they've both been fighting with the wrong hand, so they switch their swords over, and the battle gets really intense . . . that one?"

"What? Yeah, I remember. For the love of . . . so?"

"Well, I don't know if you realized this or not, but I'm not right-handed." She released her hold on him and waved the hand that had been working its magic on him, her right hand.

"Aw, jeez." He couldn't help but laugh.

"I'm going to hop over there," she said, pointing to his other side. She rose onto her knees and, with deliberate slowness, hiked the skirt of her nightgown and lifted her leg over him. As she was straddling his hips, something terribly naughty seemed to occur to her.

What blood was left drained out of his face when he read the expression on her face. "Norah . . . baby, no. Remember our promise. I've been thinking of booking us a hotel room in Vancouver or something nice for . . . I mean, I don't care bu—Norah!"

She rested one hand on his chest, her touch so light it tickled his skin, and he shivered. She sighed as she lowered her hips.

"I don't have a condom. For the first time in my godforsaken life, I don't have a damn condom!"

"Relax, honey," she said. "I don't have any intention of spoiling the perfect evening that you want to plan for us. A promise is a promise." She crossed an *X* over her heart.

"Good, 'cause . . . wait a minute . . ."

She smiled broadly and settled on him—her unimaginably soft, unimaginably wet labia parting deliciously over the underside of his thick, hard shaft.

His back arched at the profound sensuality of the act. True to her word, he remained outside her body, but he couldn't imagine an embrace ever being more intimate.

"Whoops," she said, her voice was husky. "I slipped . . . sorry." She moved her hips and he could feel every fold and petal of her against him.

He saw that this was no longer just for him. Her face was the picture of desire, her lips parted slightly and her breath came in slow shallow pants.

She took one of his hands from her hip and brought it to her breast.

He didn't need any more urging than that. His fingers groped hungrily for her. He pulled the neckline of her gown to the side, freeing one wondrous mound before bending her over him so that he could take it in his mouth.

She gasped and quickened her gyrations, and he knew she was close.

He recognized his own building excitement and tried to push it back, not wanting to crest first, but before he could finish the thought, she stiffened and her long, soft strokes reduced to tiny, almost indistinguishable vibrations. Her head lolled back on her shoulders and a low, feral wail erupted from the centre of her. Her orgasm thrilled him beyond reason and his own came long before hers had subsided.

She collapsed on top of him, breathless and whimpering softly.

Feeling the relief and animal contentment flood him, he grasped her to him, pushing her hair from her face, and kissed her repeatedly.

They held each other, sighing intermittently, until finally, she lifted her head from his chest and smiled.

"Sorry. I slipped again . . . and again . . . and again."

Chapter 13

She jerked the door of his trailer open and stomped inside.

He had been standing by his printer and jumped, whipping his head around at the source of the commotion.

"So I'm going through the café, dealing with the breakfast crowd, right? Doing my thing. I walk past this table of guys, most of them I've known my whole life. And I kinda hear them mumbling as I go past, but whatever. Then Floyd, this idiot who's half deaf so he shouts all the time to compensate, pops off, 'I guess she must be gettin' some.' About me, right? And they start to snicker. Naturally, ha-ha, my dad is sitting behind him and he stands up and starts to say something appropriately macho, and they're all, 'Sorry, Vic, I didn't know you was there.' Well, I turned around and informed them, not so politely, I might add, that Vic wasn't their biggest problem." She was spent. She noticed he was looking at her with a concerned, yet somewhat amused expression on his face.

"So what did you do?"

"I did what any red-blooded Canadian woman would do. I ripped him a new one and then called his wife and told her what an asswipe she was married to."

He chuckled and pulled her into a hug. "I don't get it. You've told me how you grew up around all those boys. You must have heard talk like that before. It's, you know, it's what we do."

"Yeah, sure, I was always hearing stuff like . . ." She dropped her voice an octave and feigned an interesting drawl. " 'Sure, she looks pretty good now, but I bet she'd look even better with my cock in her mouth. Yuk, yuk, yuk.' "

David burst out laughing.

She clicked her tongue and turned away.

"Sorry, sweetie, but that's a good one. Not that it's something I'd say . . . ever." He cleared his throat.

She cut him a look that left no doubt—she was *not* amused.

"I am sorry, that wasn't very nice. What were you doing anyway?"

"What?"

"What were you doing that made them think that you were, you know . . . ?"

A light pink flush rushed over her cheeks. "Nothing. I dunno. I guess . . . maybe I was . . . singing." Her voice petered down to a barely audible mumble.

"Sorry? What? You were singing?"

"Yes. Maybe. Brett and some of the people at work . . . they've been teasing me. I seem to be . . . I don't know, singing . . . a lot."

"Interesting. Like what? Top forty? Show tunes?"

"No. Mostly this old Blue Rodeo song, 'Lost Together.' It's a . . . I like it."

He smiled and pulled her close again and sang softly in her ear, " 'Strange and beautiful are the stars tonight, that dance around your head. In your eyes I see the perfect world. I hope that doesn't sound too weird . . .' " He pulled back to look at her. "That one?"

"Yeah, that one."

Imagine that. He can sing, too. I wonder if he ever gets sick of being perfect?

"But why did you get so pissed? Though you're adorable when you're angry, it's not like you to let crap like that get to you."

She laid her head against his shoulder and relaxed in his embrace. "I don't know. I guess . . ." She started to laugh.

"What?" he asked.

"I guess it's because it's not true."

"How's that?"

"Well, if you're going to have people talking trash about you, shouldn't you at least be doing what they say you're doing? I mean we kinda are, but not . . . oh, never mind."

"Well, honey," he said, his arms open wide and a huge smile on his face. "If there's anything I can do to help, I'd be only too happy . . ." He backed her against the table, pulled at the waistband of her jeans, and tugged the hem of her shirt.

She laughed as she pushed away his hands and tried to dodge the kisses that landed on her face and neck.

He ran his hand up her bare back and plucked at the closure of her bra.

She squealed and twisted in his grasp, but that only seemed to encourage him.

He pushed her onto the top of the table, scattering paper cups and pens every which way.

They laughed together as he climbed on top of her and pinned her arms down. Then, as if a switch was flipped, their mood changed. The laughter died and was replaced with something else.

She watched as his gaze went from hers to her breasts, pushed up and nearly out of her shirt's neckline. He looked back to her eyes, and his expression was one of pure desire.

"Oh, Norah," he moaned and possessed her mouth in a kiss so fierce and passionate she could hardly contain her own fire.

She wrestled her hands free of his grip and pulled him closer, her legs reaching up to imprison his hips tightly to hers.

The same hand that had playfully pushed up her shirt before repeated its trip, this time in earnest. He slid his fingertips along her ribcage, and she shifted his weight to one side in order to allow him a clear path. He took full advantage. His hand closed over her breast with such tenderness that she wasn't sure it was there until she felt his fingers under the lacy fabric of her bra searing her nipple with their caress. She gasped, dug her heels into the back of his thighs, and moved against the hardness that made its presence known, even through their clothing.

Then, as quickly as it began, it subsided. As though all at once, their sanity had returned, she let her head fall back to let her mind clear, and he raised, ever so slightly, to take his weight off her.

"If you're going to stop this, you'd better go now," he whispered in a voice so husky that she barely recognized it.

She nodded and almost painfully rolled from under him, slid off the tabletop, and began to rearrange her clothes.

"Jesus, you're actually going to leave?" His eyes were wide with disbelief.

She looked at him, still leaning over the table for obvious reasons, and suppressed a smile. "My darling David, if and when we do this—and believe me, I'm a big fan of the idea—it can't be like this . . . on a table in your trailer. Not the first time, anyway. Maybe the eighth or ninth . . ." She wanted to lighten the mood. "Didn't I hear you say something once about Vancouver?"

He collapsed dramatically onto the table, dropping his head with a pitiful thud, then another, then another.

She winced.

"Right, right. Fair enough." His voice echoed against the tabletop. He forced himself up and slid into one of the chairs. Leaning forward with his head in his hands, he rubbed his face and then peered up at her. "Please understand. I have no intention of pressuring you. None. This whole waiting thing was my idea in the first place, after all. Damn it to hell."

He took a brief cleansing breath. "The thing is, I lost my virginity when I was fifteen, and since then, I've never waited more than a couple of days to get a woman into my bed . . . not bragging, just stating a fact. We're at three weeks here—happy anniversary, by the way. And again, no pressure, but maybe it's time we discussed whether or not we've reached the point that we were talking about when we first set down our boundaries. Maybe get an estimate, an approximate, even."

She stood stock-still and without meeting his eye whispered, "Soon."

"Soon? Sorry, baby, but how soon?"

She headed for the door. "Soon, okay?" She had her hand on the doorknob but his voice stopped her.

"Norah. Is there something . . . something you're afraid of?"

Her mind raced as she tried to think of the answer to his question. Finally, she whispered, "Yes."

****

She walked across the lot in a daze. Her mind was churning over everything as she tried desperately to sort it all out.

She'd answered his question honestly, but she couldn't say just what it was that she was afraid *of*. Every time she had considered taking their relationship to its next physical step, she had been gripped with a sense of panic that overrode her desire for him.

Perhaps it was the old, *what if it's a letdown after all this buildup?* She was pretty sure that was rubbish, though. She believed that it would be incredible, like everything else that had come before.

So . . . what?

She'd become some sort of sexual slave to him?

Hardly.

There was always the possibility that she was simply terrified of being left without him at some juncture, and having to settle for little or nothing for the rest of her lonely, bitter life. She was half joking, but only half. There was a good deal of truth in that statement. Even if he were to disappear today, she knew she would have a pretty terrible time of it. The cold hand that closed its icy fingers on her heart at the mere thought was clear confirmation of that.

The logical side of her brain tried to argue that at least she could put this dry spell behind her in a way that promised to be amazing.

Sure, Norah, that's why you want to make love with David, because you haven't been laid since Ella was conceived and your prospects are dim, at best. Get it while the gettin's good! It has nothing whatsoever to do with the fact that . . . that you're totally and completely in love with him.

She'd said it. Even if it was only to herself.

She hadn't dared to before now, knowing the sheer stupidity in having allowed this to happen. He'd be gone in three weeks. Maybe they'd reconnect when she was in New York after that, but maybe not. She'd known from the beginning that this was temporary, yet she'd let herself get involved to the point where thinking about what her life would be like once the film wrapped for good reduced her to tears.

What to do?

Would telling him that she couldn't go on, and ending it, save her any pain? She doubted it very much. Would giving in to what her heart, not to mention other areas, wanted more than anything, cause her more agony than she was currently bracing herself for? Again, highly unlikely.

It was very much what she'd said to herself at the beginning of this roller coaster ride: best to jump in with both feet, rather than live with the regret of having done nothing. So perhaps, in fact, she had better, as Mona would say, "Shit or get off the pot." And, as she had no desire whatsoever to get off this particular pot, well, maybe it was best to end the metaphor there.

She was so caught up in her own thoughts, she was unaware that Jason had been yelling at her from across the compound until the on-set dresser tapped her on the arm and pointed.

"Hey! They're viewing some of the edited stuff from scene fifty-seven in the playback trailer. They want your input."

"Um, which scene is fifty-seven?"

"The, you know, love scene."

"Ah, sure. Who's all there?" she asked, trying to sound as if she were only slightly curious.

"David, of course. Anita, she's the editor. Jozef, Nick, and Dennis. I think that's it."

"Oh, Dennis is back." She tried to quell her anxiety at seeing David so soon after their talk.

"With pictures of the new baby."

"Great! I'm on my way."

****

Most everyone was seated when she arrived, except Nick and Dennis who had propped themselves up against the back wall. She caught David's eye, and he raised his eyebrows in polite acknowledgement. She nodded and moved to stand beside Dennis.

"All right, Dad, let's have a look," she said with a smile.

Dennis whipped out a small photo album, stored for quick and easy access in the pocket of his hoodie, and beamed as Norah flipped through them, *oohing* and *awwing* in all the right places. She gave him a big hug and congratulations as Jozef, David, and Anita finished their quiet conversation and indicated that they were ready to begin.

Anita was a woman in her mid-to-late fifties, who had clearly spent too much time in darkened rooms. Her skin had a slightly ghoulish pallor, her long hair was pulled tightly back in a tortuous knot and kept out of her way at all times. She spoke about everything in very technical terms, as if she didn't have a lot of practice with other forms of conversation.

"Norah, you'll want to sit up here." David indicated the chair next to him, which was closer to the screen.

She was happier where she was, in the back with the cool kids, with a bit of distance between her and David, but she figured she shouldn't make a fuss. "Oh, okay."

Anita hit a button and the scene played out before them. It wasn't perfect yet, according to Anita's cryptic comments—something had yet to have the thingamabob running behind the doohickey. Nonetheless, it was really exciting. Postproduction had done some colour alteration so the images were duller than she remembered. It was impressive, though. Wayne and Clare's first interactions in the scene had just the right amount of tension. Anita had left the takes as long as possible, so it felt as if Wayne's movements were stalking around the apartment. The business with the coffee cup was bang on, and she smiled with satisfaction.

Man, I looked like hell.

Norah had unconsciously pulled the neck of her shirt up while watching, so her eyes peered over the top as a kind of nervous reaction to seeing her image up on screen. The sound had been added as well, so when Wayne got up and turned on the radio a familiar love song from the 80s crooned.

"It's too bad that we need to be period specific," David said. "There's this song by Blue Rodeo that would have worked perfectly."

Convinced he was making fun of her, Norah glared from the corner of her eye and bit her tongue to keep from firing off a sarcastic barb. She focused her attention back on the screen.

As Wayne knelt in front of Clare to comfort her, kissing away her tears, Norah's heart actually ached for them.

Brilliant.

Then their kiss grew in intensity, and the buttons of her shirt were undone.

Wow!

Nick softly wolf whistled behind her. All heads turned, and he shrugged.

On the screen, Clare allowed her plaid overshirt to fall down her arms, and Norah's eyes grew wide at the clear view of her nipples straining against her tank top.

Note to self—parents must never see this film.

Nick called out, "Hey, Rothe. You're kinda hot."

"Costello." David glared at Nick, the warning clear in his tone.

"What? She is."

"Shut up," whispered Dennis.

The scene sizzled, no question. Norah wasn't sure which was harder to watch—Wayne's hand on the outside of her shirt, openly stimulating her nipple with his fingers, or his other hand underneath her shirt, doing the same thing.

New note—parents, Brett, Ella, and certainly Aunt Peg must never see this film.

She had barely finished the thought when Clare's top was lifted, totally exposing her left breast for a second before Wayne's mouth covered it.

Norah's eyes slammed shut and her head withdrew completely inside her T-shirt.

New, new note to self—no one I know or ever hope to know can ever see this film.

David yanked on her shirt, forcing her back to the viewing.

She shifted in her seat and cleared her throat.
I can do this. I'm an adult.
The scene progressed, the number of cuts increased, and emotions heightened. The music took on a very subtle, almost spooky quality. As Clare committed her final act of betrayal against Wayne and he exploded in a rage, the raw pain on both their faces was exaggerated by rapid camera moves and disjointed splices, sometimes overlapping. It was a cinematic view into Wayne's demon-infested world. Simply done, but very effective. As the camera slowly faded to black, with Clare folded in agony on the floor and weeping, tears found their way down Norah's face as well.

Anita stopped the playback and rambled some gobbledygook about pacing and the other whatchamacallit. She offered an idea in her strange film-speak to overlay images of the murders as a way to further demonstrate Kosma's frame of mind. She hit a few more buttons in rapid succession and the playback rolled from the point of Clare responding to Wayne's kiss, which was the first catalyst for his imminent breakdown.

For a fraction of a second, the audience saw an image of a woman, a micro-clip from the first murder. It was so brief, Norah wasn't sure she saw anything at first. The next trigger point had a slightly longer clip, and so on, until the point that Clare unfastened his jeans. Then there was a rapid montage of killing, screaming, and death. Anita hit a button and waited.

There was silence as everyone digested the new edit.

"Well?" David asked of no one in particular.

Jozef was the first to speak. "Is powerful, ya. It tells story very clear."

"I dunno," said Nick, his head tilted to the side. "There's something . . . I dunno."

"Dennis?" David asked.

"It's very well done, Anita. Quite chilling, using the clips in a transparency state so that you can still see the action under it. To be honest, though, I think we've seen it, or something like it, too many times before. What do you think, Norah?"

She sat and weighed her words. "Many years ago, I read a play that was going to be produced in the city. Lovely show, even though there wasn't a part for me. There were a series of monologues within the script that had the actors stepping outside the play, if you will, and addressing the audience."

"Soliloquy," said Dennis.

"Pardon?"

"That's a soliloquy, not a monologue."

"A soliloquy is to yourself—"

"No, a monologue is—"

"Monologue is to the audience or another character. 'To be or not to be' is a soliloquy. 'Speak the speech, I pray you' is a monologue."

"Guys, please," David pleaded, rubbing his eyes.

"Anyway," Norah said. "There were these beautifully written *speeches* that went a long way to telling the inner stories of the characters. Now, I went to see it because I had friends who were in it, and was horrified when the first speech began and a screen came down. There was a slideshow of images correlating to the story the actor was telling. 'I ran into my ex-wife today', and you saw a photo of a pissy-faced woman in a car. It was awful."

"I don't understand," Anita said.

"I'm not being clear. What was so wrong was that the director didn't trust the actors with the imagery. He didn't trust them to be able to tell the story without the use of a technique, a crutch, a chintzy device. I'm not saying that this is any of those things, Anita. I agree with Dennis, it's very artfully done. But ultimately, I think David's a good enough actor and has done a more than credible job of pulling off Wayne's struggle without the . . . smoke and mirrors. For what it's worth, I thought the first edit was perfect."

"That's what *I* meant to say," Nick said.

Everyone chuckled.

"Right," David said. "Thank you, Anita. I think we'll go for the first one, but I really—"

"Ooh, how about—never mind, sorry." Norah clapped her hand over her mouth like a child who had spoken out of turn.

"No, go ahead," David said and nodded.

"It's—I got this picture in my head just now. Tell me to butt out, if you like, but in the courthouse, during the final summations as the defense attorney is giving the speech about Wayne's innocence, it might be cool to do something like that there, you know? The lawyer saying he didn't do it, meanwhile all these images are running through Wayne's head. It's not taking away from your performance, 'cause basically you're just sitting there thinking, right? It's this really cool juxtaposition."

"Isn't that an oxymoron?" Nick said.

"You're an oxymoron." Dennis snickered.

David smiled.

Anita smiled.

Jozef smiled.

They all looked from Norah to each other and back again.

"Is better." Jozef clapped his beefy paws together as if a gavel had lowered to declare it so.

"Okay." Anita packed her bags. "But you've gotta film it first. Make me a good long shot, and keep it simple. And make it wide. I can tighten it in the lab."

"No problem." Jozef grabbed a couple of her cases and helped her out to her car.

Everyone was quiet, mulling over what they'd seen.

Finally, Nick broke the silence. "So are you guys fighting, or what?"

"Pardon?" David asked, his face showing clear shock.

Norah stiffened.

"You know, a lovers' quarrel. It's all *cut the air with a knife* stuff in here."

"You're kidding me, right? You know?"

Norah covered her eyes and shook her head.

"Fuck, man, everybody knows. Did you think you were keeping it secret? Remind me to never tell you one of mine. You guys suck."

"I hope it's nothing serious. You guys are great together."

Dennis, ever the romantic.

"We're not—we're not fighting. We're . . . discussing something."

"Ah, sex."

Dennis, ever the letch.

Nick laughed. "Really?"

Norah stood up and turned to confront them. "No, not really! In fact, we were talking about how we're going to go to Vancouver for the long weekend where we'll . . . have . . . lots . . . lots and lots of amazing sex. So there, you pair of buttinskies." She nodded her head, tacitly putting an end to the conversation, before storming out of the trailer and heading for her own. She left three astonished faces in her wake.

As she made her way across the lot, she was aware of her legs shaking so badly that she had difficulty climbing the steps to get in her door. Once she'd slammed it behind her, she paced and replayed all that had been said. In less than a minute, a very expected knock came—one single tap, and he was inside and closing the door behind him, a look of shock and wonder on his face.

"Goddamn it, David. After all the trouble we went to—"

"I know, baby. Believe me, I know."

"Nobody ever said anything—"

"To me, either. I mean, Jozef told me that Kat thought there was something going on, but he didn't seem to believe it. It doesn't matter, Norah. I wanted to keep it quiet at the beginning because I didn't know where it was heading, and it might have been embarrassing for you."

"More so for you."

David frowned. "What do you mean?"

"Nothing."

Where did that come from?

"Norah?" He tried to take her hand, but she pulled away and sat down on the sofa.

"It's nothing, David." She felt his concerned eyes on her, and she looked up. "I'm sorry. I'm sorry I've made such a fuss about . . . everything. I can't explain it."

"I'd like you to try."

"Why?"

"Because you seem to be struggling with something, and I'm sure it has to do with me, so I want to be—it's like you're leaving me out."

"I don't want you to feel like that," she said.

"Then tell me." He waited.

Her voice sounded so small when she answered. Even to her own ears.

"It's just that I want you so badly I'm afraid of what it'll do to me after." She wanted to add "when you're gone," but she couldn't force the full admission of her fears and insecurities out of her mouth. "It sounds pretty lame when I say it out loud," she said with a half smile.

He walked to the sofa and sat next to her, pulling her onto his lap. "No one can say what'll happen, you know that. But you've never struck me at the sort of woman who doesn't take a chance because you're afraid. You're one of the ballsiest broads I know."

She laughed and he held her closer.

"Can you tell me what it really is?"

She hated hurting him, but her sense of self-preservation was stronger. "David, I'm just incredibly nervous. It's been such a long time for me and . . . that's all. It's stupid, really."

"Okay, sweetie."

He knows I'm lying.

"I won't push. You'll be ready when you're ready. Just let me know." His disappointment was palpable.

"What do you . . . read-ready for what?"

"Vancouver . . . or wherever."

"David, I meant what I said in playback. We're going to Vancouver this weekend. Don't you know that?"

"Oh, it would be so mean to be joking right now."

"I'm not joking. Book your room."

"You're serious. You're not playing with me?"

"Not yet." She smiled her flirtiest smile. "By the way, have you had your tests? I remember you mentioning condoms before, but I could certainly live without them if you're, you know—"

"I'm all clear, and I've never gone without them but, boy, I'd sure love to, with you."

"Good, then."

"Oh, baby," he whispered against her mouth, then he kissed her long and deep.

She relaxed into his arms and kissed him back until she thought her heart would burst.

"It's going to be so great." He leaned in to kiss her again, but a firm knock broke the mood.

Out of habit, she started to get up, but he held her in place and looked at her pointedly.

"Come in," she called out.

Jason opened the door and didn't bat an eye at the two of them cuddled up together. "Excuse me, Norah. David, the crew will be back from lunch in five, and Norah, wardrobe is looking for you."

"Be right there," David replied.

"Me, too."

"Roger that." Jason backed down the steps and closed the door behind him.

Norah and David looked at each other and, considering the ridiculousness of the situation, simply shook their heads.

"Well, I should get to wardrobe."

"And I better call my travel agent."

She smiled, blushing slightly. "I guess we don't have to hide anymore, so that's good. I mean, not that we'll be making out on set or anything."

"That might be fun. I'm still blown away that no one ever said anything until today."

"I guess that means it hasn't gone beyond here, which is pretty amazing when you think of it."

"I'd like to think they respect our privacy, but still . . ."

Arm in arm, they left her trailer.

****

Nigel Coombs put down the handset of his phone, his face a study of practiced calm.

"Mr. Coombs?" Natalie, his assistant of seven years and one of the few people who would be comfortable enough to pry, addressed him with formal concern.

He smiled icily in her direction. "It would seem that our David Raurke has got himself a girlfriend."

Chapter 14

David awoke with that irritating sense of the unfamiliar—unfamiliar bed, unfamiliar sounds, unfamiliar fragrances—and then the anxious feeling as someone moved beside him.

A warm, soft body spooned against his back, while a silken arm burrowed under his and a small, delicate hand caressed his chest. A smile grew on his face as the unfamiliar became very familiar and a welcome nibble moved across the back of his neck.

"Hey!" The shout just behind his ear jarred him fully awake.

The arm was gone, the body was gone, and the nibbling was certainly gone as the woman clambered over him, bounced across the bed, and off the other side.

She ran for the window and threw open the draperies, fully blinding him with the brightness.

"We're here, we're here, we're here!" She squealed with glee, clapped her hands, hopped up and down like a small child on Christmas morning, and flung open the french doors.

He laughed softly, delighted with her excitement, and wondered if he should join her on the balcony or see if he couldn't lure her back into bed.

We're here . . . no need to rush.

Her nice bottom, covered only by a nightshirt, pointed temptingly in his direction. He stifled yet another impulse and embraced her from behind, leaning over her back to share her view.

English Bay. He'd heard her speak of it so often and had seen numerous photos of it pinned to the corkboard in her office and stuck to the refrigerator with magnets.

He felt her inhale the fresh ocean air and then noticed something warm trailing along his arm. Looking down, he saw a drop of moisture followed closely by another.

He moved to face her, unwilling to break the spell this place had on her by pulling her focus from it. He stroked her wet cheek with the back of his knuckles, and she looked up, her expression a mixture of joy and gratitude.

She stood on her tiptoes, wrapped both her arms around his neck, and molded her body to him. "Thank you so much," she whispered, her lips tickling his ear. "I can't tell you how much it means to be here with you."

He drew back to gaze at her again, touched by the appreciation he read there. He was touched by everything about her. He knew, without any doubt, that he was in love with this woman. The thought felt so foreign that he couldn't imagine actually saying it to her, despite the fact that, in the very next breath, he wanted to scream it from the rooftops. He believed he had known from the first day that everything was about to do a one-eighty on him, and it had scared the hell out of him.

He had changed. That was not in question. He'd become steadier, less prone to agitation and impatience. Directing had become easier, not casual or indifferent in any way. In fact, it seemed the cast and crew had become more inclined to go out of their way for him, and the mood of the set was one of pride, dedication, and fun. He knew that a lot of that had to do with Norah.

But the most profound differences were thoughts of the future—*his* future with this woman. It was no longer simply about a day or weekend opportunity to be with her, but what was possible for the next month, the next year, and—in those rare, unguarded moments—for the rest of his life. That frightened him as well. He knew it was ridiculous. He wasn't a kid anymore, and avoiding commitment, though formerly a full-time job, had long since lost its charm.

Along came Norah—a short, curvy, spitfire with a smart mouth and an even smarter mind. She didn't take his crap, made him laugh till he ached, and kissed him till he ached more. He didn't know what kind of demons he'd have to battle to make sure his lily-livered ass got kicked through this particular door, but battle them he would. He knew she was more than worth it. If he screwed it up . . . well, he refused to think about it.

These next few days would be days of play. No movie, no Whitecourt, no Ella, bless her. No distractions, no demands, nothing but a mini-holiday full of sunshine, walks on the beaches, excellent food, and best of all, the fulfillment of a very special promise.

From the moment she told him that this would be the weekend that they would consummate their relationship, he had happily laboured to put all the pieces into place. Most of the details had been worked out during the long nights when they had been apart and he'd lain awake in his hotel room fantasizing.

As they stood on the balcony with English Bay spread out before them, happiness shone in her eyes and he wondered how he'd managed to put thirty-eight years behind him without her.

"So what do you want to show me first?" he asked.

She raised an eyebrow. "Well, jeez, you've seen almost everything. Oh! You mean in Vancouver?"

He chuckled.

"Well, that depends. What are our . . . plans?" she inquired with a touch of shyness.

"I thought it might be nice if we picked up some things for a romantic dinner and fixed it here," he said casually, and fought to keep a straight face.

"Oh, well then, Granville Island Market it is."

****

The market wasn't on an island so much as a jetty under the Granville Street Bridge. Formerly a boat port and train depot, which busily moved goods from sea to shore and beyond, the few acres of land was dedicated to a hotel, a number of artist workshops and schools, a couple of world class restaurants, an excellent marina, and one of the best markets for fresh foods of every kind, arts and crafts, fine jewelry, and virtually anything else your heart desired. It was constant hive of activity as vendors went about their business, tourists collected gifts and goodies to take back home, while steadfast locals—refusing to let the summer crowds daunt them—tracked down the perfect ingredient for the perfect meal.

Norah and David were on the hunt for fresh pasta.

On their third lap of the market, she pursed her lips in frustration. "Damn it, I could have sworn it was this way."

He spotted a stall with knots of colourful noodles twisted together behind a cabinet of glass.

"No, the better one is . . . somewhere else."

"Don't worry about it, hon. We'll find it."

"I'm sorry. I don't mean to get so crabby. It's just . . . this was my home, and I miss it so much. I want to show you the best possible time, not to be bumping you into walls like a couple of rats in a maze."

"Cheese."

"Sorry?"

"Didn't you say we needed cheese?" He pointed to another stall, its display cases sprawling with every possible variety of cheese.

"Perfect. These guys make a smoked apple Gorgonzola that'll knock your socks off."

"Hey." He pulled her to him. "You knock my socks off. Don't worry about the rest of it because I *am* having the best possible time."

She gazed up at him with relief and gratitude. "Thank you. I think I might be a little bit nervous."

He smiled. "So am I." He knew the little white lie had been the best thing for her. Fact was, he wasn't the least bit nervous. Maybe he should be, all things considered, and he hoped it wouldn't set in later.

Wouldn't that be the kicker—finally get there, only to get a case of the flops.

He shuddered.

They picked up the Gorgonzola and a couple of other cheeses that they'd sampled, including a nice wedge of Asiago, before they finally found the elusive pasta stall and decided on a bag of gorgeous ravioli stuffed with chicken, black olives, and pine nuts. They chose some plump tomatoes, fresh garlic, onions, peppers, and a few other things to make their sauce, as well as a nice variety of fruit.

He didn't want to tip his hand about having done any preparation, so he stopped at the wine boutique situated in one corner of the market and selected a few nice bottles.

"You know, you don't have to get me drunk," she murmured as she wrapped her arms around his waist.

He chuckled and winked at her. "Maybe it's for me."

She laughed and stepped across the hall to the tea shop.

While he paid for the wine, he sensed a small fuss stirring in the dining area to his right. At first, he thought it was just the usual—a few people maybe thought they recognized him. He carried on with his business, thanked the clerk, and crossed the corridor to join Norah, who was filling her shopping bag with a few dainty bags of dubious-looking leaves. He wrapped his arm around her, guided her away from the commotion building behind them, and cast a glance over his shoulder.

It's happening again.

His jaw tightened.

During the last ten years, every time he'd appeared in public with a woman, he had been faced with disdain. How dare he find happiness, how dare he share his life with someone, how dare he not be alone? It frustrated the hell out of him. He had buddies, film actors, who were married or in long-term relationships, and while there might have been an initial furor, it quickly died down and they were left alone. Why wasn't he allowed?

Once, when a woman had left him over it, he'd asked his sister what it was about him. The lady hadn't been anyone he'd imagined anything long term with, but a nice, agreeable person who had been publicly raked over the coals one too many times and had gone screaming in the other direction.

"You belong to everyone," Beth had answered sagely.

"I don't know what that means."

"You're very accessible. People—more accurately *women*—think they know you. In their minds, given the opportunity, you would be with them. They're convinced of it. You've no business being with whateverhernameis when you're meant to be with them."

"So they'd rather I was alone for the rest of my life?" He had half laughed, feeling defeated.

"I'm afraid that may very well be the truth of it. Now, that doesn't mean to say that you need to buy into it. It's your life, David, and the sooner you show them who's boss and live the way you want, the sooner they'll start to respect that and back off."

"If not?"

"If not, you've had a good run. Go into directing where you're less in the public eye. It's what you want to do ultimately anyway. The main thing is, don't let them tell you what to do."

"How about the woman?"

"What woman?"

"What woman? *Any* woman. Who would submit to that kind of constant public scrutiny and abuse?"

She had smiled. "David, have faith. She's out there and she's going to love you enough to walk through fire."

He cast a glance at Norah as he walked her out of the main market, and wondered if she was the firewalker his sister had predicted for him. She had courage—no question—but there had been times, brief flashes, where he had sensed insecurity. It was only natural, no one was completely confident all the time, but it worried him. He had a sneaking suspicion that it wouldn't be long before she was tested, and the knot in his gut told him she might not stand up to it as well as he needed her to.

Don't worry about that now. Not this weekend. Not today. Time enough for that later.

She steered them into the loft space across the parking lot, and they picked up a couple of cool kitchen gadgets. In another artisan boutique, they found a beautiful, hand-thrown bowl for Peg. He suggested that it might not travel well, and they decided on a pretty woven shawl instead.

In the last shop they visited, David found a lovely necklace—a fine chain of complex links and a tiny pendant, made from a plate of brushed, imported silver with a profile of a curling shell pressed into it. He hoped it would remind Norah of their time here as he fastened it behind her neck. It cost nothing, but the look in her eyes as she touched where it lay at the base of her throat told him all he needed to know. It was priceless.

****

When he suggested a walk later that afternoon, she practically dragged him by the hand out of the lobby, past the bemused concierge, and into the park at the edge of the bay. She was sure he'd seen bigger beaches, more exotic, more glamorous, but she was certain that there was not a place on Earth that met the simple beloved-ness of English Bay.

They watched the children play, building castles and splashing in the waterways, and Norah felt a pang as she imagined what fun Ella would have here.

"We'll bring her next time," David said.

She wrapped her arms around his waist, astonished at his sensitivity, and relaxed into his hug.

The sea wall had been Norah's favourite place when she lived here. She had spent hours traversing this path, and she couldn't be happier than walking, nuzzled up against this wonderful man. Every so often she caught the eye of a person passing them and was sure they recognized David, though he gave no sign of even noticing. She was pleased at how comfortable he was out in the open with her. They were taking a chance, despite the ball caps and sunglasses, but he had been right before—she needed to learn to deal with it. They walked for nearly an hour, stopping here and there to scramble along some rocks, investigate a particularly interesting plant, or pet a dog that someone was walking.

She took him beyond Second Beach, past the busy swimming pool, and along another stretch of wall. They continued along the path with benches placed every twenty paces or so, each with a dedication plaque on the backrest. She led him to her favourite bench—the one she sought out whenever she was here. It told the brief story of a beloved husband, father, and grandfather, and the years that he'd lived. It was nestled against some tall trees, one with a heavy overhanging bough providing coziness and protection against the wind.

They sat and talked and laughed, enjoying long moments of comfortable silence, with her head resting against his shoulder and his lips finding her brow or temple or cheek or mouth. She couldn't imagine being happier.

"Well, I'm going to leave you to it for a while."

"Oh! I can go, too. Are you cold?" She felt a slight chill with his arm gone from around her shoulders.

"No, no, I'm fine. I have a few things that I need to take care of back at the suite, though, so . . ." He took her hands in both of his. "I'd like you to stay here and relax for, oh . . . another half hour or so, then make your way back to English Bay, take a moment, and then have a little look in your bag."

She automatically reached for her purse, but he stopped her with a grin.

"Not yet. Patience," he chided. "So, half an hour here, then to the beach before you open that okay?"

"Okay," she answered reluctantly.

"Promise?"

"I promise."

"Right then." He leaned close and kissed her deeply.

She held him around his neck, cherished the feel of his lips, and smiled as he made his way back along the sea wall. She was thrilled by the sight of his strong back and his familiar pace as he moved along the walk. She knew she could recognize that stride anywhere now, and she took comfort in that kind of intimacy.

Once he disappeared around a bank of trees, she returned her attention to the ocean. She remembered the many hours spent here, telling the ocean her troubles, and how insignificant it made them feel in comparison. Today she had no troubles to tell. Even her nervousness dissipated with the receding waves.

She touched the pendant he gave her and felt a flush of warmth rush through her. She tried to imagine what he was doing at the apartment and shivered with anticipation. He'd gone to a lot more trouble to arrange this weekend than she had realized.

She checked her watch.

Fifteen minutes?

Her fingers worried the clasp on her purse, and she chastised herself for even thinking about cheating. In her head she heard him calling her a naughty girl and she grinned.

She flirted with some of her dimming memories for something that might come in handy over the next few hours, but dismissed the effort. Every second of intimacy that she'd shared with David so far had come naturally, without contemplation or plan. So would this.

Finally, her time was up, give or take a minute. She resisted the urge to jog to English Bay but only because she didn't want to tire herself out too early.

Save your strength.

She grinned at her own joke and found herself unwilling to meet the eye of any of the passersby, convinced they'd read her thoughts and be shocked.

She came around the bend toward the bay and spotted the perfect place to sit on the beach. She settled in, flung open her bag and found her surprise. There, plain as day, was an envelope of beautiful handmade paper the colour of lilac.

How he'd managed to get it in there, she could only guess. She had gone through her purse a dozen times at the market. And when they'd gone for sushi, she remembered getting her cell phone to check her messages. It had to have been when they had unpacked the groceries. She'd left it on the counter and gone to use the washroom before they left for the beach. When she'd come out, he was holding it for her at the door.

Sneaky bugger.

She carefully removed the envelope. Her name was scrawled across the front in his bold hand and she hugged it close for a moment, smiling like a loon. She savoured the feeling of anticipation before sliding her finger under the seal and popping it open. Withdrawing the paper, she tenderly unfolded the sheets. Her heart raced as she read.

> My darling Norah,
> I understand why you get that faraway look in your beautiful eyes when you speak of this amazing city. It's a special place, made even more special by all that it means to you. Thank you for sharing it with me.
> Tonight I want to share everything I am with you. I have looked forward to this evening more than you could possibly know, and I can hardly wait until you are in my arms and we are together completely.
> You have brought peace, contentment, and indescribable joy to my complicated life, and I want to show you just how happy you've

made me.
Now, my sweetheart, if you would, please close your eyes for a moment and think about the hours ahead and know that I am doing the same—we share the anticipation and the promise of a perfect night—then take one last look, and say good night to the sea.
I await you with all my heart,
David

She read and reread the letter as the tears flowed freely, and her heart overflowed with emotion. She tucked it back into its envelope, then did as she was bid and closed her eyes and dreamed—of him, his arms, his hands, his mouth, his strong, firm body.

She opened her eyes and was in the process of sharing a secret smile with the waves, when something caught her attention—a sailboat anchored in the bay, close enough that she saw the small dog standing on the bow as a couple of people unfurled its sail. There was something odd about the canvas. It wasn't the proper shape, and it didn't display the typical design or ID numbers, but words.

"Oh my God!" She clapped both her hands over her mouth.

There, in black and white . . .

Norah, my love—
Come. Be mine.

She turned, dumbstruck, toward the condo.

As though she'd summoned him, there he was, leaning on the balcony railing and looking unbelievably powerful and sexy. He waved and blew her a kiss then, with one last smile thrown over his shoulder, he disappeared inside.

She squealed and turned back to the sailboat, fumbling frantically in her purse, this time for her camera.

Photographic proof or it didn't happen!

She was checking the playback screen for clarity when she heard a woman to her left ask, "Are you Norah?"

Startled at first, Norah realized she was referring to the sail. "Yes, I am." She took another shot for good measure.

"Wow, you've got yourself some kind of fella there."

"Honey, you have no idea," she said and giggled, before whirling around and dashing to the front door.

Save my strength, be damned.

Chapter 15

The concierge greeted her at the door and opened it for her.
 She said a polite hello as she rushed past him for the elevators.
 "Miss?"
 She turned, and he held out another familiar lilac envelope. This one was smaller, still with her name on the front. She took it, smiled her thanks, and opened it before she'd even pressed the call button. Inside, she found the card for unlocking the door to the suite and a small note.

> Come upstairs to where I wait
> And use this key to cross the gate.

 She hopped up and down, giggling like a schoolgirl. She blushed as she glanced toward the doorman, who was trying his best to keep a straight face.
 He's seen it all, I'm sure.
 After what felt like nine hundred hours, the elevator doors opened, she leapt inside, and pounded on the button with relish.
 On the sixth floor, she flew out of the lift and to the door, fiddling with the pass card. Naturally, she dropped it twice and swore under her breath, finally managing to swipe it properly. She turned the knob and swung the door open to the sound of soft blues playing. Straight ahead of her on the hall table stood a bouquet of flowers. Hundreds of glorious blooms in all the colours of the rainbow stood nearly her height above the tabletop. The perfume was intoxicating, and she inhaled deeply as she touched the blossoms. She caught sight of another envelope propped against the bottom of the vase. She glanced around for him, but he was clearly drawing this out.
 Fair enough.
 She opened the third envelope.

> I long to hold you next to me,

To kiss your lips, but first,
Go in the fridge where you will find
A drink to quench your thirst.

"Oh, this is too much." She laughed.

She skipped into the kitchen, and took a thorough look around. She couldn't see anything out of place, but she could, however, smell something.

You don't live with a chef without developing a nose for it. Is that balsamic? Certainly garlic, onion, and something sweeter . . . was that?

She opened the door to the fridge and peered inside. There, on a silver tray, a tall fluted glass of white wine and a small delicate bowl of huge strawberries dipped generously in . . .

"Chocolate! Ooh, yummy." She placed the tray carefully on the counter and noticed another envelope tucked between the glass and the bowl. She smiled, enjoying the game, especially since there were treats involved. She took a generous sip and an equally generous bite of strawberry and, keeping sticky fingers away, drew out the note.

Our love nest might be in the sky
But I will take you higher.
Return to the hall where you will spy
The flames to light your fire.

"Hmm. This is getting good."

Clutching her drink and snack, she backtracked to the foyer. A gasp caught in her throat. Where there had been only a dark corridor before, a trail of tea-light candles staggered down both sides of the wall and led an enticing path to the master bedroom.

"Wow."

Her mind raced.

How did he possibly . . .

She hadn't heard a thing. She bit her bottom lip and walked slowly past each light, careful not to disturb the flames.

When she reached the bedroom door, she stopped and knocked softly. There was no reply so she tried again.

Still nothing.

She turned the handle and stepped inside. The same music from the foyer piped in here. There was a cloth of some sort on the bed, a splash of colour, and another envelope. She walked to the bed and recognized the shape of one perfect, long-stemmed, red rose. It lay on top of a magnificent, cashmere bathrobe, in the softest shade of gray. Upon closer inspection, she noted a pair of small fuzzy ballet-style slippers standing ready on the floor. She sat down on the bed, placed the wine and fruit on the bedside table, and read the next note.

Come on in, the water's fine.
We've known love in this setting.
Bring your berries, bring your wine,
And get a thorough wetting.

She threw back her head and laughed. She gathered her robe, slippers, rose, and—as instructed—her wine and strawberries, and padded into the bathroom.

"Oh, David." She sighed.

Another two dozen tea lights sparkled everywhere, mostly around the tub, which was near to overflowing with bubbles and toasty warm water, if the steam on the mirrors was anything to go by. More vases of flowers had been placed next to the bath, along with small bowls of them on the shelves, and blossoms trailing along the top of the half-wall.

She set the wine and berries on the ledge next to the tub, undressed quickly, tossed her clothing into a pile by the door and sank cheerfully into the water.

He must have been planning for days, weeks even.

She was flattered beyond belief. How he managed the sailboat, she couldn't even guess. The envelope left with the concierge would have been easy enough, but when did he have the flowers delivered? He hadn't had that much time between getting back to the condo and her arrival. The logistics boggled her mind.

She thought about washing her hair, but decided against it. She did give herself a good scrub and soaked a bit more. She looked around the bathroom but didn't see another note, and she wondered if he was in the bedroom waiting for her. She pulled the plug, dried completely, then moisturized before applying a little bit of makeup and fixing her hair. One final look in the mirror, and she tiptoed back into the bedroom.

He wasn't there, but there had been changes made. The lights were dim, the curtains drawn, the bed invitingly turned down. On the bed, replacing the robe was another note and a gown of some sort. It was long, nearly sheer silk, hand-painted in a dozen or more jewel tones and watered pastels. The sleeves were loose and, as she stepped into the skirt, she noticed that it was cut on the bias and was full and flowing, yet somehow, the top came up spare. It plunged to her waist, and was held together with a couple of hooks and a prayer.

"Naughty boy."

She approached the full-length mirror next to the wardrobe and gasped at what she saw there.

I'm . . . beautiful.

The garment brought out the colour of her eyes and set them off as if they were lit from within. The skirt billowed out behind her as she moved and gave the illusion of floating. Her heart ached as she thought of him composing poetry and shopping for dressing gowns when he'd been so

busy with filming.
Well, I reckon I better make it worth his while, huh?
She threw her cashmere bathrobe onto a chair then picked up what she imagined must be the last note.

> Come to me, sweet Norah, by flames do I wait.
> My own passions burn for your kiss.
> Join me in body and spirit and love,
> This night we will know only bliss.
> Allow me to take you where only we two
> Exist as we fuse into one.
> I'm aching to move in you till I am spent
> While your fire outshines the sun.

"Is it hot in here, or what?" she whispered.

She read the note a couple more times and decided the flames he was waiting by had to be one of the fireplaces.

She glided down the hall in search of the first fireplace and noted the tea lights had been removed.

Good idea. This gown, those candles . . . me. Norah flambé isn't the kind of hot entrance I want to make!

She entered the dining room but it was empty, with no sign of anything out of the ordinary. She turned back to the hall and walked toward the living room.

As she approached the foyer, which was all but dark, she caught a glimpse of movement beyond. Firelight danced on the walls and a low Spanish guitar filled the air. Her vision was momentarily obscured by the hall table full of flowers, but at long last, she saw him.

David sat on the floor in front of the fireplace, one elbow leaning on the sofa seat, the other draped over his knee. He wore dark chocolate brown silk pajama bottoms and a short coffee and cream coloured robe, left untied and falling open.

He is achingly gorgeous.

She stood in the entryway staring at him—this magnificent man who wanted her, wanted her enough to do all this.

They locked eyes and shared a smile.

****

"My God, Norah." His voice cracked.

I've never seen anything . . . she's beautiful.

"Thanks for the threads."

He smiled, recognizing her defense mechanism kicking in, and crossed to her. Using only his fingertips, he traced a path along her thigh, her hip, and rested on her waist. The fineness of the silken fabric made it feel as though he touched her through smoke. He leaned toward her until he was close enough to touch her lips with his. He couldn't stifle the moan of desire as she laid her cool hand against his bare chest, nor could he stop the lingering kiss that held him in place like a magnet. He curled his toes into the carpet as if that somehow grounded him, yet had to force himself to part from her. He had every intention of drawing this evening out as long as possible.

"Hungry?" he asked.

"Starving."

The *double entendre* made him glower at her through narrowed eyes. "Have a seat," he commanded, and gave her bottom a smart smack as he made his way past her to the kitchen.

He returned with a huge tray filled with wonderfully aromatic things. He placed it close to the hearth then hurried back to the kitchen for a few more items.

On the tray was their hard-won pasta and sauce, grilled peppers, a small wooden plank covered with lox and capers, a bowl of green olives stuffed with sun-dried tomatoes, another plate with beef carpaccio, and an assortment of crackers. He returned with an ice bucket of chilling champagne and two flutes, and in his other hand, a smaller tray with pieces of fresh strawberries, banana, apple, kiwi, and mango surrounding a small ceramic bowl on a stand with a burner beneath it.

"Chocolate fondue," she said. "Oh, David, you've made chocolate fondue."

"First things first, honey." He shook open their napkins and poured glasses of champagne. He struggled with what he wanted to say to her, but he decided that simplest was best. "Thank you for being here with me." He clinked his glass against hers, but she stopped him with a hand on his wrist before he could take a sip.

She raised her glass and toasted him. "There's nowhere on earth I'd rather be than with you here tonight. You've brought magic into my life, David Raurke. You've reawakened dreams that I'd put to bed years ago, and have made all things possible. You're one of the best things that's ever happened to me. Thank you for bringing me to this place."

He couldn't look away from her as the declaration he wanted most to say caught in his throat. Instead, he clinked his glass against hers.

They ate dinner with their fingers, feeding each other from time to time.

Afterward, he moved the dinner tray to the kitchen then returned and gave the chocolate she had been drooling over a stir.

"I can't believe you went to all this trouble."

He tried, but failed to suppress a grin. "Well, I figured the fondue fit in with the theme of the evening."

"I know I'm going to regret this, but what theme is that, David?"

"I'm glad you asked. Tonight is all about introducing something firm . . ." He impaled a strawberry. ". . . to something warm and wet." He dipped up and down into the bowl of liquid chocolate, all while leering at her.

Her fork hit the tray with a clatter as her face fell into her hands.

He laughed uproariously.

I love it—she's thirty-four years old, and I can make her blush like a virgin.

He'd gone through another strawberry and half a piece of mango before she recovered enough to put her hands down.

"You're basically a bastard."

"Very likely."

He watched her slowly run her fork through a slice of kiwi, which broke apart as she tried to dip it.

"I swear, if I get chocolate on this gown, I'm going to kill myself." She chased the wayward fruit around the inside of the bowl.

"Here, let me." He scooped it out with a combination of fork and fingers, and then carefully passed it between her waiting lips.

She nibbled the kiwi then suggestively licked the chocolate from his fingers.

In his mind, his fingers were no longer his fingers and, when she smiled wickedly, he knew he'd given his thoughts away.

He cleared his throat and attempted to clear his brain as well. He had one last, small gesture coming up, and he was getting unexpectedly anxious.

She had put down her fork and seemed to be concentrating on her glass of champagne. Taking her lead, he removed the tray onto the hearth and slid next to her. He sat on his heels, his hands on his thighs, looking at her expectantly.

"What?" she asked.

"Wait just a moment . . ." He cocked his head to the side.

A long space of dead air followed the last song, and Norah looked from the stereo back to him.

"What?"

And then it began—the folksy guitar introduction of Blue Rodeo's "Lost Together."

Her eyes sparkled as the tears welled up. "Oh, David," she whispered.

He smiled and helped her to her feet. He drew her close, felt her skin beneath his fingers. With only the wisp of a dress between them, they swayed to the gentle ballad. He held her hand tightly in his and kissed each finger in turn, while she caressed his chest with her cheek and slid her other hand under his robe and over his back.

As the last strains of the song washed over them, he pulled back from her. He sought out her eyes, hoping she would see the love in his that he hadn't been able to put into words. Without a word, he squeezed her hand and slowly led her down the hall.

"Are we there yet?" she asked, recalling for them both their first date and the long drive home.

He chuckled in spite of not wanting the tension broken. "Norah . . ."

"I'm just saying. It's a very long hall."

He turned to her and brought his hands up as if to strangle her.

"Sorry." She clamped her lips together.

He shook his head as the moment passed, grabbed her wrist, and dragged her along.

They reached the threshold of the bedroom and faced one another, as if two jumpers on a precipice. The point of no return was just beyond the doorway.

He took her face in his hands, a silent question on his lips but one he couldn't bring himself to ask in case the answer was no.

"I'm sure." Her simple reply stilled his worry immediately.

He watched from the doorway as she preceded him into the room. The soft overhead lights made her look almost luminescent as she floated around, lighting candles and stopping his heart. He met her by the bed.

He smiled and leaned down to kiss her forehead, then her temple, then her cheek, then her jaw, then her neck. He took her face in his hands once more and tipped her chin to meet his kiss full on, gently at first, then that unmistakable rush of passion that always overtook him when her lips moved over his in that certain way.

He pulled away before the madness could descend completely, and took a deep breath. With deliberate slowness, he gave in to the urge he'd been fighting through dinner, allowing his fingertips to graze her barely concealed breasts. Shivers coursed through her as he carefully lowered one side of her gown over her shoulder and kissed the bared flesh, before uncovering the other and sharing attentions on that side as well.

She sighed, tilting her head to give him free rein. Within moments, she slid her hands under the collar of his robe, over his shoulders and let it slide down his back. She planted kiss after burning kiss across his bare chest, and he reveled in the view of it as his hands buried themselves in her hair.

He eased her from him, and with painstaking slowness, coaxed her gown further down her arms, revealing her breasts to his gaze. He cupped them in his hands, delighting in the tactility of her nipples under his busy thumbs.

She moaned and leaned against him again, cutting a searing path from his chest to his stomach with her naked flesh. She moved lower until her head was even with his waist and her hands found their way to his erection.

His breath came in short gasps as she stroked him through the silk of his pajamas. Anticipating her intentions, he stopped her short as she deftly untied the drawstring.

"You can't." His voice was husky even to his own ears.

"Sure I can. Just watch me."

A chuckle bubbled up in his belly while the sultry gleam in her eye turned his knees to water.

"I know, but . . . I won't make it. Rain check?"

"Possibly." She smiled, then rose with a look of wanton victory, released the ties of his pajama bottoms, and let them pool around his ankles.

"Well played." In retribution, he reached out to the closures around her waist and, with a snap of his fingers, sent her own garment floating to the floor.

She gasped. "How did you—gosh!"

His grin was his only answer. With a lusty growl, he swept her into his embrace.

She squealed in reply and hung on with fingers deep in the muscles of his back.

He swung her onto the bed, and they landed diagonally, facing each other. "Kiss me," he demanded.

And she did. Her mouth moved over his with such skill that he was convinced, and not for the first time, that his lips were created for hers alone. Her tongue moved delicately along the tip of his before exploring further and deeper. The boldness of her touch on his face, his chest, his stomach, and with cool confidence between his legs, drove him wild.

He grabbed her wrists before it was too late and guided them above her shoulders. Confining her beneath him, he feasted on the vision of her. He whet his appetite on that sweet spot at the base of her throat where his pendant lay, before he sampled her lovely breasts. He inflamed her own hunger by devouring first one, then the other, then back again in his endless craving for her. He savoured the salty sweetness of her soft belly before he moved between her thighs. Her back arched and her hands knotted in the sheets as he placed dozens of the most intimate kisses upon her.

She gasped. "Hey, no fair."

"Who said anything about being fair?" He used his lips and tongue in a merciless dance on her willing flesh. He felt the tension build in her, and she tilted her hips as if to better guide him to her climax. Instead, he retreated and, replacing his mouth with his fingers, he continued the arousing stimulation of her slippery, satiny folds.

"Ah, David. That feels so good. Please, don't stop."

"But I must."

"Huh? Um, why?"

"Because I'm going to come inside you now." He whispered against her ear, and her whole body trembled. "And I want us to come together."

"Oh."

Something was wrong.

"What's 'oh', baby?"

"Nothing. You go ahead."

"Norah . . ."

"David, you want to have a conversation right now?"

"I think I might want to have *this* conversation. What's 'oh'?"

"Ugh. I . . . I've never . . . not that way."

Her half sentences kicked in. "You don't orgasm during intercourse?"

"Nope. Never. Sorry."

"You're telling me this now?" He rolled onto his back.

"Well, I didn't think it mattered. There are certainly other—*does* it matter?"

"No, honey, it doesn't matter." He pushed up to his elbow to face her. "It's just . . . okay, here's my problem. I'm a 'ladies first' kind of guy."

"Okay."

"But when you come, it's like I can't . . . not."

"Yeah, I noticed that. I thought it was kinda great," she said with a grin.

"Don't you see the problem, though?"

"Oh. Well, I guess you're going to have to get over yourself and go first. Just don't forget about me."

He mulled that over a bit, then shook his head while pulling her back into his arms. "Nope, we're just going to have to make this work."

She laughed. "So what? You're going to bully me into a vaginal orgasm?"

"If that's what it takes."

"Okay, big man, do your worst."

He silenced their laughter with slow, deep, moist kisses. Their naked bodies entwined, their hands explored one another, arousing and rekindling the flames of their passion. When he was certain he couldn't bear another moment, he shifted on top of her, careful to keep his weight on his elbows.

She parted her thighs.

They gazed into each other's eyes and shared the moment before everything changed, the moment they'd anticipated for so long.

He guided himself to the glistening entrance of her, taking a moment before easing in, just a fraction. He stopped, waiting for the quickening to subside before he glided in a bit more and stopped again.

She tilted her pelvis, causing him to enter her faster than he'd wanted.

"Stop that." His lips curled in a devilish smile.

"Why? Why are you . . ." She was almost incomprehensible, caught in the heat of the moment, and he loved her even more.

"Listen, listen to me." He waited until he had her full attention.

She blinked and relaxed under his stare.

"You are . . . you are the last woman that I am going to make love to for the first time. Do you understand me?" His voice was choked with emotion.

She nodded as small tears pooled in the corners of her eyes.

"So you'll forgive me if I take my time?"

She nodded again.

He kissed her eyes, her mouth, her neck, then slid in a bit more, resisting the overwhelming urge to thrust his entire length repeatedly into her, dying a little with every delicious inch of her wrapped so tightly around him. He was amazed at the amount of control it took not to erupt, and he was trembling with exertion.

She calmed him by stroking his brow with a cool hand and whispering sweetly.

Finally, unable to resist another second, he plunged into her as far as he could go and they shared a gasp of pleasure.

She hooked her heels behind his thighs and held him fast, smiling wickedly.

His breath was ragged, and he felt their hearts pounding together, chest to chest.

She tightened herself around him in an intimate hug, forcing a moan out of him.

"You are a naughty, naughty girl."

"So punish me already." She teased and released her lock on him.

His eyes bore into her with unabated lust and, taking up the gauntlet, he moved inside her in slow, rhythmic strokes. She was silken and glorious and he couldn't sink far enough into her. She yielded to his invasion, and he thrilled at how completely he filled her, feeling a nearly unbearable friction deep within her, feeling a tightening, pressure building and blood pulsing.

Feeling . . . feeling . . .

"David!" she cried, her eyes wide.

"Norah, what is it? Am I hurting you?"

"No, no . . . don't stop! For the love of God, don't stop."

Puzzled, he slowly regained his momentum, sliding out nearly to the head before driving back into her. He raised high above her so he could watch her face, still not sure what had caused her exclamation.

She threw her head back, her eyes glazed over, her lips parted as her breath left her in tiny whimpers. Her fingers clutched firmly on his buttocks, encouraging his pace and the depths he breached, then she removed one hand to stimulate her own nipple.

The sight nearly drove him to the brink.

Her moans intensified. "Oh, David . . . I don't believe . . . please, oh please . . ."

He realized what was happening and forcibly reined in his own escalating arousal to maintain his tempo. "Tell me what to do, my love, tell me," he urged.

"Just . . . just a bit, I don't know . . . f-faster."

He quickened and shortened his strokes, inciting a response that confirmed his instinct.

"Yes. Oh, David, yes."

The world fell away. There was only her, soft and yielding beneath him, and his engorged member as it coaxed, lured, and pulled from her sweet depths an almost unbearable burn to match his own. He built on it, stroking steadily, mercilessly, permeating her entire body with everything he had.

She gasped and twisted beneath him, her eyes tightly shut. All at once, with an expression of utter surprise on her face, she imploded beneath him.

He watched as her orgasm engulfed her, listened to her cries of ecstasy as her back arched and pulled him even deeper inside her, felt her grip and release him in a maddeningly erotic pulse. He surrendered, unable for another second to deny his own release. He accelerated his thrusts until the fire shot through him like lava, and ejaculated with more force than he thought possible. He cried out but continued to pound into her again and again, unwilling to let the sensation diminish.

It did, however, and he felt every muscle in his body wither with relief and fatigue. He lowered back to his elbows and sought out her eyes but was shocked to find them overflowing with tears.

"Oh, baby." He pulled her close and felt her arms tightened around his neck. "Please, don't cry."

"Damn it." She still clung to him. "How am I supposed to live without you now?"

He chuckled, sure she was kidding. She had to know that there wasn't any force on heaven or earth that would take her from him.

Chapter 16

Sometime around four in the morning, he was pulled from a well-deserved slumber with her hand luring him to arousal.
"Hello?" he asked groggily.
"Oh, hello."
"Something on your mind?"
"Shhh. Go back to sleep. I want to try something."
"Pardon?" He rubbed his hands over his face, fully awake now.
"I wasn't kidding when I told you that that has never happened to me before, and I wanted to see if it was, you know, a fluke or something."
"And you thought I'd what? Sleep through it?"
She giggled. "I guess . . . I dunno."
"You goof. Why not just wake me?"
"I didn't want to bother you."
"Oh, for fu—Norah, pay very close attention to what I am about to say, all right? Any time. Any place. Have I made myself clear?"
"Yes, sir." She saluted.
"Okay. Now then, where were we?"

****

She learned that it was not a fluke. She learned that every time David penetrated her, within a half dozen strokes, her climax followed. She learned that it didn't matter the position, the time of day, the piece of furniture they were on, or up against, or bent over, or under, intercourse with David brought on a raging explosion of sexual ecstasy. She came . . . and she came . . . and she came . . .
And he loved it.
Sunday morning over breakfast, while watching her scarf down pancakes, he grabbed her and pulled her over to him, impaling her on his erection like some half-human primate.
Mental note, replace that chair.
He'd never known a woman so responsive, at least not one that wasn't

trying for an acting award. With Norah there was a pleasurable pressure on his penis, a torrent of juices, and a beautiful flush that covered her chest afterward. Pretty tough to fake.

He had become insatiable.

They'd showered, and he had cashed in his rain check from the night before. Her eagerness alone had inflamed him to near madness, and he'd finished them both when he had laid her out on the tile floor and taken her with the shower jets raining all over them. What had started as nap time quickly became a wake-up call with his mouth between her legs. And later, when he had been cooking dinner and she'd sat on the countertop eating grapes, he'd looked over to see her slowly opening her knees with an enchanting come hither look in her eyes.

And so it went.

By the time they left the apartment Monday afternoon, they looked like two people who hadn't had a holiday at all, but they also looked like they didn't care.

****

They had arrived back in Whitecourt on Monday night. She had gone to her house to reunite with Ella, and he had headed to his hotel as he had a very early meeting the next morning with the department heads, and he really needed the sleep.

Peg had already put Ella down for the night so Norah had to be content with placing a soft kiss on her brow and watching her sleep.

Norah had unpacked and set aside the gifts from Vancouver and had just gotten changed into her nightshirt when the phone rang. She grabbed it before it woke Ella.

"Hello?"

"Hello."

He sounded so far away, and her heart caught in her throat. "Hey . . ." She struggled for something charming or witty, but her mind was blank.

"How's Ella?"

"Fine, but she was sleeping when I got home."

"That's too bad. So . . . um, did you get unpacked?"

"Yes, a minute ago. We didn't get anything for Brett so I thought I'd give him those kitchen thingies."

"Okay, but won't he mind that they've been used?"

"They've not been used, they've been *tested*."

He chuckled. "Sounds good to me."

She pulled down the covers, climbed into bed, and turned off the bedside lamp before he spoke again.

"This was such a mistake."

Her gut tightened. "What was?"

"Coming here. I'm not going to get any sleep. What did you think I meant?"

She felt her head spin with relief as her body sagged into her pillows. "Nothing. I don't know. Just take a few deep breaths to relax. You'll sleep."

"What time is your call?"

"Not until ten."

"Nice. How'd you manage that?"

"Don't tell anyone, but I'm sleeping with the director."

They laughed softly together.

"Well, not tonight you aren't."

"Maybe tomorrow."

"Definitely tomorrow."

"Okay, then. I'll see you in the morning. Get some sleep."

"You, too."

She couldn't seem to hang up the phone and sat quietly holding this small piece of him near.

"Norah?"

"Uh-huh?"

"Nothing. I'll see you in the morning. Good night."

"Good night, David."

****

He hung up the phone and pounded his head into the hotel bed where he lay, completely frustrated. He rubbed his hand across his face, rolled off and stood in front of the mirror. "Norah, I love you," he said, as though rehearsing his lines. "I love *you*, Norah. I. Love. You . . . I, you know, I've kinda fallen in love . . . oh, for Christ's sake." He drilled the heels of his hands into his eyes and started to undress. He glanced in the mirror and glowered at his reflection. "Stupid ass."

The next two days on set were crazy. David's morning meeting had been a collaboration of idiots. For all intents and purposes, he hadn't felt all there and had hoped that the rest of the team would pick up the slack.

Not friggin' likely.

Jozef had arrived twenty minutes late, fallen into a chair, and announced that he had just spent the past "three days *fuckink*," and no one was allowed to ask anything of him. Geoff had taken his first holiday in eight years to Mexico, and suffered a terrible sunburn after he'd fallen asleep on a dingy. Grace had started an herbal detox program in an effort to live healthier, which had resulted in her getting up every fifteen minutes to use the bathroom. Upon exiting she'd give a meaningful look to the room and announced, "Do *not* go in there!"

No one had.

Of course, lighting was a day behind because set dec was a day behind, because paint was a day behind, because carpentry was a day behind . . .

"Does anyone have any good news to report?" David asked, and watched as several pairs of eyes shifted furtively from person to person.

Grace was helpful between potty breaks. "All right then, let's bring in a few more day calls for carpentry and paint. Set dec won't need extra, they'll just end up getting in each other's way, and lights will step up to the plate when the time comes."

"Day calls from the city?" Jason asked, pen poised over his clipboard.

"No, go into town, get them to sign waivers. I mean, we can keep within the lines and still get this done."

"Let's make this happen, please," David said, before dismissing everyone.

Once they'd left, he rubbed his eyes and basked in the quiet.

No one asked him how his weekend had gone. No one cared that he had spent *"three days fuckink"* and couldn't make a decision if his life depended on it. Still, he couldn't help smiling every time an image from Vancouver crept into his mind. He checked his watch. Norah wasn't due for over an hour. He'd try to get a few things taken care of before she arrived.

****

Tuesday was a very busy day, as was Wednesday. There were no stolen moments in trailers, lingering kisses behind craft services, or even a hand held in chairs during a changeover. David arrived at Norah's late and too tired to eat. If he was lucky, he had just enough time to enjoy a few minutes of play with Ella, if she happened to still be up, before he grabbed a hot shower and collapsed into bed, instantly falling asleep. There was no sex those first nights back, and fatigue and work frustrations were taking their toll.

I just need to get to the weekend and everything will be back to normal.

****

She sat cross-legged on the bed, the tabloid cover staring up at her. A fuzzy, grainy shot, likely from a cell phone camera, of her and David walking along the sea wall last Saturday. David had his arm around Norah's shoulder and gazed out into the ocean looking reflective and handsome. She had her arm around his waist and was gazing up at him adoringly, like a lovesick schoolgirl.

BEAUTY AND THE SHE-BEAST.

David had called five minutes ago to say he was on his way over. He hadn't mentioned whether he'd seen the article or why he was coming, but she had a pretty good idea.

"Norah!" David shouted from the downstairs hall, the door slamming behind him.

Norah jumped. She hadn't expected him so soon. Her voice stuck in her throat as she heard him stomp around the main floor then race up the stairs.

"Norah! Where are you?" He appeared in her doorway, face flushed, and had a stranglehold on a newspaper clutched in his hand. "Why didn't you answer?" He caught sight of the tabloid in her lap and his head dropped. "Oh, honey. I thought I'd get here before—how did you get it so fast?"

She found her voice somewhere. "Mona brought it over."

He blinked. "Mona? Your *mother* brought this to you?" He snatched the paper out of her lap.

"Yeah, isn't she great?" she asked, her voice dry with sarcasm. "She'd bought up every copy in the store, so of course, I had to reimburse her. She didn't want to be embarrassed at her next cribbage tournament, you see, and she wanted to know if I thought this would blow over before she and Vic shift to Phoenix next month. I mean, she can't buy up *every* copy. I don't have that kind of money." She laughed bitterly.

He dropped to his knees and took her hands. "Sweetheart, I'm so sorry."

She gestured to the paper he'd brought in, lying crumpled on the floor with the other. "Where did you get that one?"

"The hotel. I went back to get my schedule and was walking through the lobby—"

"Alan has that in his lobby?!"

"No, he was unloading the papers and magazines for the rack and was standing over this bundle. He had this look on his face like, I dunno, shock maybe. I went over to see if he was okay, and all he could do was point. I grabbed this one, and he took the rest out the back to burn them."

"Good guy, that Alan. I dated him a bit after high school." She said it almost as an afterthought.

"I thought you were with Nathan all that time."

"We broke up a lot. You know—on again, off again." She felt as if she were talking to a stranger.

"Right."

It was as if they didn't know what to say to each other.

She felt as if she'd been beaten up. She was so hurt and angry, not because they'd come after her—she figured that would happen eventually. It was inevitable. But they'd put a stain on that day, and that was unbearable.

He pushed a strand of hair behind her ear with a tender smile. "You look like hell," he said.

"Well, that should make this easier then."

"Make what easier?"

"Look, David, I promise I'm not going to make any trouble. I know we've got a couple more weeks before you wrap here, and I've got my shoot in New York after that, but . . ." She hoped he would take it from there and save her from saying the words herself. Instead, she watched the colour drain from his face.

"Norah, you sound as if we're breaking up."

"You sound as if we're not."

He doesn't look relieved. I thought for sure he'd look relieved.

In fact, he looked as if she were speaking a foreign language. She tried another approach. "It's just that—does it really make any sense to—" She waved at the tabloid trash on the floor. "—with all that now?"

He stood over her. "What are you talking about?"

There was anger in his voice, and it frightened her, but she had to push on. "In a few weeks, the movie is going to be finished, and you're going to go back to Hollywood or Europe, and all that, and I'm going to . . ." She couldn't stop the tears that filled her eyes or keep the strangled edge from choking her. "I'm going to come back here."

He placed his hands on his hips and stared at her.

"Damn it, David, we have to be realistic. Your life is not in Whitecourt, Alberta!"

His hands dropped to his sides, his face fell, and his beautiful brown eyes were suddenly moist. After a painful moment of silence, he whispered, "Yes, it is."

****

"What did you say?" she asked.

He walked to the settee by the window and collapsed onto it. He put his head in his hands and tried to quell the flood of emotions that threatened to burst out of him.

I screwed it up.

"Baby, I'm so sorry." He looked up at her, his face a picture of sorrow. "I've been . . . I've been a coward, such a fucking coward. I talked myself into believing that you knew, and that I didn't have to say it." He started to pace the room. "But that's not entirely my fault." He wagged a finger at her. "I mean, you're such a smarty-pants and always seem to know what I'm thinking or how I'm feeling so I was, I guess, counting on you to figure it out." He stopped pacing and sat down hard on the bed, making her bounce idiotically. "But that's not fair. I know that's not fair. And it's so stupid, it's been right there," he said, gesturing to his mouth with his thumb and forefinger. "Right there, and I couldn't. I don't know why. I've never felt anything clearer in my life." He flung his body back on the bed. "Why couldn't I just say it?"

I'm raving like a lunatic.

She sat stock-still, as if she was afraid to move. "Couldn't say what, David?"

He turned to look at her, so small and vulnerable. He'd hurt her and for what? To save his pride?

A fat lot of good my pride's going to be if I lose her.

Even if he came clean, he couldn't be certain that she'd forgive him.

Why should she, after what I put her through?

The memory of the first time they'd made love flashed in front of him.

Her clinging to him afterward, crying openly, and . . .

What did she say?

How am I supposed to live without you now?

He'd thought she was joking. He put his hands over his face to hide his shame.

He cleared his throat, lifted himself up, and turned her to face him. "What I couldn't say, what I should have said, what I should have told you is . . ." He took a deep breath and looked into her frightened face. "I love you."

Something flickered in her eyes but she remained still.

"I love you, Norah. I have been in love with you since . . . well, a long time. And I'm so sorry. I should have told you. You deserved to hear it. You deserve so much. More than my . . . stupid pride worrying—I guess I didn't feel—I worried that I'd look like a dope, but you've always been—argh!"

He saw her face soften, a shadow of a smile teased him, and her eyes overflowed.

He took her by the shoulders . "Norah, what I'm trying to say . . . you see, this is why I'm an actor, I need some other poor slob to write dialogue for me 'cause I suck at it."

A small laugh burst out of her.

"Norah, my love, my life *is* in Whitecourt. If you and Ella are in Whitecourt, that is where my life is. If you are in Hollywood, Europe, or Timbuktu, that is where I will be because you *are* my life."

She left him hanging for less than a heartbeat. "Oh, David," she sobbed and threw herself into his eager arms, flattening him onto the bed.

He clutched her to him, awash with relief, and sent out a silent thanks for whatever he had done right to deserve this woman.

"David, I love you, too. I love you so much. I was so afraid that this was . . . I mean, I knew it was nice, fabulous, and even that it was special for you. I didn't think, didn't dare hope that, that it could go beyond—"

"But, Norah, what about what I said? What I said Saturday night about you being, you know, the last woman that I would make love to for the first time. Did you think I was handing you a line?"

"No, no, not at all. I knew you meant it, you know, at the time. I thought —I just figured that even if that ended up being true, you still had a lot of, well, ex-girlfriends, that maybe . . ." Her voice got smaller and smaller until, by the end, it was little more than a mumble.

He pushed away from her as if doused with ice water. "That is a shitty thing . . . Jesus, Norah!"

"I know. I'm sorry! I couldn't believe that anything else was possible. It just . . . a future between us seemed too complicated."

He lay steaming at her, and it took a few minutes before he calmed down and was able to consider it from her point of view. His previous lifestyle— one short-term relationship after another—hadn't been any kind of a secret, and he sure hadn't done his all to make her see that he was in this one for the long haul.

He got furious with himself this time. "All right. All right, I understand, I guess. And my life *is* complicated, and I'm sorry about that, too. But I need you in it, so one way or another, we'll have to make this work." He rolled toward her and lifted her chin to meet her eyes. "And I promise that a day won't go by that I won't tell you how much you mean to me so you never have to doubt us again. I promise. Okay?"

"Okay," she replied, sounding relieved.

"Will you forgive me for being such an ass?" he asked.

"Not just yet. I think you've got some serious sucking up to do first." She grinned at him.

He threw back his head and laughed. That grin alone had the power to turn his insides sideways. He'd come to learn that there was a lot of promise in that grin.

He pushed back her hair and kissed her as he'd never kissed her before. He was hers completely, and from this moment on, he would let that cover him like a warm blanket. He would never again stand up against his feelings for her, would never again deny them the pleasure they took in simply being with each other. There, in her arms, as her hands reached under his shirt and caressed his yearning flesh, as his fingers tore at the zipper of her jeans, his desire for her crashed down around him and he happily surrendered to it.

****

Sex was different for men than women. That notion wasn't a new idea. Sex in a casual relationship, as opposed to a loving one, was different. Again, nothing new. What was new was making love with the person that you love and knowing they love you in return. A feeling of power. Not power *over,* but from within.

David felt as though a weight had lifted the moment the words *I love you* had left his mouth.

Maybe it was a newfound confidence, but David saw a light turn on in Norah. There was an exciting inner strength brewing. She no longer simply accepted his kisses, his touch, his body. She demanded them with a fierceness that perhaps she had been too shy to reveal before. She left him breathless and gasping for air.

He laid back and let her punish him with her mouth and hands, delirious in his love for her. She rode him like pure fury, and the sight of her above him, her hair clinging to her glistening face, drops of perspiration running in rivulets between her lovely breasts as they danced in his hands, drove him to the edge of insanity. She permitted him no tender manners, no *ladies first* etiquette.

He knew she was going to come when she damned well felt like it, thank you very much, and if he didn't have the sense to get his rocks off when the opportunity presented itself, then tough luck. He knew he deserved this sweet abuse and took it like a good sport. He took his brain out of the game and relaxed into the physical sensations she hurled upon him. When her rhythm altered, he knew she was close and that he'd better get on the ball.

Their frenzied cries rang out at the same time, and as her rapture lasted a good deal longer than his, he was able to enjoy her finish before folding her to him and covering grateful kisses all over her face and shoulders.

"I love you, I love you, I love you." He laughed, stunned by the irony that he couldn't stop saying it now.

"Um, David?"

"Yes, my love."

"Getting a little boring." Unable to hold a straight face, she burst out laughing.

He growled, rolled over on top of her, and pinned her down. "I'll show you some boring."

They laughed together at the bad pun.

"Hey, hold it. Ella's going to wake up from her nap in a minute. In fact, I'm surprised we didn't wake her."

"The kid's cutting me a break. I'll have to get her some ice keem," he said, chuckling at his use of Ella's words.

"Do you mind keeping an ear out for her while I grab a quick shower?"

"What about me?" he asked, and poked out his bottom lip for effect.

"Now I think we both know that would turn into a very *long* shower. You can wait your turn." She smiled, winked, and disappeared into the bathroom.

****

When she emerged a few minutes later, the room was empty. She stepped across the hall, peeked into the nursery and found David on the stool beside the crib, his arms folded on the safety rail and his chin resting on his wrists. He was looking thoughtfully at Ella while she slept, a slight frown on his brow.

"David? Is she all right?"

He jumped then smiled. "Yes, she's fine," he whispered. "I'm sitting here, looking at this tiny girl and I want to, I don't know, take care of her, protect her somehow." His attention turned back to Ella, and Norah's heart ached with happiness.

She came up behind David, put her arms around his neck and kissed him tenderly on his cheek. "You're my hero, you know."

He held her hands tightly to his chest and sighed deeply.

****

Nigel Coombs' long, manicured finger reached out, talon-like, for the intercom button on his phone.

The silken reply was immediate. "Yes, Mr. Coombs?"

"Giselle, please get David Raurke on the line for me."

"Right away, sir."

He clicked off and returned his attention to the latest tabloid spread on his desk.

"So, little She-Beast, what are we going to do with you?"

Chapter 17

The last two weeks of the Whitecourt leg of shooting for *Kosma* had been typical, if there was such a thing. The local crew from the city and the town itself had chatted excitedly about their next projects, if they were lucky enough to have one, or lamented the fact if they didn't. Albertan cast members, mostly bit players or extras, had either looked forward to getting back to their less glamorous lives, or wondered—like millions before them—if the bright lights weren't indeed worth pursuing.

Heads of production and the actors who would be moving on to the States faced this last, small chunk of time with mixed feelings. Some had been happy to be heading back, nearer to family, the hustle and bustle of a big city with lots of off-hour diversions and sushi on every corner. Others were going to miss this little town. They'd become accepted by and friendly with many of the residents. They enjoyed the anonymity that grew out of constant exposure, and had become used to the simple generosity that came from simple folk.

For David, the end of shooting in this hot, sticky, dusty little town—thick with flies, mosquitoes, and the inability to do anything on a large scale, or quickly—brought on a maelstrom of feelings. For the most part, he was excited about the move. The New York scenes were going to be challenging, requiring all his skills as a director, and the opportunities to learn and grow in all the directions that he wanted. Also, most of his friends were in the New York area, and he was looking forward to getting together with them, knocking back a few, and catching a game or two. And Beth lived in Long Island with her husband and kids. He had missed her this trip, mostly because he'd had so much to talk to her about. Bending her ear face-to-face was high on his list once Stateside.

But this was the place where it all began. Every time he thought about saying goodbye to Norah tomorrow, he felt as if he'd had the wind knocked out of him. She'd be joining them in fourteen days, and he would be coming back here once the film was in the can, but as he packed up the few belongings he had left in the hotel, the task weighed on him.

Over the few last weeks, he had shifted more and more of his belongings to the house, and since the afternoon that they'd declared their love for each other, he'd spent every night in her bed. He had sworn he'd be hanged before he'd sleep in this godforsaken room without her. It had occurred to him, on more than one occasion, to invite her here for a break and some fun, sleazy hotel sex, but Ella had become such a part of his life, and knowing he was going to miss her almost as much as her mother, he was loath to spend a night away from her either.

He'd even managed to snap the photo that he'd wanted from the start—Norah leaning over Ella sleeping in her crib, her lips touching the toddler's head, and the pale glow from the nightlight illuminating them. It had turned out beautifully, and he'd pledged to get a copy printed, matted, and framed for her as a gift.

So while he knew the next little while was going to be a bit bumpy for both of them, he was determined to push through it with a positive attitude, knowing that the best was yet to come.

****

Norah put on her bravest face. Only those who knew her best—David among them—realized her true inner agony. Many Whitecourt residents' chins wagged daily over what "that poor girl" must be going through. They knew what had happened the last time she had put her man on a plane.

This last afternoon, as she waited for David to finish at the hotel and bring his things over, she barely held it together. They would have a few brief hours together before they had to be at the wrap party, then one last night in each other's arms. In less than twenty-four hours, he would be gone—and the idea devastated her.

****

Brett found Norah stretched across her bed, her head resting on her folded arms, looking every bit like she had as a teenager when some angst-inducing incident had sent her into seclusion from everyone but him.

"I have this overwhelming urge to put on a Bon Jovi album and roll us a doobie." He leaned against her doorjamb.

"I never smoked pot," she said.

"Of course you didn't," he replied, before crawling up and sitting cross-legged next to her. "So tonight's the big send-off?"

"Yeah, they've rented Legion Hall, of all places."

"I know. We're catering."

"Right. I remember. Well, it'll be a nice evening."

"Will it? I mean, for you?"

She stared at him. "It'll be fine." She shrugged.

"What time does he leave?"

"Are you *trying* to start something?"

"No, I'm—"

" 'Cause, if you want to start somethi—"

"Norah, I'm mak—"

"It's not like it's not tough enough . . ."

They sat, silent, arms folded and staring in opposite directions.

"Why are you so freaked?" he asked.

"Why shouldn't I be?"

"He's going off to do his job, and in a couple of weeks, you're going to join him. I would have thought you could use the rest, personally." He shuddered as he recalled the noises that had been coming from across the hall.

"It's not that simple." She seemed determined to be miserable.

"Sure it is. It's only more complicated if you want it to be."

"You don't know what you're talking about."

"Then enlighten me. There's a chance I can help, you know."

She sighed and appeared to soften a little. "It's just that, I'm worried that as soon as he's back in his world that he'll . . ."

"Drift away?"

"Yeah. I mean, he told me that home is wherever Ella and I are, but . . ."

"You've decided he's a liar."

"Don't be an ass. I don't think he's lying, it's just that—"

"Oh, I see. You think you're such an unremarkable person that as soon as you're out of his sight, you'll be out of his mind."

She sighed again. "I know he loves me. I don't know if . . . if all of this will be as . . . important once he's somewhere else, with other, you know, people around, other influences."

"Other women?" He watched her swallow hard. "So you think that he's had a nice time playing house in Hicksville, Albert-ee, and that as soon as his back is turned he's going to . . . what? Turn his back?"

She groaned and flopped onto her side and pulled a pillow over her head.

"All right." He sighed, lifting a corner of it. "There's something you don't know."

"What?"

"I promised him I wouldn't tell you, but I think you should know."

"What?"

"I mean, my loyalty is to you, not him. Right?"

"Brett . . ."

"Although, it really involves Ella more th—"

"Ella? Brett, for pity's sake!" Pillow forgotten, she pushed onto her elbows.

"All right, he had me sign this document—"

"Sign? What on earth are you signing?" She sat upright.

"I need you to let me finish."

"Sorry, go."

"Okay, where was I? Right. Last week he asked me to meet him at the café—"

"What for?"

"Norah."

"Sorry."

"Anyway, he brought this document, this very legal docum—"

"You keep saying document! What kind of document, and what does it have to do with Ella?"

He fixed her with a stony stare, leaned back on the bed, and pretended to be interested in picking invisible lint from his cardigan.

"All right, I'm sorry. Please finish. I won't interrupt, I promise."

He gave her the once-over. "Fine, but this is your last warning." He turned to her. "He'd had his lawyers, or whatever, draw up this trust fund thing for Ella."

Her eyes were huge and questioning but she held her tongue.

"Anyway, he wanted *me* to sign on as executrix, that way he wouldn't have to tell you. But you've gotten so 'waa-waa-waa, he doesn't care about me, waa-waa,' that I figured I'd better tell you if I'm ever going to get any peace."

She contemplated him through thinly slit eyes. "May I speak now?"

"Sure."

"Wh-what—?" She sighed then cleared her throat and tried one more time. "What sort of a trust fund? Why?"

"Well, he told me he was nuts about Ella. Fine, obviously. I certainly couldn't argue with him there. Then he said that he knew what a struggle it had to have been for you, you know, the whole single mother shtick, and that he would like to make things a little easier on you for later. I read it, and it's really smartly drafted, you know. A portion for when she graduates high school, should she want to go on to university or travel or whatever, then another portion when she's twenty-five, and another when she's thirty."

"Good God, how much money are we talking about?"

"Enough," he said with a nod.

"Brett!"

"No way, I've told you what I did so that you'd stop squirreling away for her and worrying about whether or not he's a stand-up guy. I'd have to say he's pretty stand-up."

"But then why not be the executrix himself?"

"He made it so that it had nothing to do with the two of you. Isn't that fab?"

"Yeah, it's real fab. So, in other words, when he decides to dump my ass, Ella won't suffer as a result of it." She retreated to her cocoon under the toss pillows.

"Yeah, but . . . no!"

Oh shit, I fucked it.

"No, see, he didn't want you to know, and if it hadn't been for my total inability to keep a secret, you never would have. Nobody's getting dumped! What he did say, in fact, was that it might change your relationship if you knew. He didn't want to make you feel like you owed him something or were . . . you know, obligated . . . somehow. It sounded so much better in my head."

"Well, now I don't know what to think." Her voice came out from under the bedding, muffled and fuzzy.

"Oh, crap! I thought you'd be all, 'he loves me, and he loves my baby . . . ooh, ooh, I'm going to do all kinds of things that'll keep Brett clinging to his headphones another night.' "

"Don't worry, you'll be getting more than enough sleep soon enough."

****

David's dealings with the wrap-up took longer than he'd hoped. There were a thousand idiotic details at the location that needed finalizing before the circus finally pulled out. Once everything had been squared away, he spent a moment inside the now vacant soundstage and allowed himself a little quiet reflection. Some good work had been done in here, no question, not that there was a shred of evidence left in the building to show for it. The place had been swept clean—no sign of a cable, a wire, or even a fragment of coloured gel. He felt a lump in his throat. Never taken to moods of sentimentality before, he was irritated by this rush of nostalgia.

It's nothing but a big, empty, smelly barn!

But it was the big, empty, smelly barn where he'd met her. He recalled the picture of her at the table, looking so small and shy, his intake of breath as she had looked up at him when he'd first approached, and how he had fallen victim to her and those lovely, lovely eyes. He smiled as he remembered the panic that had gone head-to-head with the comical desire to kiss her in front of everyone before he'd even learned her name.

Norah, Norah Rothe.

He smiled one last time before closing the door on one of the sweetest chapters of his life.

****

When he arrived at the house, Norah was upstairs and Peg was in the kitchen, so he took the opportunity to get in a quick cuddle with Ella while getting a read on Norah via her aunt.

"She'll miss you, is all. We all will, won't we, sweetie?" she said as she gently tugged on Ella's leg. "But Norah's strong, she'll throw herself into Ella and the café, and before she knows it, she'll be on that plane herself. Well, we all will."

"I'm glad you decided to come, too."

"I couldn't see her going two whole weeks without her little chickadee. And it would be too hard to concentrate on her work if she was worried about some Yankee stranger taking care of Ella. Besides, I've never been outside Alberta, and I've become fond of the crew. I'm looking forward to it."

Suddenly, there was a loud bang and a louder, "Goddamn it!" from upstairs.

"I'm just not looking forward to the next couple of days."

"Any advice?" David asked, as he handed Ella over to Peg.

"She needs to know you're feeling the same things. Don't give me that face. I know it sounds ridiculous, but a woman apart from the man she loves is a terrible thing."

He thought how Peg had been apart from the man she'd loved for . . . forever, and it made him sad for her. He gave her a quick kiss on her blushing cheek and then took the stairs two at a time.

He peered into Norah's room and found her looking defeated on the foot of her bed, in nothing but her bra and panties, with a half dozen clothes hangers and an armload of garments piled in her lap.

She looked up and saw him standing there, and gestured toward the wardrobe where the clothes rod had come loose from the brackets and dumped everything onto the floor.

He stepped over to it, twisted and fuddled a bit, and got the errant rod back in place. "I don't know if I'd hang anything until I've had a chance to put in a screw or two."

"I'll do it. I'm going to have a bit of extra time on my hands." She focused her attention on laying her dresses across the chaise as carefully as her mood would allow.

He came up behind her and gently held her arms.

She stiffened.

"Honey, why don't you come to New York early? There's nothing saying you have to wait until you start work."

She turned in his arms, and he thought he saw some tension leave her face.

"You're going to be busy. I can't leave the café for that long. Besides, what about Ella and Peg? No, don't be—I mean, thank you, but please, don't buy into my bullshit. I don't have a single reason to be this nuts, I just am." She threw the last blouse on top of the pile.

"You don't have the market on it, you know? Being nuts, I mean. The thought of sleeping alone for two weeks has me nearly out of my mind."

"If I get a vote, I'd rather you were out of your mind than any alternative you might think of."

He smiled. "I'm not thinking of anything beyond what I'm going to do to you the night you get off that plane." He pulled her into his arms and sighed with relief when he felt her relax against him. "Now, you'd better finish getting dressed, or my filmmaker's instincts will be tempted to show you a preview."

Brenda J. Brown

****

Two hours later, they were on the lower floor of the Whitecourt branch of the Royal Canadian Legion. It would have more aptly been called a *basement* with its low ceilings and support pillars standing in less than opportune locations that forced the dance floor off-kilter. The décor had clung firmly to the fifties, with its wood paneling amidst the chipped stucco and multi-fleck industrial carpet, heavily stained and threadbare. Unseasonable Christmas lights dangled haphazardly on the walls, accompanied by plaques, framed photos, and newspaper clippings paying honour to the Whitecourt veterans of the second World War. For entertainment, there was a shuffleboard, a half dozen dartboards, and a homemade piano, which would come in handy should Dennis get juiced enough to play. It was large enough for all the cast and crew, as well as a few of the more supportive locals, and they promised to have enough beer on hand to float a boat.

By the time David and Norah made their entrance, the room was a din of jovial conversation and music. People pooled in the same cliques they'd been found in on set—carps with carps, set dec shared a long table with paint—the hatchet buried at last—and Jozef held court with lighting and camera. Norah caught Brett's eye as he swept around the room, directing how the buffet table should be placed. He had gone to so much unnecessary effort, since the masses swept down on the platters of exquisite food like locusts, tossing aside the edible blossoms, and pillaging the shrimp platter a fistful at a time.

"Pearls before swine," he muttered as he fled back to the kitchen for reinforcements.

Dennis and Nick waved them over, and David helped Norah into her seat before pulling up a chair next to her. He poured them each a sleeve of draft from the pitcher in front of Nick, who'd jokingly assured them the glasses were "clean-ish", and they chatted amiably. Grace joined them with a platter of appetizers that she'd scored off the "fruitcake with the apron."

David's beer ended up back in his glass.

Norah put her hand on his lap, and with a smile, indicated it wasn't worth embarrassing Grace over.

Before too much beer had been consumed, Jason called the room to attention. Once everyone had quieted down, he spoke up. "I hope everyone is having a good time."

Whoops and hollers filled the room.

"This party is from the producers of *Kosma*, to thank you for all of your hard work and support over the last two months. So, without further ado, our revered director would like to have a word. David Raurke, everyone."

There was an explosion of applause and whistles.

David stood and tried to bring the room under control. He gripped the back of his chair, raised his head, and met the eyes of his audience.

"I have to tell you, when locations first came to me recommending Whitecourt, Alberta, for an eight-week shoot, I didn't hold out much hope."

A round of hearty chuckles scattered over the room.

"However, I was very pleasantly surprised. We couldn't have dreamed of a better location to tell our story, a harder working crew, or a finer bunch of people. You've been a top-notch team, and I hope I get the opportunity to work with you again. You all know I have my own personal reasons for having a soft spot for this little town." He smiled at Norah and placed a hand possessively on her shoulder amidst a chorus of cheers and wolf whistles. "But professionally, I thank you all for making my job so much easier, and frankly, for making me look pretty damn good."

A loud round of laughter broke out, and David raised his glass to the room.

Just as he sat down, Norah turned and kissed him firmly.

"What was that for?" he asked.

"Do I need a reason?"

"Never."

Before long, they'd gone through the food and beer on the table, so David crossed to the bar for refills. Within a minute of his departure, the next song started up, and there was no mistaking the familiar folksy guitar.

Norah turned toward the dance floor and found David waiting, a warm smile on his face.

Her eyes locked on him as she moved across the floor.

They were either unaware or didn't care that they'd become the focus of the crowd. Conversations ceased, a few couples stopped dancing, and one or two bystanders even inched closer to watch.

Norah crossed the space between them and, when she was within arms' length, he held out his hand.

David drew her in to him, his free hand warm and firm on the small of her back, the other holding her hand against his heart.

Her left hand wound around his shoulder and stroked the back of his neck with her fingertips.

He cradled her head under his chin, and she melted to him. He inhaled the scent of her, committing it to memory along with the way she felt and the sound of her heart beating, while the music washed over them. The dance itself was incidental.

Soon they would have no choice but to face the reality of being apart, but for now, for this dance, for the walk up the porch steps and then her front staircase, there was no one in the world but them. As they peeked in on the sleeping Ella, there was no city on the other side of the continent waiting for him. As they crossed over the threshold of her bedroom, there was nothing but their love, and so it was within these precious moments that they existed only for each other.

Chapter 18

Brett came up the front steps with more care than usual. He seldom left the café before three in the afternoon, but today he decided to check in on his sister.

David had left this morning.

Brett had said his farewell to him before going to work, and could see that the fellow was in for a tough time.

Brett knew he'd be fine. David would be busy from the second he landed, and there was nothing like throwing yourself into work to keep your mind occupied. Norah had the hard part, stuck here in Nowheres-ville. The circus had literally pulled out of town and left her behind.

He braced, prepared to find her in the fetal position in the middle of her bed, weeping pitifully. He sighed and reached for the doorknob.

The next two weeks are going to be such a bore.

He cracked open the door and was nearly blasted back out as mega-volume, vintage Madonna vogued through him.

Cool . . . sort of. But what the hell?

He crept through the front hall, into the living room, the dining room, and kitchen.

Nothing.

He climbed the back stairs, peering up as he went. The baby gate at the top of the landing clued him in that the pooper was around, so he checked Ella's room.

The munchkin was busy with her books and looked up at him with a big grin. "Unky Bett. Wha' doing?"

"Hey, stinker. I just came to say hi." He squatted down in front of her. "What are *you* doing?"

"Ewwa ree."

"Are you reading your book? What a clever girl."

"Yeah," she said.

"Where's Mama?"

She pointed her chubby finger across the hall, and she resumed turning pages, immersed in the story she'd had read to her a few dozen times.

He ruffled her hair then got up and ventured over to Norah's room.

It looked as if her closets, wardrobe, and dressing table had imploded. The contents were spewed over every possible flat surface. While he stood there wondering what could cause such destruction, a shoe came whizzing past his head, then another, the third barely missing him. "Hey!"

Norah stuck her head out of the closet. "Hey, yourself. Why are you home so early?" She ducked back in, reemerging a moment later piled high with a stack of shoeboxes, biscuit tins, and plastic bags, which she hauled to the chaise and dumped unceremoniously on top of it. Dressed in her droopiest sweats and covered in perspiration and dust, she turned to her brother with a smile of satisfaction on her face.

"I thought I'd—what were you doing in there?" he asked and looked around, wondering if he had the right house.

She cocked an eyebrow at him. "Masturbating, Brett. I've been masturbating in my closet all day. I had to throw all my clothes out in order to have enough room."

The visual disturbed him and he shook his head to clear it of the unpleasant imagery. "Fine. So how are you?" he asked, perching on the only clear patch of bed.

"Good." She reentered her closet, lobbing suitcases, overnight bags, backpacks, and gym totes onto the floor.

"Are you sure?"

"Sure, I'm sure." She came out again with hat boxes precariously stacked and obscuring her face. She set them carefully in the corner. "The wrap party was a lot of fun. The food was terrific, by the way."

"Thank you."

"We came back here, made beautiful love, all night long . . ."

I know, he mouthed, the ick-factor apparent in his face.

". . . had a lovely breakfast together with Ella after you left, and then Jim picked him up around eleven."

"And . . ."

"And? And he was on his way. He called from the airport a couple of hours ago to tell me he missed me already and that he'd call again when he landed." She dove back into the closet, this time with a large black garbage bag in tow. "Do you have anything for the Salvation Army?"

"Maybe. I'll have a look in a sec. So you're okay? Really okay?"

He strained to hear her muffled voice from his perch on the bed. "Look, Brett, I appreciate your concern, honestly, and don't worry, I've had my little sniffle. All right, I sobbed the house down for about half an hour. But then I thought, this is silly, it's only for two weeks. *Less* than two weeks, really, when you consider that in one week I'm going to start getting all excited about leaving. So I thought this is a great opportunity to get to some of the projects that I've been putting off, you know, since I've been so busy with the film. And here I am. Damn, how did I get so much crap? Anyway,

I've already shampooed the upholstery downstairs, so be careful where you sit. Once I've cleared this away, I'm going to do the same to Ella's room. She hardly has anything to wear anymore. Her drawers are crammed with clothes that are too small, and I figure I'll make a list of the stuff she needs so she and Peg can do some shopping in New York while I'm shooting. Isn't that a great idea?"

"Yeah, great. Can I give Peg my list, too?"

Norah laughed. "Anyway, you're sweet to check up on me, but I realized that I was simply overreacting, and what with the phone and e-mails, it's going to feel as if he hasn't really left at all. For the most part, anyway."

"Okay, well, good. I guess I'll go to my room and see what I can part with. Call me if you need me."

****

Norah continued to purge her shelves and cubbies. The lovely cashmere robe that David had given her in Vancouver hung on the closet door, reminding her that she to get rid of her old ugly one, even though David had looked so cute when he'd turned up for breakfast in it, scaring the bejeezus out of Brett. She chuckled at the memory, and pretty sure she'd hung it in her bathroom, she reached behind the door, grabbed hold, and hauled it toward the giveaway bag.

She stopped short.

She didn't have her old robe. She held the one that David had bought for himself when they'd gone shopping in the city together so many weeks ago.

She gathered it to her face and breathed deep. His scent clung to it, and she smiled. She knew he'd left it deliberately to assure her that he'd be back. In lieu of chair space, she curled up on the floor with the cherished robe in her lap and allowed her memories to wander.

****

"So what are we buying?"

She reached between the front seats and hauled out a clipboard, which she handed to him.

"Man, this is a lot of stuff. Do you do this every week?"

"Yep. It's a bit less during the winter, but not by much."

What is he doing here?

She glanced at him from time to time, under the pretext of checking her side mirror.

God, he's handsome, and so unbelievably sexy.

Her face flushed as an image from the day before, in the bathtub, came to her unbidden.

"Are you all right?" he asked, his voice full of concern.

"I'm fine."

Embarrassed, but fine.

"Are you sure? You know you're blushing, right?"
"No, don't be—"
"Why are you blushing?"
". . . ridiculous."
He was laughing, and she was sure he'd guessed where her thoughts had taken her.
She felt as if she was naked all over again.

****

They arrived at the gigantic warehouse store after a very pleasant drive filled with stories and laughter and little girl giggles.
They plunked Ella into a cart, grabbed a flatbed wagon, and got down to work. This was a job that Norah generally hated, but with David along it was more enjoyable than she thought it could be. He was like a kid in a candy store—or, more to the point, a man who didn't get out much, in a store the size of an airplane hangar, packed floor to ceiling with goodies. More than once she had to curb his rabid consumerism.
"David, what are you going to do with a multispeed juicer in your hotel room?"
"But look at all the stuff you can make. I'll keep it at your place and make us smoothies in the mornings. Would Ella like a yummy smoothie?"
"Oday!"
"See?" He stashed it in the cart beside the portable Blu-ray player, the bulk pack of rechargeable batteries, two one-kilo bags of beef jerky, six pairs of black socks, an atlas of the world, and one handsome, bronze-coloured chenille bathrobe. She made him go back for another cart.
Norah was looking forward to getting home and having a nice dinner by the time she got into the line for the cash registers.
"God! Sheila, do you know who that looks like?"
The conversation from the two women behind Norah caught her attention.
"Who? Who are you talking about?" asked the one Norah assumed was Sheila.
"That guy over there with the little girl."
Norah looked surreptitiously to her left.
There he was, holding Ella in front of a million-inch-wide plasma television that had some animated program playing on it.
Glancing over her shoulder under the guise of straightening her collar, she ascertained that sure enough, he was the guy the women were referring to.
"Tell me he doesn't look exactly like David Raurke."
"What? Oh, yeah, I guess. Wouldn't that be something though?"
"Mm-hmm."
"What would you do if it was?"

"Well, I'll tell you . . ."

And she proceeded to do just that—in alarmingly uninhibited, pornographic detail.

Norah felt her face flush again and had to clamp her own slack jaw forcibly shut on more than one occasion as this woman described, in only slightly hushed tones, the acts that she would be too willing to perform on that man, should he in fact turn out to be the heavenly David Raurke.

Horrified, Norah watched as David made his way over to her with Ella and a stack of Blu-rays in his arms.

Oh well, at least my life is never dull these days.

"We found a couple of movies I don't have. Okay, more than a couple." He added them to the pile.

Norah leaned against the cart, half an eye on the two open-mouthed women gaping quite candidly in his direction.

"Hey, how ya doing?" he inquired politely.

Nothing.

"Oh, look! Hot dogs." He pointed in the direction of the concession. "Do you want one?" he asked Norah.

"Nope, I'm good thanks." She smiled at his enthusiasm.

"Ella, should we get a hot dog?"

"Chips!" she demanded.

"Do you want some chips?"

Norah nodded, and they strode off. She looked at the women who were turning their dumbstruck expressions back to her, and decided to have a little fun.

"Boy, I'll bet you're really embarrassed right now? Yeah, I can imagine. I wouldn't worry, though. I won't tell him anything about, you know, that stuff you said. Oh, if you don't mind though, that one thing you mentioned . . . would you need a real motorcycle, or could you use something like a chair? I mean, it's not like you could actually ride it doing that, right? Just curious, ya know. Sounded interesting. Okay, nice talking to you."

Neither woman made a sound throughout the entire exchange, even when Norah started through the checkout.

When David joined her and insisted on paying for everything, despite her protests, she noticed that they had disappeared.

"What are you grinning about?" David asked.

"Your Norah was naughty," she confessed, eyes wide in contrition.

"Naughtier then yesterday?" he whispered against her cheek, which flushed again.

"Maybe not quite."

****

"Now that's what I expected."

Norah looked up at Brett from where she sat cradling David's robe in her arms, a secret smile on her face. "I love him so much."

"I know you do."

"It's going to be a long two weeks."

"I know that, too."

****

David left the antique shop in the Village, having just purchased two frames —art deco for Norah, and simple wood grain for himself—for the photos he'd taken of Norah and Ella, along with instructions on how he wanted them restored and matted with a special linen paper that they were going to have to send away for. That done, he headed to the restaurant on the corner to meet Beth for lunch.

She was already seated when he arrived, and rose to give him a full and enthusiastic hug. "You're late," she chastised.

"Sorry. I had an errand." He took a chair after helping her back into hers. "You look marvelous."

And she did. Nearly his height, Beth Raurke, who'd kept her maiden name after she'd married the renowned structural engineer, Richard Bharma, was a striking woman with intelligent wide-set eyes, fine sculpted brows, and lovely mouth always ready for a smile. She shared her brother's strong jawline and sense of humour.

"What time did you get in yesterday?"

David shook his head. "I can't remember . . . late. I haven't righted myself yet."

"How many times have you called her?" she asked with a grin.

David signaled for the server and shot her a glare. "Don't start. This is hard for me."

"I can tell. But she's here in two weeks, isn't she?"

"Two weeks yesterday. No, the day before . . . two weeks Friday. We'd like a bottle of the house white, please. Do you know what you want to eat?"

Beth shook her head.

"Please give us a minute."

They cracked open their menus as the server scurried off.

"So how many times?"

"Beth . . ."

"I'm just curious."

He laid down his menu and sighed. "All right, I tried once from the car on the way to the airport but couldn't get a signal, for some stupid reason, but I did get through before boarding. I called again when I got home, because I told her I would, you know, to let her know I'd arrived safe, and that's all."

"What. Nothing today?"

"There's a two-hour time difference. I was out of the apartment early, and

I didn't want to wake her. Listen, one of the reasons that I asked you out today was to help me take my mind *off* how much I miss her. I can't very well do that if you've got me talking about her all the time."

"Well, hell, the only reason I accepted was so I could get a handle on how besotted you really are, and I can't very well do that if you don't talk about her."

"Well then, this is a pretty pointless meeting for both of us."

"No kidding. How's the salmon?"

"Really good the last time I had it."

"Good. I'll have that." She shut the menu and put it to the side. "Mother and Dad are coming."

He dropped his menu in a panic. "What? Here? For lunch?"

"No, you ninny. In a couple of weeks. You know, after 'two weeks Friday'. They want to meet her."

"How exactly did they know when she'd be here?"

She swallowed. "I think they read it in the trades."

"You are a bag." He turned to the flustered and fawning server. "I'll have the swordfish, please, easy on the butter, and my troublemaker of a sister will have the salmon."

"With the potato rather than the salad, please."

The server stammered her thanks then proceeded to break the cork and spill wine on Beth's table setting.

David laughed as he helped mop her up.

"Cheers." Beth said, lifting her glass. "It's always a pleasure going out with you. I either get vilified or christened."

****

The first Friday after David had left, Brett phoned Norah in a panic—the power had gone out at the lumber camp, and they decided to bus the workers into town seven hours early. Brett wouldn't have his staff in place until the dinner rush, but there was guaranteed to be a full house at the café any minute, so could she come in and cover them?

Norah didn't bother to track down Peg since she knew Friday was mahjong day. Instead, she hurried Ella over to her parents'.

Vic and Mona might not have ever been in the running for Parent of the Year awards, but they had—to Norah and Brett's astonishment—morphed into the most nauseatingly doting grandparents this side of, well . . . anywhere. Whenever they were within earshot of Ella, it started—the cooing and the kissy noises and the baby talk. All of which had Norah craving an insulin shot and Brett dry-heaving by the door.

Once she'd thrown Ella in their door, she raced off and pulled up at the rear of the café as the last of the mill crews spilled onto the streets. In the café, it was, as Mona used to put it, a total shitstorm.

The only servers left from that morning were Andrea—a heavily pregnant school chum of Norah's, just weeks away from popping her fifth—and Tina, who had been on the floor since Mona and Vic first started the place. She was scrawny and feisty like a bantam rooster, and twice as mean. In the old days, she constantly had a cigarette hanging from her lips, the ash promising to season whatever she was delivering to the tables. Now, she'd be out back three or four times an hour, having a puff. She'd been encouraged to retire a hundred times, and a hundred times she'd threatened to throw herself in the deep fryer first. She loved her job and swore to keep working or die. Brett figured she'd meet her end when her varicose veins finally exploded through her support hose.

Brett was on the line with Frank Cardinal, a local Metis Indian of few words, with a dry sense of humour, and real finesse with any blade. When Norah came in through the back, he was going through the yams like a chop saw for Brett's special fries, and her brother was doing his weird and wonderful dance between the grill, the fryer, the burners, and the block.

Norah could watch Brett for hours . . . but not today. She was almost knocked over by Tina as she made her way to the front. The woman's hands were loaded down with five plates, and a bottle of ketchup under her arm. Andrea was trying to lean sideways into the deep freeze for the ice cream when Norah smiled and took the scoop off her.

The café sat forty-six, so it could only get *so* busy before they were simply full, and they were all grateful the deck was closed due to rain. Still, every time someone vacated a table, there was another ass in the chair before the tab was paid. The men were rowdy, loud, and looking for a good time. They shouted to each other from across the room, told a variety of off-colour jokes, and frequently tipped over their drinks.

The three women fell into a cooperative rhythm, and after four hours of fairly serious mayhem, it started to peter out as the fellows eschewed their dining experiences for the bar, since beer and the prospect of getting laid were next on the agenda.

The evening staff arrived, and stared wide-eyed at the aftermath before they jumped in, served the remaining tables, cleared the dirty plates, and wiped down the counters.

Andrea was seated at once, her feet put up on a chair, and a hot cup of herbal tea placed into her hand with orders to rest.

Norah was on her knees, restocking the beer cooler, when a pair of worn, orthopedic shoes appeared in her periphery.

"Tina?" Norah asked, as her gaze traveled the scary journey up those marred and scarred legs, perma-stained apron, past the wattle, and to a face with a perennial sneer.

"He's at it again."

"Who? Brett?"

"Yep."

"At what?"

"He ain't feedin' us."

"The hell you say!" Norah was tired, aching, sweaty and, having skipped her lunch to work in this stinking pit, starving. She rose, determined and loaded for bear.

Brett looked braced for the onslaught but, having put out a couple of hundred meals, not about to be pushed around.

"Tina told me the most ridiculous thing," she said with a dangerous smile on her face. "Something about the staff not being served lunch after being hit by the lunch rush from hell, but I told her that wasn't possible because my darling brother, whose ass I just helped pull out of the fire, was not about to let a homicidal senior citizen, a prep cook who could stick him with a paring knife a dozen times and be back on the reserve before his body hit the floor, a woman who is about two hundred weeks' pregnant, and his darling sister go hungry unless he wanted to be fed his own fucking teeth!"

"Frank . . ." Brett never took his eyes off his sister.

"Chop or julienne?"

"Your choice, man."

She turned on her heel and headed back to the cooler. She couldn't remember the last time she'd raised her voice to anyone, let alone Brett, and she was feeling the heat of a couple of dozen eyes on her. The staff and patrons seated at four different tables had been privy to her outburst and watched her closely. She sighed as she realized that she was only at the halfway point before seeing David again, and she had already gone postal.

She wondered, for the hundredth time, what he might be doing right now. It would be evening soon in New York, and according to his phone call last night, they would be setting up for their fifth night shoot. It made keeping in touch difficult since they'd been on set until sunrise. Sometimes he'd call, but with her just waking up and him nearly exhausted, there wasn't much talking. It would be easier when he was back to day shoots since he'd have his evenings free. If he didn't find other things to do.

She imagined him hanging with the friends he'd told her about at a sports bar or a club. She thought of the attention he'd attract by the beautiful east coast women. She thought of them sending over a drink, or asking him for a dance and rubbing up against him . . .

Stop it, Norah. He's in the same relationship you're in, and didn't you just spend the last four hours up to your boobs in men, some of them really attractive, all of them horny as hell? Any one of them would have been only too happy to take you for a spin if you'd done so much as return a smile. But you didn't. And neither would he.

She'd known that she would miss him, but she hadn't been prepared for the physical ache that overtook her every time she thought about him.

One more week. One week from this moment, and you'll have arrived and be on your way to his apartment.

Her tummy flip-flopped, a small smile graced her lips, and she even considered making an apology to Brett.

"Excuse me."

She looked up from the last can of pop to see a couple standing at the counter. "Sorry. May I help you?"

"Two lattes, please." She took their money then turned to the cappuccino machine and started making their drinks. The strong black coffee was filtering through and she was nearly finished steaming the milk, when she turned to ask Andrea a question and in doing so, tipped the milk jug, pouring scalding milk over her right hand.

"Norah!" Andrea cried out, rushing to her side. She helped her set the jug down as carefully as possible to avoid further disaster, then dragged her to the sink. "Here, get that under cold water. I'll finish with their order."

Norah cursed her clumsiness while the water took the edge off the burn. A flash of *déjà vu* hit her full in the face. The memory of Clare and Wayne, that shoot, and those amazing first days—discovering the nuances of the scene, the screwups and ensuing laughter, and the payoff of seeing it in the playback room later, played like its own movie before her eyes.

She stood at the sink in the café her parents had shackled her to, and noticed the sight of her hand cooling under the water was beginning to blur.

"No point crying over steamed milk," Brett said. He'd obviously come up front to see if she was all right and found her weeping . . . again.

"Fuck off." She sniffed.

"The mouth on her."

They chuckled.

She turned off the water and took the towel from him as he led her to the office in the back. It was a dingy little room, not much bigger than a closet, but was brightly lit and painfully organized. She sat behind the desk and reached into one of the drawers for the first aid kit.

"So let me guess. You miss David, and your life here is pointless."

"You forgot the part about how my brother's a bitch and my hand hurts." She applied burn ointment.

"Right. Sorry." He sat across from her, resting his chin in his hand, and studied her. "You can leave, you know."

"I know. They're caught up. I'll pick up Ell—"

"That's not what I meant. I mean you can leave Whitecourt."

"I know. I'm gone in a week."

"Oh, do try and keep up." He sighed and rolled his eyes. "I mean, you can leave Whitecourt, leave the café, for good. Go. Take Ella. Live your life. Be with David, be a movie star, do whatever. Just get out of my hair."

She snorted. "Yeah, right."

"You think you're the only reason this place stays open, don't you?"

"Pretty much, yeah."

"Yeah, well . . . you're probably right, but it's time I figured it out." He got serious, which got her attention. "Norah, I've leaned on you my whole life, and that's not fair. I know my . . . lack of business acumen—"

"You mean your total irresponsible ineptitude?"

He closed his eyes for a moment, pursed his lips, took a dignified sniff, and tried again. "My lack of business acumen has kept you from the life you wanted, took you from Vancouver, all that. I will say that if you hadn't come back, you wouldn't have gotten pregnant with Ella, and you wouldn't have met David, so you're very welcome, by the way. But now all that good stuff is there for you and so . . . you can leave." He dismissed her with a wave.

"Brett, how—"

"It doesn't matter. All that matters is, it doesn't have to be your problem anymore. I'm twenty-seven years old. It's time I stood on my own two feet, don't you think?"

She stared at him, not through the eyes of his big sister—the person who looked out for him and took care of him—but through the eyes of someone who, for his sake if not her own, wanted and needed him to grow up.

"I guess. And by the way, you're thirty-one."

"Shut up."

"You shut up."

"You shut up first."

"Fine."

So much for growing up.

****

The concierge at David's Manhattan condominium held open the door as he left the building with a jaunty, "Good evening, Mr. Raurke."

David grinned and waved in return.

It was Saturday evening, and he was meeting Oliver, Terry, and a few of the other guys at one of their favourite haunts for a steak and some brews, and he was stoked. He'd been hard at it all week. He knew he had some good stuff in the can, but it seemed like such an uphill slog. The crew was much more unionized here, and it made a difference. You'd never see a grip help out set dec or vice versa, so a lot more time was spent waiting for the right person to show just to get a frigging piece of furniture shifted. It was maddening.

Night shoots didn't help the lack of camaraderie. Once they wrapped, everyone headed for bed, so there was no real socializing. Maybe things would brighten when they moved to days, but taking the shoot to the streets was a recipe for aggravation, too—ill-timed car horns, or some jackass waving at the camera, could push even the most patient of men to the edge. But if he had to put it down to one thing, he wasn't having any fun, and that sucked.

He refused to put it all onto Norah. After all, he'd had fun before he met her.

He decided against a cab so he could enjoy a brisk walk, clear his head a little, and put himself in a better mood for tonight. He pulled up his collar, trying to keep the wind off his ears, and wondered if Norah would know to bring warm clothes for her and Ella. He reached into his pocket for his cell and had nearly completed dialing when he heard it.

"David Raurke, as I live and . . . pant."

Holy crap!

"Corrina. Wow. How are you?"

"Better than you remember." Corrina Biblios made a show of pulling him into a firm, lingering hug. Her glossy, heavily tinted lips brushed intentionally against his cheek, and he was reminded of all the shirts he'd had to throw out from lipstick stains permanently embedded in the collars when they'd been together.

He pushed her back with gentle force. "Let me have a look at you."

Good save.

"Stunning as always, Corrina."

It was true. Corrina was tall, leggy, and blessed with the finest traits of her Greek heritage. Her wide eyes were blue as the sea, dark, wavy hair tumbled unrestrained well past her shoulders, and a strong, straight nose sat regally above a full, sensuous mouth.

"Why, thank you," she said. "It's been ages. How long are you in town for?" She ran her tongue across the front of her top teeth, and he remembered how he used to think that was sexy. Now he found it obvious and off-putting.

"I'm shooting for three more weeks and . . ." He could tell she'd tuned him out already as she glanced over his shoulder for . . .

Someone she'd rather fuck. Someone who maybe recognizes her. Someone who might give a shit.

He rambled for a bit and submitted to her irritating scrutiny, all while wishing he had Norah on the phone instead of making small talk with this small mind.

"Well, what are you up to right now?" she asked, cutting him off. "I'd love to catch up, talk about the old times, maybe even relive a moment or two . . ." She leaned closer in a way that she, no doubt, thought was provocative.

"Sorry, I'm meeting up with some friends, doing the guy thing. Maybe some other time, though." He pried her fingers from the lapels of his coat, gave her a polite kiss on the cheek, muttered a quick, "I'll call you," and backed inside the building.

Close one.

He looked at the phone still in his hand and heard his name being called yet again, only this time from far more welcome quarters.

"Peter. Hey, buddy!" He half jogged to meet his friends.

****

Norah and Brett had curled up under cozy blankets with a bowl of popcorn to watch the latest entertainment reports for some shot of Byron Robbins, whose newest flick was hitting theatres and had Brett all aflutter. The breaking story, however, had nothing to do with Byron or his upcoming release. It was a series of shots taken with a telephoto lens from across a busy street in New York City.

David Raurke walking.

David Raurke greeted by Corrina Biblios in what looked like a pair of nine-inch heels.

David and Corrina hugging.

David and Corrina still hugging.

David and Corrina . . . still hugging.

Wow. Would ya look at that.

Talking, smiling, smiling, more smiling.

Corrina hanging off David like a bad smell, and David kissing her.

The shots were enthusiastically expounded on by a sickeningly perky narrator only too thrilled to speculate on old flames rekindled and what a beautiful, glamorous couple they made.

About ten seconds into the broadcast, Norah stopped chewing and just stared.

"You can't be serious." Brett drooped with exasperation.

"Hmm?" she replied, the soggy popcorn in her mouth giving her the impression that all her teeth had gone soft. She reached for her smoothie to wash it down, rather than cause Brett to gag by spitting it into her napkin.

"I mean, obviously it was all her going *yummy, yummy, yummy* and him going *ick, leggo, you skank.*"

"I'm sure you're right." She was sure. He wasn't hugging her back, the kiss was clearly a kiss-off, and he'd told her all she needed to know about his relationship with Corrina. "It's just, you know, so frigging public. Everybody is going to see these bloody pictures and they're all going to wonder and gossip and stir it all up. 'Poor, poor Norah, alone again.' You know? It just pisses me off."

"Once it's out that he's with you, this shit'll stop."

From your mouth to God's ears.

****

Meanwhile, back in New York, David did a little praying of his own. A frantic phone call from Beth had alerted him, and he turned on the television to see photos of him and Corrina on the street the night before plastered across the screen on one of those bullshit entertainment shows.

What to do.

Do I call Norah, give her the heads-up or will that look like I'm trying to cover something? Do I wait for her to call? Should I say that I didn't even give it a second thought? That's the truth of it, after all, but will she see that or will she—oh, for Christ's sake, just call her.

"Hellooo."

"Hey, Brett. It's David."

"Well, hello there. How's our man about town?"

Shit, he saw it.

"Oh, I'm good, I'm good. How are things there?"

"Things are dandy. Norah and I were just enjoying your little photo spread on TV. Quick question. Are your hands really that small, or do they just look that way against the background of Corrina Biblios' ginormous ass?"

David chuckled and scrubbed his hands over his face as his whole body sagged in relief. Brett wouldn't bust his balls unless Norah was all right. "Aw, Brett, I've missed you, I really have. But then my aim's never been great. Could you put her on, please?"

"Coit-inly. Hold, please."

David was shortly treated to a second show when he heard Brett shouting.

"Hey, Norah, honey, it's David on the phone. Put down the rifle and come talk to him, why don' cha? That's a good girl."

Norah was giggling as she took the phone from him. "Hey, handsome."

"Hey yourself, baby. Brett's having a good day."

"Yes, well, nothing like a laugh at someone else's expense to put a spring in his step."

"You're okay though? I mean—"

"David, you're going to run into ex-girlfriends from time to time. It's no biggie."

He wasn't completely convinced. He couldn't help but think that he'd be a bit bent out of shape if the tables had been turned and photos of her getting groped by an ex turned up on network television, but he was proud that she was pushing through it. "Do you have any idea how much I love you?"

"I dunno. You might have to show me when I get there . . . a couple hundred times or so."

"Just five more sleeps, baby, and make sure you do sleep between now and then because I promise, you won't be getting much once you land."

He heard her sigh and hum softly before she asked the one question he'd been asking himself since the day he'd arrived in New York.

"Are we there yet?"

Chapter 19

NORAH ROTHE.

Norah spotted the sign just as she, Ella, and Peg headed toward the baggage carousel. It was held aloft by a large, uniformed fellow with a peaked cap and a large, open face. She was so relived to be back on terra firma that she greeted the man with a big hug.

Roscoe, David Raurke's personal driver, stiffened, likely taken aback by the gesture, but waited Norah out.

Once she released him, she patted his arm and apologized. "Don't mind me. We're Canadian. It's just our way."

His good-natured grin let her know he was game to play along, and he cast a welcoming smile to Aunt Peg.

"Don't get your hopes up," she said, and they all enjoyed a chuckle while he helped collect their suitcases and made their way to the car.

Norah started up a string of chatter on the long drive into the city. Now that her nerves from flying had subsided, her nerves about seeing David again got the best of her.

Peg simply wanted a cup of tea in a chair that wasn't hurtling her through the air, and Ella was a jumble of fatigue, plugged ears, and restlessness.

They pulled up in front of David's building, and Norah's mouth dropped open. He had told her he had an apartment in Manhattan, but for some reason she had pictured a small rustic loft, not this.

The concierge opened the door before the car fully stopped, and Norah carried Ella onto the carpeted walkway under the awning as Roscoe held out a hand for Peg. He told them he would bring the luggage up as soon as he had the car parked, then got back behind the wheel. In the meantime, the doorman showed them inside and, per David's instructions, handed over his suite number and a pass card.

The awestruck trio entered the elevator, which shot them to the ninth floor with lightning speed.

Peg wondered out loud if the world would never settle beneath her and smiled bravely at Norah as she swung open the door to David's suite.

"Jesus, Mary and Joseph . . ." Peg whispered.

Norah could not help but be impressed. From the large, open foyer, the kitchen was to their immediate right and beyond that a dining area with seating for eight at a large square table. To the right of the dining room were double doors that led to what she assumed was the games room that David boasted of. The living area was to the left, with generous seating and the highlight of the apartment—four large-paned windows with a view of the park. The short hallway directly in front of them likely led to the sleeping quarters.

Norah wandered slowly about the living space and took it all in. She smiled at a framed photo of David, Norah, and Ella that had been taken at the Whitecourt set—Norah sitting on a fence and David, with Ella happily on his shoulders, leaning his elbows on it next to her. All looking in the same direction and smiling broadly.

What a nice looking family.

There were other photos of people she didn't know but was sure she'd heard of. There were several of Ella scattered here and there, and on his desk near the first window, a close-up shot of Norah alone, eyes slightly lowered and giving the appearance of gentle reflection. She couldn't remember when the picture had been taken. It was quite lovely, and it touched her that he chose to have it here where he would see it so often.

Peg called out, "Do you think he'd mind if I made us a cup?"

Norah smiled again, ran her finger along the top of his desk and then crossed to the kitchen to join her.

"When I spoke to him last night, he said to make sure we make ourselves at home. Apparently, Ruby—she's the housekeeper—is visiting her niece who's just had a baby, otherwise she'd be here to greet us."

The two women dug around searching for a kettle or some such, as Roscoe came in with the bags on a rolling rack. He pointed out a nifty gadget situated next to the stove that dispensed boiling hot water with the press of a button, and then showed them where David kept the tea things.

Leaving Peg to it, Norah scooped up Ella, who was in need of a change, grabbed one of the carry-on bags, and followed Roscoe and the luggage down the hall.

Their first stop was a smaller guestroom on the right. Norah pointed out Peg's bags and they moved across the hall to a very small room that David had set up with a toddler-sized bed, a small chest of drawers, a nightstand with a lamp, and an activities table with all manner of blocks, train tracks, and drawing implements.

Norah smiled, delighted at the obvious trouble he'd gone to in order to make Ella feel comfortable for two short weeks. Delighted, but not surprised.

Roscoe set down Ella's belongings and told Norah he'd take the remaining cases to the master suite at the end of the hall.

She thanked him and then got on with the business at hand. Once Ella had been freshened up and was making herself busy with her new toys, Norah ventured down the hall.

His bedroom was pure David. A heavy, king-sized mission-style bed dominated the room. Beautiful lamps with solid amber shades promised a warm glow from the bedside tables, and a soft brown leather sofa in sat invitingly in a corner. The bric-a-brac and art work from local craftsmen of the countries he'd visited during his career were scattered on shelves and hanging on walls. Each one carried a story behind its acquisition, she was sure. He had sweetly labeled *His* and *Hers* on alternating drawers of the massive mule chest sitting against the wall.

Another photograph of Norah held a place of honour on the bedside table. This one she remembered him taking in Vancouver. She had on the cashmere robe, which had slipped off one shoulder, and she was looking at the camera dreamily. He would see it before turning out the lights every night, and she held her hands over her heart to keep it from bursting out of her chest.

Once she'd unpacked, she reentered the common area and was pleased to see Peg nesting contentedly in one of the oversized armchairs, sipping her tea. She entered the kitchen where her own tea was cooling and investigated possibilities for dinner.

Roscoe was seated at the island and explained to Norah about the location where *Kosma* was currently shooting. Since he liked to be early, he would leave as soon as he'd finished the mug of tea Peg had poured for him.

Norah was in the middle of preparing him a sandwich to take with him, under his halfhearted protests, when his cell phone rang.

"Roscoe here . . . yes, sir, Mr. Raurke."

Norah looked up with a smile.

"Yes, we arrived about a half hour ago. All settled in. Yes, sir . . . oh, I see . . . yeah . . . yeah, I can do that. Should I put her on the line? She's right here."

Norah had become concerned by his demeanor. "Hello, David?"

"Hello, my love. How was the flight?"

"Stupid question, David." Norah hated flying with a passion.

"Right, sorry. Welcome to New York, honey."

"Thanks. It's pretty great to be here. Is there something wrong?"

"Just that it looks like the day could run longer than we thought. Naturally. We did such a great job of it earlier today that it only made sense to shoot one of tomorrow's scenes. The upside being that we'll be even further ahead, but it'll mean not wrapping until around ten or so tonight."

"Oh well. Obviously, I'll wait up."

Despite orders, she hadn't gotten a great deal of sleep since they'd spoken last Sunday. What with studying her lines, worrying about the flight, and fantasizing about seeing him again, she hadn't slept five hours a night, and now that they'd finally gotten here, she was weaving with relief and fatigue. What little adrenaline she had left was fizzling, and she was concerned that her lover was going to come upon her snoring away in a chair.

"Well, I was thinking maybe Roscoe could drive you out here now. You could watch the shoot, meet the new crew, hang with Judy, that sort of thing. That way at least, I can have you in my arms within the next hour, and maybe we can make out in the car on the way back home."

I'm awake.

"Perfect. I'll change my clothes, get Ella settled with Peg, and then Roscoe and I will be on our way."

"I can't wait."

"Me, too." She handed the phone back to Roscoe and ran for the bedroom. "Peg?" she called out.

"Of course, I don't mind, dear. You run off. Ella and I will have us some supper and very likely be asleep before we've finished it."

"Bless your heart. Roscoe, give me five minutes."

****

Kosma shot in a number of areas within New York where the real Kosma's crime spree had cut a swath of terror in the mid-eighties. The two-month shoot in Whitecourt had saved the production millions of dollars, allowing these location shots, which authenticated the picture and would give it a genuine flavour. The area they headed to was in a field near New Jersey, with the Hudson River in the background and the always-recognizable Manhattan skyline in the distance. Visual effects would make the adjustments for changes to it in the last quarter century or so, deleting the buildings that had gone up since then and poignantly recreating those that had come down.

Roscoe parked on the far side of the circus. Norah's excitement and enthusiasm had kept him in stiches the whole drive in. She was practically airborne as he led her across the compound but they were forced to stop a half dozen times by familiar faces greeting her with hugs and friendly hellos. She engaged everyone with a bit of a chat but was squirming with impatience to get on her way, and Roscoe couldn't suppress yet another chuckle as he watched her.

As they entered the fringe of the shot, a PA signaled for them to stop as the cameras were rolling.

Norah was able to make out Keith operating the steady cam as one of Kosma's victims tried to flee from her attacker. She caught a glimpse of David standing near the camera to give the actress a focal reference, and her heart hammered.

He called cut and turned, checking the crowd behind him as she imagined he'd done at the end of every take for the last half hour.

She brushed past the PA and strode toward him.

David froze where he was, his eyes locked on her, and a warm smile spreading across his face.

She was semi-aware of ribs being nudged, whispers, and meaningful glances exchanged among the crew.

David Raurke's girlfriend was on set.

David crossed the last dozen paces and pulled her forcefully to him, nearly crushing her. She made no protest as her arms went around him and her fingers tangled deep in his hair.

She half laughed, half cried into his neck, her feet dangling above the ground as he held her viselike against his body.

"Oh, Norah, Norah, Norah . . ." he murmured close to her cheek, lowering her to the ground.

He didn't release her, nor did she loosen her hold on him. They never considered the idea of separating, even for a second. Without being conscious of it, or of the stir they were creating, they stood locked in their embrace for several minutes. They didn't even kiss but began to sway back and forth ever so slightly instead, almost creating a bookend to their dance at the wrap party two weeks ago.

Has it really only been two weeks?

Norah brushed her lips against his ear and felt the shivers pass through him.

"Stop that, or I'll take you right here in the grass," he whispered.

She giggled and resisted the urge to move her hips across his.

They broke apart slowly and reluctantly with deep sighs.

He took her face in his hands and gazed at her eyes. "Did you miss me?" he asked.

"Meh, you know," she answered nonchalantly with a shrug.

There was a bit of restlessness around them, and they became acutely aware they were holding things up.

"Let me get this shot in the can, then we can grab a coffee."

"Is that what we're calling it now?" she asked.

He laughed and walked her to the chairs with his arm about her waist.

****

David glanced to the clock on the bedside table. It was after one, and Norah was out like a light already. Their reunion lovemaking—wicked in its intensity—had sapped her last ounce of strength. He smiled, happy in the knowledge that they had many, many nights of long, lingering loving ahead of them.

He watched her sleeping form. He lifted a strand of hair off her cheek and laid it to the side, his tenderness for her filling him. The light from the window cast a soft glow across her, and he discovered, to his amazement, that he wanted her again.

Let the poor woman sleep, David.

He flopped on his back and tried to will himself to relax and drift off but it was no use, and he reassumed his vantage point, unable to keep his eyes off her.

The covers rose and fell across her chest with her breathing, and he was hypnotized by the rhythmic movement. Without conscious thought, he drew the sheet down to her waist so he could feast his eyes upon her naked breasts. He recalled their incredible softness, then—unable to resist their allure—traced their outline with a featherlight touch. He watched as goose flesh appeared, and he slowly swirled a finger around the peaks, fascinated by the quick hardening of each sweet bud. Before he could stop himself, he lowered his head until his lips were close enough to kiss one, his tongue moving in tiny, gentle rings around it.

A small sigh escaped her in her slumber, and it excited him beyond measure.

His hand circled her silken stomach many times before desire overcame him, and he ventured lower. The juices of their last joining still clung to her and allowed his fingers to slip easily in and around her velvety folds, and he permitted himself a long, leisurely exploration of her.

A low moan of pleasure came from far inside her, and she stirred, moving instinctively with his touch.

His want of her drove him mad and he lured her into a deep kiss, and her tongue moved dreamily in his mouth.

She gasped, her voice drowsy and low. "David, what are you doing?"

"I'm sorry, baby, I can't help it." He moaned against her throat as his lips tasted her skin. "I need you. I need you so much."

She rolled lazily toward him as if in a dream. She slid her leg up and around his hips and her hand crept along his chest to his firm abdomen and further until her fingers enclosed around him, rock hard and straining toward her. She then moved the sensitive tip along her vulva, rubbing it slowly front to back over and over again until he begged her to stop. Relenting, she guided him at last to her welcoming entrance.

Engorged to bursting, he plunged inside her, and they both cried out. She moved with him, hastening the ache that built in his loins. He struggled for a slower tempo, desperate to prolong the ecstasy, to stave off his release, and savour the perfection of this embrace. Somewhere in his conscious brain, he sensed her resisting his languid pace, and they engaged in an erotic battle of sensual lingering versus a hot, pounding fuck. Just as he thought he had her on the ropes, she put her luscious mouth against his ear.

"David, I want you to listen closely." With wantonness he didn't know she was capable of, she regaled him with a torrent of vividly suggestive phrases, detailed carnal demands, and sexually explicit imagery bordering on depraved.

His facial expression went from shock to stunned to weakened resistance to complete surrender.

Within mere moments, they lay entwined and slack with exertion.

"Where in the hell did you learn to talk like that?" he asked between his gasps.

"Have I bruised your delicate sensibilities?"

"No, I-I never imagined. I mean, you never have before, at least not . . . nothing like that."

"Yeah, I've had a lot of time on my hands thinking about you the past two weeks."

"Really? Cool."

"I'm glad you liked it."

"I did, believe me. But tell me, do you think we'd need a real motorcycle for that one thing or could you just use a chair?"

****

Norah waited at her first position for the next shot. Back in her grubby, oversized jeans, steel-toed boots, and her old friend, the flannel overshirt, she felt right at home.

They were filming in the New York Naval Shipyards in Brooklyn, near the Battery. It was the stand-in for Todd's Shipyard in New York, which had been torn down in 2006 and replaced, oddly enough, with an IKEA.

She stood at the foot of the stairs leading off one of the loading docks, kicking her feet together to ward off the nip in the air. In front of her was the Hudson River, busy with cheerfully lit boats chugging up and down its grimy length. There was little foot traffic at this hour but what was there was held in check by roadblocks on both sides of the dock, manned by PAs as well as city police for extra security.

Norah breathed deep the smells of this city. Granted, she wasn't in the most savoury neighbourhood, and her deep inhalation was rewarded with the stench of raw and rotting fish, burning crank case oil, and urine, but she couldn't have been happier.

She was within spitting distance of a city she'd dreamed of visiting her whole life, and she was shooting a film!

And then, there was him.

He sat in his chair and signaled an AD, consulted with Judy, and crossed to Jozef, who was yelling at a grip about where to refocus a lamp. He returned to his chair but was back up a half second later to check in with Grace, got partway back before he turned on his heel, and bounded off in another direction.

She watched his frenetic movements with amusement and pride. Every so often he'd look in her direction and they'd share a smile before they went back to what they'd been doing.

Yep, life is pretty darn good.

The new crew had been a bit cooler than the one back home, but they were professional toward her and she with them. She saw what David had meant in his phone calls—this lot wasn't nearly the fun the other had been, but it didn't matter; the department heads were still in the mix, having a laugh and keeping things running.

Bernice, her stand-in, had run the blocking for her earlier, but when it came time for Norah to rehearse the walk, Jozef hadn't been satisfied with the shadows and wanted to rehang a couple of lights.

Norah toyed with the idea of keeping warm in her trailer but was so pumped up just being there that she decided to tough it out.

Jason jogged up a moment later. "Hey, Norah."

"Hey, Jason. Are we nearly there?"

"Nearly. Can I bring you a cup of tea?"

"That would be lovely, thank you. Just su—"

"Sugar, I know." He grinned and ran toward a tent.

She smiled, not at all surprised that among the million details that boy kept crammed in his head, how she took her tea was one of them.

"Finals," Grace called out. She used her outside voice since she didn't care for bullhorns and she needed to cover a lot of ground. The location was a full city block wide with four-story warehouses on one side and the river to their backs.

Amanda, the on-set hairdresser, and Everett, from makeup, swarmed around her.

She climbed up to the top of the stairs in order to get a continuous run at it, waited through the rolling sequence, heard David call background to action and then cue her.

"Norah, action."

Clare clumps down the stairs, fastening her flannel shirt up to her chin before yanking her gloves out of her pocket and jamming her hands into them. She turns, as she has a thousand times before, and proceeds briskly along her route. She reaches the corner in under a minute and makes another left turn.

"Cut. Print that, I guess."

"One more time, boss?" Norah requested, as she returned from around the corner.

"Do you need it?"

"I dunno. I don't think . . . didn't feel right."

"Okay, back to firsts everyone. Let's take one more for good measure."

They recreated everything, only this time Norah let Clare's moroseness sink in a bit deeper. Though subtle, the result was a much clearer picture of who Clare was. A stranger passing her in the street wouldn't have given her a second glance. Someone walking behind her might have wondered if she was someone who'd been beaten down a time or two . . . or ten.

****

"Cut. Print that one for sure. When she's right, she's right. Check the gate, please." David crossed the street to meet Norah as she reemerged from around the corner.

"Gate's clean!"

Grace called for the next set up.

It would be at least an hour before they'd be shooting again, so the couple planned on grabbing a hot drink and hanging in Norah's trailer until needed.

"Sorry about that," she said to David, as Jason walked up with a cup of tea. "Thanks, J. I should have got that the first time."

"Honey, we scheduled twenty minutes for that shot and you got it in about five. I wouldn't worry about it." He grabbed a coffee off the craft services table, and they weaved hand in hand around the grips carts, props wagon, and dresser dollies, before a less than discreet conversation stopped them dead in their tracks.

"I only took this job because I'd heard he was directing. I thought I'd at least get a chance to blow him or something. What the hell he's doing with that little troll is beyond me."

It was followed by a couple of nonspecific grunts.

Norah had no idea what to do.

Evidently, David did. He dropped her hand and stepped around the trailer, his jaw tight with rage, and found Norah's stand-in holding court with a couple of the female grips and, whether she knew it or not, kissing her career goodbye.

Their faces blanched when they saw him, but the grips had the good sense to beat it around the other side. The offender was frozen where she stood.

"Bernice, isn't it?"

"Uh, yeah."

"Aren't you supposed to be on set now?"

"Right." She stomped out her cigarette. "I was having a quick—"

"Before you go, let me try to explain something to you, even though I expect you're too thick to comprehend it."

Her eyes widened.

"First, I don't know where you get the gall to imagine I'd let you within a hundred feet of me. I can only hope that before I reached that level of desperation, someone would be compassionate enough to shoot me."

Norah had stayed where he'd abandoned her, out of eyeshot but not out of earshot. She winced at David's words.

"Second, and this is the part that I doubt you have the brains to grasp, but I'll let you in on it anyway. Call her whatever your ego needs to make you feel better about yourself, but if you'd spent just five minutes of your bitter life talking to Norah you'd understand exactly why I'm with her and maybe be moved to do something about your own existence."

Bernice stared, blinking at her shoes.

He tossed his head, indicating she should get back on the set.

She started to make her way past him, but his voice stopped her once again.

"Don't come back tomorrow."

She drooped and slinked around the corner, only to come face-to-face with Norah.

It made an interesting picture, as they were identical height, hair colour and length, and dressed exactly the same. Bernice blushed into her hairline and dropped her head, bracing for the onslaught that never came.

"Come back tomorrow, Bernice." Norah's wasn't unfriendly, but firm.

The woman's head shot up.

David came around the corner having heard the exchange. "Norah, what are you doing? She's not coming back."

"Yes, she is. Bernice, get to set. Quickly, they're waiting."

"No, she's not."

Bernice looked back and forth between them like a spectator at a tennis match, clearly unsure which way to turn.

Norah put a hand on her shoulder and lightly shoved her in the direction of the set. "Go. It's all right."

Bernice fled toward the set, and Norah strode past David in the direction of her trailer. She'd made it almost ten feet before she heard his footsteps hard behind her.

"What the hell, Norah?"

"Not here, David."

"Fine."

They reached her door, and he held it open for her before swinging himself in.

She unsnapped her flannel top in one quick movement and began untying her heavy boots.

David stood with his hands on his hips, apparently awaiting her explanation.

She sat in a chair to pry off the footwear and finally met his eyes. She made no attempt to conceal her barely contained temper.

"Listen. You've got no business being pissed at me," he declared with, what rightly enough, was a pretty good defense. "I get to fire people, Norah, I'm the director."

"Then behave like one."

"I beg your pardon?" David's jaw dropped.

"You didn't fire her as the director, David, you fired her as my boyfriend. You can't do that."

"She . . . she behaved inappropriately toward one of my actors, that's—"

"Then write her up. Report her to her union. You can't fire someone for being a bitch. There wouldn't be a soul left on a soundstage . . . anywhere!" She had him there. She threw her boots by the door and flung herself down onto the sofa.

He ran a hand roughly through his hair, a gesture she'd come to know meant he was confounded by something. After a minute, he lowered himself into the armchair across from her. "All right, you're right. I'm sorry."

"Good."

There was a long, painful pause in which neither spoke.

Norah blatantly avoided his gaze and slumped deeper in her seat.

"You're still mad at me. Why are you still mad at me?"

"Because, David, you can't . . ." She struggled for the words to describe her feelings. "You said it yourself. People are going to say things to me—*about* me—horrible things. Are you going to keep attacking people on my behalf? Do you think that's actually going to make them think, *gosh, she must be really swell after all?*"

"No, but . . . I can't just stand there and let—"

"You have to. Don't you? Isn't that what you said, that I have to handle it, not you?"

"Yes, I know. I did say that."

"So?"

"So . . . I didn't love you then."

She looked at him, sitting there so crestfallen, and crossed to sit on the coffee table in front of him. She pulled his hands onto her lap then lifted his face to hers. "I love you, David, and I'm not ashamed to say that what happened tonight upset me. I love you enough to face it when it happens again, but you have to have faith in me to stand up to it on my own."

"Why do you have to do it on your own if we're together? Do you actually expect me to stand back and—"

"If they're ever going to respect me, isn't that exactly what you have to do?"

"Maybe." He sighed. "I can't promise I can do it, though."

"Can you promise to try?"

He nodded slowly. "I can promise to try."

She crawled onto his lap and his arms reached hungrily for her.

They sat for a long time as their breathing synced up and everything else fell into place.

****

"Who all is going to be there?" she asked as she flattened the fabric of her linen pants over her backside and checked her reflection in the mirror again.

David drifted into frame and helped her with her efforts. "Um, Carol and Ben—"

"That's Carol James, right?"

"Right, and Ben is her crazy stuntman husband. Then there will be Terry—"

"Terry Micks? Jesus, really?"

"And whoever he's dating at the moment. My buddy, Oliver—"

"I remember you telling me about him."

"And his wife, Kate. Mike and Cora, I've known them since high school. And, of course, my sister, Beth, and her husband, Richard."

Talk about a trial by fire.

Tonight she would be introduced to David's people, or a faction of them, anyway. A cornucopia of the very famous, the sort-of famous, and the never-want-to-be famous. All of them he'd known for years, all of them totally devoted to him, and all of them eagerly awaiting the arrival of the woman he'd been seeing.

She wasn't worried about meeting the men. Men, she never had any trouble with. In fact, she had hoped that she'd be doing this over a friendly game of poker and bullshitting through a fog of cigar smoke and beer foam. At least that way she could have been stuffed into a pair of comfy pants and a T-shirt rather than making herself nuts over which blouse to wear with which earrings.

David, on the other hand, had very likely grabbed whatever was on the closet floor from last week and still managed to look devastating.

He can really piss a girl off sometimes.

She knew it was the thought of facing the women that made her want to throw something. She knew they'd be giving her the once-, twice-, and thrice-over, checking for flaws, chinks in armor, hidden agendas, any sign of weakness or inadequacy. But she knew how important this was to him so she was determined to give it her best effort.

"You look perfect," David said, using the voice that one reserves for people on ledges and the very insane. "They're going to love you."

****

And indeed they did.

The dinner party had been held at Carol and Ben's condo, which was just across the park from David's. Roscoe had been given the night off so they'd taken a cab there, and Beth and Richard drove them back at the end of the evening, with promises between Beth and Norah to get together later in the week.

Norah had to admit, her nerves had been unwarranted in the end. She had been met with graciousness and friendly smiles, even from the ladies who were delighted that their darling David had finally met someone with a brain in her head, a clever quip on her tongue, and appeared to be able to keep him in line while still loving him to bits. They had dealt with one pointless woman after another and were uniformly convinced that this one was a keeper.

There had been stimulating conversation all through dinner, sprinkled with often-told tales of David's mishaps and misadventures that had brought on gales of laughter. Norah had contributed a lively yarn or two of her own, bringing the house down with the retelling of her and Brett's rescue mission to save her journal from David's evil clutches. She smiled again at the memory.

****

David couldn't have been more pleased with the evening. Everyone had been great. Word had obviously gotten around that he had found someone pretty special, and it pleased David to see how ready his friends were to accept Norah, based on nothing more than that she made him happy. Once Norah had loosened up and realized it wasn't the Spanish Inquisition, she had been her charming, funny, delightful self.

He had watched their faces closely as Norah had spoken, and had been thrilled by their reception of her—Beth especially, who had caught David's eye and smiled at him with a barely perceivable nod.

She approved.

"Did you have a nice time?" David asked as he held the covers back for Norah to slide in beside him.

She cuddled close, rubbing her cheek against his shoulder. "I had a lovely time. You?"

He held her tightly, a foolish smile pasted on his face. "I was so proud of you I thought I would burst. That was a pretty tough crowd you came up against, you know."

"I liked them very much."

"And they liked you."

"What if they hadn't?" She asked after a long moment of silence during which he'd nearly drifted off.

"Hmm?" he mumbled, as he had nearly drifted off.

"What if they hadn't liked me?"

"They did like you."

"But what if they didn't?"

"I would have had to dump you."

"David!"

"I wouldn't want to, honey, but there are ten of them, and only one of you."

"You know, Mike told me that if you gave me any trouble, I was to let him know, and he'd rough you up for me."

David laughed, having no trouble imagining his ham-fisted friend saying just that. "Yeah, well, you can tell Mike that I happen to know you like the trouble I give you." He rolled on top of her and pinned her to the mattress. "And if anybody's going to get roughed up, it's going to be you."

She giggled then put on her best Brooklyn accent as she pulled off a pretty fair imitation of David's buddy. "Yeah, well, you talk tough, you douchebag, take-it-up-d'ass, bastad, but I'm wondrin' if ya got d'balls t' deliver."

David chuckled, took her hand, which he had been detaining on her pillow, and placed it on the area in question, causing Norah to laugh uproariously.

"You tell me, baby. You tell me."

Chapter 20

On Saturday, David declared that he would be taking advantage of his star status by bringing the whole of his management team into their offices on a weekend.

The receptionist, Giselle, highly professional and highly polished, greeted them with an equally polished smile.

"Good morning, Mr. Raurke. What a pleasure to see you again. Mr. Coombs is waiting for you and Miss Rothe in his office. May I offer you a beverage?"

"Thank you, Giselle, no. But if you could do me a favor?"

"Certainly, I'd be delighted."

"I'd love to take Norah to The Loeb Boathouse for lunch. Could I ask you to reserve a table for us, please? With a lake view, if possible."

"Oh, I'm sure for you it will be no problem."

"That's the thing. Could you make it under another name? We'd rather not take the chance of being interrupted if we can avoid it."

"Very good. I'll make it under Mr. Coombs' name, shall I?"

"Perfect, Giselle. I appreciate it."

"Think nothing of it." She was dialing before they disappeared behind the double oak doors.

Norah swallowed her inappropriate compulsion to giggle and took everything in.

Walls of glass and cherry wood panels surrounded them, as did the team—a good half dozen people ranging from early twenties to midforties, immaculately coiffed and manicured, all suited, bespectacled, and bathed in the very finest names in designer fashion. A formidable group, to say the least.

Then there was Nigel, president and CEO of this, one of the most powerful and influential talent agencies in the world. Its clientele were the *crème de la crème* of the entertainment industry, from actors, to pop stars, to fashion models. Being represented by Coombs Elite was a sure sign you were either on your way up or already there.

The Wrong Woman

The man himself was more than a figurehead. He stood six-and-a-half feet tall, was lean of frame and long of limb. One might even say lanky, but never to his face. He had a thick mane of silver hair, which was worn long with Samson-like vanity. His suit was a perfect cut of Italian silk in a shade just this side of black, a midnight blue kerchief—the mate to his neck tie—peeking from the breast pocket. One might guess he was in his fifties, but he had a light in his ice blue eyes that sparkled with a kind of ageless vigor. His face was long, like the rest of him, but with an undisputed sensual attractiveness.

He was reclined in a Corbusier armchair, one endless leg crossed over the other. When his guests of honour entered, he unfolded with graceful ease to greet them, his thin lips curled into a smile, revealing too white, too even teeth.

"My dear, David," he said, his smooth voice stubbornly retaining the upper-crust British accent of his youth. He clasped David in a handshake with a hug, then stepped back as if taking inventory. "I believe you've gotten even more handsome, though I would never have thought it possible. And this . . ." He turned to Norah, who, with some effort, stifled the urge to slip behind a piece of furniture. ". . . must be the reason. Norah, Norah Rothe, how wonderful." He had gripped her by her shoulders, surveying her from head to toe, like something he was considering trying on. "David has told me so much about you. I can't tell you how pleased I am to finally have the honour. Our little group has been simply abuzz since news of you reached us. We've all been left wondering about the ingenious lady who finally snared the elusive David Raurke."

Am I supposed to thank him? He makes me sound like a scheming little floozy.

She glanced at David, who was kicking the rug with the toe of his shoe, embarrassed, as though he'd exposed her to an overly exuberant uncle. She settled for civility in the end.

"Well, I'm happy to meet you, too."

"Allow me to introduce you." He guided her to the ensemble, each standing in turn to shake her hand as their names and job descriptions were announced.

Elegant yet guarded smiles bid her well, but she was glaringly aware of each of their eyes raking their individual paths over her as she passed from one to the next, and felt like the mouse in the snake pit.

Primary among the team was Jasline, an immaculate-looking image consultant, and Antony and Laurence, the head publicists. The rest had titles and designations that Norah had never heard of, but she was led to believe that if she was very lucky, they were the people in whose hands would lay her hopes and dreams.

"Won't you please sit? Did Giselle offer you a drink?"

"Yes, thanks, we're fine." David led Norah to a space on the couch that had been eagerly vacated by two of the lesser echelon, and sat beside her, taking her hand for support. "I've briefed Norah on your reason for wanting to meet with her, beyond trying to spin the fallout from when . . . well, the shit hits the fan."

"Yes, yes. All the unpleasantness with the press." Nigel had coiled himself back into his chair and was piercing what little calm she had left with his unrelenting stare. "Pardon my . . . scrutiny, my dear. It is an unfortunate side effect of my profession. I must, you see, assess a potential client's qualities—their attributes, their flaws, work with what they have, develop what they need, and eliminate what they don't."

Something about that last bit sent a chill down her spine, but she pushed it aside before she could dwell on it.

"I mean, you should have seen our David here when I first took him on. Sideburns, my dear. They looked like small, hairy, trouser legs clinging to his face."

The room chuckled amicably, and even David laughed, blushing slightly at the memory.

"Sideburns?" Norah smiled and fixed him with a dubious grin.

"Oh yeah, baby. They were the cat's ass. I'm thinking of growing them back."

"You do that."

They both knew full well he'd wake up in the middle of the night with a razor at his jaw.

Nigel returned order to the room. "Anyway, as you can see, he turned out quite nice in the end."

An uneasy quiet descended.

Norah looked to each person in the room, and it became very clear the purpose of this meeting and the principal question on everyone's lips. "But what on earth are you going to do with me?"

David turned slowly toward her.

Her tone was low and detached. She wasn't so much asking a question as speaking the mind of the mob.

Nigel's slow smile stretched the width of his face. "David said you were bright."

"What's going on?" David asked, sounding like the guy who didn't get the punch line to a joke.

"Everything's fine, honey. I present a slightly bigger challenge than they had anticipated. Don't I, Mr. Coombs?"

"Nigel, darling. You must call me Nigel. We're all friends here, and as friends, we must be honest with each other. It's true, you might not be exactly what we expected, but tell me, my dear, do we look like we're not up for a challenge?"

She scanned the faces raptly staring back at her. "No, I'd have to say this lot could manage anything."

"But how about you? How will you . . . manage?"

"Try me." She had no idea where she got the nerve to talk to him like that, but she felt as though she stared down the barrel of a gun and could either beg for her life or coerce the shooter to turn the weapon over. She didn't like the feel of the first choice, and as much as anything, she had to prove to David that she was up for a fight.

Nigel's smile dissipated a fraction. "Do you know what you'll be coming up against?"

"I have a small idea."

"Do you know what the public will do to you once your relationship becomes common knowledge?"

"They're going to eat me alive." She stated it simply and without reserve.

Nigel's smile broadened again. "Do you trust me?"

Now, there's a tough one.

Every instinct she had about this guy told her he was bad news.

But . . .

She glanced at David, who hadn't taken his eyes off her since this exchange began. "David trusts you."

"And that's good enough for you?"

"That's right."

Nigel studied her, unblinking. "Very well. Ladies and gentlemen, where do we begin?"

Norah permitted herself to breathe again.

David sat back and stared at her, something incomprehensible in his eyes.

Had she overstepped? Had she sounded arrogant? Presumptuous? Was he ever going to stop looking at her as if he couldn't remember her name? Then a smile touched the corners of his mouth and spread across his handsome face, and his eyes filled with a kind of wonder as he reached for her hand and brought it to his lips.

I think I might have passed!

Jasline eyed Norah while consulting her notes, and was onto her third recommended cosmetic procedure when Norah interrupted.

"I'm sorry. I respect what you're trying to do here, and I appreciate your efforts, I really do, but let me get a couple of things out of the way here. I haven't any false modesty nor am I self-deprecating. I know exactly what I look like. I have no desire to make your job any harder than it already is, but I need you to know my boundaries. You may pluck, cut, colour, exfoliate, paint, and polish me. You can bend me, stretch me, send me to yoga, or Pilates camp. I'll take voice lessons, dance lessons, etiquette lessons or . . . whatever the hell. What is *not* going to happen, however, is there will be no surgeries, no needles, no suction, no implants, no . . . none of that crap. I realize that may put a damper on your game plan." She singled out Jasline, who looked stricken. "But look at it this way, anybody can make Corrina Biblios look good." She felt David stiffen, and she gestured to herself as a whole. "But make this red-carpet-worthy, *then* you can call yourself an artist."

There was a moment of deafening silence, and then the room erupted in a flurry of ideas and strategies.

Jasline permitted an actual smile to grace her polished features, then started speaking intensely and perhaps even a little enthusiastically with her colleagues.

David reached over and ran his hand through Norah's hair.

She met his eyes for a moment before she stole a glance at Nigel, and she caught the briefest glimpse of . . . something in his expression, before his classic charming smile fell into place. She grabbed on to David's hand, held tight, and hoped she was wrong.

****

She followed David out of the main entrance of Loeb's, filled to bursting with a splendid lunch. From the moment they had arrived and she had spied the beautiful flowered terrace reflected in the lake, she had been giddy with excitement. She couldn't stop staring out the window.

He couldn't stop staring at her.

They'd taken their time, held hands, and savoured every morsel from appetizer to dessert. Their conversation had been relaxed, full of laughter and plans for the rest of the weekend. As they had drained the last of their coffee, their most immediate plan was to sneak back to his apartment for a few leisurely hours in bed.

They had sent Roscoe on his way, after he'd dropped them off at the restaurant, so had planned on a happy stroll home through the park. The weather was crisp but manageable, and they had just finished fastening up their jackets when all at once they were set upon. No less than three dozen members of the press descended on them like a tidal wave and surrounded them, expertly cutting off any route for escape.

There was nowhere to look where the bursts of light didn't blind them. Nowhere to turn where a microphone wasn't shoved in their faces and questions were hurled at them from every quarter, ranging from typical inquiries to coarse and derogatory cross-examinations.

"David! Is it serious?"

"Have you been seeing each other long?"

"What will your fans think of you taking yourself off the market?"

"What's her name, David?"

"How do you think this will affect your box office sales?"

David, one arm around Norah, turned them back toward the restaurant but that way was solidly blocked. He thought to redirect them through the throng toward East Drive, when he recalled there was no vehicle traffic allowed through the park on weekends. He tried to placate the horde with a smile and a series of brief answers to the more benign questions. "We're very happy. We met several months ago . . . on set. Her name is Norah Rothe, Norah with an *H* and Rothe with an *E*. You'll want to remember that, she's a great talent. Just wait until the picture is released in the spring . . ."

Norah held on to him while David tried to shield her from the worst of it, as he kept his own rising panic under control.

He spotted the Boathouse shuttle. The driver had apparently watched the onslaught and stood on the running board, waving them over. Without tipping his hand, David sent a quick nod to the driver and subtly redirected Norah in his direction.

She was white with fear.

The din as each reporter tried to be heard over the other was dizzying. Most of the questions were unintelligible but the more malignant ones began filtering through.

"So, David, this could mean an end to your career. Is the sex worth losing everything over?"

"Yeah, David. We've never heard of her. Exactly what did she do for the role?"

Norah spun out of David's grasp and turned on the reporter, causing renewed interest on the part of the paparazzi. She could barely focus on her verbal attacker with the flashes going off at such a sickening rate. "What the hell kind of a question is that? You don't know me, and you haven't any business saying something like that."

"Do you really think anyone's going to care if you're a big deal on screen? The only thing anyone will know is you're the broad fucking David Raurke."

"You miserable little scum-sucking—"

Norah started to charge him, but David grabbed her by the elbows from behind and physically restrained her, all but dragging her toward the shuttle, which had cut a slow path through the melee, nudging the more belligerent members of the press out of the way,

"Norah, let's go." His command came through gritted teeth.

"Do you kiss your daughter with that mouth?" came a female voice from the swarm.

She broke free of David's grasp and turned on them again, her face flushed with rage, the cameras going off so often it was nearly a steady stream of brilliant white light.

"Norah, now!"

The van pulled up, and David managed to get the door open and literally threw her inside before he jumped in and slammed it behind them.

The driver inched along with determination and plenty of horn until he had them at last on the Drive.

David was generous with his gratitude and his wallet, then gave his address before he lapsed into a monstrous silence.

****

Norah shivered on her side of the backseat, the twelve minute drive seeming to last an hour. She stared out, unseeing, and tried to quell the pounding in her chest and her head. She felt the fury emanating from the man beside her and was certain that his temper was fixed on her. For him to be angry at her after what had just happened was unfathomable.

At long last, the cab drew up to David's building and, without waiting, she threw open the door and stormed past the doorman.

David caught up to her at the elevator, and once they were shut inside, he turned on her. "What the fuck was that, Norah?"

"David." She tried to force some measure of calm into the bedlam.

"What did you think you were going to accomplish—"

"—please don't yell at—"

"—behaving like some hooligan—"

"—me. You're on me about my—"

"—where was your head? They're going to have a—"

"—behavior? Where the hell were you?"

"—goddamn field day! Where was I?"

"Yeah!"

"I was stupid enough to let you handle it, wasn't I? Isn't that what you wanted? *Isn't it?*"

The force of his last interrogative forced Norah back against the wall. David stood so close his breath was hot on her face and the wrath in his eyes all but shattered her.

The doors slid open.

He blinked, then stepped off and reached over to keep the doors from closing on her.

She considered not following him, but some sense of clarity was returning, and she knew that running away was not an option. At the very least, her child was in there.

When they entered the suite, Peg and Ella sat at the dining table making a soupy mess of finger paints, and Ruby, back from helping her niece with the new baby, puttered in the kitchen.

Norah reined in her emotions long enough to greet her daughter with a kiss on the top of her head before excusing herself from Peg's questioning eyes, and fleeing to their bedroom.

David had lingered by the door, hanging his coat in the front closet, but was on her heels before she had a chance to slam the door behind her. "Stop it, Norah." He shut them in quietly and kept his voice low but deadly serious.

She hated the telltale blurring in her vision, cursed her fear and her anger, and willed herself not to cry.

Why, when things fall apart, does it feel like we have nothing to hold it together? Is it just me?

She had felt abandoned in that onslaught. She hadn't understood why he hadn't fought them with her—not for her, but by her side.

Christ, we've been together a week and already we've fought twice! Both times over the same thing: strangers putting me down.

He had been right, though. She had asked him to let her handle it, and a pretty piss-poor job she'd done of it.

How should I have dealt with it?

She knew she had gotten the role in *Kosma* based on the talent David had seen in her and nothing more.

Should I have laughed it off? Made a joke?

It might have put the mob off balance long enough to come up with a more civilized retort than the one she'd offered.

David was waiting.

She wasn't sure for what. An apology? Maybe. An explanation? She hadn't one. A promise to behave herself in the future? She couldn't be sure he wanted one.

What a fucking mess.

In the end, she surrendered to the truth. "I'm sorry. You're right. I did want to handle it, but clearly, I wasn't prepared . . . not for that. That's no excuse, though. It's just I . . . damn it, I'm proud of the work I'm doing, and for someone to suggest . . . I mean, don't they have enough, they have to invent . . ." She shook her head, lowered it in defeat, and awaited his next barrage.

It never came.

****

David took her "I wasn't prepared" comment like a punch in the gut. He recalled the hours and hours of instruction by members of Nigel's entourage when he was first finding his way into columns and magazine spreads. What to say, how to stand, which questions to avoid and why. How to be gracious without being condescending. How to be interesting without sounding pompous. How to leave a question unanswered without coming off as evasive, leaving them fixated on the story behind the evasiveness. Norah hadn't had the luxury of such instruction. She'd been thrown into the fray without a single weapon.

He dropped his own head in shame. "It wasn't your fault. It's mine. You *should* have been prepared. I should have prepared you. Nigel and his bunch taught me the ropes way back when. There's no telling the trouble I would have gotten myself into otherwise.

"I'm sorry I yelled, baby. I had no business getting mad at you. You keep getting thrown into one clusterfuck after another, and you've been doing— you've been amazing. You really have. That fiasco this afternoon . . . how could I have expected you to act? I would have done the same thing, no question."

It had been such a lovely day.

He worried about how much more he could expect her to take. How many more lovely moments would get shat on before she threw in the towel?

Their perfect weekend in Vancouver had been marred by that piece of shit tabloid, the joy she got from her work had been slapped down by some trashy stand-in. And today, a successful meeting that signaled the beginning of a real career for her, followed by an exquisite lunch promising an even more exquisite afternoon . . . demolished.

"Am I worth it?" he asked.

"What?"

"All this bullshit. Every time we take a step forward, someone or something drags us two steps back. And I wish I could say it'll be over soon, but frankly, I don't see it ever ending, not so long as we're in the business. Maybe it's because it's new. Maybe once we've been together awhile it'll die down, but honey, you've got to know it's going to get worse —a whole lot worse—before it gets better. You need to decide."

"To decide what? If you're worth it?"

He nodded, not meeting her eyes.

"Oh for Pete's sake, David." She threw her coat on the arm of the sofa.

"Don't dismiss this, Norah. Don't dismiss me."

"I'm not dismissing you. It was a stupid question. I mean, how would you feel if I asked *you* that? After all, I'm the one causing you all these problems, right?"

"No, you're not causing anything. It's one of the downfalls of the job."

They were quiet a moment.

She sat next to her coat and removed her boots.

He crossed over and sat against the other arm.

"What if I wasn't in it?" she asked, not looking at him.

"Wasn't in what?"

"The business."

"Forget it."

"Now who's being dismissive?"

"Norah, you can't be serious."

"Why can't I? The film wraps next week, and I'll be done. There's no reason to think there will be other jobs, and if there are I'll . . ."

He knew how badly she wanted this career, but he knew she wanted him, too, almost as much as he wanted her. Could she possibly need him in her life enough to give up her dreams to make it happen? There were no guarantees in this line of work, and she might even be resigned to the possibility that this film would truly be the only one for her, something nice to look back on. He loved her too much to leave her in any doubt.

"I'm going to show you something." He walked to the door and picked up his briefcase. He took out his laptop, sat back down next to her, and fired it up. "Anita sent these to me Thursday. I only glanced at them yesterday, but there's one I think you should see."

Anita had burned her latest editorial efforts onto a Blu-ray and sent them to him for his comments or approval.

He browsed the menu for the scene titles and found the one he was looking for. He clicked on it, then hit play.

The shot opened on the front of a classic New York City newsstand, where Clare was reading the latest on the serial killings taking place in the area when a shadow fell across the page.

As the scene unfolded, Norah watched the gentle timidity of Clare against the sensual charms of the cunning psychopath. Wayne looked stunningly handsome. An almost bashful smile played across his sexy mouth from time to time. Then there was Clare—dowdy, downtrodden, and bowed, yet somehow completely entrancing. It was a long, captivating scene where much of the characters were revealed. Their rapport built, and it's made clear why they end up reaching for each other.

Even Norah had to admit that, although David was the far more experienced film actor, she had nothing to apologize for.

"I had to work my nuts off just to keep in the picture," David said with a laugh. "I've sent some of your stuff around to a few people, people who count . . . besides Nigel. I didn't trust my own judgment, you see, but they all say the same thing. There's nothing stopping you, honey."

She sighed. "So what do we do . . . about *us?*"

"What can we do? We accept the fact that we're going to be waist deep in it for a while, and we make a plan."

"A plan?"

"What to do next time because, unfortunately, there will be a next time. We need to prep you, teach you how to keep your head, and we'll be fine."

"That sounds a bit simplistic."

"It isn't. It'll be hard work, but it's not impossible, and it's not forever. This is a great business, Norah. There's not much about it that I don't love, even the day-to-day frustrations, and when I see something like this . . . " He gestured to the image frozen on the laptop. "It's so . . . gratifying, so rewarding. I can't imagine myself doing anything else." He turned off the laptop, slid over to Norah, put his arm around her, and tilted her chin until her eyes were on him. "I can't imagine myself doing anything else, and I can't imagine myself loving anyone else. I'm sorry this happened today. I'm sorry our day was spoiled, and again, I'm so sorry I got so angry. I wasn't mad at you, I was—"

"I know." She stroked his face and leaned in to kiss him.

He sighed deeply and enveloped her in his arms, and she let herself be absorbed into his embrace, the madness of the day all but forgotten for them both.

****

"Norah, my dear, please sit down. I have some very good news."

David had taken a call for her yesterday afternoon from Nigel's assistant. They had wanted Norah in for a meeting at her earliest possible convenience. It was midway through the last week of shooting, but she had been able to get away during lunch. In order to save time, she had arrived in full costume, but since Clare was testifying in the trial scenes, she was dolled up a bit at least. Her hair had been restyled slightly and she had on a pair of khakis and a black V-neck sweater.

"I like good news," she said, shifting in her chair under the direct gaze of his posse. They met in Nigel's personal office this time, and though lush and impressively outfitted, it lacked the vastness of the boardroom, and she found herself feeling nervous and claustrophobic.

"We've decided to represent you," Nigel declared, reaching for two envelopes—one thick, one thin. He handed her the thin one. "Our standard contract. Read it, have a lawyer look at it, whatever you like. I think you'll find it holds the usual fine print traps and treacherous loopholes. Tell me, do you have full custody of your daughter?"

"Excuse me?"

The team laughed, and she realized she was being had. She managed a chuckle but vowed to give that contract a very good going over.

"Seriously, Norah, since your last visit I've contacted Ramone Bartolini, and he has a magnificent part for you in a film that goes into production in France in three months." With a flourish, he handed her the second envelope. "You'll be teamed with your old friend, Nick Costello. The two of you will be playing a pair of rogue intelligence agents during World War II, a kind of *Casablanca* meets *Bonnie and Clyde*."

She was nonplussed.

Is this actually happening?

"Nigel. I'm . . . I don't know what to say. Wow, you guys really earn your ten percent."

"Twenty, actually, but who's counting?"

She half smiled. "Right, well thank you. Thank you so much. What do I do next?"

"Nothing, my dear. Someone from Ramone's office will be contacting you in the next week or so. Get that contract back to us as soon as possible, and you'll be on your way."

"No kidding? Wow. My head is spinning." She took a quick look around the room. "Well, I know you're very busy, and I need to get back to set so . . ." She clutched the two envelopes and pushed her chair back.

"One moment, please, Norah. There is one other matter I'd like to discuss with you."

"Okay, sure." She stifled the instinct to cut and run.

"Everyone," he said, addressing the minions. "If I may please have the room."

They stood as a unit and filed quickly and wordlessly out the door.

"There. Isn't that better, just the two of us?" He stared at her.

"There was another matter?" she prompted.

"Yes, quite. You are a get-to-the-point kind of woman. I like that." He crossed to an elegant table that served as a bar arrangement and gestured with the decanter of amber liquid. "Would you care for anything?"

"No, thank you."

He poured himself a glass. "Norah, I'll be frank. I think you're a huge talent. What is it they say? The real deal. An agent such as myself can wait a whole lifetime for someone like you to cross his path. It doesn't happen very often."

"Thank you very much. I guess you're very lucky." When he looked at her questioningly, she replied, "It happened with David as well."

"Mmm, yes. Don't get me wrong, my dear. I adore David. Everyone adores David."

"Well, David is adorable."

"But he doesn't have nearly your skill."

"Pardon?" She felt her hackles rising.

"Norah, there's no need to get defensive, believe me. David and I have had this discussion a number of times over the years, from the first time he sat down across from me some twelve years ago now. I told him he wouldn't win any awards, but he'd definitely pack the houses."

"But he *has* won awards. Lots of them."

"Yes, but after a point, they are as much to do with popularity as anything else, and as you well know, David is very popular. That was my job. Not that I take full credit, mind you. David is a very easy man to promote. He's excellent on set, easy to work with, he turns in a good performance in the end, is charming during the press junkets, shows up at the premieres and award ceremonies looking dashing, and has never lost his temper with the paparazzi."

That was aimed at her, but she lowered her eyes and let it slide.

"He doesn't drink to excess, at least not publicly, or do drugs, he doesn't drive recklessly." He took a small sip of bourbon. "And until now, he's never been involved with the wrong woman."

She absorbed his last statement with unsettling stillness then slowly raised her eyes to confront the person who had just vindicated every suspicion she'd ever had about him. "How's that?"

"Norah, as I said before, friends must be honest with each other. This thing between you and David simply must end."

"This *thing?*"

"Please, don't play the wounded virgin with me. You're not a child, and I refuse to speak to you like one."

She was taken aback by his change in attitude. She felt exactly like she was being scolded by a parent.

"I am, however, going to address you as the woman you are, a talent this movie generation has hardly seen, with a future that will put the dreams you've had so far about fame and fortune to shame."

She swallowed hard. "So long as I quit David."

He smiled, and she wondered why he had never struck her as a viper before now. "Yes, I'm sorry. I won't lie to you and tell you I'm a romantic.

Never have been, and it's served me well. But I do accept the fact that you and David love each other. I've known him a long time and have never seen him happier. I also know, regrettably, that it cannot—*must not*—continue."

"Why?"

"I can't tell you that without hurting you."

"I'll risk it."

He considered her for a long time. "All right. You're common. You're not tall enough, young enough, thin enough, beautiful enough, or . . . unsullied enough."

She raised her eyebrows in question.

"I'm sure she's a lovely child, but the unwed single mother scene doesn't read for David's particular biography. For your own, that's quite another story. Coupled with the fact that you're an extraordinary actor, it'll make you a star. But that doesn't alter the fact that you're an ordinary girl. You don't suit him, you're—"

"The wrong woman."

"Yes."

"I see."

"See, I told you. I've hurt your feelings."

"Not at all." She shook her head slowly, letting it all sink in. "What would David have to say about all this, I wonder?"

He smirked. "Is that intended to frighten me?"

It was actually, but he didn't wait for her response.

"By all means, let's involve him in our little *tête-à-tête*. Or you could let me save us all the time. He would sit there, like you are now, and declare his love for you a thousand different, heart-wrenching ways. He'd call me all manner of nasty names, many of which would be quite fitting, then he'd take you by the hand, toss me my pink slip, and the two of you would storm out of my office forever. Shall I tell you what would happen after that?" He took her silence as consent. "It would begin with a lot of bad press being sent your way. That would happen almost immediately. In fact, you've already had a taste, haven't you? For the record, I don't think you're a 'she-beast' at all."

The memory of that headline caused her to wince slightly.

"David would do his best, be very protective of you, at first, but after awhile, it would naturally start to wear on him. Always having to defend your relationship, going on the talk show circuit, telling the world over and over what a delightful woman you really are. At some point, the comedians would undoubtedly kick in with cruel witticisms about David coming to the rescue of his very ordinary girlfriend.

"And naturally, you can say goodbye to any hope for a career yourself. No one will know you for your gift or accept your talent, they will only see you as the woman who tried to, pardon me, fuck her way to the top. You will go down into obscurity as that very commonplace woman who David Raurke lost his head over once, before he came to his senses. Now, wouldn't that be a terrible waste indeed?

"Then there will be the other women because, with David, there will always be other women. He'll put up the good fight, but, my dear girl, you haven't seen it. He's like a bloody rock star, really. They turn up under the beds in the hotels, find their way into his trailer. I remember one, years ago, fell out of his luggage at the airport. He's only human, after all, and I think if you consulted your heart, you'll find that you've always known you wouldn't be the one and only. For some men, it's simply not possible. There will always be someone a little more . . . appealing around the corner.

"So there it will be. David's career will be damaged—not beyond repair, certainly, but scarred nonetheless—and here you'll be, tossed over, very likely out of resentment or boredom or a desire for someone else, and you'll have nothing—no career, no David."

"I'm sorry, all this because I'm not a twenty-four-year-old, five foot ten inch, size two beauty queen with a certificate of . . . virtue?"

"I don't write the rules, Norah, never forget that. I am not your enemy. I do know the game, however, and how to play it. It's true that what I'm asking of you will still mean no David, but at least if you move quickly, you'll be out before any damage is done to either of you. I know you care enough about him that you'd hate to see him dethroned, even temporarily, and how terrible would it be to know that you caused that kind of injury to a life he's worked so hard to cultivate?

"So unless your plan is to take him back to, where is it—White . . . *Court* —so that the two of you can run your little café together in anonymity for the rest of your lives . . . no, I thought not. Well, you're a smart woman, sensible. I am sorry to be the bearer of such unpleasantness, but it has been my job for over a decade to protect him, even against himself. It has been far from the easiest part of my day, especially when it has involved hurting someone decent like yourself. But the fact that he is the star he is, and enjoys the career he does, should prove to you that I've only ever had his best interests at heart, and you can rest assured that it is my most fervent plan to do the same for *you*.

"Now you may take as much time as you wish to think over what I've said, but I think you'll come inevitably to the same conclusion. Best to get it over with quickly, the sooner the better, so we can get on with the business of making you a star."

****

The new location was at the New York City Criminal Court building, shooting the final trial scenes. It meant long days, but they were inside where it was warm, and with limited action, they'd been clipping along at a pretty good pace. All the exteriors had been shot, and they were using an old courtroom and a couple of hallways that hadn't undergone renovation for the interiors.

Norah made her way onto the set as if in a dream. A very bad dream. Dennis and Nick were next to the craft services table as usual, and she joined them.

"Did I miss anything?" she asked, as she automatically fixed a cup of tea.

"No," Dennis said, stirring his own drink. "Just a couple of shots of the jury, Nick and I in the gallery, and David at the defense table."

"Hey!" Nick nudged her arm. "I got a call from Ramone Bartolini last night. Is it true?"

Norah flushed a bit, unaware that the news had reached reality so quickly.

"Yeah, I guess it is. Nothing official yet, I mean the papers haven't been signed but—"

"What's this?" Dennis' curiosity was piqued.

Nick put an arm around Norah's shoulders and announced, "My girl and I are going to be kicking some French ass in a few months. Bartie called me to see what you were like to work with. Naturally, I told him you was a total ballbuster. Nah, I told him he couldn't ask for better. We're gonna have such a blast!" Nick pulled Norah into an enthusiastic hug and swung her around.

"Let go of my lady, Costello. If I've told you once . . ." David approached the scene with some amusement, though Norah was less amused. "Hey, baby." He kissed her. "How'd it go?"

"Good." She nodded. "Really good."

"Good?" Nick played up mock outrage. "Tell him about the film."

"I'll tell him later, Nick."

Grace called places and Nick and Dennis made their way back.

"What film?"

"Later, okay?"

"Sure, okay. Are you all right?"

"Uh-huh. Just kind of overwhelmed."

"You look sad, honey." He took her face into his hands and looked down at her with concern. "Everything's coming to an end, isn't it?"

"What?" Her heart skipped a beat.

"We wrap in a couple of days. Is that what's getting you down? I know I'm getting bummed."

She swallowed hard and forced a weak smile onto her face. "Yeah, I guess so."

"It's one chapter, baby. We've got a whole book ahead of us."

She nodded and he hugged her for a moment.

"Places, please." Grace's voice was more insistent, so David and Norah broke apart and entered the set.

****

They were headed home when Norah told David the news—getting signed with Coombs Elite and the film with Bartolini and Nick in the new year.

He was thrilled for her and suggested they go somewhere nice to celebrate, maybe call some of the gang to join them.

She couldn't face it and begged off, claiming she was tired and just wanted a quiet dinner at home with the family.

He agreed, since they had an early call the next day, and he wanted Ella to be part of the fun as well.

The rest of the drive was spent with David chattering excitedly away while Norah tried to swallow the lump that felt permanently lodged in her throat.

He offered to courier the contract to his lawyer first thing so that Norah could get it signed and back to Nigel by week's end. She wouldn't want him to change his mind. "Not that he would," David chuckled.

No, wouldn't want that.

Chapter 21

"We need to talk."

The four most dreaded words in the relationship lexicon, and David had just been subjected to them.

The film had wrapped right on schedule. The party had been a real barnburner with a couple of days spent decompressing and tying up loose ends. David had tried to talk Norah into staying longer in New York since they'd had so little time, in the scheme of things, to have a real look around, but she'd been strangely eager to return home.

She hadn't been herself for the past week or so. He'd initially thought it was due to wrapping *Kosma*, but with another movie in the works, he'd dismissed that reasoning early on. There had been no denying it, however, she'd been sullen for days, turning up late for the wrap party then begging off early. She had been ill. She'd assured him she wasn't pregnant, but she couldn't or wouldn't offer any explanation.

He'd briefly wondered if he'd done something, but the way she clung to him every night and made love with a fierceness that left him gasping laid that concern to rest. It was as though she couldn't get enough.

In an effort to get to the bottom of whatever was eating her, he'd made the arrangements, and they had arrived in Whitecourt two days ago. But things hadn't improved. In fact, she'd grown snappish and withdrawn.

He was a patient man, but he had his limits, and the strain was getting to him. More than once he'd tried to talk to her about it, and she'd put him off, but it seemed she was finally ready to clear the air.

Brett and Peg had taken Ella over to her grandparents', so this was the first time they'd been alone, really alone, since they'd gotten back. He'd been going over an editing schedule that had been e-mailed to him that morning from Anita, when Norah stepped purposefully into the living room. The look on her face sent a chill through him, and without knowing why, his hands trembled as he put his papers down.

"Okay. What's on your mind?"

"Here's the thing." She stood, her hands on her hips, her breath quick and shallow. She shook her head slightly and wouldn't meet his gaze. "I thought this could work, but now I know it can't. I guess you really can't have your cake and eat it, too."

"Am I supposed to know what you're talking about?" He tried to smile through the panic that was reaching up and threatening to close his throat.

"I've wanted to be a working actor all of my life, David. I've never made any secret of that."

"No, you haven't."

"And now with Nigel taking me on and the Bartolini film, it looks as if that actually might happen."

"It is going to happen, honey."

"But here's the thing, we've only been together for three months." She sounded as if she was discussing having the car serviced.

"What does that have to do—"

"I'm saying that I can't have both."

The hand that had been reaching for his throat grabbed him by the chest and squeezed hard. Her voice sounded as if he was hearing it from under water. "I don't understand."

She gestured to the world beyond. "They won't let me have both."

"Jesus, Norah. I can't believe we're having this conversation again. Who said you can't have both? Fuck 'em!"

"That's easy for you to say. You've arrived. You've made it, and they don't hate you. They will *never* hate you. They will never vilify *you* on the streets. They might think, okay, he's gone a little crazy but he'll come to his senses. Me, I'm the enemy. I'm the one that took you away from them, and they will never accept me, never accept me as an actor, never accept my work so long as I'm with you."

"Maybe not right away, but after a while, they'll leave us alone. Damn it, we've been over this!"

"David, I'm thirty-four years old. I should be nearing the end of an acting career, not trying to start one. I've only got ten or twelve years before the world decides that I'm over the hill, if that. I am not going to get another chance."

"No. I cannot believe . . . you would walk away from us? From what we have, from everything we share just so—"

"Just so that I can have the life I've dreamed of ever since I was a kid? How can you be so selfish?"

****

It was intended to hurt him, and by the look on his face, she knew she had hit her mark.

It had been a week since her meeting with Nigel, and she felt as if a parasite had been eating away at her ever since. She'd built up to this confrontation dozens of times but had chickened out. Nigel had been right, though. Waiting hadn't made it any easier.

"Norah?"

She knew she needed to end this, that there couldn't be any room for argument, but the sight of him standing there so wounded, the raw pain in his eyes, and knowing she'd caused it—was anything worth that?

She'd been over this a million times in the last seven days. She had to remember who she was doing this for. She wouldn't damage the career that he'd worked so hard on, nor would she suffer the way he would look at her once it had happened. She stiffened her resolve.

"David, believe me, I get the irony here. You give me my big break, and then I give it to you up the ass." She forced a laugh and hoped it sounded convincing. "Look, I'm sorry, but I'm not prepared to give up everything I've ever wanted just for a good fuck."

He reared back as though she'd struck him in the face and fixed her with a look of frigid loathing so pure that she wasn't sure he wouldn't return the blow. Instead, he turned away from her and took a couple of disoriented steps. He seemed to gather himself up and even calmly collected his papers from the coffee table, and slid them into his briefcase. Then, as though it were any ordinary morning, he walked out the door but slammed it shut with such force that it rattled every window in the house.

She dropped, trembling, into a chair as her legs finally gave way. Her breath came in gasps as if his leaving had taken the very oxygen she needed to breathe. Her vision started to swim and a bitter, metallic taste found its way into her mouth. She bolted to the powder room and vomited violently and then dry heaved until her ribs ached and her head throbbed.

She began to cry—not the controlled, delicate weeping of the movies, but a soul-shattering wail. Again and again, she dragged air into her lungs, only to have it wrenched from her by her own agony. That was how Brett found her, hours later, still sitting on the floor next to the sink, in a dark house. Her breaths were jagged gasps and pitiful moans. Her face was streaked with tears that ran unchecked. Her eyes looked right through him as he stared at her from the bathroom door.

"Jesus, Norah," he whispered. "What the fuck?"

****

David stumbled down the front steps and grabbed for the latch on the gate. That's when he noticed he had somehow had the forethought to grab his coat from the foyer on the way out. Good thing, since his car keys were in the pocket.

He climbed inside the rental car, his hands frozen to the wheel and his guts churning. There was some kind of whine tearing through his brain. He had no clue what had happened, no clue where he was going, only that he had to move, get away from here.

As he drove along the main street, he knew the Legion was to his left and

the theatre to his right, and a little farther ahead was the café.
Maybe Brett—no, he's at Vic and Mona's and...
David slammed on the brakes. A child, about nine or so, was crossing in front of the car. He hadn't seen her and almost hadn't stopped in time. He saw her little face with its frightened expression, and he felt sick. He had to pull over before he killed someone. He'd been heading for the highway toward the airport but maybe this was a sign, and he should stay close in case...
In case, what?
He couldn't think. He needed to stop and figure shit out. He saw the hotel he'd stayed in before and parked around the side.
In case she comes looking.
Just inside the back entrance, he peeked into the lobby. Alan was at the desk.
Thank heaven.
David waited until he was sure there wasn't anyone else around, then crossed quickly to him.
Alan looked up and smiled broadly. "Hey, David. Nice to see . . ." Alan's smile waned.
Whether it was years of experience or the look on his face, David didn't know and didn't care.
Alan reached for a key and handed it to him. "I take it you're not here?"
David shook his head. "No one's gonna be looking for me." Hearing the truth out loud stung. "I am going to need a drink pretty soon, though. Can you send something up?"
"A double?"
"A twenty-sixer."

****

He thanked Alan silently for not giving him his old room. He might have gone berserk. He put his briefcase on the desk and rummaged through it in a panic. His luggage was still at the house—just clothes, toiletries, and a few books, but nothing much since they'd only planned on staying a week. He sagged with relief when he confirmed that his briefcase held his laptop, important production papers, and his passport. If and when he did decide to get out of Dodge, the worst thing would be to have to ring her for something.
Okay, maybe that *wouldn't be the worst thing.*
His legs folded under him.
He hadn't cried since he was seventeen, when the family had had to put their dog down. At the time he had been certain that he would never recover.
He recognized that feeling.
The ludicrousness of the situation hit him—he was, at nearly thirty-nine

years old, suffering his first heartbreak. Sure, he'd had disappointments of a romantic nature, but nothing he hadn't been able to shrug off after a day or two. This was certainly making up for it. Memory after memory crashed over him with the force of a stampede—their meeting, their first date, their first kiss, laughing on set, the afternoon in the bathtub, playing with Ella, Vancouver. One after another pounded him senseless.

He had his face buried in his hands, barely keeping the sobs in check, when a knock came on the door. He'd sprung to his feet and made it halfway across the room when he heard Alan's voice on the other side.

"David, it's me."

The disappointment knocked the breath out of him. He collected himself as best he could and opened the door. Alan had a shopping bag in one hand and a small brown paper bag in the other, which he handed off.

David took the bag and withdrew the bottle. "I asked for a twenty-sixer."

Alan shook his head and stepped inside, uninvited, shutting the door behind him. "That'll do the job. Twenty-six will very likely kill you." He cocked his brow. "David Raurke ain't dying in *my* house."

The same age as Norah, Alan was a tall man—six foot at least, and built like someone who worked out in his spare time. Not classically handsome, but he had an appealing face and a soft gentle manner. He'd been a gracious and obliging host while David and the movie crews stayed here. Everyone liked him and knew that he kept their comings and goings to himself and tenaciously guarded their privacy.

Alan nodded to the salty fare as he unpacked chips, pretzels, and other various snacks. "You should try and get some of this in your belly. You'll hate yourself a little less in the morning."

"I don't think a bag of chips is going to save me from that, bud," David said with a sardonic smile. "You want one?" he asked, indicating a second glass.

"No, thanks. I don't do that anymore. I liked it a little too much in my twenties." He perched against the dresser and crossed his big arms. "Was it the publicity that did it?" Alan asked after a moment.

David sank into the chair and with a smile that didn't reach his eyes asked, "Do I have the look of a man that's been handed his walking papers?"

"A little. I figured whatever it was couldn't have been your idea, or you'd have kept driving. In fact, I doubt you would have come back to town at all if that was where your mind was taking you."

"You're a smart guy. What else have you worked out?" It wasn't a hostile question, just honest curiosity.

Alan shrugged. "I dunno. Norah's a tough bird, but after that newspaper bullshit and that stuff on TV with you guys in New York, all those photographers and reporters . . . I can't see anyone standin' up under that for very long."

"Anything else?"

"Well, at first, I figured it might be another woman."

"Really."

"Well, they was always all over this place while you was here. I don't know how many'd come to the desk, sayin' they was reporters, or that they worked for you and needed to get something from your room. Then there was the others. They didn't make no bones about what they was doin' here, and *what* they was willing to do to me for just letting them near you. Shit, was enough to turn a guy around."

David chuckled and relaxed as the liquor steadied the shaking in his hands. "Did you ever . . . you know?"

"What? Me? Hell no. I got me a nice girl down Mayerthorpe. She'd friggin' skin me if I even thought about it."

"No, Alan. It wasn't another woman."

"Oh, well, that's good. Norah's a good person, and I wouldn't be likin' you nearly so much if I thought you was messin' around on her. It used to really piss me off when Nathan'd step out, but he'd lay low for a few days, and then go beggin' around till she took him back. I thought maybe you had the same idea."

"Nathan cheated on Norah?"

"Yeah, all the time. Nice guy though, Nathan. He used to drive my mom into the city for her doctor's appointments the year I lost my license. Whenever you needed him, he was there. I guess that was kinda the problem." He smirked. "He was a good looking son of a bitch, that's for sure, maybe even prettier than you. And the girls were nuts over him. I guess he was only human, but still . . ."

"But Norah always took him back."

"Yeah, well, like I said, he was a real charmer. She chucked him for good, though, just before she left for BC. He followed her out there once, like a little puppy, but she sent him back with his tail between his legs. I always figured he married the Olson girl out of spite."

David had more or less stopped listening.

"Well, I'll leave you to it."

You gotta respect a guy who knows when to make an exit.

"Alan?"

David's voice stopped him as he reached for the knob.

"What broke you and Norah up? She told me you dated for a while."

Alan smiled softly. "Yeah, that was a long time ago. She was a nice girlfriend. The kind of girl you can watch a game with on a Sunday and then hit the sheets with during halftime." Alan blushed. "Sorry, man, I shouldn't have said that."

"Don't worry about it. As you said, that was a long time ago."

"Right. Anyway, it never would have lasted, her and me. This is my home, but Norah, she was never going to stay here, never seemed to belong. I'm surprised she's lasted as long as she has. Ever since we was kids, there was always something special about her. She had a kind of . . .

shine about her, made the rest of us look dull by comparison. You know what I mean?"

David nodded and returned his focus to his glass. "Yes. Yes, I do."

Alan crossed to the desk, and scrawled on the notepad. "That's my cell number. I'll be on the desk till ten o'clock, but you can reach me on that anytime. You need me, David, you call me, y'hear?"

"Thanks, Alan. You're a good man."

And then he was alone.

****

Norah blinked.

What . . .

Something in that slant of light forced her back to the surface for a closer look.

Everything was soft and white—the draperies, the bedding, the paint on the walls. Everything but the shadow in front of her. It was a man.

"David . . ." Her voice croaked on the single utterance.

He quietly shut the magazine and leaned into her. "Norah, it's me, " Brett said.

"Where am—"

"You're in the hospital, honey. Don't you remember?"

She tried to sit up. "Ella! Where's Ella?"

Brett pressed her shoulders back on the pillows. "Ella's fine. Nothing's happened to Ella. She's home with Peg. Everything is fine."

Relief washed over her and she sank into a moment of confused peace. Then tiny tendrils of memory reached out for her, grabbing hold, and everywhere there was pain. Every recollection made her consciousness draw back as if burnt. Everything was very much not fine.

"Why am I . . . how did I get here?"

"I'm sorry. You were just so . . . I didn't know what else to do."

****

When Brett had found her that evening, his first instinct had been to run away and let Peg handle it, but he'd held his ground. He had called out to Peg to take Ella upstairs. Brett's tone had been enough to alert her, and Peg came to investigate. The briefest look in Norah's direction had told the story, and she returned to the foyer, gathered Ella in her arms and rushed upstairs with promises of a warm bath.

It had taken a great deal of coaxing to get Norah off the floor and into a chair. She had been shaking and couldn't even hold the tea or the brandy he'd offered. He had tried to talk to her, first softly, then firmer, in an attempt to snap her out of it. Peg finished bathing Ella and had her occupied with something before she'd ventured back downstairs.

"Oh, my darling girl. What has happened?"

The Wrong Woman

"Three guesses." Brett scoffed.

"Has she said anything?" Peg stroked her brow, peering into her face as if she'd find an answer there.

Brett shook his head. "What should we do?"

"I don't know. You don't suppose . . . she didn't take . . . something?"

"No, I checked around. There's no sign. Do you think I should take her in, I mean—"

"I know. I suppose it wouldn't hurt to have a doctor look at her. Would you like me to take her, dear?"

Brett looked determined. "No. Stay with Ella, I'll do it."

They'd bundled her up and placed her in Brett's car. As he walked her discreetly toward a side door of the hospital, they were met by a blessing.

Dr. Connie Benson had been on her way home and stopped in her tracks when she saw them. She and Norah had been in high school at the same time—Connie had been two years ahead and had tutored Norah in science one year. They'd renewed their friendship when Connie had returned to Whitecourt to set up her practice.

"What's this?" she asked, as she took Norah's other arm.

"We're calling it exhaustion," Brett replied.

Connie checked Norah in under an assumed name and assigned one nurse per shift, those who could be trusted to keep their mouths shut. She examined her as Brett shared the little he had in the way of history.

He made no mention of David, only that she'd been hard at work on the film in New York until a few days ago.

She gave Norah a mild sedative and spoke to Brett in hushed whispers. "Technically she *is* exhausted. I'd never go so far as to call it a breakdown, but it's serious, and she does need to rest. Lots of rest."

"How long should she stay?"

"Normally, I'd say three or four days, but I can't promise to keep this under wraps for that long. It's a small hospital. I'd suggest you take her home tomorrow, maybe later in the day, and make sure you keep her quiet. I'll give you my private number, and I'll swing by the house every day to have a look."

"Thanks, Connie. The press are hard enough on her without this getting in the papers. You know how they'd blow it up."

"Sure. Anything for Norah. We're all so proud of her. You don't think David Raurke will be by to see her, do you? I could help sneak him in—"

"No, that's not likely. He's back in the Big Apple doing some . . . director stuff, you know."

She had lifted an eyebrow. "Oh, sure. Oh, well, too bad." She took another peek at Norah and headed out the door.

****

Norah didn't remember any of it—not Brett finding her, being admitted,

Connie. She didn't remember anything beyond David slamming the door. "How long have I been here?"

"Since yesterday. You get to come home later today, but you're going to have to stay in bed and rest for a while."

Not a problem.

"Where . . . do you know where he is?"

"Alan called me last night, told me he'd checked in. He wanted to know how you were."

"David did?"

"No, honey . . . Alan. Alan wanted to know how you were."

"Oh. What did you tell him?"

"I asked him to tell me how whatshisface was first."

"And?"

"Well, Alan said he was probably drunk and destined to wake up in a pool of his own vomit. I said you were the same. Just as a joke."

Norah didn't laugh. "Is he still . . ."

"No, Alan rang before I came here. He checked out after lunch and left a forwarding address for his things. Alan said if you wanted, he would come by the house and pick it all up. Send it on for you."

"That's very thoughtful. We should maybe think about letting him do that."

"It's already done. Peg packed everything up, and I dropped it by the hotel on my way here. We didn't want you to have to deal with it when you came home. Is that all right?"

"Yes, it's fine."

She tried not to think about what it would be like to go home to find all traces of him swept away, as if he'd never existed for her.

Norah saw Brett watching her every move. "Brett?"

"Yes, sweetie?"

"Brett, I need to tell you . . ." She felt the latest round of meds kicking in but fought against their sweet pull.

"You can tell me later, you need to sleep now."

"No, I have to tell you . . . now."

Brett took her hand and leaned in.

****

Seven weeks later, David sat in Anita's studio in Queens, going over final edits. He was in the *throw yourself into work* phase of healing which, although therapeutic for David, was a real pain in the ass for everyone around him.

He laboured tirelessly over every detail, supervised every aspect of postproduction, insisted on being consulted on each decision, and bitched incessantly whenever there was a corner cut.

"Anita, I don't know what we're trying to say with this. It hasn't any flow at all. I thought we talked about this. It needs to flow."

Anita had become a bundle of nerves and frustration and seemed unable to communicate on any level whatsoever. David watched as she flipped madly through her notes.

Jozef came to her rescue. "No, Dafid, you are wrong. This scene need the choppy for, what you say, contrast to later. Remember, you say here is de . . . de . . ."

"Descent into madness," Geoff said.

"Yes, that's it. Descent into madness. Descent—not flow, descent is chop, chop, chop." He pressed his point with the accompaniment of judo gestures.

Anita slapped her notepad on the bench in front of David with a victorious flourish.

He read it and his own words came back to haunt him. He nodded begrudgingly. "Right. Sorry, Anita. I could have sworn—"

"Don't worry about it, David, it's—"

David couldn't bear to hear one more person making excuses for him. "What's next?" He caught Anita making worried eye contact with the others. He bit his lip to keep from shouting. "C'mon guys! Let's do this."

Anita's fingers flew over her control board.

Wayne and Clare walk along a quiet New York street together, chatting amiably. The couple stops, and he leans against a railing, taking her hand and pulling her to stand between his knees. A few whispered words and Wayne tries to kiss her for the first time, and she timidly lets him. It is barely a kiss, a mere brushing of lips before she pulls away. She shyly smiles at him and backs up. He watches her walk up the street with a kind of astonished happiness reflected in his eyes.

Anita was explaining something about the shot, but David wasn't paying attention.

The playback ran past the call for cut, and he watched as Norah ran back into the shot and threw herself into his arms. He remembered the exact moment. How it had nearly knocked them both over the railing. He watched as the onscreen David picked her up and threatened to drop her over the edge. Their laughter and her screams echoed through the fade out.

Anita's hand slapped the stop button, but it was too little, too late.

They sat in terrible silence. Then David rose quickly and grabbed his cup. "I need another coffee, anyone else?" Without waiting for an answer, he strode through the soundproof door, and left the others hanging uncomfortably.

****

It was less than a week before Christmas, and only two weeks before she left for France to shoot the Bartolini film. Norah took a bit of time between learning her lines and getting packed, by trying—for Ella's sake—to appear enthusiastic about the holidays. Brett wrapped presents on the coffee table, with Ella's help of course, and Norah hung garlands around the hall. One of those tear-jerking Christmas movies warbled away on the television. On the surface, it all looked very festive.

"Day-day!" Ella shouted. "Mama, Mama! Look, Day-day!"

Norah drifted into the room and stared, wide-eyed, in the direction of Ella's chubby finger pointing straight to the screen.

David stood at a press podium announcing the upcoming release of his new movie, *Kosma*, due out next spring. He fielded questions about the subject matter of the film and whether or not Hollywood would ever grow tired of seeing women as victims in cinema.

"While I was doing the research for the film, I learned that many of the victims were criticized for having fallen for the charms of this man. I think this goes a long way to explaining that."

"Is the killer, and indirectly his crimes, glamorized?"

"We do not glamorize Wayne Kosma at all. We merely represent him as a human being, a grossly damaged human being, but still just a man in the end. As for the other part of your question, how can you possibly glamorize rape?"

Good one, David.

The ache in Norah's heart caught up with her. She forced herself not to think about how handsome he looked in his suit and tie, how the smile he flashed the reporters went straight into her soul.

"Look, Mama. Day-day." Ella grinned and clapped.

"Yes, honey, I see." Norah smiled but never took her eyes off his face.

"Is it true there's a love story between the killer and one of his victims?"

"Yes, rather, no . . . the woman in question was never one of his victims, but yes, there was a relationship."

"There was a rumor that life was imitating art, David. You were romantically linked for a while with your costar. Do you have any comment?"

David had obviously prepared for this question because he didn't miss a beat. "The actor you're referring to is Norah Rothe, that's Norah with an *H* and Rothe with an *E*. She was a huge asset to the film. When you meet her, get her to tell you the story of how she was cast. There's a movie right there."

"But was there a romance, David?"

He smiled his most charming smile. "You guys should know you can't believe everything you read, because most of you are writing it."

Amused laughter broke out from the assembly.

"Norah and I are just friends."

It rolled off his tongue so easily she winced.

"One more question, David. What are you doing over Christmas?"

Norah was certain this was a question he hadn't prepared for as a shadow of something darkened his eyes.

He recovered quickly. "No plans really. Just family and friends, getting drunk, that sort of thing. That's all. Thank you, everyone. Good afternoon."

Brett clicked the remote, and the television went black.

"Where Day-day go?"

Norah leaned down to ruffle Ella's hair, her gaze still fixated on the blank screen. "David's gone, honey."

Chapter 22

David stood at his desk in his temporary office in the building that played host to the production staff for *Kosma*, situated in the meatpacking district of Manhattan.

Under orders to supply him with any and all press related to the film, one of his assistants had presented him with piles of local and foreign news reels, magazine articles, radio tapes, and newspaper clippings. He had sorted through one stack of stuff in front of him and was moving on to a second. He discarded most, but set a few of the more interesting or better represented ones aside for his permanent file.

One cover story caught him short. A French magazine he'd never heard of featured a story about a film being shot in Provence. There was Norah, holding Ella, walking along a charming European street with Ramone Bartolini's arm around her. Ella held her hat against the wind and looked adorably stubborn about it, while Norah and Ramone appeared every inch the celebrities in their sunglasses and Euro-trash jeans. It was a full-page, full colour photograph, so clearly the locals viewed this as a big deal. He cursed his inability to read the language, but did pick out *Kosma . . . avec David Raurke* along with her name in the article.

He sat heavily into his chair and wondered who could translate it and resist fixing him with that pity-filled gaze that he'd grown so sick of over the last three months.

Even though he knew better, he allowed his gaze to return to the photo. Norah looked good, really good, like she'd always been a star. She was watching the ground in front of her, clutching her daughter close as they tried to navigate around the paparazzi. Ramone, meanwhile, was smiling smugly at one of the cameras.

I hate him.

He hated this feeling even more, but he wasn't ready to admit that just yet.

One of his assistants walked in.

"Hey, Shasta, can you read French?"

"Me? No. I can barely manage English. Call for you on three, boss. It's Nick Costello."

David's head shot up. "Thanks." He reached for the receiver. "Nick?"

"Yeah, fuck you, too."

Oy.

"What's up, Nick?"

"I don't know, Raurke. Just when I think I got this world by the ass and it's all figured out, someone comes along and screws with my head."

"Nick, can I help you?"

"No, but maybe I can help you."

"How's that?"

"Well, here's the deal. I heard you and Norah hit the skids before I left the States, right? I got no details, but I figure, since she's been dragging her ass around here like *Dawn of the* freakin' *Dead*, and you being such a pussy hound, that you dumped her for another piece."

David was so at the end of his rope with this guy. "Is this going somewhere?"

"Hold your horses. Now I'm talkin' to Dennis yesterday, you know, shootin' the shit, and he fills me in. That it was, in fact, Norah who dumped *you*. Well, you coulda knocked me down with a fuckin' feather. So now I gotta decide whether or not to let you in on a bit of info."

"Is this the part where I'm supposed to say, 'Please, oh please, Nick, tell me'?"

"You're a real smart-ass, boss, that's why I like you. So, I'm gonna tell you. I don't know whether or not you've seen it, but there's a thing running in one of these Frenchy magazines here, and it's some bullshit about Norah and Bartie."

What are the odds?

"Yeah, I've seen it."

"Well, it's just that. Bullshit. He told me he's been pitchin'. Why not, ya know? She's a nice broad. But she's not swingin'."

"Is that so?"

Nick laughed. "That's right, Raurke, you play the tough guy. I thought you'd wanna know. I been where you are. Just coz *you* ain't doin' 'em anymore doesn't mean you want anyone else doin' 'em."

David had to smile. "How is she?"

"She's all right. Gotten a bit skinny, I don't like it. She's fuckin' killin' it on this picture, though. She's handin' me my balls daily."

They talked a bit longer, about the film, about France, about when Nick would be coming back to the States to do promos for *Kosma*.

"Yeah, boss. We'll get drunk and get laid, okay?"

"Sounds good, Nick. You take care and watch out for those French women."

"Ooh-la-la, Raurke, ooh-la-fuckin'-la."

David laughed as he hung up, and though he wouldn't have admitted it to anyone—least of all himself—he was glad to learn that Norah wasn't involved with that pretentious knob. He still wondered what the article was saying about *Kosma,* though. David considered having one of the assistants put out the call to a French teacher or something. He looked up to make the request when his heart stopped.

"What are you doing here?"

Brett looked down at him, dressed like the textbook tourist complete with guidebooks and camera bags. "Hello to you, too."

"Has . . . has something happened?"

Brett smiled.

Asshole.

"Everyone is fine. Well, not really fine. Ella is sad."

"Why is Ella sad?"

"Because her mother is sad."

David stiffened his back. "Brett, I'd like you to leave."

"No, you don't. You say you do, but you don't really."

"Don't I?"

"No, because then you wouldn't hear what I have to say."

"I'm not interested in what you have to say."

"Again, you say that but—"

"Brett!" He slammed his binder on the desk with a crash. "Get out."

"Now, David, listen to me." Brett sat across from him and crossed his legs. He removed his gloves and said, "You can ask me to leave, which naturally I won't do. You can even have security haul me out of here, which actually might be fun. Yes, you go ahead and do that. But then you'll spend the rest of the day wondering what it was that I came all the way to New York to tell you. A week will go by, and I'll be gone, and you still won't know what was so important that I'd fly halfway across the world to tell you. That's how it will go, week after week, year after year, eating away at you until you're an old, old man. Then on your death bed, in your shame and regret, you'll call out my name, and you'll die, never knowing the one thing that I wanted so badly to say. And because your very last word will be a man's name, everyone will think you were, in fact, a fegeleh."

David smiled and sank into his chair in defeat. "You make a compelling argument."

"Don't I? I think I would make a fab lawyer. Only I can't do the double-breasted thing. It makes me look hippy."

"You've got five minutes."

"You're not going to buy me lunch?"

****

Fifteen minutes later, they had ordered and David sat fidgeting across from Brett, staring him down.

Brett seemed completely undaunted as he took in his surroundings in the brightly lit café. "So this is nice. I'm hitting as many eating establishments as I can while I'm here, that way I can write the trip off as research." He sipped his cocktail.

"Brett, I swear to God—"

"Fine, fine. Have it your way." He leaned in conspiratorially. "I know you think you know what you think you know, but in fact, you're wrong."

David sighed and put his head in his hands. "What does an embolism feel like?"

Brett made face. "That didn't come out quite as I'd intended. Let me start again."

"Please."

"I know what happened that afternoon, you know, the day of the big kiss-off."

David clenched his jaw. "So?"

"I also know it was a lie."

"What was a lie?"

"Every word she said, pretty much."

"Look, I don't know what you're going on about or why—"

"The *what* is I'm here to tell you that your breakup was part of a huge, horrible plot, and the *why* is . . . well, you still love each other, and I think everyone should be happy."

"Okay, you're full of shit, and I'm a fucking idiot for giving you the time of day. I'm out of here." He said it, but he appeared to be welded to the chair.

"David, David, David. Of course you still love her. You've been apart nearly as long as you were together, yet you're still so angry with her, aren't you?" Brett waved his hand, signaling he had permission to not answer, as if he could. "For her part, you should know, she's a mess. It's like talking to a shell. She's put up a good front and has been working crazy hard on the Bartolini film—"

"I heard."

"Hmm?"

"I hear things. I can't help that I hear things."

"No, of course not, but don't you think it's a shame that there's all this hurt for nothing?"

"Okay. Now I need you to tell me what you meant with that plot comment, and I need you to make it quick 'cause I don't know . . ." His voice choked off as though someone had him by the throat.

"Right. I'll give you the abridged version. Your agent-slash-manager-slash-spawn-of-Satan convinced Norah, in no uncertain terms, that staying with you would ruin you, that you'd be the laughingstock of Hollywood for being lured into the clutches of some ambitious little upstart. As if that wasn't enough, he made certain she knew that it was inevitable that you were going to dump her ass for some long-legged, glassy-eyed, star-fucker anyway so she might as well save herself, and you, a world of pain and pull the plug before she'd caused your career irreparable damage."

The wheels spun wildly behind David's eyes. He replayed everything that had been said that day, weighing it against what he had just heard. He was prepared to believe anything, anything short of Norah having been temporarily replaced by a pod person, that would reduce that day and all the days that followed into nothing more than a bad dream. But what this lunatic was suggesting was beyond science fiction.

"No! It isn't possible. You weren't there. She's not that good an actress."

"David. You, of all people, know better than that."

Touché.

"All right, then. Nigel would never have said that, and even if he did, why wouldn't she have told me so that we could, I don't know, confront him together? I could have at least told her it wasn't true, that it didn't matter if it was . . . that nothing . . . that nothing was worth losing her." David was barely holding it together.

"Listen, I can't tell you what's going on in the mind of your high-priced pimp. Maybe it's the power, the money. Who knows, who cares? And I can't say for sure why she didn't come to you first. My guess is because she was afraid you'd talk her out of it. You see, David, she honestly believed what he told her. He's your agent, after all, and, supposedly, only looking out for you, right? Why would he lie? Trust me, there is nothing short of being convinced that staying with you would ruin your life that would have forced her to say the things she did. It would have to be at least that serious for her to, well, go on without you."

"She told *you,* though. Why didn't you come to me sooner?"

"She doesn't know she told me."

David shook his head, confused.

"Oh, boy. Look, I don't know if she'll ever forgive me for what I'm about to say. And I don't mean that in the, *Here's Brett, the little drama queen blowing things out of proportion again* way, but the, *Goodness, how lovely! Are those* my *balls on that platter?* way. But you need to know. You see, David, letting go of you nearly killed her. Okay, that's a bit of an exaggeration, but I did have to put her in hospital. They kept her sedated at first, just so she'd rest, and while she was zoned out she told me what happened. I didn't come to you earlier because I knew she wouldn't put herself through that kind of hell unless she knew what she was doing. Norah has always been the strong one. She was the one always holding *me* up, so I trusted her instincts. Also, she made me promise not to tell you unless . . ."

"Unless?"

Brett bit his lip. "She was completely devastated you see. It was . . . if not for Ella . . ."

"Brett, unless what?"

"I wasn't supposed to tell you anything about what had happened unless she died. She was never really in any danger of that, not really, but have you ever—" He clapped one hand daintily over his mouth.

"Have I ever hurt so bad I didn't think I'd live through it? Yes, Brett, I have." That admission took the last bit of strength David had.

"So that's why I had to tell you, don't you see? Even if it meant, well, pieces of me being served up *en croute*. Not because I've come to embrace the fact that I'm really crap at keeping promises, but because you needed to know the truth, and more importantly, you need to do something, David. You need to fix this."

****

David's hands shook so bad he was unable to open the door to his apartment. Finally, he slowed his breathing and got a grip on himself long enough to get inside. He hoped some measure of familiarity and security would stop the ringing in his head. Every answer that he now had gave birth to two more questions in a circuitous maze of dialogue—what she had said to him, what Nigel supposedly said to her, what Brett repeated back and around and around and over and over.

He paced around the living room, sitting down only to spring right back up and start pacing some more.

"Ruby!"

"Yes, sir, Mr. Raurke."

He looked at her helplessly for several seconds before he realized that he had no idea what he'd wanted.

"May I make you a drink, sir?"

"Please," he said, relieved that he'd found her something to do and that he'd soon have alcohol.

She made it a hearty one.

Bless her.

"Thank you," he said as he took it from her and drank it down gratefully. He passed it back to her, the request for another in his eyes. He noted, absently, her lips pressed thin in disapproval.

Poor old girl. Things were just getting back to normal, weren't they?

While she scurried back to the bar, he fell into a chair with his head in his hands, and let the liquor work its magic to smooth his jangled nerves.

By the time the second drink was in his hand, the shaking had stopped, but the ache in the pit of his stomach was larger and harder to ignore.

"Sir, is there anything I can do? Anyone I can call?" The woman wrung her hands.

"No, thank you. You can go."

"Sir . . ."

"I'll be fine, Ruby, please."

She backed slowly from the room.

She'd given him an idea, though, and he crossed to the phone and hit a single button.

"Hello?" His sister answered after two rings.

"Beth . . ." Again, he found himself reaching out to someone but at a loss about what to say.

"David?" she asked, alarm in her voice. "David, what's happened?"

"I don't know what to do."

"Where are you? Are you at home?"

"Yes."

"Don't move. I'm on my way."

He hung up and sat back in the chair with his drink and the first small stirrings of hope.

Help's on the way.

****

David was still slumped in the same chair when Beth buzzed up just over an hour later. He was a couple more drinks to the better but had spent the time well. In an effort to not hurl a heap of incomprehensible babble at Beth the moment she arrived, he'd recalled and compartmentalized all the relevant information that he either knew or had been told.

He watched as Ruby answered the door, and his sister squeezed the older woman's arm as she passed her coat and bag over, thanking her.

He tipped his glass in her direction as Beth crossed to him.

"Holy shit," she said, immediately ascertaining his condition.

"Yep."

"I'm going to go out on a limb here and guess this has something to do with Norah." She sat facing him on the ottoman in front of his chair.

David smiled. "Her brother paid me a visit this morning."

"Brent?"

"Brett."

"Right. So, what did he have to say?"

During the sorting of facts, David decided he would have to go a bit further back in the story than simply this morning. He started with the conversation he'd had over the phone with Nigel just days after he and Norah had returned from Vancouver.

****

"Hello?" David had been going over the schedule for the following week in his trailer, looking forward to the next two days with Norah and Ella, when his cell phone rang.

"Please hold for Nigel Coombs," said a silken voice from across the continent.

David's eyebrows went up in surprise.

"David, m'boy. How are you?"

"Fine, Nigel, just fine. How's life in the Apple?"

"Marvelous. We're anxiously awaiting your return. When may we expect

The Wrong Woman

you?"

"A week tomorrow. To what do I owe the pleasure?"

"Well, I have a rather nasty bit of tabloid on my desk at the moment, and I thought I'd better get some information, considering the phones have started ringing off the hook."

David winced. "Sorry about that, Nigel. I guess I should have called earlier."

"Never mind, dear boy. I expect it's nothing but another bit of fluff to sweep under the rug. Don't give it a moment's worry."

"Um, that's not quite the case this time, Nigel."

"Really? Well, I'm all astonishment. Do tell."

David filled his agent and manager in on the basic details, Norah's part in the film, how brilliant she was, how she came to be part of it, and how they were in love.

"David, I couldn't be happier for you or for the very clever girl who has conquered the unconquerable. Will she be coming to New York with you?"

"A couple of weeks after we get set up. She's shooting a number of scenes there. Why?"

"Perhaps I should meet her here. Does she have representation?"

"Um, no actually. Just a cursory contract that she signed on the day we cast her. It was all kinda rushed."

"Brrrr. That's the sort of talk that sends a fellow like me into fits. No, no, if she's as talented as you say, then we simply must have her. Don't you agree?"

"Well, I think that'd be great. I can send over some footage so you can have a look. Other than that, should I just bring her by once she's in town?"

"Certainly. Give us a call, and we'll set up a proper meeting. I'll introduce her to the team, and she can see how things are done in the big city."

"That'll be fine. Thanks, Nigel."

"Happy to do it, David. Any friend of yours . . . well, you know the song."

"Yes, I do."

"David, if you could . . . one other little matter. This ghastly gossip and whatnot. Is there anything about the lady that I should know? You understand, so that I can best protect you both? Forewarned is forearmed, and all that."

David said he couldn't think of anything in particular unless the single mother thing was going to be a problem, but since Ella's father had died—in combat no less—he couldn't see a worry there. He reiterated what a huge talent Norah was, that she was a wonderful person, and that he'd never been happier.

"Then that's good enough for me. Leave it in my hands, David. I shall make all this unpleasantness go away."

"I'd appreciate that, Nigel."

"David, it's what I do."

****

Beth remembered walking her children to school the week the photograph had caught her attention from the front of her local newsstand and brought her to a screeching halt. Her heart had caught in her throat as she'd read the headline.

Christ, was he never going to catch a break? And that poor woman.

She'd had a number of phone conversations with David at that point and was looking forward to meeting Norah, sure he really had something this time. It had been a favourite topic of conversation whenever she'd talked with their parents or one of the old chums.

Well, it was a good test. If she can stand up against Beauty and the She-Beast, then maybe she's got the stuff to walk through fire.

****

"But what does Nigel have to do with this?" Beth asked, once David had finished relaying the phone conversation to her.

"I'm getting to that." He narrated the details of their meeting in Nigel's office. How impressed Nigel and the team had appeared to be with her, how she'd answered all of his questions with courage and conviction and how, in general, he'd thought it to be a very good interview. He went on to describe how, a couple of hours later, they had been mobbed by the press coming out of the restaurant where they'd lunched, and how badly that had gone. "In retrospect, I'm sure Nigel tipped them off."

"He told the press where you'd be? Why would you think that?"

"At first, I thought someone from inside the restaurant had given us up, but then I remembered I'd had his receptionist make the reservation for me. She would have told him, for sure. Also, Nigel knew that Norah had never been briefed on media protocol, you know, measured responses, when not to answer, that sort of thing. Jesus, Beth, you should have seen it. It was a nightmare."

"But why would he do that?"

He shrugged. "To shake up her confidence. Maybe to try to make her look bad in my eyes, I don't know. He wanted her gone, I know that for sure now."

"But didn't he get her the Bartolini film?"

"Yeah, but I think that might have been his plan B if he couldn't get her to come around to his way of thinking. That way, at least she'd be three months in Europe while I was stuck here editing. Maybe he hoped the separation would do the trick."

"But . . . what? You're telling me he got her to come around to his way of thinking?"

David got up and made himself another drink, and poured one for her as well. He'd never gone into detail with Beth about what had happened at the end of his and Norah's relationship. He'd never revealed to anyone what she'd said to him that day. Beth had just accepted the fact that something truly awful had happened, that her beloved twin brother and best friend had been devastated, and that it was all a terrible shame.

He sat back down and stared intensely into his drink, like millions of men before him, seeking courage from within the liquid. By the time he'd furnished her with the portions of the dialogue he'd committed to memory, and ended with his hasty exit out of Norah's front door and life, Beth had tears falling down her face from the raw pain in David's eyes.

"Oh, my darling, darling, David. I had no idea. Why? I can't believe . . . from what you told me, from what I know of her, none of that makes any sense."

"No, it didn't to me either, but I was too torn up to challenge it. I couldn't face her again. I just couldn't. I thought that I knew her better . . . better than myself, but that day, fuck, it was as if I'd never known her a day in my life. A total stranger who'd killed the woman I loved. Does that make any sense?"

Beth nodded.

David revealed the details of Brett's visit, how he had admitted Norah to the hospital after David had left that horrible day, and what she had told him—while under sedation—about Nigel's inconceivable betrayal.

Beth placed her hands over her mouth. "No. It's like a bad movie. Who behaves like that?"

"An agent."

Beth studied her brother. "David, what are you going to do?"

He shook his head and shrugged.

"Okay, let me rephrase. What do you *want* to do?"

"I want to kill him." His voice was chillingly calm. "I want to go into his office and wrap my hands around his scrawny neck and squeeze the life out of him. That's what I want to do." He took another drink.

"All right, let's tuck that one to the side for a moment, shall we? What do you want to do about Norah?"

He half smiled. "I nearly called her. About two hundred times since I hung up with you."

"What would you have said?" She placed her hands on his knees.

He sighed. "I dunno. That I know the truth. That Nigel is a self-serving prick, and that I don't give a flying fuck what happens to my career, that . . ." He drew his hand over his eyes as the alcohol and the agony swept over him.

"That you still love her?" Beth finished the sentence for him, and he nodded from behind his hand . . . behind his tears. "Then you need to do that."

He jerked his hand down and looked at his sister. "What?"

"Call her. Immediately. Well, maybe in the morning." She deferred to his condition.

"Nope. No way." He sat back in the chair, panic and stubborn resolve all over his face.

"Why?"

"She needs to come to me. She ended it, she needs to fix it."

"David, this isn't high school. Adults don't play *who goes first*. You know the truth, she doesn't. She's living with the bullshit that's been fed to her and still thinking she's done the best thing for you."

"No, damn it, Beth. What if she hangs up on me? What if the papers are right, and she ends up telling me she's having it off with Bartolini and that I need to mind my own fucking business. What if—"

"It doesn't matter, David. Even if it has nothing to do with the two of you getting back together again, she deserves to know what really happened. If she's going to spend the rest of her life in an industry that, frankly, makes me grateful I went into architecture, then she needs to know that there are people like Nigel in it. And at the very least, she needs to know what he's done so that she can get out from under him. Now! If I'm any judge of character, David—and I think I am—she's in worse shape than you. Don't interrupt me! She's in worse shape than you because she's in shambles as a result of a decision she's made, one she has to live with every single day. You're living with the consequences. I know that seems like a fine distinction, but it makes a difference when you think there are two people laid out bleeding, but she's the one who pulled the trigger."

She sat back, letting him chew on that a moment. "What are your options here? Ignore this information and continue as you have for the last three months? Why on earth would you let her go on thinking that you're better off without her, when, clearly, you aren't?"

"Pardon me, sir."

David and Beth both jumped at the sound of a third voice.

Ruby stood a few feet away, neither knew for how long, with a courier package about a foot square and nearly six inches deep in her hands. "This just arrived for you. It says rush delivery, and so I assumed it was important or I wouldn't have—"

"That's fine, Ruby. Thank you."

She handed the package to Beth who passed it off to David.

A distraction might do him some good, seeing as how they'd both been so immersed that neither had heard the buzzer in the first place.

Beth crossed the room and poured them both a glass of water. "What is it?"

"Probably books. I'd ordered a couple of biographies about Kosma ages ago, not that they'll do much good now. Final edits are nearly finished."

He carried it to the bar and used the blade from the corkscrew to undo the wrapping.

Beth stood nearby, watching.

"Oh no. God . . . no." David had taken the bundle apart to reveal two similarly sized items wrapped in tissue. He had one nearly uncovered when he all but collapsed on the bar.

Beth reached for him and took the half-wrapped bundle from his hand.

Inside were two beautiful antique picture frames—one elegant platinum and the second of thick, polished wood. Each had soft linen matting and a photograph of a lovely woman kissing a sleeping child. Beth recognized them at once and, with tear-filled eyes, looked over at the ruin that was once her brother.

She set the photos of Norah and Ella gently down on the bar and pulled David into her embrace. "David. Please, darling. Tell me what I can do."

He clung to her for a moment and then pulled away, a new look in his eyes, one of fierce determination and focus.

This needs to stop and it needs to stop now.

"Please, help me get my family back."

****

Nigel Coombs held the meeting in the cherry wood paneled conference room. Handsome ergonomic chairs surrounded an impressive table made out a single slab of black, rough-cut granite. He sat at the head, flanked by five heads of publicity, two image consultants, a private photographer, and three junior managers from his own organization.

There was a miserable-looking rock band about town that had a certain something and had piqued Nigel's interest enough to take them on for a limited contract. He'd try to make the proverbial silk purse out of a reasonably talented, though scruffy and undisciplined, sow's ear. If it came to nothing, well that was all part of the game, but with the help of this lot, they may well come to something. At the very least, he anticipated getting his initial investment back a couple of times over, and that was all right for a few days' work. The image consultants were having a dreary argument about haircuts when a fairly distinctive disruption came from the direction of the lobby.

The double doors at the end of the room burst open and David Raurke stood, eyes ablaze and framed in the doorway like some demonic painting as he scanned the room for his target. The receptionist trembled behind him and looked with desperation in the direction of her employer.

"That's all right, Giselle. I always have time for David." Only Nigel knew of the cold hand creeping down the back of his neck at the sight of his most lucrative client standing there looking all but completely deranged. "Ladies and gentlemen, I believe you know, or know of, David Raurke."

Everyone had turned to David at the moment of his explosive entrance, all openly astonished at such a display, all secretly hoping that they not be banished, as this promised to be interesting.

Alas, it was not to be.

"Perhaps you could all wait in the outer offices for a moment while David and I have a word."

The assemblage rose and filed past David, casting curious looks in his direction before the last one out secured the doors behind them.

David hadn't moved a rigid muscle since he'd come through the doors. His eyes had locked onto Nigel like heat-seeking missiles.

Nigel Coombs was in his element. Having been in this industry for over thirty years in one form or another, the tantrums of petulant actors had become all in a day's work for him. He wasn't a fool, though, and was very much aware that the next few minutes had to be managed with great care. "David, won't you have a seat? A drink, perhaps?"

David shook his head.

"Very well. Let's cut to the chase then, shall we? I assume, by your barbaric demeanor, that this has something to do with a female. Our Norah would be my guess. Tell me, has she finally impressed you with tales of Nigel, the big bad wolf? Rather ungrateful of the little chit, after all I've filled her dance card for the next eighteen months. She's going to be in an Erickson next summer, and that took some string pulling, I don't mind telling you. So tell me, my boy, have you descended upon me to, how is it they say, clean my clock? Is that it?"

David stalked to the end of the table opposite Nigel and placed his hands on it. His voice was glacial. "First, she is not *our* Norah. Second, I've not talked to her in nearly three months. Third, Erickson would be lucky to get her, and fourth, and let me make this perfectly clear: I. Am. Not. Your. Boy."

Nigel was grateful indeed for the sixteen feet of solid granite between them. "Then what is the problem, David? As well you know I have a large number of very expensive people outside waiting for you to come to the point."

"Why did you do it? And how could I have been so fucking wrong about you all these years?"

This really was too tedious. If she didn't tell him, she must have told someone who told someone.

Pity.

He'd thought her more tight-lipped than that, considering he'd motivated her with enough self-centred material that she'd come off looking ruthlessly ambitious for casting David aside for her career. She was either stupid, with which he hadn't any patience, or clever in a way that he hadn't anticipated. Either way, he'd deal with her in due course. For the moment, he had an exceptionally valuable commodity staring him down, and he needed to extinguish this particular fire before it spread beyond his control.

"How do you like your house in the Hollywood Hills, David? How about your apartment here in Manhattan? Your home in Ireland? Really more of a castle, isn't it? Are you terribly fond of the cars? The motorcycles? The yacht? How do you stand on the public adoration? The women crawling out of the woodwork? The talk shows beating down your door for an appearance? The scripts landing on your desk daily? You've been a very, very lucky man, David. You've had everything you've ever dreamed of land on your doorstep, and that is almost entirely due the efforts put into your career by this office. By *me*. It hasn't always been easy, and it hasn't always been tidy, but it has been done because that is the way a movie star is made."

"You . . . you destroyed Norah and me for the sake of some property and a couple of jobs?"

"Don't be naïve. You are not merely an actor, David. You are the result of thousands of hours of strategy, manipulation, and politics. You are the product of my particular machine, David, my finest work, I'm proud to say, and I have no intention of having you brought down by that common little Canadian bumpkin."

****

That was all he needed.

He'd spent nearly a third of his life under the control of this man, and part of him had been clinging to the hope that there had been some sort of misunderstanding, but no. He considered how many other ways this vulture might have used his influence to alter the natural course of his life.

That can wait.

"I wonder, can you even conceive of the possibility that being with someone, making a life with them, having a family even, could matter more than all the things you mentioned, or are you such a . . . such a . . ."

"Bottom feeder?"

He's nothing if not helpful.

"Thank you, bottom feeder—that you believe it's all just some kind of illusion or make believe, possible only in the films you send us up for? That it doesn't actually exist, or if it does, that it simply doesn't matter if it happens to come up against *your* particular idea of success?"

Nigel's lips thinned into something resembling a grin. "What I believe, David, is that love, like film roles, money, and fame, is transitory, and like all the rest, if handled properly, can build on all the other assets in one's life. For example, if you have money, you can buy love. With the proper film roles, you can achieve fame. You were the product of *my* particular idea of success for many years, David, and I'd not have objected to your going dotty on someone had it increased your bottom line. But Norah? She was insupportable. Simply put, she's the wrong woman for the job."

"Really? Just out of curiosity, Nigel, who would have been the right woman?" He'd kept a close eye on the man since he entered the room, ready to catch a nervous blink, an anxious clenching of the jaw, or bead of sweat that might appear on the brow or upper lip. Finally, it revealed itself, a chink in the bastard's armour, a nervous twitch in one corner of his mouth and a nearly imperceptible swallowing. The victory was bittersweet.

"That's what I thought. You'd have made sure I was alone for the rest of my life, wouldn't you?"

"Never alone, David," Nigel said, bald sincerity sounding foreign coming from him. "You would never have been alone. I would have seen to that."

Exhaustion washed over David, diluting his rage and extinguishing the passion for revenge that had held him upright to this point. He looked at Nigel and was stunned to feel something akin to pity take the place of everything he had felt only moments before. "See to it that my contract with you is dissolved immediately. I want to be rid of you before the end of the day."

And with that, Nigel Coombs saw the back of David Raurke for the last time.

Chapter 23

She made her way across the lot, weary after a long day of shooting.

It's odd how early it gets dark these days. Then again, I suppose it's not really that *odd, seeing as it's probably getting dark just as early back in Alberta as well. Maybe it's just odd because it's ordinary. I mean, this is France! Is it possible for France to do ordinary? Is it possible for Provence to be mundane. Is it possible . . . that I am losing my mind?*

She shook her head to clear her brain of the whirl of haphazard thoughts, and reached for the latch on her trailer door. She hauled herself up the stairs, shut the door, and clicked on the small, overhead light. Peg and Ella had gone back to the hotel since the shoot had run so late. She pouted, knowing that she'd missed saying good night to the little one, but she'd be damned if she'd complain about it.

She was a working actress now. She had three projects in the works after this one wrapped, each one more exciting than the one before it. Not a single piece of film showing her work had even been distributed yet. All her good reviews and recommendations had been dispersed by word of mouth, and she wasn't about to do anything to let down the people who'd had such faith in her.

Never again.

The familiar ache returned to her chest. It had become a constant companion these last three months, and she'd often wondered if she'd simply become used to it, the way Peg had become accustomed to her grief after Eric had died.

She removed her trench coat and boots and placed them in the closet near the door for Celeste to pick up. Glancing in the direction of the table, she caught sight of the message light on her cell phone. She stepped toward it while undoing the heavy belt cinching her dress. As though in slow motion, she halted, her hands frozen on the buckle, and she panned her head over her right shoulder where her peripheral vision made out a shape.

"David." Her voice was barely a whisper, afraid to say it too loud, afraid she was wrong . . . afraid she was right.

"Hello."

She was astonished at how cool he sounded. She was astonished she was still standing. Her heart pounded so hard she could make out a distinct flutter along the front of her silk blouse.

He looked so relaxed with his legs outstretched and crossed at the ankles, his hands resting on the arms of the chair. He was partly in shadow, but still stunningly handsome in a cable knit sweater the colour of sun-dried tobacco. Norah spotted his coat draped over the back of the sofa, and at least two beer bottles on the table to his left, suggesting he'd been there for some time.

He motioned to it. "I helped myself, I hope you don't mind."

"David, what are you doing here?"

"I was in the neighbourhood."

The idiocy of that statement snapped her out of her shock. "The neighbourhood? The *neighbourhood?!*"

"Would you like a beer? I wouldn't mind another." He stood, and she realized she'd forgotten how tall he was. He completely filled her field of vision, and her breath caught in her throat.

She gestured for him to sit back down, and walked on unsteady legs to the fridge. She opened the door and, while reaching inside for the bottles, filled her lungs with the cool air. Her mind raced as she tried to come up with some reason for him to be here. She uncapped the bottles and stepped back into the lounge.

****

"How's Ella?"

She couldn't meet his gaze as she handed him another drink.

She'd accepted the hell she'd put herself through by letting him go, but she'd had a much harder time coming to terms with the fact that she'd taken David from Ella and vice versa.

She nodded while taking a healthy draw on the bottle, then answered. "Ella's great. Thanks."

"I've missed her." He cleared his throat and rubbed the chair's armrests.

She couldn't respond. It was too hard. She hadn't missed the catch in his voice.

She sank weakly onto the far side of the sofa and tried to look interested in the label on the bottle. "When did you arrive?"

Maybe he's here by accident, on holiday, meeting up with someone.

"I landed this afternoon."

Nope, he came straight here.

"I flew out of New York. Beth asked me to send her love."

"David . . . what—"

"I came from New York because I had a meeting there yesterday—at least I think it was yesterday—with Nigel Coombs."

"Excuse me, I need to get out of this before wardrobe shows up to collect it." She jumped up, set her drink on the table, and disappeared into the back.

Her hands shook as she tried to get the dress on its hanger.

What on earth could he have talked about with Nigel that immediately put him on a plane for France?

She hooked the dress on the door and took several long, slow breaths in an attempt to recover from seeing him here. She turned and there he was again, having followed her to her dressing room. "That's an annoying little habit you've developed."

He smiled that maddeningly sexy smile that had never failed to make her go wobbly, but seeing she'd been wobbly since she first spotted him, she couldn't be sure this wasn't carryover.

"I was afraid you might try to sneak out the window."

She felt his gaze as it wandered over her body, clothed only in a vintage bra and tap pants, and she recognized the heat left in its path.

What the hell does he want?

A knock at the main door and a voice calling out had Norah almost jumping out of her skin.

"No-ah, c'est Celeste. Allo?"

"Just a sec, Celeste. *Je serai sur,*" she called out, and turned back to David. "Please, give me a moment."

He nodded and backed out.

Norah hurried to the door with the dress on its hanger and a small lingerie bag.

Once Celeste had gathered the coat and boots at the door, she bid a bashful *adieu* to David, cast an impressed smile toward Norah, and departed.

Norah had changed into dark chocolate brown pants and light knit top, the colour of buttercream frosting. She sat in the dining chair and pulled on a pair of short, brown leather boots.

"Are you going somewhere?"

"Look, David, I realize you've got something on your mind, and you've come a long way, but it's late. I have an early call in the morning, and I'm too tired to play cat and mouse with you tonight. You must be exhausted after your trip. Why don't we just pick this up another day, tomorrow, Saturday even—"

"Norah—"

"David, I am one frayed nerve sitting here. Get on with it, or get out. Please." She was trying hard to portray strength and resolve, but her eyes, brimming with tears, told another story.

"I know what Nigel said to you."

"How?"

"He told me."

"Nigel told you?"

"That's right."
"He just offered it up?"
"Well, I asked him, and he—"
"No, he did not."
"Sorry?"

She fixed him with a stare, then her eyes closed painfully as if it all dawned on her at once. "Brett. He's put you up to this."

She watched him struggle at the prospect of throwing her brother under the bus. "He paid me a visit while I was—"

"When?"
"I was editing. The day before yesterday."
"Brett was in New York two days ago?"
David nodded.
"And he said what to you exactly?"
"He told me everything you told him."
"What I . . . wait, I didn't tell him anything about Nigel."
"Yes, you did. You told him what happened while you were in the hospital."

"When I was in hosp—" She wrapped her arms across her chest and folded over. The memory of that awful, horrible time was multiplied by him knowing all about it, and obliterated her control.

"It's okay, Norah. I'm glad he told me."
She stayed curled within herself and shook her head.

"After talking to Brett, I went home. I called Beth. I was crazy. I wanted to phone you, to kill Nigel . . . Beth came over, we talked, she made some sense of it, our part of it, anyway.

"I went to Nigel's office the next morning. He denied nothing, told me he did it for me, that I'd thank him later, that he had worked too hard for what I'd achieved to have it all brought down by . . . you. I told him . . . I told him that nothing in my life mattered if you weren't in it. It didn't matter if he didn't believe me." David took a shallow breath. "But then, why should he believe me when you didn't?"

She slowly lifted her head to find him still in the chair, but his hands were clenched tightly together, elbows on his knees, and his face barely masking his bitterness.

"Why didn't you believe me?" His voice had a pleading quality that nearly broke what was left of her heart.

"I did. I believed you meant what you said when you said it but—"
"That is such bullshit, Norah!"
She winced.

"You let Nigel determine my level of sincerity, my level of fidelity. *I* said I'd love you forever. *He* said, nope, end of the week, at best. So *that's* the one you went with? You actually believed him when he said that I would be better off without you, that at the end of the day my career must mean more to me? Have you ever heard a single, goddamn word that I've said to you?"

"He's known you so much longer, knew that . . . that part of you—"

"He's a fucking *agent*, Norah! He makes his living off my back, like a pimp. You know that. You're not a child."

"I couldn't go back."

"Go back? Go back where?"

"Whitecourt . . . the café . . ."

"Who said you—"

"He did! Nigel. He said in the end you'd resent me for the damage to your career and leave me. We'd only been together a few months, David. I didn't dare to dream we'd be together forever. As much as we loved each other, I didn't dare. He made a pretty convincing case about how I couldn't make a go of it acting, that I wouldn't be accepted so long as I was with you, and he wasn't far wrong there, was he? Without you, and without the opportunity he was offering me, I was back in Whitecourt, for good. Any way he spun it, I was going to be alone. I'm sorry. I really, really am, and I hate how this makes me sound, but if I couldn't have you, I had to take what I could get, to take care of me. I know you'd made arrangements for Ella, but I needed to do what I could . . ." She blanched, realizing what she'd let slip.

"Pardon?"

"Aw, shit."

A heavy silence fell over them, full of recrimination, full of blame, and, it seemed for both of them, with very little hope.

****

"Your brother is one big security breach, isn't he?"

"He's not good, but in his defense . . . he told me about the trust fund because he thought you'd look like the good guy back when I'd started having doubts. Not about you being a good guy but . . . anyway, what he accomplished instead was furthering my fear that you weren't really planning a future with us. Once Nigel got a hold of me . . ."

His face was in his hands.

Give me strength or I will surely throttle this woman!

"Why didn't you tell me? We could have worked something out."

"What? What could we have worked out?"

"I don't know. We could have kept us a secret until you'd built yourself up a bit, I could have dropped out for a few years and directed, or vanished altogether, anything. I would have done anything, Norah, if you'd only told me!"

She shrugged. "I was a woman in love and was made to believe, by someone that *you* trusted, that I was going to destroy you. That if, in fact, I *did* love you, I needed to get out of your way. How could I not get out of your way?"

They sat quietly, each absorbing what the other had said.

It was true. He had trusted Nigel and had led her to him like a lamb to slaughter. She was an intelligent woman but she'd never come up against someone like Nigel, and there was no way she could have come out on top. Hell, he'd been taking it up the ass all these years, so how could he possibly blame her for not seeing through the prick? The fact that Nigel hadn't banished her into obscurity was a bit of an oddity. Perhaps he knew how talented she was and thought he'd take his pound of flesh before he got found out. Or, more sinister and therefore more likely, he'd planned to keep her working and under his malevolent thumb for the rest of her life.

"So how does one go about dumping their agent?" she asked.

"I'll call my lawyer tomorrow, and get her started on it. Maybe we'll get a group rate. Are all your other contracts secured?"

She nodded. "All but the thing with Ralston next autumn."

"He's a friend of mine. I'll call him. It shouldn't be a problem, even if Coombs tries to cause trouble." David was confident that once the trades got their hands on how he, Terry Micks, and several other top names had pulled their contracts out of the house of Coombs Elite, anything Nigel might have to say about a green up-and-comer wasn't going to be worth spit. Norah would be safe from him.

"Thank you."

"You're welcome."

It felt odd having such a normal conversation when everything was so unsettled. He was still angry with her, though, no denying that. The last three months wasted.

All this damage, for what?

She didn't trust him to have an attention span longer than Ella's, didn't trust him even when he told her time and again how much she meant to him, didn't trust him, period.

"So, what . . ." She cleared her throat and tried again. "What happens now?"

He blinked and looked at her. "What do you mean?" He was angry enough to not make this easy for her.

"All right. What happens now between us? I want, more than anything in my life, to fix this if it can be fixed. For what it's worth, I have never, even for a second, stopped loving you, David, and I will do whatever it takes to make this right. But I need to know, please, what do you want to happen?"

He was satisfied that that had been difficult for her to say. He was pleased that she'd put herself on the line, and more than that, the fact that she was willing to open herself to his reply spoke volumes.

The worst is over.

"Norah." He had to restrain himself from charging over to her. "Two days ago, I endured your brother over lunch, which I cannot claim as a legitimate business expense. Then I nearly sacrificed my sister to the Long Island Expressway. The next day, I fired my agent of twelve years—if not performing career suicide, at least causing a scandal that'll be the front

The Wrong Woman

story for every entertainment magazine and news show for the next two weeks, and you know how I love it when that happens.

"Then I got on a plane, for nine unimaginable hours, that landed me in a country where I know exactly twelve words of the language, seven of which are requests for sex, which I don't need because the only person I want to have sex with speaks English. The idiots at the airport rent me a car with an American license because I'm, you know, David Raurke and—I'm ashamed of this part—I never learned to drive a stick, so you know that's going to cost me.

"And then I get here only to have to hide in a dark trailer for four hours waiting for you to finish playing Mata Hari, or whoever, and forced to drink this French swill they call beer. Norah, what do you think I want to have happen?"

She'd listened to his rant through suppressed laughter and suppressed tears. When he'd finished, she slowly stood and ran the short distance to him.

He met her partway, and they fell into one another's arms with an almost violent force. He crushed her to him, silently thanking God for giving him the balls to go through all this.

She wept against him.

He lowered her feet to the floor, took her wet face into his hands, and looked hard into her eyes. "I love you so much, but I need you to promise *never* to do this again, Norah. I mean it. We can get past this, we can come out of it—maybe even stronger—but you can never do this again. You can never doubt me or my love for you, *ever*. I need you to promise."

"David, I promise. I promise, I swear, I . . . vow . . . I pledge my troth, or whatever the hell. Just please, please tell me you'll forgive me. I'll never forgive myself, but I need . . . please, tell me you forgive me."

"Um, maybe not just yet. I think you've got some serious sucking up to do first."

She laughed and rained kisses on his face. "Get your coat, I've a car waiting," she said in such a way that it made him warm in all the right places.

He shrugged into his coat and helped her on with her own then stopped her hands from doing up the buttons. Instead, he slid his own beneath her coat and up under the hem of her shirt, unable to wait to touch her skin.

The sigh that escaped her went straight to his heart, and pulling her close, took her mouth with his own. Within seconds, her lips sought more of him. She deepened the kiss and flirted against the part between his lips with her tongue.

The blood started to pool deliciously in his groin, and that blissful fog descended on his brain. There was no mistaking the effect of her kiss, or the fact that the emptiness that had consumed him without it these last three months was wreaking havoc on his restraint. "You'd better be staying around the corner or we're going to give your driver one hell of a shock."

"He's a French chauffeur. I don't think he *can* be shocked."

Laughing, he withdrew his hands and put them to use fastening her coat buttons, then opened the door, and followed her out into the night.

****

The ride was only fifteen minutes in length, but it seemed to them an eternity. The suite that had been rented for her was in an ancient manor house, hundreds of years old, paint peeling in all the right places, worn rugs on the floor, and squeaky stairs leading everywhere, but it was exceptionally clean, terribly cozy, and the staff charming and eager to please.

Norah opened the door with her key, very aware of David's eager hands on her waist, of his mouth against her ear. The door creaked open, revealing Peg in the sitting room curled up in an overstuffed armchair.

She looked up from her book to greet Norah, and a look of pure pleasure lit her face when she noticed David behind her.

"David! Oh, my dear boy." She lifted herself from the chair and crossed cheerfully to embrace him. "Please tell me this means . . ." It only took her one look in Norah's glistening eyes. "Oh, God bless us. Well then, you two have lots to talk about, no doubt, so I'll just take my book to my room."

She gathered book, teacup, and shawl, all the while prattling on about how she'd always known everything would turn out all right in the end and walking toward one of the doors off the sitting room. Before passing through it, she turned to them. "It's just that nothing else was possible, you see." She grinned and closed the door behind her.

The sitting room was a bit small, but pleasantly furnished in cheerful prints and patterns with a comfy sofa, three mismatched armchairs, and a variety of small, oddly shaped tables set randomly in the area. Five doors were placed at irregular intervals around the room. The one closest was the one that Peg had claimed as her own, one in the middle Norah identified as a washroom, while she led David to a third.

The loudly protesting knob gave way to reveal a room dimly lit by a very small table lamp of a cartoon character holding up a wisp of a shade.

David's breath caught when he looked inside.

Ella was sound asleep on her side with both arms tightly embracing a long-limbed plush monkey, her face the picture of serenity and innocence.

"His name is François," Norah said, indicating the monkey. "The landlady gave him to her."

"A Frenchman? I'll be having a word with him in the morning. I guess she's talking by now, like, a lot more."

Norah nodded, feeling the full weight of what she'd denied him. "It's still mostly babble, but it catches me off guard all the time that she actually makes sense now and then."

"She's gotten so big."

"Only about an inch since the last time . . ." She couldn't get past the lump in her throat.

She kissed her daughter then watched with an aching heart as David leaned over and did the same. She moved back in the sitting room and waited for him. "I'm so sorry, David. I'm sorry for what I did to us, obviously, but even more than that, I'm sorry for having kept you from Ella."

"I wish I could say it didn't matter, but I don't hold you entirely to blame, honey. We'll just have to do all we can to make up for lost time."

To demonstrate, he drew her into his arms and kissed her with all the passion deprived them the past three months.

She molded against him.

"Where?" he moaned against her mouth.

Without releasing him, without removing her lips from his, they half danced, half staggered toward the two doors on the left wall. She had one of his arms out of his sweater by the time she needed to reach behind her to turn the knob of the door and push it open.

"Bathroom," he said, looking past her to the room over her shoulder.

"Bugger." She didn't take the time to shut the door again, but continued kissing him and dragged them to the next door. She got his head out of the neck of the sweater, and he tossed it on the floor behind him. She shook her head. "Don't drop it there. Peg . . ."

"Baby, I think she knows what we're up to. I doubt she's going to imagine we're sitting fully clothed in your bedroom discussing a tour through the wine country."

She smiled, the sound of him calling her that again filled her with joy. "David. Pick up the damn sweater."

He laughed and reclaimed the discarded item before she opened the door and pulled him inside with a saucy grin. He shut the door behind him, tossed the sweater . . . somewhere. He glanced around the room only long enough to see where the bed was, and then started gently shoving her toward it, his urgency apparent in his manner and in his pants.

"Stop pushing," she said, half whining, half giggling, and slapping at his hands. "You'd think you'd—" She gasped and her eyes widened.

No . . . I don't want to know. I don't want to know. I don't wan—

"What? Gone three months without getting laid?"

"You didn't?"

"No." He peered into her face. "You?"

"No. Of course not. I can't think . . . ever again."

"Then it's an awfully good thing we got this straightened out. That would have been a horrible waste." He slowly undid the buttons on her cardigan and his lips burned a trail along the side of her neck from her ear to her shoulder. "All those lovely, lovely orgasms bottled up forever?"

She trembled at his touch and his words. Her hands crawled sensuously over the expanse of his naked chest and stomach, and at long last, reached his belt. Her work was interrupted for a second as he pushed her top off.

He busied himself with the fastener at the waist of her slacks, but he fumbled with the foreign device, clicking his tongue in frustration.

She pushed him onto the bed in mock impatience, and he yanked his own pants from around his ankles and took off his socks, which then afforded him the opportunity to watch her undress herself.

She had the snaps undone in an instant and shot him a look as she wiggled the fastener mockingly before sliding the zipper down with maddening slowness. She stepped out of them and tossed them over a chair. With the little boots still on, she lifted one foot and placed it smartly between his legs. She laughed when he flinched, but he did his bit and removed the boot then the small sock from her, both of which he chucked across the room before he gestured for the next one.

Her eyes lingered over his boxers, and he took less than a second before he leapt up, wrenched them off, then reassumed his place on the bed half sitting, half leaning back on his arms.

She looked at him with a look of feigned wonder. "I have never known nor heard of anyone who could get out of his shorts with that kind of speed. You need to start some kind of Olympic event."

He smiled. "I'm motivated."

They laughed together and then she drank him in with her eyes.

She moved her gaze from the top of his head to the tips of his toes, lingering on some of her favourite spots, her yearning for him growing with every second of her intimate perusal.

"You've lost weight."

His assessment broke her out of her reverie. "Only about ten pounds." She could tell he wasn't pleased. "I wouldn't worry about it. As I recall, I ate like a pig while we were together. It'll be back. If you don't mind, though, I'll try to contain my appetite until *after* the film's wrapped, for continuity purposes, you understand."

"So long as that's the only appetite you contain." He grinned. "I wouldn't worry too much about it, though. I'll help you keep the pounds down if need be, for continuity purposes, you understand."

She smiled softly. "God, how I've missed you."

"I've missed you too, baby."

"What? Oh, I wasn't talking to you." With a lift of one eyebrow, she nodded at his nether region.

He fell back on the bed and roared with laughter. "Damn it, you know what happens when I laugh."

She grinned, wiggled her brows, and then crossed the small space between them.

For a person who enjoys the sexual act, there is nothing as sweet as the lovemaking that follows an argument or separation. For David and Norah, three months of living in a purgatory of empty arms and lonely beds had made them keenly aware of how great a love they had and had been forced to live without. They'd both endured endless nights of reaching over to the far side of the bed, imagining the other there, enjoying the fantasy for the briefest of moments only to suffer pitiably when the cold cloud of reality had sunk down over them again.

As Norah crawled along the bed beside him, she swallowed the memories of nights when she had turned her pillow sideways to lie against it, pretending it was him. It had been a poor, pathetic substitute, but it had served the dual purpose of taking in her tears. She straddled his waist and then lowered her head to take his hungry mouth in hers, showing him no mercy as his hands got reacquainted with her skin, his touch urgent and tender all at once. She felt him throbbing, reignited beneath her, and a shiver ran through her.

She reached behind her to unfasten her bra, but his fingers beat her to it and the straps were well on their way down her arms. Before it had even hit the floor, his hands cupped her breasts and her head tilted back as the heat scorched through her. His mouth replaced his hands, and her hips began a taunting rhythm, but her panties were most inconveniently in the way.

He flipped her—none too gently—on her back, reached down, and tore the light silk from her in one quick rending of fabric and elastic.

She gasped. "David!" He'd never shown this side of himself before. It frightened her a little and excited her a lot.

"Underwear-removing classes start tomorrow. I expect your full cooperation and attendance is mandatory."

She giggled. "Do you promise lots of homework?"

"Honey, you may never see the sun again."

She wrapped her legs around him and pulled his body where she most wanted him. Her own urgency made her bolder than ever.

He looked into her eyes as he perched on the edge of her. "Oh, Norah, I missed you so much."

Her hand stroked his face, and the emotion in her heart choked her voice. "I know, my love. I never thought . . . I dreamed so many times . . . oh, David, come inside me, please, now."

With a powerful thrust, he slid deep inside her, filling every velvet inch of her completely.

Her brain reeled in shock at how every nerve ending he touched flared up and burned. She submitted to the arousal that his body demanded of her, and welcomed the familiar feelings he revived within. The glorious ache seeped further and built relentlessly higher with an intensity that she had never known, even with him.

Her cries of ecstasy filled the room, and he quickened his tempo.

He trembled with the force of his own release and clung to her as they rode the final waves together.

****

The sense of waking to the unfamiliar filled David's bleary consciousness the next morning, though it wasn't accompanied by that foreboding feeling of dread as it had in the past. In fact, he had the distinct impression that it never would again. He rubbed the blurriness from his eyes and adjusted to his surroundings in the light of day. It was a pretty room. Feminine with the floral wallpaper and chintz bedding, and it smelled of lavender soap, fresh rainfall, and lovemaking. A delicious memory filled him and he rolled onto his side.

Norah is sleeping next to me.

He was so delirious by the realization of it that he repeated the notion in his head again and again.

He smiled and inched toward her. On one hand, he didn't want to disturb her, but on the other, he was eager for her to join him. She lay facing him, the draping of the sheet outlined the soft curves of her hips and waist. He lifted her hand from where it lay on her thigh and pressed it to his lips, his happiness nearly palpable. Carefully, he eased his way off the bed and went to the bathroom.

On his way back, he caught a glimpse of something familiar out of the corner of his eye. On the small dressing table, among her lotions, her hairbrush, and a photograph of Ella, was the coil notebook he recognized as her journal. He picked it up, ran his palm over it, and let the memories back in.

He'd disciplined himself, since their breakup, to lock out his recollections of all things Norah. He'd determined it was the only feasible course of action. Otherwise, how could he ever face an ocean view, the flickering of a candle, a walk along a river bank, or the laughter of a child?

He carried the book back to bed and examined the cover, gently running his fingertips over the beautifully embossed antique fabric. The edges of the pages were worn with turning and time, and he wondered what her entries for the past months might have been. That brought him to question that if he'd been able to chronicle that time for himself, how might they have read?

His stomach tightened.

"Do you want to read it?" a sleepy voice whispered next to him.

He turned and drank in the beauty of her dazzling eyes blinking sleepily from her pillow and her tousled hair begging for his fingers to run through it.

"I was . . . did you write, you know, since?"

She nodded. "I thought it would be therapeutic."

"Was it?"

"I don't know. It didn't stop the pain, if that's what you mean, which is what I hoped."

"I was just wondering what I would have written."

"I'm sorry, David."

He turned and gathered her to him. "Don't. It's past. Every time you say you're sorry, every time we look back and it hurts us, he wins again."

"I don't disagree, but I also think we can learn a lot from what's happened. Like how much we belong together."

"Norah, I didn't need it to happen to know that."

She stiffened in his arms. "But I did."

"I didn't say that."

"No, I know you didn't. I'm saying that I didn't completely believe that we . . . that I couldn't live without you until you weren't there. I mean, obviously I went on living. I had Ella to think about, and I had work to . . . but otherwise . . . I think I might have doubted us forever if we hadn't gone through it. I'm not saying it was the best way to accomplish it, but we're here now and, like you said, we'll be stronger."

"So that's all in here?" he inquired, gesturing to the journal still in his hand.

"Yes. Everything since I first met Ted and Steve."

"Do you—have you read those—"

"Have I gone back and read about us falling in love?"

"Yeah."

"All the time." She asked again, "Do you want to read it?"

"No, baby, it's private."

She grinned. "David, how can it be private from you? You're everywhere."

He laughed then stared at the journal some more, contemplating its mysteries and whether or not they should stay that way. "I don't know if I can face the last three months, not yet anyway, but I would like to read the stuff from the beginning."

"How come?"

"It was too hard holding on to you, the memories of you, of us, so I tried to make myself forget everything. I want to remember again."

"Go ahead, then. I've no secrets from you." She looked at the clock, gave him a quick kiss and made her way to the bathroom. "Good, it's still early. Ella won't be up for at least an hour. My call's not until one and—"

"You told me last night you had an early call." He was so absorbed in the journal he missed watching her walk naked across the room.

"Yeah, well, I lied, didn't I?" she said with a smirk. "Anyway, I'm going to run a nice bath and get myself ready. Are you hungry?"

"No, I'm okay. Besides, I'd like to wait and have breakfast with Ella."

"All right, I'll be out in a while."

He cracked open the volume and was overwhelmed by the scope of the thing. She'd written in it nearly every day since they'd met. Some days were chronicled very briefly:

> David came over for dinner this evening after shooting. I burned the chicken so I decided to take him upstairs instead. I may never learn to cook at this rate.

He smiled at that memory.

Then there were episodes that went on for pages and pages, like when they first met, and all the anxieties and excitement surrounding that day. She'd gone on to write that she'd sensed something in their very first hug, which surprised him, because he had, too.

She described their first kiss in such detail that it caused the same warm sensation in the pit of his belly that he'd gotten whenever he'd thought of it himself.

It's working! The journal is working.

He scanned a few pages, sought out particular recollections, relived them through her point of view. It was actually kind of fun.

Her writing was witty and sensitive, like her, and really, really sexy . . . again, like her. Her retelling of the events in the bathtub had him aching with arousal, and if he hadn't been so keen to continue reading, he might have climbed into her tub again, for old time's sake.

He learned about the women in the checkout at the store, the things they'd said and how Norah had reacted, and he laughed out loud. She wrote essays on how he'd bonded with Ella and what that had meant to her. She'd recalled funny dialogue between them practically word for word, and on one page, she'd copied the lyrics for "Lost Together." She had described a number of sexual encounters in painstaking detail, up to and including a page-and-a-half on how much she loved his penis.

He barely kept his eyes in his head.

He relived Vancouver through her words, and found all his poems lovingly tucked between the pages. The initial letter that he'd secreted in her purse had an aged look about it. She'd clearly folded and unfolded it dozens of times, and he was not surprised to see what looked like tearstains on the pages.

There was the business about the tabloid and the sadness of him flying to New York, and he closed the diary. He wasn't ready to walk that road yet.

He marveled at her courage, convinced that if such a thing had existed for him he would have destroyed it in his anguish, or tucked it away where he'd never see it. She had visited their joy over and over again, even though it meant returning to their heartbreak. She was his hero and, as he'd told himself a lifetime ago, she was the girl for him.

She came out of the washroom, clad in the cashmere robe he'd bought for her even though she earned enough money to own a hundred robes. It showed wear, but like the journal, she'd held on to it because meant holding on to them.

Now it's my turn to hold on.

"Marry me."

She stopped dead halfway to the bed. "I . . . I'm . . . I'm sorry, what did you say?"

"I said, marry me. As in, will you?"

"Marry you?"

"Yes."
"Will I marry you?"
"That's right."
She froze, staring, flapping. "You want me . . . to marry you?"
"That's what I said. What do you think?" He had sat up when she'd first come in, and he smiled broadly at her reaction. He couldn't blame her, since they'd never talked about it . . . ever. He didn't even know her views on the concept in general, but what he did know was that he never wanted to spend another day without her. He wanted her to be his wife, to make her and Ella his family.
"What do I think?" she asked softly, as if asking herself.
"Norah, honey, come here."
She sat next to him, an expression of wonder on her face.
"I want you to be with me, always. I want to raise Ella with you and watch her grow up. I want to be there with you when you commit Brett to an institution." They laughed together and he drew her into his arms. "Norah, my love, I want to be your husband. Will you marry me?"
Before she could answer, a soft knock made them turn toward the door.
"Um, come in."
The door squeaked open, and Peg poked her head in, said good morning, and made sure that they weren't *in flagrante* before standing back to allow Ella to enter.
"Day-day!" The toddler raced with a less-awkward gait toward them, and Norah watched David's face light up as he reached for her daughter. He heaved her up and they clung to each other.
"Peg," she called out to her aunt, who was enjoying the touching reunion from the doorway.
"Yes, my dear."
"Could you please get Brett on the phone? Tell him he's going to be a bridesmaid."
"Tell him . . . oh . . . oh, dear! Oh, Norah, really? Oh, David!" She oh, oh, oh-ed all the way back to the sitting room to find the phone.
David smiled into her magical eyes, then leaned toward her and kissed her with all the love he knew . . . all the love she'd taught him.
"When? When can we get married?" she asked. She seemed completely captivated by the idea.
"As soon as you wrap up here, I guess. Unless we want to fly everyone to France, you're going to have to wait until we're back home."
She joined Ella in the comfort of his arms, and the three of them snuggled together. Norah gazed up at David and sighed. "Are we there yet?"

Acknowledgements

To my oldest friend—*oldest* in that I've known her a really, really long time—Gaye Lepage. For her kind criticism and subtly ferocious encouragement. She had her outfit picked out for my launch party by the time I'd written the third chapter and wouldn't suffer any of my nonsense to stand in the way of her not getting there. Cancer had other ideas, however, and it is with bitter-sweetness that I've dedicated this work to her.

Thanks to Rowan Tully for her staunch support, for taking up the slack so that I could write, and for not slapping me upside the head every time I'd ask, "What part are you at?" when she'd laugh . . . or frown . . . or raise her eyebrows while reading my first draft.

To Brenda and the Budds for their formidable friendship, their boundless enthusiasm for my success, and for the all-important use of their scanner.

To my family, who are constantly bewildered by what I'll try next but cheer me on nonetheless.

A special thanks to my mother, Erna. Though she would have preferred a phone call saying that I was getting married, she was still pretty pleased about the "getting published" thing, too. Sadly, neither she nor my father, Gordon, lived long enough to hold this work in their hands.

To David Sivertsen, my sometimes love and constant friend, thanks for proofing my on-set segments to assure me that I'd gotten all the lingo down.

To Gerald Osborn, Russ Hewitt, Patti Stiles, and Karen Duncan—my 'lifers' who wanted this for me as much as I did for myself. You have no idea what having all of you in my corner has meant. I am truly blessed.

To the great, patient, insightful, talented, and hilarious DJ Gann. I don't know what I expected my relationship with an editor to be, but even in my most generous, most fantastical dreams, I could never have conjured such a woman. I have been overwhelmed by how tenderly she has guided me along, and from the first time she told me that I was "fine as frog hair," I knew I'd found a kindred spirit.

A special thanks to Amanda Hayward, Cindy Bidwell, Lea Dimovski and all the wonderful people at The Writer's Coffee Shop Publishing House. You've made this potentially terrifying experience a gentle journey, and I'm so glad that my baby found its way to you.

And speaking of babies, loving gratitude to my own little copper-topped 'Pooper' who is now nine years old and happily, able to feed herself when mum is editing.

And finally, to Tiggy and Audrey who kept me company through it all. You are deeply missed.

About the Author

Before writing *The Wrong Woman*, Brenda dabbled in a myriad of professions. She's been a waitress (back in the day before they were called *servers*), a security guard, a ballroom dance instructor, an interior decorator and design consultant, a set dresser for the film and television industry, where she is still a member in good standing, and a restaurant manager. She is currently working as a visual merchandiser for The Brick, a chain of furniture stores throughout the lower mainland.

In the midst of all that, she's been an active part of the community theatre scene doing set design but principally acting and studying most of the great works since her late teens. She currently lives in Coquitlam, British Columbia, with her beautiful daughter, one dog, and two cats.

CPSIA information can be obtained at www.ICGtesting.com
Printed in the USA
LVOW07s0504280314

379238LV00007BA/38/P